DATE DUE

D0952827

PRINTED IN U.S.A.

STRONG DARKNESS

*Published by Forge Books

STRONG DARKNESS

A CAITLIN STRONG NOVEL

Jon Land

A TOM DOHERTY ASSOCIATES BOOK
NEW YORK

This is a work of fiction. All of the characters, organizations, and events portrayed in this novel are either products of the author's imagination or are used fictitiously.

STRONG DARKNESS

Copyright © 2014 by Jon Land

A Forge Book
Published by Tom Doherty Associates, LLC
175 Fifth Avenue
New York, NY 10010

www.tor-forge.com

Forge® is a registered trademark of Tom Doherty Associates, LLC.

The Library of Congress Cataloging-in-Publication Data is available upon request.

ISBN 978-0-7653-3511-1 (hardcover)
ISBN 978-1-4668-2106-4 (e-book)

Forge books may be purchased for educational, business, or promotional use.
For information on bulk purchases, please contact Macmillan Corporate
and Premium Sales Department at 1-800-221-7945, extension 5442,
or write specialmarkets@macmillan.com.

First Edition: September 2014

Printed in the United States of America

0 9 8 7 6 5 4 3 2 1

For the Gregorys
Life's a beach

ACKNOWLEDGMENTS

Must be that time of year again, and I promise you another great ride this time. Before we start, though, I need to give some much-deserved shout-outs.

Stop me if you've heard this before, but let's start at the top with my publisher, Tom Doherty, and Forge's associate publisher, Linda Quinton, dear friends who publish books "the way they should be published," to quote my late agent, the legendary Toni Mendez. Paul Stevens, Karen Lovell, Patty Garcia, and especially Natalia Aponte are there for me at every turn. Natalia's a brilliant editor and friend who never ceases to amaze me with her sensitivity and genius. Editing may be a lost art, but not here, and I think you'll enjoy all of my books, including this one, much more as a result.

Big thanks also to Mireya Starkenberg, a loyal reader who now suffers through my butchering the Spanish language in order to correct it. My friend Mike Blakely, a terrific writer and musician, taught me Texas firsthand and helped me think like a native of that great state. And Larry Thompson, a terrific writer in his own right, has joined the team as well to make sure I do justice to his home state. I'm also indebted to my cousin George Mencoff for introducing me to the principles of the Deep Web and to *Time* magazine for publishing a perfectly timed cover story.* You'll also find more info

*"The Secret Web: Where Drugs, Porn and Murder Live Online," Lev Grossman and Jay Newton-Small, *Time* magazine, November 11, 2013

on how *Strong Darkness* came to be in my author's note that follows the epilogue here.

Check back at www.jonlandbooks.com for updates or to drop me a line. I'd be remiss if I didn't thank all of you who've already written or e-mailed me about how much you enjoyed the first five tales in the Caitlin Strong series. And if this happens to be your first to visit to the world of Caitlin, welcome and get ready for a wild ride. Right now it's time for me to stop talking so you can start reading.

P.S. For those interested in more information about the history of the Texas Rangers, I recommend *The Texas Rangers* and *Time of the Rangers*, a pair of superb books by Mike Cox, also published by Forge.

In order for the light to shine so brightly,
the darkness must be present.

—Francis Bacon

PROLOGUE

"They knew their duty and they did it."

—Ranger John S. "Rip" Ford (1815–1897)

LANGTRY, TEXAS; 1883

"Well," said Judge Roy Bean from behind the greasy bar in his cramped saloon that doubled as a courtroom, "I've researched this matter from the best resources available and have concluded that there ain't no law in Texas against killing a Chink. So with that in mind, this court finds the defendant not guilty."

The overflow crowd, hoping to a man for a quick resolution so they could get back to the business of drinking, was already applauding the verdict when Bean banged his gavel. The judge stripped off the black robe covering his bulbous frame and laid his palms atop the bar on either side of the single law book upon which he relied.

"Now," he said, slapping the wood hard enough to kick a blanket of dust into the air, "who wants a drink?"

In the bar's rear, Texas Ranger William Ray Strong was the lone man not celebrating. He stood shaking his head, eyeing the famed frontier judge who liked to proclaim himself the only law west of the Pecos. Just a few days earlier, William Ray had been summoned to an area on the outskirts of El Paso where the Chinese victim had been found hanging from a cottonwood tree. Arresting the culprit had been as easy as walking into an El Paso bar with the intention of posing some questions, only to overhear a cowboy with rotting teeth and the worst breath he'd ever smelled boast of doing the deed.

"Can I take that as a confession?" William Ray asked, approaching the table.

"You can take it as the drunken word of Cole Varney," the cowboy said, toasting him with his beer, "the only word I know."

Varney watched William Ray hitch his barn coat back to reveal his Colt Peacemaker.

"What are you, some kind of lawman?" Varney asked, drawing a collective chuckle from those crowded at the table with him.

William Ray pulled the barn coat further to reveal his Texas Ranger badge, forged out of a Mexican Cinco Pesos coin. "I suppose you could say that."

The chuckling seemed to freeze midbreath, the whole bar going silent. William Ray noticed men who'd eased their hands a bit closer to their holstered pistols draw them back, leaving those hands in evidence for him to see.

"And you, Cole Varney," he resumed, drawing close enough to stand over his suspect, "are under arrest for the murder of Han Chu."

"Was that the Chink's name?"

William Ray kicked the chair out from under Varney and he hit the floor hard, blowing out some breath that stained the air with the stench of stale onions and eggs gone bad. Light spilling from dusty tin lanterns strung overhead flickered at the impact that coughed a dust cloud into the bar's already grimy air.

"Doesn't matter if he was a Chinaman or the goddamn man from the moon," William Ray said, jerking Varney to his feet by the scruff of the neck. "You confessed to murdering him, sir, and the awful stench you give off should be enough to arrest you on its own."

"I didn't confess to nothing. Anybody hear me confess to something?" Varney asked anyone in the bar who was listening.

To a man, including those at his table who'd kept to their chairs with their hands remaining where William Ray Strong could see them, nobody answered Varney's question one way or another.

"You're under arrest, sir," William Ray said, snapping his handcuffs into place on the suspect's wrists.

"Who the hell are you?" Varney spat, clinging to his bravado.

"A Texas Ranger, and if that ain't enough for you, we can each try our guns and see who's still standing after the smoke clears."

While William Ray had been riding with the famed Texas Ranger captain George W. Arrington of the Frontier Battalion, fighting renegade Indians and Mexican bandits, a steady stream of Chinese workers had moved into West Texas to continue laying track for the Central and Southern Pacific Railroads' expanding routes through Texas and into Utah, Nevada, and California. There weren't enough workers to handle all the area that needed to be covered, and it had reached the point where the railroad companies were actually negotiating with prisons to turn their incarcerated into virtual slave labor.

When the Frontier Battalion was disbanded the year before, William Ray had found himself busting up those illegal chain gangs. But the charges never stuck and those truly responsible were too powerful and far away to arrest anyway. While that frustrated him to no end, it in no way softened his commitment to make sure the laws of the land were applied to this new wave of immigrants on both sides. As far as he was concerned, American or not, they had to be answerable to justice whether they were the perpetrator or the victim.

Chinese crews relocated their campsites regularly to keep up with track laying progress. The particular camp they occupied here in the Trans-Pecos region of Texas had served as home longer than usual, thanks to the need to build an earthen dam to help stabilize the rail bed before ties and tracks could be spiked. It had been an unusually wet year for West Texas, stopping the railroad in its tracks until the Chinese crews completed the nearly quarter-mile-long, fifty-foot-high dam.

Work on the tracks, though, still had yet to resume, the land deemed too wet to drive the ties into place to properly secure the rails. By then, William Ray imagined the Chinese had worn out their welcome as far as the locals, never known in these parts to be friendly toward strangers, were concerned. A local sheriff had called in the Rangers as soon as Han Chu's body was found, and William Ray had ridden through the night to pick up the trail that had brought him to this bar and Cole Varney.

It turned out the tree from which Varney had hung the Chinese victim actually lay in Langtry, home of the infamous Judge Roy Bean. Bean was known for hanging more than his share of men himself, just not any who were patrons of the saloon that doubled as his courthouse, which the accused clearly was. William Ray didn't expect much from Bean and, true to form, the judge didn't disappoint.

"Yo there, Ranger," he heard Bean's voice call, when he was halfway out the door in the wake of the verdict being announced.

William Ray turned slowly, watching the judge comb his long gray beard with the fingers of his right hand. "What can I do for you, Judge?"

"You're real good at holding your tongue, ain't ya, son?"

"I did my job, sir. Not for me to tell others how best to do theirs."

"No matter, Ranger. You heard me say there's no law in Texas against killing a Chink, I imagine."

"I did indeed. Imagine you got it out of that single law book of yours."

"Well, that same book's got nothing to say about killing a whole bunch of Chinks neither," Bean said, his expression tightening to the point where the spiderweb of red veins across both his cheeks smoothed a bit. "Chink ladies more to the point."

"Sounds like you're about to tell me something I oughtta know, Judge."

"I am indeed, son. Regular customer of mine who supplies beef to the railroad spilled it in the saloon just the other night 'fore he puked all over his shoes." Roy Bean stopped long enough to stuff a thick

wad of tobacco into his mouth, his left cheek puckering and then filling out with what looked like a round rock wedged in place there.
"Four Chink women he said, all killed deader than dead in the past
few weeks since the rains come, their bodies left like you wouldn't
believe. Chinks figure the rains brought something else with them."

"And what's that?"

"Southern Pacific man heard them blame a 'black guy,' meaning
we could be looking to put a nigger in our sights, if that makes any
sense."

"It doesn't. *Bahk guai* is what the man meant by those words."

"Huh?"

"Chinese for 'white devil.'"

Bean stiffened. "That ain't right at all."

"'Course the phrase could mean something else entirely, more
literal."

"Like what?"

"An actual devil, a demon."

"Well, son, I never put one of them on trial."

"First time for everything, Judge. In any event, I'll head out to
the Chinese camp and have myself a look straightaway."

Roy Bean looked as if he were running the prospects of that
through his mind. "I'm of a mind to ride along with you on this one,
Ranger."

William Ray hocked up some spittle. "Rangers are used to working alone."

"Land west of the Pecos got its own law, son, and that law's me.
Trouble here is you ain't gonna be facing Injuns or Mexicans, no
sirree. You ever get yourself snared in barbed wire?"

"Can't say I have, Judge."

"'Cause that's what this investigation is gonna be like. You're
gonna be dealing with a whole bunch of interlopers and invaders,
from the Chinese to the Southern Pacific goons, to their bosses in
starched suits coming to our land like they can do whatever they
want with it. Pays to have a man of my esteem standing by your side
with a pair of wire cutters should the need arise."

William Ray considered Bean's proposal, working his tongue around his mouth from the left to right and sweeping it across the inside of both cheeks, pushing one out and then the other. "On one condition, Judge: any man I arrest stands a fair trial."

"Aw, hell, I only sentenced two men in my whole career to hang."

"Were they guilty?"

"Close enough."

"Close enough don't cut it in my book," William Ray groused. "I can't stop you from holding your court in a saloon. But if booze dictates your justice, I'll burn the place down with you in it."

"I'm offering you a helping hand here, Ranger," the judge said, frustrated by the lack of embrace to his proposal.

"Which has got a mite too much blood on it for my tastes."

Roy Bean made a show of wiping both his hands on a vest missing half its buttons. "That oughtta do the trick. So let's ride out to that camp and catch us a killer, a demon, or a black guy."

"That's *bahk guai*."

"Isn't that what I said?"

CHINA, 1998

"You understand there is a stern price you must pay for such grand ambitions."

"*Wo yuan yi*," Li Zhen said in his native Mandarin, forcing himself to bow slightly. "I do."

Zhen stood reverently in the center of the deceptively simple room formed of a bamboo floor and walls covered in rattan and tightly woven straw. The harsh light shining in his eyes nearly blinded him while the three men seated at the table before him remained lost to darkness. Mere shadows wearing expensive dark suits, formless and lacking any texture at all, visible only in the slight motions and mannerisms they allowed themselves. A fourth chair had been placed behind the table but it remained empty.

"I am willing to offer you anything in my possession," Zhen

said to them, bowing again so they wouldn't notice him visibly cringe at this necessary show of deference.

"In your case," another voice said to him, "anything may not be enough. You are not of the proper social class to pursue such ambitions. You should consider yourself fortunate to even be permitted in this room."

"I understand."

"No," snapped the third man hoarsely. "If you understood, you would not have bothered wasting the Triad's time, *er bal wu*."

"Perhaps it is my own time I am wasting," Zhen said, hardly bothered by being called a fool.

He had been directed to this room inside a decrepit building rising from the refuse of what the Chinese government referred to as "inner-city villages." Slums like this had been settled in crumbling neighborhoods by rural migrants in search of any work the factories and plants nearby had to offer, the truly poor and destitute. Many of the homes and structures had been built illegally, the government turning a blind eye to the challenges posed by evicting and then resettling huge masses of residents. Sometimes it was easier to leave well enough alone.

"Perhaps," Zhen continued to the shocked trio seated before him, "I should be bringing this opportunity to other parties."

"You would dare disrespect us this way?" snapped the third man. "Watch your tongue or you will find yourself without it."

"I come from a neighborhood like this," Zhen told them quite calmly. "I was raised in a slum."

"As you remain in our eyes and the eyes of China. Peasant scum," one of the men hissed.

"We are well aware of your background," the man in the center, who Zhen knew to be the leader, said, sounding more intrigued than angered, "along with the areas of expertise that have already endeared you to us. Your pornography interests have yielded a great fortune. Perhaps you should consider an expansion there in an area of familiarity."

"It is another area I seek your support in pursuing."

"And what might that be?"

"The future, *shīfù*," Zhen said, careful to use the most reverent word for "master."

In China, there was no such thing really as upward mobility. The only alternative to winning the favor of the government or military for men like Li Zhen was to pursue an alliance with the only other true power in China: that of the Triad, a criminal organization with interests all across the globe that often counted the government and military as its willing partners.

"We can look out the window and see the future," the second man scoffed. "You waste our time. Go back where you belong."

"A slum like this *is* where I belong, among the dregs where Chinese society dictates I must reside. I come to you because it lies in our mutual best interests to change that. And I wish to do right by the Triad," Zhen added respectfully, "for the opportunities already afforded me."

"Then go back to make more of your dirty pictures."

"I can do much better than that," Zhen said and produced a floppy disc from his pocket; he promptly brought it to the table and laid it before the leader seated in the center. "This is merely an example."

"And what exactly does it contain?" the leader asked, holding the disc up before him.

"The product of a quest, *shīfù*, a quest that brought me to America on the pretext of expanding my interests there. A new age of communications technology is dawning that will change the world forever. And we can own that age. It can be ours."

The leader passed the disc to the man on his right.

"One disc," that man said, regarding it disparagingly. "This must be a very modest future indeed."

"I have nine more containing the greatest secrets of America's telecommunications industries, the secrets that will open the door to the future of their wireless technology. We can beat the Americans in the race to this future. They see it as a sprint, while we know it is a marathon."

"What do you seek from us?" asked the leader.

"Your backing now, *shīfù*. Your funding later."

"I'm afraid," said the Triad captain still holding the floppy disc, "backing for such an elaborate venture does not suit a man of a standing better fit for serving us with his films of naked women and sex."

Zhen remained unruffled.

"I have further demonstration of my true capabilities," he said, focusing on the empty chair set behind the table. "A shame about Governor Chen's tragic passing."

The Triad captain slammed the floppy disc down atop the table. "You dare raise his name, you dare violate the sanctity of this chamber with such a blatant disregard for our ways?"

"I understand it was a car accident just this afternoon after his driver inexplicably lost control," Zhen resumed. "You will learn that the car continued to accelerate, that its braking system was rendered inoperative. It was traveling at over a hundred and fifty kilometers per hour when it crashed into that bridge support and burst into flames."

"And you tell us this to showcase the depth of your knowledge?" the man challenged.

"No, I tell you because it could've been you, any of you. A check of the remains of the wreck's engine block will reveal my initials soldered just under the head gasket. So the three of you should count yourself as fortunate that I chose Governor Chen for my demonstration."

"Demonstration of what exactly?"

"The potential to use technology toward our nation's best interests."

"So if you were aware of Governor Chen's identity," the Triad captain on the far left started, "we can assume you know ours as well."

"A fair assumption, Magistrate," Zhen told him casually.

"You play a dangerous game," the leader said, before either of the other two Triad captains could respond. "Now it is up to you to explain why we should let you leave this building alive."

"Because, Colonel Chang, it remains in your best interests to do so. I have just demonstrated to you the power of using technology as a weapon. Multiply that many, many times and you have a notion of what backing me can achieve, the power I seek to lay at our country's doorstep with your help." Zhen bowed slightly again in feigned reverence. "But I have also come with an offering of my goodwill and intentions," he continued, "a sacrifice to the greater good of China."

With that, Li Zhen removed a picture from his pocket and held it up to the light for the Triad captains to see.

"A gift?" the leader raised, clearly impressed by what he saw.

"As is the custom of any man who comes before you."

"Even a man who would dare threaten us?"

"Especially such a man."

"You understand the consequences."

Zhen nodded. "I do, and I accept them with heavy heart but knowing mind. Regrettable, but necessary to prove my loyalty to you and to provide tangible demonstration that I love our great nation more than anything."

He stopped there to let his point sink in, taking the silence of the Triad captains for the fact this face-saving gesture had captured their interest and left them in his trust. Yet he couldn't help wondering what they'd think if they knew his true purpose in coming before them, his true goals. Zhen had killed the fourth member of their council, Governor Chen, to make one point.

And he intended to kill millions and millions of Americans to make another. Because it was America's fault he was forced to come groveling to these men to attain the power and riches that should have been his birthright.

The leader continued to regard the picture Zhen was holding. "We will require some time to consider this matter."

"I have waited all my life for this opportunity," Zhen said humbly. "I can wait a little longer for China to own the world."

Colonel Chang, the Triad captain in the center, smiled wryly. "You mean we don't already?"

"Not yet. But with America's help we will."

PART ONE

"So, the government provided for their protection as best it could with the means at its disposal, graciously permitting the citizens to protect themselves by organizing . . . ranging companies."

—Noah Smithwick (1808–1899)

I

"Sinners repent or more will die! Sinners repent or more will die! Sinners repent or more will die!"

Caitlin Strong listened to the chant repeated over and over again by the Beacon of Light Church members who'd decided to picket a young soldier's funeral here in San Antonio in pointless protest. The words were harder to make out across the street, beyond the thousand-foot buffer the protesters were required to keep, but clear enough to disturb the parents of an army hero who just wanted to bury their son in peace.

"What are you going to do about this, Ranger?" Bud Chauncey, the young man's father, asked her.

"I've requested that they vacate the premises, sir," Caitlin told the man. "My orders are to do no more than that as long as they keep their distance. It's the law."

Chauncey, who owned several car dealerships in the area, turned toward the Beacon of Light Church members gathered on a patch of fresh land up a slight rise across the road, land that Mission Burial Park had purchased in order to expand. His eyes looked bloodshot and weary, his face held in an angry glare that captured the frustration over being able to do no more about their presence here than he could for the son he was about to lay to rest. He stretched a hand through stringy gray hair to smooth it back down, but the breeze quickly blew it out of place again. Chauncey always looked so strong, vital, and happy on his television commercials, leaving Caitlin to wonder if this was even the same man. His neck was thin and marred by discolored patches of skin that looked to have come from radiation treatments. His hands were thin and knobby and she noticed them trembling once he removed them from his pockets. She caught a glimpse of tobacco stains on the tips of his fingers and nails and thought of those radiation treatments again.

"Thousand feet away?" Chauncey questioned.

"Legislature passed a law restricting protests to that distance to funerals held in the state."

Chauncey gazed back at the mourners gathered by his son's gravesite waiting for the service to begin. He and Caitlin stood off to the side of the building funeral cortege at Mission Burial Park, the cemetery located on the San Antonio River where her father and grandfather were buried in clear view of the historic Mission Espada.

"Why don't you explain that to my boy, Ranger?"

It sounded more like a plea than a question, a grieving father looking for a way to reconcile his son's death in the face of picketing strangers paying him the ultimate disrespect. Blaming gays and their lifestyle for the grenade that had taken a young man's life when he threw himself on two other soldiers to save them.

"The world might be full of shit," Chauncey resumed with his gaze fixed across the road, electricity seeming to radiate out of his pores with the sweat to the point where Caitlin figured she'd get a shock if she stretched a hand out to comfort him. "But that doesn't mean we ever get used to stepping in it."

"I'll be right back, sir," she told Bud Chauncey and headed toward the street.

2

It seemed like too nice a day to bury somebody as gifted as Bud Chauncey's son, Junior. An All-District athlete in three sports, Homecoming King, and senior class president who'd joined the army's ROTC program. He went to Afghanistan already a hero and came back in a box after his platoon was hit by a Taliban ambush while on patrol. It was bad enough when good boys died for no good reason Caitlin could see. It was even worse when it happened while a war was winding down and most back home had stopped paying attention.

Caitlin was thinking of Dylan Torres, the eighteen-year-old son of the man she considered, well, her boyfriend, as she walked toward the road and the grassy field across it that was in the process of being dug out to make room for Mission Burial Park's expansion. Bud Chauncey Junior had been barely a year older when he died and she couldn't help picturing Dylan patrolling a desert wasteland with an M16 held in the ready position before him. Still a boy no matter how much he'd been through or how many monsters with whom he'd come into contact. Currently in Providence, Rhode Island, Dylan was in the midst of his freshman football season for Brown University, and had a junior varsity game next weekend, if she remembered correctly.

Caitlin had read that Junior Chauncey had been accepted for admission at the University of Texas at Austin, where he had hoped to do the same. But Junior would never don helmet and pads again.

That thought pushed a spring into her step as she strode across the road now crammed with cars, both parked along the side and inching along in search of a space. The funeral was being delayed to account for that, giving Bud Chauncey more time to suffer and the Beacon of Light Church more time to make their presence known. Alerted to their coming, she could see that television crews from five local stations and at least two national ones had arrived first, their cameras covering all that was transpiring on both sides of the road.

Crossing the street, Caitlin thought she felt a blast of heat flushed out of a furnace slam into her. It seemed to radiate off the protesters, turning the air hot and prickly as they continued to chant. The sky was cloudless, the heat building in the fall day under a sun that felt more like summer judging from the burn Caitlin felt on her cheeks.

Caitlin recognized the leader, William Bryant Tripp, from his wet-down hair, skin flushed red, and handlebar mustache, and angled herself straight for him across the edge of the field that gave way to a drainage trench the width of a massive John Deere wheel loader's shovel. The trench created a natural barricade between the Beacon of Light Church members and what might as well have been the rest of the world, while the big Deere sat idle between towering mounds of earth set farther back in the field.

"Sinners repent or more will die! Sinners repent or more will die! Sinners repent or more will die!"

"Mr. Tripp," she called to the leader over the chants. He'd stepped out of the procession at her approach, smirking and twirling the ends of his mustache.

"It's *Reverend* Tripp," he reminded.

Caitlin nodded, trying to look respectful. "There's people grieving a tragic death across the way, Reverend, and I'd ask you again as a man and a Christian to vacate the premises so they might do so in peace. You've made your point already and I believe you should leave things at that."

The smirk remained. "Peace is what this church is all about, Ranger, a peace that can only be achieved if those who debauch and deface the values of good honest people like us repent and are called out for their sins."

"Gays had nothing to do with putting that brave boy in a coffin, sir. That was the work of a bunch of cowardly religious fanatics like the ones serving you here today."

The smirk slipped from Tripp's expression, replaced by a look that brushed Caitlin off and sized her up at the same time. "We're breaking no laws here. So I'm going to ask you to leave *us* in peace."

Caitlin felt her muscles tightening, her mouth going dry. "You have every right to be here and I'm here to protect your rights to peaceful assembly as well as the rights of the Chauncey family to bury their son without a sideshow. The problem is that presents a contradiction it's my duty to resolve. And the best way to do that is to ask you and your people to simply leave in a timely fashion."

Tripp shifted his shoulders. He seemed to relish the threat Caitlin's words presented. "And if we choose not to?"

"You've made your point for the cameras already, sir. There's nothing more for you to prove. So do the holy thing by packing up your pickets and heading on." Caitlin gazed toward the protesters thrusting their signs into the air in perfect rhythm with their chanting. "Use the time to paint over those signs, so you're ready to terrorize the next family that loses a son in battle, Mr. Tripp."

Tripp measured her words, running his tongue around the inside of his mouth. It made a sound like crushing a grape underfoot. Caitlin could feel the sun's heat between them now, serving as an invisible barrier neither wanted to breach.

"It's *Reverend* Tripp," he reminded again.

"I believe that title needs to be earned," Caitlin told him, feeling her words start to race ahead of her thoughts.

Tripp stiffened. "This church has been serving Him and His word since the very founding of this great nation, Ranger. Even here in the great state of Texas itself."

"Those other military funerals you've been picketing from Lubbock to Amarillo don't count toward that, sir."

"I was speaking of our missionary work back in the times of the frontier; the railroads and the oil booms. How this church tried to convert the Chinese heathen hordes to Christianity."

"Heathen hordes?"

"It was a fool's errand," Tripp said, bitterness turning his expression even more hateful. "The Chinese made for an unholy, hateful people not deserving of our Lord's good graces."

"But you believe you are, thanks to hurting those good folks across the way, is that right? Problem is you're not serving God, sir; you're serving yourself. And I'm giving you a chance to square things the easy way instead of the hard."

Tripp sneered at her. "Such threats didn't work in Lubbock or Amarillo and they won't work here either."

"I wasn't the one who made them in those cities, Mr. Tripp. You'd be well advised to listen this time."

"And what if I don't?"

"Sinners repent or more will die! Sinners repent or more will die! Sinners repent or more will die!"

The chanting had picked up in cadence, seeming to reach a crescendo as the funeral goers squeezed themselves around Junior Chauncey's gravesite across the road so the ceremony could begin. Caitlin watched the members of the Beacon of Light Church thrusting their picket signs into the air as if they were trying to make rain, the image of their feet teetering on the edge of the recently dug drainage trench holding in her mind.

"I guess I'll have to think of something," she told Tripp and started away.

3

SAN ANTONIO, TEXAS

Caitlin looped around the perimeter of the protesters, her presence likely forgotten by the time she reached the John Deere wheel loader parked between matching piles of excavated earth. She recognized it as a 644K hybrid model boasting twenty tons of power that could probably level a skyscraper. Caitlin had learned to drive earlier, more brutish versions while helping to rebuild a Mexican family's home after they'd been burned out by drunken kids for a pot deal gone wrong. Trouble was the drug dealer who'd screwed the kids actually lived across the street. Caitlin's father had arrested the boys two days later. Considering them dangerous criminals, Jim Strong made them strip to their underwear and left them to roast in the sun while he waited for backup to assist him in a cavity search. Jim had organized the rebuilding effort, financed ultimately by the restitution paid by the accused boys' parents to keep them out of jail. Caitlin's father had brokered that deal as well.

The hybrid engine of the 644K sounded a hundred times quieter than the roar coughed by the older version, and handled as easy as a subcompact, when Caitlin started it forward.

"Sinners repent or more will die! Sinners repent or more will die! Sinners repent or more will die!"

She couldn't hear the chanting anymore, imagining it in her mind with each thrust of the picket signs into the air. It was loud enough to keep the protesters from detecting her approach, even when she lowered the shovel into position and let its teeth dig maybe a foot down into the ground.

Caitlin plowed the growing pile of dirt forward as if it were snow after a rare Texas blizzard. The back row of the protesters turned just as the wall of gathered earth crested over the shovel. Caitlin imagined the panic widen their eyes, heard screams and shouts as they tried desperately to warn the others what was coming.

Too late.

The massive power of the John Deere pushed the earthen wall straight into the center of the pack fronted by William Bryant Tripp himself, driving the mass forward without even a sputter. The last thing Caitlin glimpsed were picket signs closer to the front stubbornly clinging to the air before those holding them were gobbled up and shoved forward.

Down into the drainage trench.

Caitlin pictured Reverend Tripp toppling in first, imagined the trench as a mass grave or, better yet, the week's deposit zone in the local landfill. Because that's where the members of the Beacon of Light Church belonged in her mind, dumped in along with the other stench-riddled trash.

Some of the protesters managed to peel off to the side to escape the John Deere's force and wrath, and Caitlin didn't brake the big machine until the earthen wall she was pushing stopped on the edge of the trench. Portions of it sifted downward, forestalling the efforts of Tripp and his minions to climb out. So she gave the Deere just a little more gas to trap them a bit longer.

Caitlin cut off the engine at that point. Her gaze drifted across the street to the funeral ceremony for Junior Chauncey, where everyone had turned around to face the other side of the road. They saw the members of the Beacon of Light Church visible only as hands desperately clawing for purchase to pull themselves from the trench into which Caitlin had forced them. She hopped down out of the cab and walked around the wall of dirt and grass the John Deere had helped her lay.

Then, to a man and woman led by Bud Chauncey himself, the funeral goers started to clap their hands, applauding her. It got louder and louder, reaching a crescendo just as the television cameras began rotating feverishly between both sides of the road and reporters rushed toward Caitlin with microphones in hand.

She leaped across the trench, brushing the microphones and cameras aside, the sun hot against her flesh.

"You're going to pay for this, Caitlin Strong!" she heard Tripp scream at her, as he finally managed to hoist himself from the ditch. "The Lord does not forget!"

"Neither do I, sir," Caitlin said calmly, regarding the dirt clinging to him that no amount of shaking or brushing could remove. It turned his ash gray hair a dark brown, making him look as if he was wearing a vegetable garden atop his head. "And you'd be wise to remember that."

4

"You know what a TV camera looks like, Ranger?"

"I believe it's one of those dark things with a man's eye stuck to it," Caitlin told Texas Ranger captain D. W. Tepper, head of Company F headquarters in San Antonio. "And in this case it caught a whole bunch of people at that funeral applauding my actions."

"So you've seen the coverage."

"Nope. I just saw the directions all those cameras were pointing in."

"All *those*?" Tepper shook his head, his expression growing even tighter. His ceiling fan spun lazily overhead, picking up the room's stray light and splashing it against the cream-colored walls stained by cigarette smoke. "How many cameras we talking about here? Or were you too busy bulldozing two dozen people into a drainage ditch to notice?"

"A trench, actually."

"So you don't dispute the bulldozing part."

"It was a wheel loader."

Tepper puckered his lips. "I gave you the assignment because I figured even you couldn't cause a storm at a funeral. But never underestimate the reach of Hurricane Caitlin—you'd think I would've learned that by now," he said, and made a show of lighting one of his Marlboros just to piss her off. "You got something you wanna say about my smoking?"

"Why bother?"

Tepper slapped his desktop with enough force to rattle his fingers. "Exactly my point, Hurricane. Now you know what it feels like."

"I thought I behaved responsibly."

"Why's that?"

"Because I didn't shoot anybody, D.W."

"No, today you put a whole bunch of live people into graves, instead of dead ones."

"At least they could climb out. Normally it's a permanent condition."

"You know what else is permanent?" Tepper said, cigarette dangling from his mouth now. "You being a genuine pain in my ass. I've tried everything, Ranger, and nothing seems to stick. You just keep writing up your own rules and the rest of the book be damned."

"You've got two boys who've been to war, Captain."

"And I'm proud as hell of them."

"So how do you think you'd feel if you were Bud Chauncey, about to lay your firstborn to rest while that Beacon of Light Church lot was chanting up a storm about God hating gays?"

"I sent you there to enforce the law, Caitlin. What's so damn hard about that?"

"William Bryant Tripp wasn't a hospitable man. He wouldn't listen to reason."

"So you hit him with a mountain-load of dirt. Is that how you deal with all the inhospitable folk out there?"

"Normally I just shoot them."

"The Beacon of Light Church was operating within the boundaries of the law it's our job to enforce, not make up as we go along."

Caitlin thought of the radiation stains along Bud Chauncey's neck and leaned over the desk far enough to pluck the cigarette from Tepper's mouth.

"I believe I was smoking that."

"You keep on smoking, D.W., I'll keep on plucking," she said, pressing it out in an Alamo ashtray now missing almost all of the famed landmark's facade because of age and use. "Maybe you should try those new E-cigarettes."

"What's that, like e-mail? How the hell I am supposed to smoke something on a computer? Close my eyes and imagine?"

"You should try it some time."

"Oh, I have, and you know what I imagine? Not opening the

newspaper to find more damage from Hurricane Caitlin on the front page."

Caitlin eased the old vinyl chair set before his desk closer to the front. "That's not what's bothering you this time."

"Oh no? What is?"

"The fact that the Rangers are going to get applauded for what I did, finally standing up to the Beacon of Light Church. You're afraid it'll encourage me."

"As in encourage you to do something you're going to do anyway, Ranger. So why should I bother?" Tepper started to reach for a fresh cigarette, than thought better of it. "How long you figure it'll be before they file a lawsuit?"

"What for?" Caitlin asked, the agitation over that morning's mere memory creeping into her voice.

"Oh, I don't know. Maybe premature burial. Some would call that a violation of civil rights."

"Tell that to the family burying their son."

"Be glad to. But that doesn't change the fact that what the Beacon of Light Church was doing was legal."

"No, sir, it wasn't."

Tepper rolled his eyes, started to reach for the pack of cigarettes nesting in his pocket but then stopped again. "Why, because you say so?"

"No, because I measured."

"Measured *what*?"

"The distance between the gravesite and where the Beacon of Light Church whack jobs were standing behind that drainage trench. Came out just short of nine hundred and sixty feet."

"I'm not following you here, Ranger."

"Law that passed the Texas legislature requires them to be a minimum of a thousand feet away."

"So they were off by forty."

"The law's the law, D.W."

Tepper massaged the bald patches of his scalp. "I'll let Austin know. But I'm taking the bills to clean the clothes those people were wearing out of your salary. And William Bryant Tripp is waiting for an apology."

"Then I hope he's a patient man, Captain, because he's going to be waiting for a long time."

"You have any regrets over this at all?" Tepper asked, shaking his head.

"I sure do, Captain: that it wasn't a sewer trench instead, so that piece of shit who calls himself a reverend would've felt right at home."

Tepper pulled something from his open desk drawer and plopped it down on the blotter right next to his Alamo ashtray.

"What's that?"

"Pocket tape recorder I bought at Radio Shack so you could listen to how you actually sound." Tepper gave it a closer look, then brought the recorder right up to his eyes. "Goddamnit, I forgot to push the record button. Damn thing wasn't even on. Aw hell, wouldn't have made a difference anyway, would it?"

"Not at all."

Tepper dropped the recorder into the drawer and leaned back in his chair, the springs creaking as it tilted toward the open office window. "You know how many times your daddy and granddaddy got their names in the paper?"

"No, I don't."

"Neither do I, Ranger, because it wasn't often enough for anybody to pay attention. If it's their tradition you're trying to live up to, you've got an awful peculiar way of doing it."

"Old Earl rode with you back when dinosaurs roamed the prairie and I don't believe Jim ever owned a cell phone. It's the age that's different, D.W., not me."

"No, Caitlin," Tepper corrected, "it's both."

As if on cue, her cell phone rang and she took the call only after seeing CORT WESLEY light up on the Caller ID. "You see me on television, Cort Wesley?"

Her mouth dropped at his response, quickly followed by the phone itself into her lap.

5

Dylan lay in the hospital bed at Rhode Island Hospital. Perfectly still, eyes closed, covered to the waist by a sheet with more wires and tubes running out of him than Caitlin could count. Cort Wesley Masters stood next to her holding his hands by his sides, clenching and unclenching his fists as if picturing what he was going to do to whoever had done this to his oldest son.

"What's a medically induced coma exactly?" he asked the doctor, who was in the midst of shining a penlight into the boy's eyes to check for a reaction.

Caitlin looked at Cort Wesley, his thoughts and fears easy to read because they mirrored her own.

Dylan with brain damage . . .

Dylan unable to walk . . .

Dylan a quadriplegic . . .

Dylan never waking up . . .

Every parent's worst nightmare, compounded by the helplessness. Standing there utterly powerless, absolutely nothing they could do other than hope.

The doctor, whose name was Hirschman, according to his tag, turned with a start. Cort Wesley had listened to his explanation of Dylan's condition that had ended moments before in silence, his question posed on some kind of delay.

"Standard treatment when a patient presents with swelling on the brain."

"Presents?"

"What our initial examination of your son determined."

Hirschman was looking at both Cort Wesley and Caitlin when he said that. Normally, being confused as the boy's mother would have brought a warm rush through her, but not today. Today was about clinging to the hope that Dylan wouldn't be in the hospital for long and beginning the process of finding who had put him there in the first place.

The preceding April, around six months earlier, Caitlin had accompanied the boy on a trip to Providence to visit Brown University where he hoped to gain admittance and play football. Barely a week later, he was accepted and had gotten some reps on the junior varsity team already this season, though he looked woefully small in his uniform when compared to other players with the physiques of professional wrestlers. She and Cort Wesley had made it out to two of the games, one with Dylan's younger brother, Luke, accompanying them.

Upon reaching her in Captain Tepper's office, Cort Wesley had explained he'd just got off the phone with Phil Estes, Brown's head football coach. All Estes knew was that Dylan had been rushed to the hospital after some kind of altercation, the details of which remained sketchy. Estes said he'd just gotten to the hospital himself, and Cort Wesley recalled the heavy echo of footsteps along a stairwell in the background of their conversation.

"I'll meet you here," Estes had told him.

"It's gonna take us a while with the flights and all," Cort Wesley replied.

"See you and the Ranger then."

6

PROVIDENCE, RHODE ISLAND

True to his word, when they arrived from Texas Estes had met them in the waiting area of Rhode Island Hospital's intensive care ward, where Dylan had been whisked after being stabilized and evaluated in the emergency room the previous night. The coach informed them about the medically induced coma, stressing that it suggested a far dire prognosis than was very possibly the case.

Possibly.

After her father had suffered his heart attack, doctors in San Antonio had told Caitlin he could possibly resume a normal life. He died in an intensive care ward pretty much identical to this one, except the waiting area had windows.

"We had meetings last night," Coach Estes, a bear of a man himself with forearms the size of fire hydrants crossed over his chest, explained to them. "As far as I can tell, the players went straight back to their dorms afterward. Dylan was walking home with two other freshmen players when he got a text and said he had to take care of something."

"Take care of something," Cort Wesley repeated, his voice sounding as if his throat had been scraped raw by steel wool.

"That's what the other players recall that he said. Their words."

Cort Wesley turned to meet Caitlin's stare, both asking themselves the same obvious question in full awareness of the fact that Dylan using those words probably meant something unpleasant.

Take care of something . . .

The life had returned to Cort Wesley's eyes, regaining their intensity and purpose in light so dull Caitlin figured she'd need a flashlight to read one of the magazines pulled from a stack of months-old selections. She could see his mind working, focus turning however briefly to what he'd do if he caught up with whoever had planted his son in a hospital bed. She stopped her thinking there.

"They didn't express any concern?" Cort Wesley asked Estes, after an uncomfortable silence. "The players, I mean."

"Mr. Masters, Dylan has a tendency to keep to himself. He's about the team when he needs to be, all business, and the truth is I've enjoyed watching him carry the ball in both practice and those JV games as much as I've enjoyed anything this season. First hit hasn't taken him down yet, not even once," the coach finished, the statement seeming to make him feel better and his warming gaze indicating he hoped it might do the same for them.

"It did this time," Cort Wesley said, his expression not moving at all.

7

PROVIDENCE, RHODE ISLAND

"Due to blunt force trauma—you mentioned that too," Cort Wesley was saying to the doctor now, the emotions shifting on his expression in such rapid fashion that it seemed framed by a strobe light.

"You want to tell us what that means for his overall prognosis?" Caitlin interjected.

"Well," Hirschman said, "the CT scan revealed no skull fracture and no damage we can detect to the brain tissue itself. He's responsive to stimuli and, like I said, inducing the coma was just precautionary, especially in light of the concussion he suffered."

"But you didn't say what caused it," Cort Wesley noted.

"We believe it was from a blow, several of them, in fact."

"Any particular weapon?" Caitlin asked.

The doctor shrugged. "That's undetermined at this time, and not for me to say."

"Then for who is it to say?" Cort Wesley said, before Caitlin had a chance to.

"That would be me," came a voice from the doorway.

8

Caitlin recognized the man standing there as a Providence police detective from her last visit to the city, when, on Dylan's visitation trip to Brown University, a gunfight broke out during a festival called WaterFire down along the city's riverfront. His last name was Finneran and he was a beefy man with red spiderweb veins growing over his ruddy cheeks, and a stomach that tested the bounds of his button-down shirt. He looked like he'd lost some weight since her last visit.

"Know the last time anybody up here killed four people in self-defense?" he'd challenged her in a quasi-interrogation at the station.

"I'm afraid I don't, sir."

"Never, Ranger, never. Looks like you've made history in a second state."

She had indeed and was very much prepared to again, as she watched Finneran wait for Dr. Hirschman to leave the room before entering.

"Please tell me I'm not seeing this," the detective said, looking like he was fighting to swallow something sour.

"We meet again, Detective Finneran," Caitlin greeted. "I'd call you by your first name, but I don't remember it."

"That's because you were too busy telling me all the things I had wrong about the investigation into the mass murder you committed here last spring." Finneran's gaze locked onto Cort Wesley, as if realizing he was in the room for the first time. "Maybe you and I should talk alone."

"Why," Cort Wesley started, "the lady scare you?"

Finneran looked back toward Caitlin. "She has no part in this investigation and I have no intention of sharing information in her presence. You want to, be my guest. But this conversation is over until she leaves the room."

Silence settled between them, the steady hum of the machines wired to Dylan the only sound in the room.

"Then I guess you might as well stop wasting your time here," Cort Wesley said finally, breaking it.

"I'm sorry about what happened to your son, Mr. Torres," Finneran resumed, caught off guard.

"It's Masters, Detective. Torres was the name of the boy's mother. She was murdered six years back now. My son witnessed the whole thing. The woman you want to leave the room saved his life that day. I'd say that gives her a stake in whatever you have to say."

Finneran's gaze rotated between the two of them, trying to figure out his next move.

"You got a superior we can talk to, Detective?" Cort Wesley continued. "Somebody who can help sort out how the investigation into a kid nearly getting beaten to death in your city should be handled."

"Don't tell me how to do my job."

"Then start doing it by picking up where we left off before you told a fellow law enforcement official to leave the room. What can you tell *us* about what happened to my son?"

Finneran made a sound that started as a sigh and ended as something low and guttural. "He was found by another student on a street near the Brown campus who called nine-one-one," he said, turning so his back was to Caitlin. "The first officers and paramedics on scene found his pockets emptied. No wallet, money, just his Brown University ID that was found by itself in a pocket."

"What about a cell phone?" Caitlin asked him.

Finneran shook his head, still not looking at her.

"Because we believe the boy received a text message maybe not too long before he was attacked," she continued, leaving out the part about Dylan leaving his friends in order *to take care of some-*

thing. She could pretty much figure how Finneran would react to that, based on their last encounter.

"It would be helpful to know who that text came from," Cort Wesley said, when the detective didn't respond to Caitlin's suggestion.

"Give me his phone number and provider and I'll get the info dumped. Might need a warrant, but they're pretty easy to come by in these parts."

"That's a relief," said Cort Wesley, as if he needed something or somebody at which to lash out.

"Your son was in a bar last night, Mr. Masters. Were you aware he'd been drinking?"

"Dylan's football coach told us they had some meetings and Dylan left with a few teammates," Caitlin told him.

Finneran turned back toward her slowly, as if the mere motion pained him. The room's dim light left him bathed in shadows and Caitlin realized for the first time since they'd arrived that the sun was long gone and night had taken firm hold of the sky.

"And afterward they must have gone to Spats."

"Spats?"

"The bar where Dylan was drinking. Underage. Were you aware he had a fake identification?"

Caitlin unconsciously sidestepped to place herself between Finneran and Cort Wesley. "How could you know that if his wallet was missing?"

"The staff at Spats remembered him."

"From last night?"

"And numerous others."

"Did they recall him drinking last night?"

Finneran looked down, then only halfway up again. "Not specifically, no."

"Then why are we talking about this?" Caitlin interjected, unable to hold back.

"Because alcohol and college kids, especially football players, leads to fights. You can do the math as easy as I can, Ranger."

"So can I," Cort Wesley said, coming forward but stopping even with Caitlin as if struck by an invisible barrier before he could reach Finneran. "Enough to know it doesn't add up."

"He's right, Detective," Caitlin echoed. "Whatever happened didn't start in that bar. It started with that text message Dylan received. What I care about is finding what that text said, where it took him, and what happened when he got there."

Finneran stiffened. "Go home, Ranger."

"You said that to me once before."

"And now you're back."

"Just couldn't get enough of your lovely city, I guess."

"You killed five men last time you were here."

"Four," Caitlin corrected.

"That's right," Finneran nodded, gloating over her having walked right into his trap. "The assault victim in that bed over there knocked the fifth into the river. So maybe you can tell me which one of you he takes after."

"How badly you want to find out?" Cort Wesley asked him.

9

PROVIDENCE, RHODE ISLAND

"You getting at something here, Detective?" Cort Wesley continued before Finneran could react.

The detective started to speak, then changed his mind in midthought. "Only that the boy was clearly no stranger to violence," he said, words aimed more at Caitlin. "By your own admission."

Cort Wesley started forward through that invisible barrier, stopping only when Caitlin reached out for his arm but ended up with only the fabric of his shirt in her grasp. She could feel the rigidity of his triceps muscle beneath the cotton that was damp with perspiration.

"You mind addressing your remarks to me instead of the lady

here, sir?" he said so calmly his voice didn't sound calm at all. "You want to insinuate that both my sons are no strangers to violence, go ahead. Truth is the two of them have been the victims of it time and time again on account of the shit I keep dragging into their lives. Please don't blame them for my issues."

Cort Wesley started to ease himself farther forward and Caitlin let him go, the tone of his voice telling her it was okay.

"But what Dylan got himself into last night had nothing to do with any of that or either of us. So I'm gonna ask you as respectfully as I can to stop looking at my son through the lens of what happened before he was a student at your college here and start looking at him as the victim that he is."

Finneran was nodding, the gesture so routine as to appear meaningless. "We've got matters well under control, Mr. Masters, I assure you of that. It's good to see the boy has the kind of family support he needs in a time like this, but I need to tell you that's where the support needs to end." He stopped, as if to let his point sink in before he finished making it, aiming the remainder at Caitlin. "Let us do our jobs, Ranger. Stay out of this and let us catch whoever put the boy in that bed over there."

"Not sure I can do that, Detective. In fact, I'm sure I can't."

"It wasn't a request. Word gets out that the Texas Ranger who shot up WaterFire is back in town and everything else will get lost in the shuffle. Might even spook the perpetrators to skip town to avoid getting shot themselves."

Caitlin glanced at Dylan, all the tubes and wires running from him making the kid look like something from a science fiction movie. His face seemed to glow with life in the room's flickering shadows, but his eyes didn't move and closer up his cheeks looked as if they'd been flushed with milk.

"You're missing the point, Detective," Caitlin told him. "You're treating this like an ordinary fight, a beating, because that's what the perpetrators want. I'm assuming there were no witnesses."

"Not a one," the detective acknowledged.

"But I get the impression he was found on a public street."

"In the bushes slightly off one."

"So maybe that text he received baited him into a trap and he was jumped. You bother considering that?"

"The investigation is ongoing," Finneran said.

Fresh tension made the veins throb on Cort Wesley's temples. "What's that mean?"

"Just what I said."

"Then I'm going to assume that keeping me in the loop on everything isn't going to be a problem."

Finneran eyed Cort Wesley closer, sizing him up. "And what is it you do exactly, Mr. Masters?"

"I live in the moment, sir, which means what I do is wait by my son's bedside to be here when he wakes up . . . and just in case whoever did this to him comes back to finish the job."

"I get the feeling you're a man who wouldn't mind that at all. Am I right?"

"I believe the same thing could be said for any man."

"And what am I going to find when I run your name through the relevant databases?"

"That I'm someone you don't want to be on the wrong side of."

Finneran was left shaking his head. He reached back for the door to widen the opening a bit more. "Do you people ever sit back and listen to yourselves talk? You want to uphold the peace wherever your boots land, Ranger, I may not be able to stop you. But you damn well better respect the laws of Rhode Island and not the ones of where you came from."

"When a boy gets beaten within an inch of his life, the law's the law, Detective."

Finneran's eyes honed in on Caitlin, Cort Wesley's presence forgotten for the moment. "In that case, I'm going to give you the rest of the day to leave this state, Ranger, out of courtesy."

"And what happens after that?"

"An indictment against you gets unsealed. For unlawful possession and discharge of a weapon, and manslaughter."

"We both know what happened here last year was self-defense, Detective."

"That will be for a grand jury to decide," Finneran told her, "if you're not gone by midnight."

10

San Antonio, Texas

"I'm not going to take attendance," Guillermo Paz said to the assembled class of Mexican immigrants seeking to learn to speak English, almost all of whom spoke barely a word of it at present, "because I don't care who you are or whether you show up or not. See, I've been on an existentialist kick lately."

The adult students were squeezed into desks in a Dorney Hall classroom of San Antonio College, featuring a clear view of the park-like setting beyond the double windows that didn't actually open. At night there wasn't really much to see, but Paz liked watching the wind whip through the elm and maple trees beyond, imagining the sound of the branches rustling together through the closed windows. Standing nearly seven feet tall, as high as the top of the old-fashioned blackboard in the front of the classroom, afforded him a good view.

Right now the only sight that view provided was of his own reflection. His shoulders and chest looked so big that it seemed the glass must be warped. No shirt he could find seemed able to confine them without pinching, becoming little more than paint layered over his skin after a washing or two. His dark, oily hair glowed in the window glass, falling in a twisted tangle of ringlets just past his shoulders. His eyes were black and in the glass their reflection showed no whites at all, as if someone had painted over them with ink. His skin seemed shiny, slathered seemingly in some mysterious sheen even though it was dry to the touch. And there was a spot on his forehead, kind of a dark grainy indentation that looked like a third eye. Paz passed it off first as a smudge on the glass and sidestepped, only to find the third eye, or whatever it was, still in place.

"I know you're all here to learn English," Paz continued. "But I'm not going to use that workbook they gave you; instead, you're going to learn English the way I did, by listening and absorbing. That's what you're gonna do as I speak. Listen and absorb, even if you have no idea of what I'm saying. *Comprendé?*"

The class nodded to a smiling man and woman, even though they didn't comprehend him at all.

"These existentialists I've been reading are mostly full of shit, but they did raise a couple good points I wanted to share with you because I think they're especially appropriate to your situation. Specifically, I mean this existential notion that there's no meaning in the world beyond that which we give to it. I've learned that first-hand and nothing could be closer to the truth. See, I used to be an *asesino*. In a lot of ways I still am except now I only kill who I want for causes of my own choosing. My choice, not somebody else's, just like it was your choice to come to this country. You see what I'm getting at here?"

The class nodded enthusiastically again, although this time a few of the immigrants seated before Paz exchanged hushed words and looked confused.

"Here's what you need to know, *mis amigos*," Paz continued. "The philosopher Kierkegaard believed that happiness was a function of man's ability to manage control of the external conditions transpiring around him. Not easy to handle, that much I can assure you, and I can see the whole concept has you a bit baffled, so let me give you an example from my own life."

Here Paz felt his mind drifting, back to the time his refusal to burn a Venezuelan village and its people had led to his exile from his home country.

"I was a much different man before I met my Texas Ranger," he told his students, "just like all of you today are much different from the people you'll be next week, next month, and next year. I looked into my Ranger's eyes and saw what was missing in my own."

Paz stopped as if waiting for his words to sink in. His students looked on enthralled, captivated, recognition flashing in most of their gazes as if they could somehow glean the portent of words spoken in a language they hardly understood at all.

"Existentialism is mostly bullshit like everything else, but there are a few things we can learn from it. Take Albert Camus, for example. He was obsessed with the myth of Sisyphus, you know, the guy condemned to keep pushing the rock up a hill only to have it roll all the way back to the bottom as soon as he reaches the top. Camus's point was that the futility of the act wasn't as important as Sisyphus finding meaning and purpose in its completion. Why else would he continue to do something he knew was pointless? You see what I'm getting at here?"

His students didn't, their expressions utterly blank.

"Okay," Paz continued, "let me put it this way. There are going to be days where you feel the same futility that Sisyphus did. But, as was the case for him, the key for you will be to find purpose and meaning, a sense of fulfillment and achievement in the completion of the simplest task. That's as good a definition of happiness as you'll ever find and it's what I want you to take from this class if you take nothing else. The language itself doesn't matter because what matters is what transpires in your own mind. Thoughts are more important than actions because they define those actions and lend purpose to them that—"

Paz stopped in midsentence, midthought. A curtain drew before his vision, trapping his students behind it and leaving Paz alone in a cold, dark place. It parted slowly, some mystical being tugging on a rope to draw it open again, leaving him looking straight at his reflection in the window. But he was gone, his very being erased from existence so he could see straight through the glass to the darkness beyond. Then something else began to take shape in place of his reflection. Obscure and unrecognizable and then licked at by flames that later burst into a bright inferno that utterly consumed whatever had been taking shape before him. The flames seemed so real Paz swung to see if the classroom might have caught fire. But nothing had changed, his students still in their seats, a few of them following his gaze toward the window as if wondering what it was he had seen.

The flames continued to lick at the world beyond the window, and Paz caught glimpses of shapes and shadows consumed within them. He squinted, hoping to better grasp the message and portent of what was unfolding before his vision. For a moment, brief and fleeting, the face of Caitlin Strong appeared amid the flames, threatened by them and yet untouched for the time being. Then the flames were gone, Caitlin Strong having vanished with them, nothing but darkness remaining beyond the window. Even the trees and campus beyond were gone, lost to a maelstrom of violence that was coming. At once, Paz felt blisteringly hot, as if the flames had found him. Just as quickly, though, he went cold, imagining the flames dying as if buckets of ice water were dumped over his person.

"*¿Son esta usted bien, Profesor?*"

"*¿Pasa algo?*"

"Yes," Paz said in English, "something is very wrong. My Texas Ranger needs me." Then he was in motion for the door. "*Clase desestimó.* Class dismissed."

I I

NEW BRAUNFELS, TEXAS

"Look at me and tell me if I seem convinced," the man named Brooks said. "That's because I'm not convinced the situation is contained at all."

Li Zhen studied him dispassionately, viewing him as no more than another ornament within the Chinese garden around which he'd constructed the American headquarters of Yuyuan, the company he'd built from the ground up thanks to the support he'd won from the Triad sixteen years earlier.

"I was not aware I needed to convince you of anything," he told Brooks.

"This is the United States, my friend, not China. An innocent kid getting the shit kicked out of him tends to rub people the wrong way here. Last time I checked, it was called a crime."

"You can make your point without sarcasm or such unfortunate language."

"Really?" Brooks asked him. "Because you don't seem to be getting my point at all."

Brooks towered over Zhen's diminutive stature, with broad shoulders barely contained by the white dress shirt that fit him too tightly in the neck. His head too was large, his skull looking almost simian in shape beneath hair cropped so close that his scalp burned red beneath the sun, the shading exaggerated by the milky paleness of his skin. He looked like a man better suited for a military uniform, in contrast to Li Zhen's perfectly fitted Jhane Barnes suit that elegantly covered his athletic frame. It was the only brand Zhen wore, in recognition of the fact that Jhane Barnes was the first major label to relocate its apparel manufacturing to China.

And an American label at that.

"You seem unimpressed, my friend," Li Zhen said, trying to keep the disgust he felt for the man from creeping into his voice.

"With your efforts to reassure me that things haven't spun out of control here, you're damn right." Brooks was sweating despite the coolness dominating the air, even for October in Texas. "You should have told me the truth about the girl, Li. Holding back serves neither of our interests."

"Personally or those of our countries?"

"What's the difference?" Brooks smirked. "And that's the point I'm trying to make here."

Zhen knew "Brooks" wasn't the man's real name but didn't care about that any more than he cared about the man himself. He was a distraction, a part of his overall operation to be tolerated as necessary and placated as much as possible.

"Did you think we wouldn't find out the truth?" Brooks, or whoever he really was, continued. "We're pretty good at this stuff. You should keep that in mind."

"I have, my friend," Zhen said, his voice calm in a cold and disinterested manner. "I always do. The girl will be found."

"Which implies she hasn't been yet. That's why I'm not reassured by your insistence that the situation is contained, especially since your efforts ended up putting an innocent kid in the hospital. It's only a matter of time." Here, Brooks enunciated his point by tapping his watch, further annoying Zhen.

"A matter of time before what?"

"Your indiscretions lead back to you. And if they lead back to you, there's a risk they could lead back to us, and that's a risk we cannot accept."

Zhen simply shook his head, seemingly unmoved as he gazed about the garden. "All this beauty and you seem not to even notice."

The Yuyuan Gardens, as Zhen had come to think of them, formed an elegant testament to a tradition dating back thousands of years in his home country. A classical mix of tumbling waterfalls, flowering plants, and thickly lavish vegetation all laid amid beautiful layered stone and rock of varying colors and sizes keyed to the particular area of display they inhabited.

"What's that have to do with anything?"

Zhen smiled, enjoying the fact that the American believed he, and his people, were in charge, just as the Triad had upon their initial meeting. "I built this garden because I wanted the employees of Yuyuan to find true beauty just steps away from their offices. Because in this beauty they will find purpose to their work. They will know that while their individual contributions might seem to mean nothing when compared against the greater whole, each of those contributions are actually like all of the flowers you see around you. Each one adds its own element of beauty. Remove it and the garden suffers. But in beauty, there is also danger."

Zhen strolled on, leading the American along the garden's winding paths, the flowers they passed so beautiful that they looked part of a landscape painting dropped onto the scene instead of grown there. He caught his own reflection in a still stream, feeling he had not aged a single day in the sixteen years since his new life had begun. He wore his still thick hair slicked back. His complexion was unmarred by wrinkles and his skin tone even except for a tint of red that seemed to perpetually flush his cherub-like cheeks.

Zhen stopped before a nest of beautiful red, pink, and white flowering plants. "This is oleander, among the most beautiful flowers known to man," he told Brooks. "But also among the most poisonous. Just breathing in the aroma from a strain as pure as this is enough to induce symptoms that include heart palpitations that can lead to death if not treated almost immediately. There are stories of besieged Chinese villages burning fields of oleander to forestall the approach of their enemies, sometimes turning them back altogether."

Brooks nodded impatiently. "So your point is that the girl is beautiful and dangerous. I get that, Li."

"Actually, that's not my point at all. In the case of oleander it is not the flower that may cause death, it's the ignorance of the man unaware of the danger it portends. Do you see my point?"

Brooks smirked again. "Let me make *my* point, Li. Your whole operation here is under my control and my discretion. We may serve each other's needs, but it happens on my terms. Is that clear?"

Zhen bowed slightly in feigned reverence again.

"What is it that old Chinese curse?" Brooks asked him. "'May you live in interesting times,' isn't it?"

Zhen just looked at him.

"Well," Brooks continued, "I suppose we're both cursed, aren't we? That's a point we need to keep in mind in the hope the day never comes when we find our interests opposing each other."

At that, Li Zhen reached up and pulled an entire oleander flower, stem and all, from its bush.

"For that day," he said, handing it to Brooks.

* * *

Li Zhen remained alone in his gardens for some time after Brooks departed, stroking the oleander petals as if the flowers were pets, enjoying the risk he was taking by sucking in their deceptively dangerous aroma. Finally he entered the building through a private entrance and stepped into an elevator cleverly disguised as a closet. The compartment swept him downward through four stories of hardened concrete to make sure the true purpose behind Yuyuan's very existence was never detected by spy satellites orbiting hundreds of miles in space.

The elevator opened onto an underground floor that made up a single cavernous space that could have been part of a brokerage house or call center, except its stations were unmanned. Everything in Li Zhen's true headquarters, the ultimate product of his initial meeting with the Triad captains all those years ago, was automated. And everything keyed off two dozen wall-sized monitor screens that provided the floor's only light until sensors picked up his movements and activated the dull fluorescents recessed overhead. Each screen represented a region of the United States, all of them showing a constant scroll of numbers rolling from top to bottom. Those numbers, collected and received from a pair of satellites launched by the Chinese government, were then programmed into the drive of a supercomputer that powered the various substations lining the floor before terminals that might as well have been manned by ghosts. Their screens glowed eerily, the collective light forming a kind of haze in the floor's dehumidified air that seemed thick enough to touch.

The total count, according to the central monitor, had exceeded a hundred million for the first time two days ago and was already a hundred and twenty-five million now. And before too long, Li Zhen fully expected that number to double to nearly two hundred and fifty million.

Representing eighty percent of the United States population.

All of whom would be dead in a week's time.

PART TWO

When we see him at his daily task of maintaining law, restoring order, and promoting peace—even though his methods be vigorous— we see him in his proper setting, a man standing alone between a society and its enemies.

—Walter Prescott Webb, *The Texas Rangers*

12

"*. . . if you're not gone by midnight, Ranger.*"

Finneran's threat seemed a better fit for the Old West, but Caitlin knew it was to be taken seriously nonetheless. The last thing she needed, especially in the wake of plowing members of the Beacon of Light Church into a drainage trench, was to get embroiled in yet another fiasco certain to draw unwelcome attention to her and the Rangers.

From Rhode Island Hospital, Caitlin and Cort Wesley went to Spats, the bar just off the college-dominated Thayer Street, where, according to Detective Finneran, Dylan was last seen before he was attacked.

"Sure, I remember him," the manager, a stout muscular man named Theo, said, handing Dylan's picture back to Cort Wesley. "Comes in a lot with his friends. Always smiling. Good with the girls."

"He was in here with some friends last night," Caitlin picked up. Theo's olive skin and slight accent made her peg him as being from the Middle East, Lebanon or maybe Turkey. "Before he was attacked."

"Oh, man," Theo said, shaking his head. "Just goddamn awful. . . ."

"My son," Cort Wesley said, still holding the picture.

Theo shifted his shoulders and stretched his arms, trying to find comfort in the sports jacket that fit him too snugly. "For what it's worth, I'm sorry."

"For what it's worth, what was an eighteen-year-old kid doing drinking in a bar?"

"Nobody said he was drinking."

Caitlin let her eyes drift over the tables squeezed below the bar area beneath a host of wide-screen televisions where kids who looked to be little or no older than Dylan were filling glasses out of tall plastic tubes with beer foam clinging to the empty portions. "What else do people do here?" she asked Theo.

"You didn't let me finish," he said. "Sunday night that kid— Dylan—came in here and met some friends at a table in the back over there and ordered a tube."

"One of those," Caitlin said, pointing toward the tables in the lower area of the bar where a hockey game was projected on one screen and a basketball game on the two others. She didn't notice who was playing.

"Yes. But before it got to the table, a girl showed up. Dylan must have recognized her because he joined her at the bar right away."

"You tell this to the Providence police detectives?"

"Sure. They asked the same questions you are pretty much."

"Did it look like Dylan was expecting her?" Caitlin asked, thinking of the text message Dylan supposedly received.

"I couldn't say. Sorry."

"Can you describe the girl?" Cort Wesley asked him.

Theo hedged.

"What's wrong?"

"I just want to choose my words carefully here. The girl wasn't a Brown student. Only time I ever saw her she was alone and not just here either."

"What are you getting at?"

"I manage the place across the street too. I've seen her at the back bar there, when we open it as a nightclub called Viva. I had her pegged as, well, a working girl."

Caitlin and Cort Wesley exchanged a wary glance.

"That's why I noticed when she walked in here last night," Theo continued. "College kids aren't her kind of crowd, especially a kid like your son who could probably have any girl he wanted. I don't know how old she was, but I'd guess twenty-four, maybe twenty-five. Always very well dressed. Reminded me of a model, something like that."

Caitlin could see Cort Wesley's mind veering in a different direction.

"How'd my son get in here exactly, Theo?"

"He's got an ID."

"A fake ID, you mean."

"They all have fakes, Mr. Masters."

"Dylan didn't have one when he left Texas."

"You sure about that?"

"Could you describe the girl for us?" Caitlin interjected, before Cort Wesley could respond to Theo's challenge.

"Are you a cop or something?"

"Something. A Texas Ranger."

"You got any jurisdiction up here?"

"So long as Providence is part of the United States. You mind describing the girl now?"

"Long dark hair, not much over five feet tall. Very beautiful and exotic-looking," Theo finished. "Oh, and she was Chinese."

Caitlin felt her cell phone vibrating in the pocket of her jeans and drew it out. "It's Paz," she told Cort Wesley.

13

"How's the boy, Ranger?"

"How'd you know to ask, Colonel?"

Of all the relationships Caitlin had ever enjoyed, the one she maintained with Colonel Guillermo Paz was by far the strangest and most inexplicable. It had begun under violent circumstances over five years ago now with them on opposite sides and had continued with them having joined forces ever since.

Paz, a former colonel in the Venezuelan secret police and Hugo Chavez's personal attack dog for a time, said it was because he'd seen something in Caitlin's eyes that had changed his life forever. He seemed single-mindedly and resolutely committed to protecting her at all costs to himself. That protection now extended to Cort Wesley and his two sons and probably anyone else who was important in Caitlin's life. When a secretive hit squad had attacked Caitlin, Cort Wesley, and his boys on the streets of a Texas town, Paz paid a visit to the squad's headquarters in Houston where he proceeded to pour an experimental explosive down their throats that blew them up from the inside. When a kill team composed of Mexico's worst killers launched an attack during one of Dylan's high school lacrosse games, Paz rode to the rescue wedged out of a sunroof firing twin assault rifles. The list went on.

The colonel had a small private army in his charge now, operating under the auspices of a Homeland Security spook whose name varied by the assignment and who believed Paz was beholden to him, whereas Caitlin knew Paz was beholden to no one. They didn't see each other very much but he always seemed to know when she needed him, or was about to.

"I had a vision," Paz told her. "I used to see things only in my dreams, like my mother, who had the sight. But now I get them when I'm awake too. I saw the outlaw's oldest boy in this one consumed by flames."

"Dylan was attacked last night. He's in a hospital in Providence, Rhode Island. That's where Cort Wesley and I are right now."

"Providence, Rhode Island?"

"The boy goes to school here now, Colonel. College."

"I'm teaching at one of those myself now."

"Really?"

"English to those who don't speak it yet," Paz said, not bothering to elaborate further.

"What else did you see in that vision, Colonel?" Caitlin asked him.

"This is just the beginning, Ranger. But I don't think I'm telling you anything you don't already know."

"What about a young Chinese woman? Anything about her?" Caitlin asked, not believing she was actually posing the question.

"Not that I've seen yet," Paz told her.

He tried to recapture the broader message of his vision in his mind. But it was more a series of still shots than a moving portrait, denying him a clear picture. Then he recalled what had come after the flames had receded, leaving a scent on his nostrils like scorched wood and earth and flushing heat through his blood that made his skin feel oven-baked. He'd gazed out the window at nothing where the shifting trees enveloped the parklike grounds of San Antonio College beneath a moonlit sky, nothing at all.

"Darkness," Paz heard himself say softly.

"Say that again."

"I saw darkness, Ranger."

"Nothing we haven't seen before, Colonel."

"This is different. You've heard of the existentialist philosopher Martin Heidegger?"

"Only that the Nazis were rather fond of his teachings."

"That's because he wrote extensively on the connections between being and action, that by undertaking actions which do not
support that being a man risks degeneration. Heidegger believed
the wasteland was not so much a place as a state of mind we effectively banish ourselves to if we don't stop resisting the nature of our
being and just accept it."

"What's the point here, Colonel?"

"Goes back to the point you raised about the affinity the Nazis
held for Heidegger. They saw in his writings moral justification for
their actions because they were acting upon the natures they perceived themselves to possess. Following the path they were meant
to take. You see where I'm going with this?"

"Nazis represent as dark an evil as man has ever known," Caitlin
assumed.

"There's a new darkness coming," Paz told her. "I saw it take the
outlaw's boy in its grasp when he crossed its sweep. Be warned that
it's not about to stop with him. This darkness is hungry for more
and I could see no end to its reach in my vision."

"There's something bigger involved here. That's what you're
saying, Colonel."

"Isn't there always?"

14

PROVIDENCE, RHODE ISLAND

Theo provided Caitlin and Cort Wesley with the names of the two
Brown University students Dylan met up with at Spats the previous
night. He also provided one of their phone numbers and the information that neither played football, in contrast to Coach Estes's
assertion that Dylan had been with some fellow freshmen players
prior to the attack.

"Are we in trouble?" Salaar Khan asked when they met in the

Delta Phi fraternity house lounge, inside a brick-walled quadrangle draped in ivy where Greek life on campus was centered.

"That depends," Caitlin told him and fellow Delta Phi brother Ross Julian beneath the glow of a video game frozen on a big wide-screen television hanging from a wall over the room's fire-place mantel.

"Is this official?" Salaar picked up. "I mean, you're a Texas Ranger and this is Rhode Island."

"We're here because Dylan's my son," Cort Wesley interjected.

"Do we need a lawyer?" Salaar asked.

"What did I just say?"

"We heard what happened," Ross said, speaking finally. "How can we help?"

What struck Caitlin most about these two Brown University juniors was how young they looked. Then she thought of Dylan lying in a hospital bed and started to feel the heat building inside her again. The video game frozen on the mounted wide-screen television looked to be one of those shoot-'em-ups where players with soldier avatar figures got points for each kill. She'd seen Luke playing similar ones, cringing every time a fake gunshot rang out through the surround sound, wondering what it might do to the video-game industry if every player had to witness what real violence looked like. Luke, Cort Wesley's fifteen-year-old younger son, was enrolled at a Houston boarding school now, and she found herself starting to worry whether something bad was about to befall him. Maybe she should've asked Paz about that too.

"You were with Dylan in Spats last night," Caitlin said, after clearing her throat in the hope it might do the same to her mind.

"He showed up there after his football meetings," the one named Ross said.

"But this isn't the football fraternity. Have I got that right?"

"You do," Ross told her. "Football players join Thete—Theta Delta Chi. Dylan will probably end up there, but he fits in better here."

"Get back to last night," Caitlin told him. "You said you met up with Dylan after his football meetings."

"We didn't exactly meet up with him," Salaar answered instead. "We were already inside when he arrived. He sat down with us, but he was waiting for a girl."

Cort Wesley eased himself forward on the couch he'd pulled out and tilted on an angle so he and Caitlin could better face the boys. It still smelled of fresh leather. Caitlin noticed that the room's sole light, other than that emanating from the television screen, spilled from two tracks missing half their fixtures.

"This would be the Chinese girl we heard about," Cort Wesley said to them both. "Was she his girlfriend or something?"

Ross and Salaar looked at each other, then shrugged in virtual unison.

"Something," Ross said.

"And what's that exactly?"

"Definitely not his girlfriend," Salaar tried to elaborate.

"I believe we're straight on that much. Now tell me what's bothering the two of you about this. What's got you so uncomfortable?"

"He recognized her," Salaar managed, while Ross was still collecting his thoughts. "From another night, the first time he saw her."

"Recognized her from where?" Cort Wesley asked them.

The two boys looked at each other, as if to determine who would answer.

"From where?" Cort Wesley repeated.

"A video," Salaar responded.

"The kind you may not want to hear about," Ross added.

15

They watched what could only be described as a pornography video right there, projected wirelessly via laptop onto the widescreen mounted over the fireplace. Caitlin told Salaar to hit pause as soon as the young Chinese woman made her first appearance, still fully clothed.

The bar manager's description didn't do her justice. Her beauty was as natural as it was ravishing and exotic. Her black hair was long, tumbling past her shoulders in light waves. Her complexion seemed fair and pristine, like a porcelain statue until the screen froze on her smiling, which exaggerated her beauty and made her look a notch beyond seductive.

Caitlin supposed that was the point. She hadn't had much dealings with pornography, Internet or otherwise, but any experience was too much. Especially when it involved what could only be equated as a modern form of slavery. A seminar Caitlin had taken last year at Quantico pegged human trafficking as a thirty-five-billion-dollar-a-year international industry with the vast bulk of that being spent in the United States. That seminar had provided samples of various brands of pornography, and as things went, this looked relatively high-end as opposed to the underground variety that ranged from kiddie porn to even higher up on the demented scale.

The film featured credited names that were almost surely fake and a grabber of a title, *Pumping Iris*. Caitlin guessed that the Iris of the title was the very girl with whom Dylan had left Spats the night before.

"Any way you can lift a still picture off this?" she asked Salaar.

"Sure. I can isolate it and e-mail it to you. Or print it out if you can wait a few minutes. The quality won't be great, though."

"It'll do and I'd like you to jot down the URL link to the video," Caitlin said, standing up and turning her back to the screen. "And we don't mind waiting at all. I appreciate your help, both of you. I'm sure Dylan would too. Isn't that right, Cort Wesley?"

He grunted something, still coming to terms with all he'd learned about his oldest son, then nodded with apparent reluctance.

"We'll wait down here, if that's okay."

"Fine," Salaar said with Ross nodding behind him, the two of them relieved to be able to make their exit. "Just be a few minutes."

Caitlin turned off the television as soon as they were gone. "I know what you're thinking, Cort Wesley."

"Don't even go there, Ranger."

"When did you start drinking exactly?"

"Why is it always your job to defend Dylan?"

"That doesn't answer my question."

"I was different."

"You sure were. Boone Masters had you working with his crew boosting major appliances out of warehouses when you were, what, fifteen? Took all of that long before Dylan got himself kidnapped and went up against a serial killer because we dragged him into our shit."

"I get the point."

"I don't believe you do, Cort Wesley. I seem to recall you saying you started drinking whiskey around the same time you rode in the back of your dad's truck holding the fridges in place. I don't see a problem with Dylan doing it in college along with pretty much all the rest of the population. I think you're more bothered by this fake ID thing because it reminds you how young he is and how much you miss him, especially with Luke off in boarding school. You think I don't feel the same way?"

Cort Wesley made a point of checking his watch.

"What are you doing?" Caitlin asked him.

"Finneran gave you until midnight to get out of Dodge. I wanted to see how much time you had left."

"And that makes me figure I should take you with me when I go."

"Why exactly?"

"You want me gone so you can handle this your own way."

"I'll handle it my own way, whether you're here or not."

Caitlin checked her phone to find a call from Captain Tepper that had come in while she and Cort Wesley had been questioning the two Delta Phi fraternity brothers.

"Get your butt back in the saddle, Ranger," his message started, choppy and stiff the way all his voice mails were. "We got ourselves a genuine serial killer. I need you back here."

"You smoking right now, D.W.?"

"See the influence you got on me even from a thousand miles away?"

"I'm guessing you already heard from the Providence police again."

"Yeah, a pissed-off detective who told me he gave you until to-night to leave town. I laughed and warned him that he issued his ultimatum to somebody who bulldozed the last person to piss her off into a drainage ditch."

"I was looking forward to what he was going to do when I'm still here tomorrow."

"Didn't you listen to my message, Ranger?"

"We've had serial killers in Texas before, D.W.," Caitlin told him.

"Right. Before, as in a hundred and thirty years ago, on your great-granddaddy William Ray Strong's watch."

Caitlin knew there was only one case he could be talking about, the legendary one that had seen William Ray Strong paired with none other than Judge Roy Bean.

"And if I wasn't of reasonably sound mind," Tepper continued, his voice scratchy from cigarette smoke, "I'd say the same killer's back for an encore."

16

Judge Roy Bean rode out to the Chinese camp alongside William Ray Strong, the Ranger keeping his pace slow since Bean looked like a man ready to be thrown well before his horse reached a gallop. They hitched their horses to posts under the watchful, suspicious gazes of the Chinese milling about, their eyes widening at sight of William Ray's Texas Ranger badge proudly displayed on his lapel.

"Anybody here speak good enough English to understand what I'm saying?" Judge Bean asked them.

Many raised their hands, all of them tentatively.

"We're here about the killings of your women and need to be pointed in the right direction."

Those who understood him took Bean literally and pointed off to the right, toward a single structure on the camp's outskirts perched in the shade. The judge and Ranger had just started that way when a thin woman with ash gray hair gathered in a bun grabbed hold of William Ray's arm.

"My daughter," she said in what sounded more like a plea, squeezing his arm even tighter. "My daughter."

William Ray saw the sadness of mourning in her eyes and nodded. "I understand, ma'am, I understand," he said, hoping she did as well.

The woman released his arm, looking no less sad as she bowed repeatedly. "Thank you, thank you."

She moved aside so the two men could continue on, followed the whole way by even more curious stares. The mud-strewn center of the camp was dominated by canvas tents stained dark and dotted with clotheslines, fire pits, and several larger tents, these strung over heavy posts and served as a school for the children and a cafe-

teria where the workers ate breakfast and dinner. William Ray and
the judge noticed a few whites mixed in among the Chinese, talking to them with Bibles held in their grasps and crucifixes dangling
from their necks.

"Missionaries," Bean noted, "trying to turn the Chinks' skin
white."

This vantage point afforded a clear view of both the earthen
dam up the river to the north and the actual worksite several hundred yards to the south, where Southern Pacific personnel were visible as mere specs checking to see if the land was dry enough to
resume work. Normally this time of year the land would be parched,
a veritable dirt and gravel bowl laid over a landscape so flat that
walking it bored a man's feet, William Ray's father used to say. The
railroad had chosen, for precisely that reason, to originate this northern spur of the Trans-Pecos line here. The unseasonable rains had
taken everyone by surprise, and William Ray heard it told that it
had actually been one of the Chinese who suggested the dam's construction based on a similar experience he'd had on a railroad worksite in California.

A Chinese man was busy writing something out on an oblong
board placed upon an easel in the lee of a grove of trees. William
Ray figured it must be the coming week's work schedule, and he
took his hat off, along with the judge, when they got close enough
to the man to block out what little light streamed through the trees.
He worked with paint and brush, an artist more than a laborer,
looking up after he finished the line he was working on.

"I'm Texas Ranger William Ray Strong and this here's Judge
Roy Bean," William Ray said by way of greeting.

The man regarded them suspiciously. "Did the railroad send
you? Are you going to arrest us all?"

"No, the railroad didn't send us, and that would depend on what
you did."

"We went on strike. After the railroad refused to pay us for
building their dam for them. They are very angry, but so are we
over them breaking their word."

"Never trust a man in a suit, friend," said Judge Roy Bean, hitching his thumbs in his vest pockets. "And it's these murders of your women we're here about, not this here strike."

The man's expression brightened immediately. He reached and shook each of their hands, clearly grateful for their presence.

"Call me Su," he greeted in perfect English. "All the Americans do."

"We were directed to you, sir," William Ray told him.

"The railroad does not care about the killings. They have done nothing about them, even before the strike."

"That's why we're here, Mr. Su. Because we do and we will."

"Just Su," the man corrected. "Please."

"Okay. Su."

"What can you tell us about the victims?" Judge Bean asked him.

"Four women so far. Every few days these last few weeks. Always found dead. Always the same. Always killed at night. One found in camp, one just outside it, and two nearer the head of the tracks," Su finished, referring to the congested temporary town set up where the rails currently ended.

"What were they doing there at night exactly, sir?" William Ray asked.

"Some of our women have taken to providing service to the workmen. To bring in extra money."

"Whores, in other words," elaborated Judge Bean.

Su didn't bother to argue his point.

"Anybody ever see anything at all?" William Ray asked him. "Maybe somebody who didn't belong who might have done this."

Su stiffened, black paint dribbling down off his brush to stain his otherwise perfect chart. "Not who," he said. "*What*."

Su led the Ranger and the judge through a camp William Ray found surprisingly well maintained, right down to the clapboard outhouses the Chinese workers had built themselves with no assistance or funding whatsoever from Southern Pacific. The camp had a seasoned look to it, populated no doubt by Chinese who'd been in the United States and working the rails for some time. That explained the organized nature of the surroundings and why, unlike every other Chinese worker camp he'd ever been in, this one featured children rushing about, their bare feet churning through the mud that speckled their faces.

"The latest woman murdered was last seen alive hanging laundry after another storm passed. A few hours later, her body was found just like the other three."

"And how's that?" William Ray asked him.

"Better you see, Ranger," Su answered, leading them on.

Judge Roy Bean pushed a thick wedge of chewing tobacco into his mouth when they reached a lone tent set way back from the others, in the camp's shadiest and thus coolest spot. The Chinese had built the bulk of this particular camp in the heat of the Texas sun, but that also brought them closer to the river swelling over its banks. Fetching the pails of water needed for a camp of maybe five hundred residents was no small task, making the heat better to brave than the endless succession of treks.

Su parted the flap and held it open, eyes tilted almost reverently downward as William Ray and the judge entered. The stench assaulted them immediately, like spoiled meat spilled from a grocery wagon left to roast on the street. Enough to tell William Ray the woman had been dead for a day, maybe two at the most, as he moved ahead of the judge toward a wooden slab of a table that still smelled like fresh lumber.

Su pinned the flap open behind him so the light could shine into the tent. Wooden shelves dominated the square structure, lined with knickknacks and trinkets that all looked handmade. William Ray's eyes were drawn first to a series of finely stitched dolls lining the upper reaches, each unique and personal as if possessing a soul made of stuffing.

"I make toys for the camp's children," Su explained. "Often I make too many."

The dolls were beautiful, the Ranger thought, but somehow sad, as if to reflect the general plight of the Chinese who'd worked the rails almost since the first tracks had been laid on the Transcontinental Railroad. Amazing how changing the placement of a few threads could create virtually any emotion in such seasoned hands. Too bad the feelings of real people, not just elegantly embroidered dolls, could be affected as easily.

William Ray also noticed several intricate creations, including a series of train cars carved out of wood in the process of being painted. And on a table set in a darkened corner, he saw what looked like a scale model of the river and the recently completed dam.

"It was your idea," he said, realizing. "Building the dam, I mean."

Su nodded humbly and bowed slightly. "I am something of an engineer. But more recently I am, how do you say, a coroner."

William Ray moved his gaze toward the outline of a body evident beneath a water-stained canvas blanket. He eased the canvas back, peeling it away as respectfully as he could.

"Holy hell," Judge Bean muttered, taking off his hat. "Am I seeing this wrong?"

"Nope," William Ray told him, "that's the back of her head all right."

It was facing the wrong direction, the victim's hair falling over the nape of her neck where her face should have been.

"Looks like it was cut off and sewn back on," noted Bean. "Backward."

"But the way the blood settled here, here, and here tells me he broke her neck or strangled her first. Then he cut off her head and sewed it back on." William Ray looked toward Su who'd remained by the tent flap, his eyes distant and distracted as if he was hearing what he'd already determined for himself. "Were the others found like this?"

"Almost exactly. Their bodies are in the ground now."

"Before you reported the murders?"

"We did report them, to the chief of the Southern Pacific railroad police."

"He do anything about it?"

"Yes. He told me to leave his office."

The stitching on the woman's neck and throat, William Ray noted, was irregularly spaced; the thick, jagged lines marked by makeshift black thread that looked more like twine. Thick trails of dried blood ran from each stitch. Something made him want to turn the woman's head back around the way it should be. Instead, though, William Ray peeled more of the canvas backward; bundling it over the corpse's thighs to expose her midriff and private area, he set to examining.

"What is it you're doing there, Ranger?" Judge Bean asked him, his stomach gurgling audibly with distaste at the scene.

"There's bruising here but no swelling," William Ray reported, angling his frame to block view of the woman's body from Bean. "That tells me the killer likely violated her after she was dead." Then he looked toward Su. "How old was this girl, sir?"

"Nineteen, Ranger."

Bean's features tightened enough to close his eyes halfway, mouth wrinkled in disgust. He blew out some hot breath. "What do you make of him sewing her head on backward before he stuck himself inside her?"

William Ray smacked his lips together, thinking on that. "Only thing I can figure is he didn't want her to see him doing it, dead or alive."

Judge Bean looked toward Su. "That a Chink thing or something?"

"It wasn't a Chinese who did this," Su told him calmly.

"Son, I don't see any other way whoever did this could move about so close to the camp without drawing notice."

"Unless it was invisible."

"*It?*" from William Ray.

"The land is angry over what we've done to it, Ranger. The Indians you've been to war with left many burial grounds behind that we've ravaged in laying track. Maybe one of them finally got angry."

"But that's not what *bahk guai* means, is it?"

Su glanced toward Roy Bean, as if the judge's presence was keeping him from elaborating further. "Death follows in the wake of the White Devil, these victims only adding to his tally."

"Make you a deal, Ranger," Judge Roy Bean offered outside the tent, the two of them glad for the fresh air after soaking up the spoiled, sickening stench that continued to cling to their nostrils like prairie dust. "You catch him, and I'll hang him."

"Might be a good idea to give the sumbitch a trial first, Judge."

"That never stopped me before," Roy Bean winked.

William Ray considered Bean's proposal, working his tongue around his mouth from left to right and sweeping it across the inside of both cheeks, pushing one out and then the other. "Is what you said really true, about only hanging one man?"

"Sentenced two. The other escaped 'fore I got the chance."

"That don't answer my question."

"It's a fact, yes, though I don't suspect I'd want to see it written down nowhere. Man don't got much to stand on 'sides his own reputation."

"In that case, I'd be glad to have your help, Judge," William Ray told him.

"Then what say we head back to the Langtry saloon and do us some drinking?"

"Rather we have ourselves a look-see down at the head of the tracks."

"Fine by me," Judge Roy Bean said, "long as we drink up afterward."

"I'm buying, Judge."

"Didn't you hear?" Bean grinned. "All drinks are free on hanging days, son."

"Gotta catch the sumbitch first."

"A mere formality," the judge followed.

17

PROVIDENCE, RHODE ISLAND

"What's the connection with this new serial killer?" Caitlin asked, after Tepper finished a part of the story she'd long forgotten.

"What do you think? We got the bodies of five women scattered across the southern part of the state, all with their severed heads sewn back on their necks facing the wrong way and all raped postmortem. Department of Public Safety has assigned the case to the Rangers."

"Lucky us."

"Lucky *you*. This thing goes public, the whole damn state crawls under a bed until they find out a bona fide gunfighter is on the job. So the Department of Public Safety wants me to put that well-earned reputation of yours to good use."

"I'll take the first flight out of Providence tomorrow morning."

"There's one leaving out of Boston in a couple hours. Get you in the air before midnight."

"Sorry, Captain, I won't be able to make it."

"Why?"

"There's something I gotta do first."

18

Dylan was dreaming, at least he thought he was. He felt something cold grasp his hand, tried to squeeze back but couldn't. Then remembered it didn't matter because he was just dreaming.

"I'm sorry."

Or was he?

"This was all my fault."

Because the soft voice in his ear felt very real. It sounded like Kai and he wanted to tell her she had nothing to be sorry about; maybe he did tell her, because he felt something squeeze his hand harder.

"Can you hear me?"

Kind of.

"Squeeze my hand back if you can."

Sorry, no can do. Hey, am I dreaming or are you really here?

"Say my name."

Kai.

"Say my name."

Kai. Can't you hear me?

In his mind, Dylan remembered spotting her across the nightclub floor, the blueish translucent lighting almost identical to how they'd shot the last scene of the video from which he'd immediately recognized her. Like there wasn't any doubt and no coincidence at all. It was the same girl from the video, *Pumping Iris* or something, in the flesh only covered up. Wearing skintight jeans that looked painted onto her perfect lines, coated with something shiny so they were more like leather than denim. She looked really athletic and for some reason Dylan pictured her on horseback. Made for a great opening line.

"Say, do you ride?"

The way she looked at him made him feel like an idiot, a loser, and he regretted even coming over until she grasped his arm tenderly and then stroked it.

"I'm sorry I got you involved in this," he heard her say now, wherever he was.

But Dylan was thinking about how he'd taken her back to his room. He'd had more than his share of girls in high school, but nothing like this with a room all to himself and no fear of his brother, father, or Caitlin walking in on him. He'd never been with a girl before already wrapped up as a fantasy in his mind. Couldn't believe it was really the girl from the video that had been spreading around Delta Phi. And, truth be told, he hadn't known for sure she was a professional, or what that meant exactly, until they were back in his room for a night that couldn't have been better if his imagination had conjured up the whole thing. They'd finally drifted off to sleep together around dawn and Dylan woke up to find Kai gone, realizing he'd already missed his first class.

It was the next day that he began to realize she was in some kind of big trouble, figured it out only when she began to pester him about Caitlin Strong after spotting her in pictures in his room and on his phone wearing her Texas Ranger badge. At first she thought it was a Halloween costume, didn't think a woman could become a Ranger.

Boy, could I tell you some stories . . .

And Kai pestered Dylan to do just that, something clearly on her mind the night they'd met up at Spats just before he'd been jumped.

"I'll make it up to you," Dylan heard her saying now. "I brought you something so when you wake up you'll know I was really here."

But where was he? Where was *she*?

He heard her speak but couldn't respond, as if in some deep sleep from which he couldn't rouse himself.

"I promise," she said. "I won't let you—"

She stopped there, her voice immediately replaced by those of his father and Caitlin approaching the room.

19

"You can still make that flight tonight," Cort Wesley told Caitlin as they entered Dylan's room.

"I need to see him again before I head home."

"Expecting a miracle, Ranger?"

"He's gonna be just fine without one, Cort Wesley."

As they reached Dylan's bed, to find a pink rose sitting atop his covers, Caitlin caught the reflection in the window glass of a figure darting out from behind a door down the hallway. It was just a glimpse, but enough to identify her as a young woman who matched the description of the Chinese girl from the video and the bar.

"Stay with him!" she instructed Cort Wesley, as she burst out into the hall.

Caitlin swept her gaze in the direction she thought the young woman had fled, then remembered it was a reflection, meaning she had it backward. And sure enough a shape crashed through an exit door into a hospital stairwell halfway down the hallway in that direction instead. She charged after her, the door just closing when she reached it.

Caitlin had her gun out by then, more instinctive than anything else, as she followed the echo of footsteps downward, passing level after level. She was gaining no ground at all. The echo of her steps ended with the thump of another door crashing open, Caitlin heading down the last flight to see the door leading into the hospital's engineering room just swaying closed.

She shouldered through it before it sealed, any potential sound of footsteps lost to the hum, whir, and grind of machinery, fans, air exchangers, and pumping apparatus. Caitlin felt as if she'd been dropped into some horror movie with the killer certain to lurch out from behind a rusted baffle or drop down from the steam pipes hissing overhead.

Instead, she spotted the young woman speeding through the clutter of the floor with a dancer's agility.

"Stop!" Caitlin yelled, picking up the chase but gaining only modest ground. "Stop!"

The clanking and rumbling of machines drowned out all other sound, this level empty save for the two of them so late at night. Huge fans spun on both sides, making her feel as if she'd landed in a world of giants, air forced up through the network of flexible and tin ductwork. She smelled grease and oil and the distinct scent of what could only be WD-40.

Up ahead the young woman found her path blocked when the passage narrowed to the width of a massive exhaust fan placed to drain heat from the potentially stifling confines around them. Caitlin thought she had her then, realizing only in that moment she was still holding her SIG at the ready. She left it in her grasp as she picked up the pace, closing the gap further, when the young woman grabbed what looked like a broomstick from the floor and used it jam the fan's blades still.

Caitlin lit out into a mad dash, as the young woman squeezed through a gap that looked much too narrow to accommodate even her lithe frame. But she made it somehow and charged on without seeming to even have missed a step.

"Stop!" Caitlin shouted, reaching the seized-up fan to realize the gap was too tight for her to squeeze through in pursuit. "Wait!"

The young woman turned at that, slowing her pace enough to meet and hold Caitlin's gaze. Then her eyes moved to the pistol Caitlin was still holding; just then the broomstick snapped, the fan started spinning again, and she was gone.

"We gonna tell Finneran about this?" Cort Wesley asked her when Caitlin made it back upstairs to Dylan's room, still struggling to get all her breath back.

"Why bother?"

"I wonder how long she was in the room before we got here."

"Nobody at the nurse's station noticed a thing."

Cort Wesley looked back at Dylan, as if something may have changed in his condition in the past fifteen seconds. "You get a good look at her, Ranger?"

"I think so."

"What's that mean?"

"Something about her eyes, the way she looked at me when she saw my gun. I've seen it before, a few times anyway."

"Saw what exactly?" he asked her.

"I think she wanted me to shoot her, Cort Wesley," Caitlin said, her gaze joining his on Dylan. "I think she wanted to die."

20

SAN ANTONIO, TEXAS

"The American police refuse to remove the protesters," the head of Yuyuan's security detail told Li Zhen as they approached the stage hastily erected for the occasion. "They claim they have the right to peaceful assembly."

"Then let them learn of a future they can do nothing about," Zhen said.

He let his gaze drift to a scraggly bunch at the rear of the dignitaries, officials, and invited guests assembled for the ceremony. Each of the protesters held a torn, tattered piece of the Chinese flag, waving them in the air as if this were some American sporting event.

Zhen couldn't help but smile smugly. "They deface the symbol of our people without realizing how beholden they are to us."

Zhen continued shaking hand after hand of those gathered on Alamo Plaza for the ribbon-cutting ceremony, turning away to steal the moments he needed to spray his hands with antiseptic cleaner and rub them dry before returning to the task at hand. Finally the head of Yuyuan's public relations department, who'd coordinated the event with officials in Texas and Washington, eased him aside and then up toward the podium that had been placed upon the stage. Far more people had shown up than expected, drawing a cringe from Zhen when he emerged from his limousine. China was a culture steeped in secrecy, while the United States prided itself on just the opposite. He wondered how it was possible anyone ever got anything done here, as Yuyuan's PR chief backed off to leave him alone behind the microphone.

"I would like to thank you all for coming," Li Zhen greeted into the microphone without further delay.

The milling crowd swung toward him in uniform fashion, a few of them still speaking in hushed tones. Zhen resisted the temptation to cease his address until all were quiet and no lips moved. But he remembered the lesson of congeniality and the politics in play that were never a concern back in China, where the only audience that mattered were representatives of the government and military. And before he could consider the matter further, the protesters began waving their pieces of the Chinese flag higher in the air to further mock him.

Zhen scanned the crowd and found Brooks lurking near the rear not far from the protesters, a caustic look on his face as if he were sucking on something bitter. But he spotted something else as well that grabbed his eye and made him forget all about the fragments of his country's flag flapping in the breeze: a group of high school girls on some kind of field trip that had coincidentally brought them to the Alamo this morning. They were dressed like an assemblage of dolls in white blouses and plaid skirts that hung high on their thighs, porcelain dolls like the ones his oldest daughter had once collected and were still arranged just as she'd left them back in China before her death.

"This is truly a glorious day for both our nations," he continued. "I am Li Zhen, CEO of the Yuyuan Corporation. My company has been welcomed by the people of Texas into this wonderful state, a favor we intend to repay many times over given this opportunity we consider a great privilege."

Louder applause filtered through the crowd. Before him, two more members of the Yuyuan public relations department stretched a red ribbon between two stakes that had been hammered into the soft earth of Alamo Plaza. But Zhen's gaze again drifted well past it to that group of high school girls clustered near the back, the lips of their skirts tossed about by the breeze revealing even more of their shapely thighs. He suppressed a shudder, the air suddenly alternating between waves of heat and cold, as if the sun itself was betraying him. In his mind the many others gathered before him for this momentous occasion could read each and every one of his thoughts, and Zhen imagined a curtain drawing across his mind to keep his most base secrets safe.

"There are those in this country who would chastise and target China for our self-interested pursuits, just as there are those in China who choose to do the same with the United States. On the field of business, though, we stand side by side to make ourselves stronger through an honest and fruitful association, born of supply and demand. There is demand for a fifth generation wireless transmission network and Yuyuan has been graced with the privilege of supplying it to the betterment of all Americans. We were not selected because we were the lowest bidder or even the only company in the world capable of achieving such an arduous and unprecedented task. Yuyuan was selected because we were the best suited for the task, and we are grateful for the opportunity to prove this to all in this great country."

Li Zhen fought to keep his eyes off the cluster of schoolgirls and failed completely. In his mind they were all naked now, mocking him in the rear of the crowd. Spectral shapes leering at him lasciviously, wetting their lips with their tongues and spreading their legs, the stiff breeze tossing their hair from one side to the other and back again. How many girls little older than this had he put on film to be immortalized and celebrated forever? Zhen's mind began to wander once more, taking him back to the times before his initial visit to the Triad, to when he was a different man entirely. *Peasant scum*, one of the captains had called him.

True enough then, he supposed, but not now, not ever again.

And yet to the befuddlement of Yuyuan's public relations people, Li Zhen decided to end his planned remarks early and stepped out from behind the podium. From there he made his way down off the makeshift stage toward the ribbon strung before him, intending to continue the ceremony without a microphone on ground level where the spectral schoolgirls would be harder to glimpse and thus tempt him. He recalled an old Chinese proverb that warned only the man who crosses the river at night knows the value of day, just now grasping its meaning. He had spent so long in the night that renouncing its darkness had become impossible. If he couldn't resist the sight of the uniformed schoolgirls, he must deny it to himself here in the day.

"Today I am proud to announce that the first segment of the new five G, fifth generation, wireless network is fully operational." Zhen accepted a pair of scissors from the head of his PR department and eased the twin blades over the red ribbon. "Let this be a symbol of a new beginning," he proclaimed proudly, "a new road that will take us into a bright future full of life and promise for our two peoples."

And with that Zhen drew the scissors closed and felt them slice through the ribbon effortlessly. Applause rippled through the crowd and more mindless handshakes followed, while his attention was drawn to a school bus to which the schoolgirls, fully clothed once more, were now headed. Then a shadow crossed before him and he looked up to find Brooks standing there.

"You have absolutely no fucking idea what you've done," the big man sneered.

Zhen felt his heart skip a beat over being caught in the act of leering at the schoolgirls. In just a matter of days now, Brooks would be dead, the schoolgirls too probably, and another quarter billion of Americans with them.

"You better hope what you pulled in Providence was worth the shit storm you've unleashed."

"Sometimes your American idioms are lost on me," Zhen said, breathing a sigh of relief.

"Then try this, Li. Of all the people in the world you don't want to piss off, you picked the absolute worst two."

PROVIDENCE, RHODE ISLAND

Cort Wesley was sitting by Dylan's bedside when the sun rose high in the morning sky over the city of Providence. Caitlin had already left to return to Texas, their final conversation in the wake of her failed attempt to chase down the Chinese girl somehow responsible for Dylan being here starting out terse but finishing the way they always did.

"I overheard your call with Tepper," he told her.

"How much did you hear?"

"Enough to know something's going on at home that needs your attention."

He could see Caitlin hedging. His dad had been something of a gambler, a magician working the cards as well as a dice mechanic who thrived on ripping off mopes too distracted to follow his hands. Boone Masters had spoken to him a few times about "tells," how he selected his marks from the varied candidates who submitted their applications just by showing up. Boone could read a man by his actions and mannerisms, most having more than their share.

Well, Cort Wesley knew Caitlin Strong had only one such tell: the way she twirled a finger through her hair, sometimes nibbling at the strands with her teeth. She'd get fidgety and her eyes would start looking past him, seeing other things.

"I can handle everything on this end," he continued. "It's long past midnight, Ranger."

"I just can't get the way that girl looked at me out of my mind."

"Describe it."

"Pleading. And she recognized me, Cort Wesley. I'm sure of it, just like I'm sure she was almost ready to talk before she ran off."

Once Caitlin had left, Cort Wesley's thoughts veered the way they always did when he got scared or angry: to taking a two-by-four with rusty nails hammered through it to whoever had done this to his son. It was the only way he knew to deal with the tide of violence that always seemed to find him no matter his resolve to avoid it. It was, Cort Wesley supposed, his tell. For so many years in his life, first in Army Special Forces and then as a much-feared enforcer for the Branca crime family out of New Orleans, violence had been a first resort, not a last. It came naturally to him and he saw no reason to resist the temptation, couldn't have even if he wanted to.

And that made Cort Wesley wonder if the last five, six years had been a lie. That he'd fooled himself into believing it was possible to reconcile the worlds he moved in and the dueling instincts that battled to control him. Suddenly he smelled talcum powder and fresh root beer and turned toward the window to find old Leroy Epps standing there, winking his way.

"How you be, Bubba?"

22

PROVIDENCE, RHODE ISLAND

"Been a while, champ," Cort Wesley said to the ghost of the man who was the best friend he'd ever had.

Epps grinned, showcasing the full rows of teeth that alternated between shiny white and the decaying brown Cort Wesley remembered better. *"Too long. How is it you only see me when times are tough, the world turned all upside down on you?"*

"I don't know."

"Believe I do, 'cause them's the times you start looking outside yourself for answers and your gaze turns naturally to me. Just like it used to when we was inside the Walls together."

Epps held a bottle of root beer in a thin, liver-spotted hand. His lips were pale pink and crinkled with dryness. The early morning light filtering through the window cast his brown skin in a yellowish tint. He'd been a lifer in the brutal Huntsville prison known as the Walls, busted for killing a white man in self-defense; his friendship and guidance had gotten Cort Wesley through his years in captivity. The diabetes that would ultimately kill him had turned Leroy's eyes bloodshot and numbed his limbs years before the sores and infections set in. As a boxer, he'd fought for the middleweight crown on three different occasions, knocked out once and had the belt stolen from him on paid-off judges' scorecards two other times. He'd died three years into Cort Wesley's four-year incarceration, but ever since he always seemed to show up when needed the most. Whether a ghostly specter or a figment of his imagination, Cort Wesley had given up trying to figure out. He just accepted the fact of his presence, grateful that Leroy kept coming around to help him out of one scrape after another.

His old friend extended the bottle of root beer out toward Cort Wesley. *"Say, you want a swig?"*

From this angle, a measure of the sun's rays seemed to pass straight through him. "No thanks, champ. You enjoy it."

"Don't seem like you be enjoying much right now. You know the amazing thing about where I be these days?"

"What?"

"You can't see better really, just farther and deeper. By deeper, I means on the inside and out. And right now, old Leroy can see you making bad thoughts in your head."

"Can't hide anything from you, can I, champ?"

"If it's in your head, you might as well write it down on a chalkboard from where I stand."

"What is it you see?"

"You fixing to scramble a whole lot of people's brains. I remember how you used to deal with the shit of the world on the inside. Nothing seems to have changed on the out."

Dylan snorted, something like the noise he made during nightmares hatched in the first few months after watching his mother murdered five or so years ago now. Cort Wesley glanced over, watched his son's eyelids seem to dance. A good sign, he hoped.

"One thing has," he told Leroy, leaving his gaze where it was.

"You think the reason for the thoughts you got matters?"

"As a matter of fact, I do. I think it matters a whole lot."

"A man ain't allowed to determine the circumstances of his own changing. In for a penny, in for a pound—you reading me here, bubba?"

"Not really.

"Goes like this. You think the cause changes things, but it really don't since the only change that matters is the kind that happens real deep inside a man at his core. You remember me telling you about that?"

"Ilk you called it."

"Damn straight I did, 'cause that's what it be. You're a much different man today than you were when I had feet that made marks in the sand. Except when you dig down real deep where it takes someone like me to see what's going on. Down there you're the same and that's the way you're thinking right now. I ain't blaming you none—it's the way you deal with things, how you keep control by knowing what you can do when push comes to shove. I just want you to know the cost."

"What's that?"

Leroy drained the rest of root beer, his thin neck expanding like a snake swallowing a rodent, and then laid the empty bottle down on the windowsill. *"Only way a man can change who he be is down at that core with his very ilk. Everything else is for show, and the problem is it seems you gotta step into the kind of shoes I'm wearing now to finish the job. So I guess my point is don't look for it, bubba, but be ready when it comes."*

"Whatever you say, champ."

"Doesn't sound like you mean that much."

Cort Wesley's gaze veered back to Dylan. "Somebody put my boy in a hospital and damn near killed him. Caitlin and I think it may have something to do with the porn industry and prostitution."

"How is the Ranger?" Leroy asked, the whites of his eyes brightening.

"Same as ever. Just like me."

"You say that like it's a bad thing."

"Isn't that what you just told me?"

"Which I take to mean you weren't really listening. No matter. What I say'll make sense to you soon enough, but I imagine some heads will have to get cracked first."

"Nothing new there, champ."

"Every day is new, bubba, every hour and minute too. That's what you learn where I'm at, where time don't have no matter at all. Like I told you, I can't see better, just farther but, man, what a sight!"

A doctor he hadn't met yet, wearing a white lab coat, pushed the door to Dylan's room all the way open and entered, startled when he saw Cort Wesley seated in the chair.

"You must be the boy's father."

Cort Wesley rose, his knees cracking, noticing that Leroy Epps was gone. "I am. How's my son?"

"As his neurologist, that's what I came to check," the doctor said, moving to the bed. "We should begin to see some improvement today."

"He made a sound. His eyelids were fluttering. I think he was dreaming."

"That's good," the doctor noted, and held Dylan's one eyelid open and then the other while shining the light into them. Then he looked toward the window, face tilting in surprise. "Where'd that come from? Haven't seen one of those since I was a boy growing up in the South."

Cort Wesley followed his gaze and saw the bottle Leroy Epps had drained still sitting on the sill.

"Authentic Hines Root Beer with old-fashioned sassafras as

the primary ingredient," the doctor continued, shaking his head nostalgically. "Brings back memories, I'll tell you. Almost like seeing a ghost."

"I know what you mean," said Cort Wesley.

23

SAN ANTONIO, TEXAS

The serial killer's latest victim had been found in a room at the Menger Hotel that overlooked the Alamo. According to Bexar County medical examiner Frank Dean Whatley, the unidentified young woman was presumed to be a prostitute for reasons he didn't elaborate on right away. Her body had been removed hours prior to Caitlin arriving on the scene but the wall behind the headboard was splattered with blood and the bed sheets were covered in it.

Caitlin stood in the doorway for a moment, picturing the scene in its original form; the victim with her head cut off and sewn back on backward, raped postmortem.

Just like the victim William Ray Strong and Judge Roy Bean had examined in a camp occupied by Chinese workers building the Trans-Pecos rail line in 1883, without benefit of crime scene technicians, DNA testing, blood splatter experts. Or lights and sprays that could reveal hidden blood and semen. Hard to believe a case ever got solved in those days, but the Texas Rangers had solved plenty of them anyway.

"We pulled a sample of the stitching he used off the carpet," Whatley reported, having inched up closer to her. "Step into the room and I'll run the numbers for you."

Frank Dean Whatley had been the Bexar County medical examiner since Caitlin was in diapers. He'd grown a belly in recent years that hung out over his thin belt, seeming to force his spine to angle inward at the torso. Whatley's teenage son had been killed by Latino gangbangers when Caitlin was a mere kid herself. Ever since then, he'd harbored a virulent hatred for that particular race from the bag boys at the local H.E.B. to the politicians who professed to be peacemakers. With his wife lost, in life and then death, to alcoholism, he'd probably stayed on the job too long. But he had nothing to go home to, no real life outside the office, and remained exceptionally good at performing the rigors of his job.

Whatley had seemed to resent Caitlin in her first years as a Ranger, warming up to her only after they'd worked closely on a few cases together. Caitlin always let him know how much she appreciated his persistence and professionalism, inevitably treating the victims of violence with a dignity that belied the coldness of his office. He'd purchased floral bed linens with his own money to better dress the steel slabs on which he performed his autopsies, because he believed those with the misfortune of ending up there deserved at least that much comfort and respect.

Caitlin entered the hotel room, feeling immediately chilled, and wondered if it was the product of illusion or a literal change in temperature from the hall. The room looked lifted straight out of the mid-nineteenth century when the hotel had been built, outfitted with furnishings that included a four-poster bed, velvet-covered Victorian couch, and marble table. A framed colorful tapestry map of Texas from around that time hung over a dark-wood desk.

The Menger was proclaimed "the finest hotel west of the Mississippi" almost since its first day in business and, according to the information Caitlin had pulled up on the Internet, had played host to the likes of Sam Houston, Robert E. Lee, Ulysses S. Grant, and numerous presidents. It was even said that none other than Teddy Roosevelt recruited several of his Rough Riders in the hotel bar. The hotel's majestic facade and beige-tone design, together with its original wrought-iron balconies pitched beneath striped awnings that looked like wagon canvas, made it an apt complement to the historic Alamo located directly across the plaza.

Caitlin could hear Whatley's labored breathing just to her right. "You know, my great-grandfather came up against an almost identical killer in 1883."

"You mean the case he supposedly worked with Roy Bean? I thought that was just a legend."

"Maybe so, like everything else. But there's plenty of facts to support it really did happen."

Whatley took out his handkerchief and mopped his brow of sweat, even though the room was chilly. "Well, I got some facts for you too. The victim wasn't carrying any ID and AFIS came up with nothing when we ran her prints. But if she was a prostitute, I'd say we're looking at very high-end, even exclusive."

"What makes you say that?"

"We found her clothes hung neatly in the closet, name-brand designer the whole way. Her grooming was perfect and she carried a small bottle of perfume in her purse that cost more than I make in a week."

"So she had a purse, but no identification."

"Killer must've removed it. A souvenir probably."

"Well, I hope it helps us catch him, Doc."

Whatley frowned and dabbed some more sweat off his brow. "The preliminary autopsy I conducted revealed fracturing of the hyoid bone and broken blood vessels in her eyes consistent with being strangled to death before she was beheaded. The cut was jagged and, I'm only guessing here, done with some kind of sharp, serrated knife like you might see a butcher use to trim filets. But, judging by the irregular slices, a butcher would have been much finer in his work."

"You said you found some of the thread he used when he stitched it back on."

"It was more like a twine, maybe a tightly woven yarn. I haven't identified the material yet, but I can tell you it was found at the crime scene in Houston too."

"Houston," Caitlin echoed. "Where else?"

"Laredo," came the voice of D. W. Tepper from the doorway,

"to go with Lubbock and Amarillo. Is five still your favorite number, Ranger?"

"I don't recall it ever being my favorite number," Caitlin told him.

"I'm talking when you were a girl. Everything had to be in fives. Know why? Because that's how many shells fit into a Colt Patterson revolver, the first pistol Earl Strong taught you how to shoot."

Whatley looked toward Tepper. "Am I done here? I got a ton of work waiting for me back at the lab."

"You got any more questions for the good doctor, Ranger?"

"Just one," Caitlin said, turning back toward Whatley. "Your autopsy reveal any semen inside the victim, Doc?"

"No, and I wouldn't expect there'd be."

"Why's that?"

"Because the man who raped her didn't do it with his johnson. Near as we can tell, he did it with a soldering iron. Guess the only good thing about us not being able to identify her is that we don't have to explain all that to her next of kin. Long way to ship the body in any event."

"What's that mean?"

"The girl was Chinese."

24

SAN ANTONIO, TEXAS

"All five victims were Chinese," Tepper told Caitlin, after Whatley had taken his leave.

"Just like William Ray Strong's case in 1883 . . ."

"Another reason why you're the only one for the job, Ranger."

"I assume you dusted the outlets nearest the bed for prints, Captain," Caitlin said.

"We did and there weren't any." Tepper felt about his pockets, not realizing he was already holding his pack of Marlboros in hand. "But heat marks indicate the soldering iron was probably plugged in when it was inserted into her. You can see why I was adamant about asking you to come home."

"Because I know something about electric tools?"

Tepper's expression crinkled in displeasure. "Because Austin figured we needed to put the right face on this."

"Me?"

"People of Texas are sure to feel safer knowing that you're on the job."

"The ones I haven't shot anyway."

"How many of those are left? Ten or twelve maybe?"

Caitlin looked back at the blood staining the sheets, back wall, and floor. "How do the other four killings compare to this one?"

"I got Lieutenants Berry and Rollins sorting through that now. Looks like the pattern's pretty much identical, although the other investigations all seemed to miss out on one thing Doc Whatley figured out in the time it takes me to finish a Marlboro."

"This is a nonsmoking room, Captain," she said, watching him tap the pack.

"You see me striking a match, Ranger? Let it go, will ya?"

"Soon as you give up that nasty habit, I'll be glad to."

"Tell me how our serial killer could be repeating history, how he came by such specific knowledge that's not written down anyplace I've ever seen."

"Maybe he had a grandfather like mine who told him the tale."

"Either way, he's got intimate knowledge of events from 1883."

"A connection to the railroad would be the most obvious conclusion."

Tepper flashed her a wink, popped a cigarette into his mouth but didn't light it. "Glad you figured that much out all on your own."

"What is it you're not telling me, D.W.?" Caitlin said, recalling how cryptic he'd sounded over the phone as well.

Tepper moved to the desk over which hung the framed tapestry map of old West Texas. "Houston, Amarillo, Lubbock," he said, touching each city through the glass, "San Antonio, and Laredo. That line I just drew look familiar to you?"

"I'm not following you, D.W."

"Take a closer look, Ranger."

Caitlin stepped back and did, seeing the map in a whole new way and feeling her eyes widen. "Oh, God," she realized. "It's the original rail line built by the Southern Pacific."

25

NEW BRAUNFELS, TEXAS

"I'm impressed," the big man said, over the steady drone of the machines in the secret underground level of Yuyuan.

"Your skills in killing are matched only by your loyalty, Qiang," Li Zhen said, moving a hand out from behind his back toward one of the computers inputting information fed by his orbiting satellites. "But in less than a week's time, I will be able to kill thousands with a simple touch of a key."

"And yet you still require my more old-fashioned services," Qiang told Zhen.

"The two targets are threats we must eliminate to ensure we encounter no setbacks."

The big man nodded, letting his eyes run along the walls of numbers rolling down the screens taking up one entire wall of the sublevel. He regarded them diffidently, seeming to forget they'd ever been here as soon as he turned away.

Qiang was big *everywhere*. A tower of muscle wrapped into a black suit, shirt, and tie that hid all but a single line of tattoo ink that pushed itself up over his collar. Li knew Qiang's entire body would be covered in ink, each drawing etched into his skin telling a different story of his background, lineage, and experience with the Triad, still the most powerful criminal organization in China. Like organized crime in America, the Triad had been targeted relentlessly by law enforcement, ultimately moving their efforts underground. Men like Qiang became ghosts, lost to their families who were under constant surveillance and adopting the philosophy that they were already, for all intents and purposes, dead—at least the men they had been were. The men they were now had no families, no history, no friends, no relationships. They had only the Triad.

"Qiang" wasn't his real name, but one appropriated because it meant "strength" in the Chinese language. Qiang's father had been one of Li Zhen's closest associates, the man who had guided him through his formative years when the highest echelon a peasant scum could reach in China was in either gambling or pornography. Thanks to Qiang's father, Zhen had ended up in pornography, taking over the entire business when his mentor fell ill. Near death, he'd asked Zhen to pledge that he'd look after his son, a wish Zhen was more than happy to grant for his own selfish reasons, given Qiang's reputation as a violently effective enforcer even when barely out of his teens.

"You are prepared, then?" Li Zhen asked him now.

Qiang looked away from the wall he'd taken to studying again. "I have two teams moving into place, ready to act as soon as I give the word. I need only one more thing from you."

"Name it."

"Camellia flowers from your gardens for the strings they produce," Qiang finally said. "I want my men to partake in the traditional ceremony as my ancestors did before they set out in battle."

"This isn't just a battle, my friend, it's the beginning of a war."

Qiang looked down at the keyboard over which Zhen stood. His spine stiffened, making him seem even taller. "*Qǐshì*," he said.

"Chinese for apocalypse," Zhen translated, "because that is what I'm bringing to America."

Li moved to another terminal attached to a screen with only four numbers frozen upon it and depressed the Enter key.

"And what was that?" Qiang asked him.

"A test, my friend, a test."

PART THREE

"We had a little shooting and he lost."

—Anonymous Texas Ranger

26

Guillermo Paz sat seething behind the wheel of his massive, customized pickup truck currently stuck in traffic on the 410 heading out of San Antonio. He lived in a cabin on a lake he'd bought with cash from his American employer at Homeland Security, a long way from growing up in the La Vega slum of Venezuela that was built on a hillside so the raw sewage could run downhill.

Traffic started moving, then snarled to a halt again almost immediately in all three lanes. Paz cringed behind the wheel, squeezing it so hard he could feel the leather starting to crack. He was coming from the other English class he taught to recent immigrants at San Antonio College and it had gone no better than the last.

"Today's lesson is on delusion," he started the class off by saying. "Pay special attention now."

He paused, the entire class nodding and smiling as if they totally grasped what he was saying, except for one woman who was texting on her cell phone. Probably his only student who deserved an A.

"See," Paz continued, "I thought I'd found the answer to what I'd been looking for in existentialism. That term was coined by the

French, you know, and I started turning away from the Germans to Sartre and a little Camus for the spiritual message I was somehow still missing. That's what life is about—searching, even if you don't find what you're looking for. But I thought Sartre's premise that meaning exists out of nothingness—it's there for us to create of our own making—made a whole lot of sense. A wonderful concept really, don't you agree?"

The class nodded enthusiastically, even though not one of his students had any idea what he was actually saying.

"Except it's total bullshit. The existentialists embraced the darkness and ugliness, and preached hopelessness, not because they actually believed it so much as it made them rich and famous amid the decadence and despair of the post–World War Two world. You see what I'm getting at here?"

More enthusiastic nods.

"So it was lies, all of it, dressed up in philosophical bullshit to sell books and pad bank accounts. And it fooled me. What was I thinking? These people don't know any more about meaning than I do. I'm starting to realize I should have faith in the lessons of my own experience and rely less on the lessons of others. Comes down to lies again, and I'm not going to lie to you or anyone else. America's not the land of opportunity anymore; there's no such thing and maybe never was here or anywhere. You're wasting your time and should go back home. *Clase desestimó*," Paz said, shaking his head in disgust as he moved for the door. "Class dismissed."

And now he was stalled in traffic, an apt metaphor for what he was feeling, like there was an itch he couldn't scratch. Paz had been a soldier before he became a killer, and what he felt now was like the final moments before a battle began. The waiting, the tension, the apprehension giving way to the reality of what was about to happen. Men who defend violence normally haven't seen and lived as much of it as he had. Very few were cut out for the kind of life Paz himself missed when he was away from it for too long. It had become like a drug to him, a fix, an insatiable addiction that defined him and left him grasping for philosophical bullshit to fall back on when his core was robbed of the adrenaline that violence sent coursing through his veins.

Maybe that's what had brought Caitlin Strong into his life. Maybe his Texas Ranger was a magnet who drew bullets toward her and Paz had latched on so he might have moral justification to dispense his own. Maybe what he'd seen in her eyes the day they'd first met with guns blazing was not emblematic of the moral core he was missing, but a mirror image he'd tried to reject. The mere possibility had chased him from the classroom an hour before and now left him cringing behind the wheel, ready to floor his accelerator and plow through all the cars blocking his way ahead on the 410.

Until he saw the minivan pulled over on a strange angle on the side of the road. At first, Paz thought the three kids hovering by the vehicle were there to help, maybe offer to change a flat tire or something. But at next glance their baggy clothes, tough-guy strut, and pistols displayed in the waistbands of at least the two he could see clearly told him they were gangbangers. Probably out for a quick score, maybe a carjacking.

Paz saw a way to scratch his itch and pulled his truck over onto the shoulder behind the minivan.

27

SAN ANTONIO, TEXAS

"That's what I like to see," Paz said, climbing out of the truck and tucking his long-sleeve denim shirt all the way into the olive drab cargo pants he liked because of the extra pockets. "Young people out doing a good deed. Think I paid you boys five dollars at a car wash to raise money for the homeless a few weeks back."

"You got it wrong, man," said the kid Paz took to be the leader, making sure to show no fear of him. At least outwardly. "Best be on your way now. We can take things from here."

Paz kept coming, reaching the rear of the minivan much faster than the gangbangers had figured. "What do you mean exactly, 'take things from here'? I'm sorry, it's my English."

The kid hitched up his pants with one hand, the other straying back on his hip to where his pistol was tucked. Paz glimpsed the second kid carrying a pistol tucked into waistband mimic that motion, and now he could see a third gangbanger was holding a baseball bat on the passenger side of the minivan. Paz heard soft sobbing and realized three kids were squeezed into the rear seat, a woman who must have been their mother behind the wheel shaking her cell phone as if that would help her find a signal or reach 911 faster.

"Oh, I get it," Paz said, stopping just outside of the range he needed. "Taking things from here means teaching these kids how to hit, right?" Then, to the 'banger holding the bat, "Hey, you got a baseball? 'Cause I think I may have one in my truck."

The leader drew his gun, held it sideways, tough-guy style, which nobody who really understood how semiautomatics worked would ever do. In Paz's experience, men who held their guns that way never fired them. It was less than a toy in their hands because, at least with a toy, you pulled the trigger.

"Oh," he went on, "I see. Not baseball, target practice. Makes sense. Fine skill to teach young people. Who taught you, *amigo*?"

"Fuck you, man!"

"Hey, talk to me like that," Paz grinned, "and I might have to ask you for that five dollars I donated at the car wash back."

"Get your ass gone or I'll blow a second hole in it, fuck wad."

"Hey, that's good English. I teach a couple classes to immigrants. Maybe I should have you in as a guest speaker."

The other two gangbangers were looking at each other, the leader trying to hold his pistol steady with its weight starting to bring the barrel down.

"Fuck you, man!" he blared. "Fuck you!"

"Sure, whatever you say. I think I know this family from the neighborhood. Let me just check to see if they fed my dog like I asked them."

Paz knocked on the rear window, angling himself closer to the leader without the 'banger ever realizing it. Paz took his gaze off him, still watching the 'banger's reflection off a window featuring a smiley face drawn in built-up condensation. The sun cut through the van from the other side of the road, ending up in the leader's eyes.

The 'banger did exactly what Paz was expecting next: eased himself a little closer, gun starting to tremble a bit. Not taking his eyes from the window until the very last moment, Paz whirled. He latched a hand onto the 'banger's wrist holding the pistol so fast the guy didn't even have the split second he needed to pull the trigger. And by the time he found it, Paz had wrenched his hand downward and to the side, the snap of his wrist breaking almost as loud as the gunshot that followed.

The second armed gangbanger had his gun out by then, and Paz used the leader's to shoot the kid's wrist, the .45 caliber slug practically blowing his whole hand off as the percussion powdered Paz's ears. Inside the minivan the kids were screaming and on the other side the kid with the baseball bat, for some inexplicable reason, started hammering it against the window. Shards of glass blew airborne, most of them raining inside the cab.

The next instant found Paz leaping onto the minivan, hitting the hood first and denting it badly before projecting himself over, the screams of the kid whose hand was halfway blown off bubbling his already rattled eardrums. He hit the ground just as the final 'banger twisted, canting his body to strike with the bat hard and fast.

He was holding the bat at the ready, then he wasn't. Because Paz had stripped it from his grasp. Kid could do nothing but watch, as Paz took it in either hand and snapped the bat in two, square in the middle.

"Man, it's a good thing you didn't try hitting a baseball with this piece of shit."

Paz watched the final gangbanger turn and rush off down the shoulder, his form shrinking rapidly to utter insignificance. Then he tossed both halves of the bat aside, listened to them clack against the pavement while the two other gangbangers battled for who could scream the loudest in pain.

Paz grinned, looked inside the minivan where the mother was now cradling two of her kids, staring at him as if she wasn't sure he was really there.

"*Clase desestimó,*" he said, and walked back to his truck.

28

PROVIDENCE, RHODE ISLAND

Wake up, bubba, wake up!

Cort Wesley heard Leroy Epps trying to stir him from his sleep in the chair by Dylan's bedside, but he couldn't make himself awaken. Going sleepless in the hotel the night before should have been nothing for a man who'd once humped four days straight through Iraq in the Gulf War without even a nap. This was different, though, and not just because he was almost twenty-five years older. There was no stress worse than worry, even battle, and worry for his son's very life gave no quarter and provided no respite.

He realized the only place he could sleep at all was here by Dylan's bedside where he need not fear the ringing of a phone.

"*Dad?*"

Cort Wesley heard Dylan calling to him in his dream, but couldn't see him anywhere. He was back playing football a million years ago in high school, only the field was formed of unlined tall grass and none of the players were in uniform. Then the scene morphed to a seaside and he found himself walking along a dock, ecstatic because he was about to take his boys fishing.

"*Dad?*"

But Dylan and Luke were nowhere to be found and, when he reached the end of the dock, there was no boat or moorings. His own father was suddenly standing there, refusing to acknowledge Cort Wesley no matter what he did. The dream ended just as their eyes met.

"*Dad!*"

His eyes shot open. He practically jumped out of the stiff chair.

Dylan was looking at him from the bed, eyes fighting to stay open. He'd interlaced his fingers near his chest, tugging at one of the zillion wires and lines attaching him to this machine or that.

"Dylan!"

Cort Wesley burst out of his chair too fast to realize his right leg was still asleep. It crumpled beneath him and he had to grab the near railing on Dylan's bed to stop from falling.

"I'm not dead, am I?" his son asked, his voice dry and cracking.

"Not unless I am too, son," Cort Wesley said, smoothing a hand through the boy's hair. He almost stopped himself, then changed his mind and went right on doing it.

"I'm real thirsty." Dylan glanced around him, starting to realize where he was.

"Yeah, you're in a hospital."

The boy's gaze found the television. "That the best you could do?"

Cort Wesley looked up at the screen, saw it was tuned to some kid's show featuring a giant red dog.

Dylan was trying for a grin when he looked back. "I was just playing with you." Then a grimace flashed across his expression. "Whoa."

"What's wrong?"

"There's something inside my dick."

"They had to put a catheter in."

"And my head's killing me. Can you get them to give me some aspirin?"

Cort Wesley watched him swipe a tongue over his parched lips, and knew he must be thirsty after getting his liquids only through a tube for a couple days now. He moved to pour Dylan a glass of water from the pitcher he'd been using for himself when he saw the boy's features lock, his groggy eyes seizing up.

"Uh-oh . . ."

"What's wrong?"

"I can't feel my legs, Dad."

29

SAN ANTONIO, TEXAS

"That's quite a story, Ranger," said the older woman dressed in denim overalls, imitating an old-time railroad engineer, after Caitlin finished explaining how a serial killer from the present was explicitly linked to one who'd struck in a camp of Chinese workers laying the old Trans-Pecos rail line for the Southern Pacific railroad.

"It sure is, ma'am. And I was hoping as a general expert on those times that you could help me make some sense out of it."

"Well, I just work at the Railroad Museum, I'm not an exhibit in it."

Sharon Yarlas wet her lips with her tongue and adjusted the red kerchief tied round her neck from side to side as if the material was making her itch. She had a big-boned frame with ample flesh riding it, pushing sixty probably with her hair an even measure of gray and black. She wore work boots that must have been hell on her feet and left her standing almost equal to Caitlin's five feet eight inches.

The museum's spacious grounds were located a short haul from Alamo Plaza in the city's Oak Grove neighborhood just short of Schulmeier Cemetery. Not far from them, a line of tourists was building for the next train ride on an adjoining track. In addition to the brief journeys aboard old-fashioned locomotives, the museum contained both indoor and outdoor displays charting the history of railroads in Texas.

"But I'm familiar with the story of those murders back in 1883," Sharon Yarlas continued. "Believe they ended up being responsible for shutting the whole line down."

"I wasn't aware of that, ma'am."

"Well, the Southern Pacific made sure nothing was ever written about them, so most of what I've learned is based on conjecture."

"In my experience, when it comes to the past, that passes for fact often enough."

The nearby train blew its whistle so loud it made Caitlin flinch, a spout of steam pouring out the engine's chimney. The coal-black, silver-fronted engine looked like a shiny dinosaur lifted from the ground and placed right here on the track beds that may well have been laid by the Chinese workers in the camp William Ray Strong and Judge Roy Bean had visited to begin their investigation.

"Well," started Sharon, "that's my train there. How about you hop on board with me and I'll tell you what I know during the ride?"

Caitlin nodded, watching four clowns in cowboy regalia that included holstered pistols mixing among the visitors waiting to board the train as well. A young boy was playfully slapping at one of them, the smallest, who kept arching backward at the last moment to agilely avoid the blow. Finally, a second clown stooped down and flattened himself out directly behind the other, and this time the young boy pushed instead of slapped. The smaller clown went tumbling over, his sneakers kicking up into the air, to the delight of all those standing in line.

"You just never know what you're going to see here," Sharon grinned, shaking her head. "Something wrong, Ranger?"

Caitlin watched the clowns staking out a place for themselves in line, still playing with the crowd, one of them juggling three rubber balls. "Guess I'm just scared of clowns, ma'am."

Sharon adjusted the kerchief tied around her neck yet again. "Why, I didn't think Texas Rangers were scared of anything."

"You'd be surprised," Caitlin told her, still eyeing the clowns.

30

PROVIDENCE, RHODE ISLAND

"Nothing to worry about," Dr. Hirschman said, continuing to shine a penlight into Dylan's eyes that had grown alert again. He had stringy hair and shoulders so bony that Cort Wesley could actually see the ridges protruding under his white lab coat. "Just like the neurologist said."

"Then why am I seeing two of you and why does my head feel like somebody took a sledgehammer to it?"

Hirschman squinted as he looked into Dylan's eyes. "Because that's pretty close to what actually happened. We were bringing you out of the coma slowly and you woke up ahead of time. What you're feeling, that's just the effects of the medication."

Cort Wesley could see the bedcovers flutter slightly as Dylan wiggled his toes beneath them.

"Yeah, it's starting to come back now." The boy winced. "Yup, I can feel the knee I hurt in practice again."

"Which knee?" Cort Wesley asked, drawing closer to his bedside. "You hurt yourself?"

Dylan shook his head. "Aren't you supposed to be a tough guy?"

"I thought you were too."

"Hey, I'm the one who almost got his brains scrambled."

"My point exactly, son. Big, tough college football player like you ought to be able to take better care of himself."

"I'm tough, but I'm not big, at least that's what everybody keeps telling me."

"Hey, Doc," Cort Wesley said, everything about the world feeling lighter, "they got something that can help the kid out there, make him bigger?"

"Yes," Hirschman said, finally switching off his penlight. "It's called genetics."

"You call Caitlin?" Dylan asked.

"Damn." Cort Wesley felt for his cell phone, finally found the pocket in which he'd tucked it. "Not yet."

"You better, or she's gonna be pissed."

"She'll already be pissed I wasn't dialing before you finished your first word."

Cort Wesley hit CAITLIN and waited for the call to go through.

Dylan looked back toward Dr. Hirschman who was rechecking all his vitals and comparing them to the LED readouts on the monitors. "Where's the other guy?"

"Who?" the doctor asked him, while Cort Wesley heard the phone ringing on the other end.

"The other doctor. He was standing in the doorway when I first woke up, when I started calling for my dad. An Asian guy."

Caitlin's phone went straight to voice mail and Cort Wesley looked back toward Dylan before leaving a message.

"Strange," he heard Dylan's doctor say. "Neither the resident nor attending assigned to your case is Asian," the doctor said. "In fact, no physician assigned to this floor fits that description at all. You must have been dreaming."

"Sure," Dylan shrugged. "I guess."

The doctor grinned and squeezed his arm. "Everything looks good. You're a very lucky young man."

Dylan nodded, forced a smile back. He and Cort Wesley both watched Hirschman take his leave.

"I wasn't dreaming, Dad," the boy said, as soon as he was gone. "I woke up and a Chinese doctor was standing there."

"Chinese," Cort Wesley repeated.

Dylan tightened his gaze, starting to realize that his father must've had a pretty good idea of what had led to his getting the shit kicked out of him. "Where's Caitlin?" he asked, looking around the room as if expecting her to appear.

"They needed her back home, son."

"Maybe we need her here too."

"Let's talk about the other night," Cort Wesley said, sitting down on Dylan's bedside. "Let's talk about this Chinese girl you got yourself mixed up with."

Dylan held his eyes closed and massaged his temples. "Later, Dad. Okay?"

"She was here, in your room."

"Who?"

"The girl."

Dylan's eyes snapped open. "Kai?"

"That's her name?"

"Kai was here?"

"She ran off. Caitlin chased her but couldn't quite catch up."

"I thought it was a dream . . ."

"What?"

"I heard her talking to me, telling me she was sorry, shit like that. I tried to answer her back but my mind kept drifting."

"She left you this," Cort Wesley said, producing the rose he'd spotted atop his son's bedcovers when he and Caitlin had first entered the room the night before.

Dylan took the pink rose in hand, smiling slightly. "That was nice of her."

"Right, nice gesture considering this girl's responsible for you being here." Cort Wesley moved right up to his son's bedside. "You ready to talk about that now?"

31

"Where would you like me to start?" Sharon Yarlas asked, after the last ticket was collected and they boarded the train.

The whistle blew two times again and the train began to rumble forward, clinking and clanking, taking Caitlin back to her visits here as a little girl when she might well have ridden in this very car. That memory got her thinking about the clowns again, something wrong about them that she couldn't quite put her finger on, and she wondered where in the train they might be.

"How about with what you know about the Trans-Pecos line in general?" Caitlin told Sharon.

"There were actually three separate short lines constructed in the Trans-Pecos region that stretches westward from the Pecos River and includes some of Texas's highest mountains and its hottest deserts. The first rail line into the Trans-Pecos was the spur that ran eastward. It reached El Paso in May 1881 and met up with the westward line from San Antonio in 1883 when a silver spike joined the two at the Pecos River."

Caitlin cast her gaze down the aisle and noticed the clowns working their way through the center car immediately behind this one, joking it up with the riders. "How about the work being done on the Trans-Pecos in 1883 in the area of Langtry?"

"That would have been the line linking up with the spurs already completed to the north. The Southern Pacific relocated the workers to the Langtry area after that silver spike was driven at the Pecos River."

"I was hoping you could tell me what happened when my great-grandfather, Texas Ranger William Ray Strong, and Judge Roy

Bean got to the main camp at the head of the track after they inspected the body of the most recent victim."

The older woman's gaze drifted, her mind flashing back to an unwritten chapter of history nearly lost to the years. "I'll do the best I can, Ranger. . . ."

32

LANGTRY, TEXAS; 1883

The chief engineer was a man named Kincannon who smelled like tar and had grease stains all over his face and bare arms. He'd torn the sleeves off his shirt to reveal beefy arms layered with bulk instead of firm muscle and had a beard he seemed fond of scratching. He carried a shovel with him everywhere he went and leaned on it like a crutch as he addressed William Ray Strong and Judge Roy Bean. Nearby, an Irish work crew was busy shoring up the ground enclosing the track bed bending north.

"I think you're full of shit," Kincannon said, spitting tobacco down into a pool of rain that had yet to dry on the hardpan of the West Texas prairie.

Judge Roy Bean ejected a wad from his mouth that landed right atop Kincannon's. "I've put men in jail for saying less than that to me."

"Only if you're really Judge Roy Bean."

"Who you think I am?"

"Don't know, don't care." Then Kincannon's big, droopy eyes turned back to William Ray. "I ain't scared of you none neither. That Ranger badge of yours ain't worth shit here. I answer to a higher power."

"Who'd that be—God?"

"Nope, somebody higher: the head of the Southern Pacific Railroad, John Morehouse. In case you ain't noticed, they run this country now. And, in case you ain't noticed, I am their duly appointed emissary in these parts. Morehouse might as well be president of the whole dang country, and that means I don't need to take no shit from the likes of you."

William Ray Strong took a step closer to the bigger man, the two of them drenched in sunlight while distant thunder rumbled in storm clouds visible over the nearby mesas. "You from Texas, sir?"

"Nope. Alabama born and bred, but I been pretty much anywhere there's track to lay, and if you knew anything outside this bone state of yours, you'd know that was pretty much everywhere."

William Ray hitched his coat back so Kincannon could see his Colt. "They don't have Texas Rangers everywhere, sir, they only have them here. So I'm going to forgive you your disrespect of both myself and the judge and remind you of one simple fact: you might not be from Texas, you might've spent all but a speck of time inside Texas, but you're here now in your position as chief engineer of the Southern Pacific and that places you in my jurisdiction where I am the law. Ain't that right, Judge?"

"A Texas Ranger tells you to kiss your ass," Bean told Kincannon, "you'd be wise to figure out a way to stick your head under your balls."

Kincannon turned his gaze away from the sun toward the Irish work crew, sneering. The worksite was located maybe a quarter mile from the Chinese camp. Besides three separate work crews, flattening and hard packing the soil bed to ready it to take track again now that the dam was finished, there wasn't much else to speak of. A pair of rectangular tents held up by thick wooden beams driven into the ground contained construction supplies and the cafeteria, respectively.

William Ray figured a smaller tent complete with flaps blowing in the breeze functioned as the camp office, another an infirmary, and a third seemed to house a makeshift church. A big steam engine with five cars sat parked at the head of the tracks laid so far and would inch forward along the two or so miles construction covered every day once the ground dried out. A host of stands and shanties from which local vendors were peddling this and that to the workers dotted the landscape as well.

William Ray could see measurements being taken and, well off in the distance, a pair of wagons toting crates he guessed contained dynamite toward a rock face the Southern Pacific needed to blast through to link up with its sister track to the north. Closer by, a crew was pushing rods into the ground to gauge soil depth in plotting the straightest route around deposits of limestone and shale.

Kincannon swiped a hand inside his cheek and emerged with a wad of tobacco that looked like moist moss. He aimed it downward for William Ray's boot and just missed.

The Ranger retrieved the wad and tucked it into Kincannon's vest pocket. "Believe you dropped this, sir."

Kincannon's breathing picked up. His eyes narrowed on William Ray, then swept to both sides as if measuring how many men in the area he could count on if it came to blows. But then his gaze fastened on William Ray's Colt instead.

"I'll talk to you," he said, prying the wad of tobacco free of his pocket and tossing it well clear of William Ray this time, "because it'll be easier if I do than if I don't."

"You hear about the murders of these Chinese women?" William Ray asked him.

"I suppose, but I didn't listen much."

"Having a killer at large at your worksite didn't concern you?"

"In case you ain't heard, the Chinese went on strike this week."

"We heard."

"Bastards ought to be grateful for having food on their plates and a roof over their heads."

"A tent, you mean," the judge reminded.

"It's them you should be arresting," Kincannon sneered. "Maybe make them see the light before things turn ugly."

"What you mean by that?" William Ray asked him.

"We're gonna fall behind if they don't smarten up. And that

means less money for everybody else, including me. I heard Pinkerton men are already en route. The Chinks know what's best for them, they better come around."

"So you never thought to report these murders to the authorities," William Ray surmised.

"You hear what I just said?"

"I must've missed the part about how you dealt with a bunch of killings."

"I reported them all right, to the only authority that matters: the Southern Pacific Railroad. You got no authority here and neither do you, Judge. This here land doesn't even belong to Texas anymore—it belongs to the Southern Pacific and the railroad makes the only law I abide by."

"What do you say about that, Judge?" William Ray asked him.

"Nothing I can say, Ranger. The chief engineer here's right, so far as the track goes. That's Southern Pacific territory for sure, the whole six-foot-wide stretch of it for as far as it goes, all the way to hell for all I care."

William Ray kicked at the dirt at his feet, fully dried since it got sun all day without benefit of shading even from mesas towering to the west. "Well, it doesn't seem like there's any track bed here."

"You're right," Roy Bean said, scratching his forehead. "This here's Texas land, which means I can issue any legal order I so choose, and right now I think I'll have every man not standing on that track there yonder thrown in jail."

"You can't do that!" Kincannon protested, starting to spit before he remembered he'd tossed his tobacco away.

"You can raise that at the hearing, son. I'll schedule it to give your bosses plenty of time to send their lawyers, say a week's time. Of course, we'll have to order you to cease and desist all work in the interim."

Kincannon stamped the earth hard enough to cough dust on the two Texans' feet. "All right, just tell me what you want."

"Any of your men show any signs of blood on their clothing?"

William Ray Strong asked him. "You catch any of them wandering around between here and the Chinese camp? Anything about any of them strike you as standing out in a way that made you take notice? Any of them have the kind of violence in their past that suggests them capable of killing women?"

"They were whores, each and every one of them, not women." Kincannon's expression crinkled. "And pretty much all the men in this camp have some violence in their past. Too many suspects for you to bother with."

"Well, I'll be the judge of that, Mr. Kincannon. What about men with prison records?"

"Imagine we got our share of jailbirds, but 'long as they do a good day's work, I let their pasts be."

"You got records I can look at?" William Ray asked.

"I got records, but not that you can look at, not without permission of my superiors at the Southern Pacific."

"We back to that again?" Judge Bean spat at him. "You seem hell-bent on pissing me off here, Mr. Kincannon."

William Ray looked toward one of the tents with flaps rustling in the late-afternoon breeze, something striking him about it. "Nice sewing job somebody did on that tent," he told Kincannon, thinking of how the heads of the victims had been sliced off and sewn back on. "You can see the stitch lines where he meshed the material together."

"You've done wasted enough of my time," Kincannon said and took a single stride with his boot, big enough to put William Ray's eyes even with his. "And I mean to get back to work now. You've wasted enough of my time and I ain't got no more to give. You hear that—"

Before he got his next word out, William Ray slammed a knee into his groin that dropped him to the hardpan where Kincannon's face went beet red under the sun, grimacing in pain and letting out huge gushes of breath. William Ray yanked him up to his knees by his mustache and stuck his Colt Peacemaker into Kincannon's mouth while he continued to gasp.

"When I remove my gun," William Ray said, conscious that all work had ceased for the moment, the entire site gone quiet with its attention turned toward whatever was transpiring here, "you're gonna tell me what I want to know or I'm gonna jam it back in and break all your teeth. Nod if you read me, asshole."

Kincannon nodded.

William Ray removed his Colt but held it firm. "Now, who's the man that sewed those tent flaps for you?"

33

SAN ANTONIO, TEXAS

"I've shot that Colt," Caitlin told Sharon Yarlas, when she finally stopped. "My great-granddad William Ray gave it to his son, my granddad Earl."

"But I'd bet you never stuck it in a man's mouth."

"No, not that gun anyway," Caitlin winked. "I still own it and it still shoots."

"Well, being old doesn't mean you can't work as well as you need to. I can tell you that much from personal experience." Sharon started playing with the kerchief strung round her neck again, taking notice of Caitlin watching her. "I'd like to go on, Ranger," she said, suddenly sounding impatient, "but the next part of the story's kind of a fog."

"You mind taking off that kerchief, ma'am?"

"Excuse me?"

Caitlin pointed toward the red cotton with her finger.

"Well, I don't see why."

"I'd like to see what you're hiding beneath it, if you don't mind."

Sharon frowned, but finally started to unwrap the kerchief with a deep sigh that seemed to compress her chest.

The glass door leading from the next car opened and the four clowns entered, yammering it up with the seated patrons enjoying the ride in odd counterpoint to what Caitlin found herself looking at.

A neat line of raw, inflamed tissue ringed Sharon Yarlas's neck like a collar. It made Caitlin think of the ligature marks she'd seen on victims of strangulation and recalled how Doc Whatley described what an awful death that was.

"Who did that to you, ma'am?" she asked the older woman, fresh laughter from the middle of the passenger car telling her the clowns were making their way up the aisle.

"It's my husband," the older woman finally said, with another sigh, her voice cracking with subdued tears. "He's not . . . well."

"Are we talking about Alzheimer's, ma'am?"

Sharon Yarlas started to take a deep breath and let it out halfway in. "Early stages. He's still aware enough to know what's happening to him, how he's deteriorating, and his lucid moments are full of anger and rage. He takes it out on me because he doesn't know what else to do."

Caitlin looked into the woman's sad, moist eyes, seeing in her a portrait of unrecognized heroism standing by a loved one no matter what because it's what people were supposed to do.

"I'd like your phone number," Caitlin told her.

Sharon dabbed her eyes with the kerchief she'd unwrapped from her neck, then looped it back into place. "I want to keep this private, Ranger."

"I understand. But there are programs and funds available in some places for those who know how to look for them. I'm pretty good at such things and, if you'll pass on that number, I'll check into things on your behalf."

Caitlin started to ease the cell phone from the pocket of her jeans to switch it back on. Her gaze spotted a father using an identical phone to snap a picture of his son between two of the clowns just fifteen feet away from her now. The train continued shimmying over the uneven track bed, bending into the curve that jostled the clowns across the aisle with the young boy still between them. As Caitlin waited for her phone to power up, she glimpsed the clowns steadying their sneakered feet and then realized what had seemed all wrong before.

Where were their clown shoes?

The sneakers were all wrong, and the presence of the clowns had come as a surprise earlier to Sharon Yarlas, Caitlin remembered as her eyes locked with one of the clown's in the same moment the two she'd lost sight of stormed up the aisle with pistols drawn.

34

PROVIDENCE, RHODE ISLAND

Dylan clearly didn't want to talk much about whatever had happened between him and the Chinese girl Kai, but Cort Wesley didn't give him a choice.

"This her?" he asked, unfolding the picture one of Dylan's friends at Delta Phi had printed out for him and Caitlin.

"I've gotta go to the bathroom," the boy said, still achy after a nurse had removed his catheter.

"No, you don't."

"What, you can read my bladder now?"

"Nope, I can read you."

Dylan rolled his eyes, the simple motion enough to send a bolt of pain that tightened his features into a grimace that straightened only when the boy settled himself with some deep breaths.

"Let me ask you a question," Cort Wesley said when he thought Dylan was ready again, leaving the picture atop his bedcovers in the same place the pink rose had been. "If this were Caitlin asking, would you answer then?"

"Probably."

"Why?"

"Because she's a Ranger."

"And I'm your father."

"You just made my point."

Cort Wesley was left shaking his head. His oldest son having been away for over two months now, since late August, left him with only the good memories and allowed him to push the perpetual conflict between them into the far recesses of his mind. Cort Wesley figured it was just part of the process of the son growing up and the father not ready to let go. He'd had so much time to make up for and Dylan's high school years just hadn't lasted long enough.

"You said her name was Kai," Cort Wesley persisted. "What else can you tell me about her?"

Dylan tried to meet his gaze.

"You still seeing double?"

The boy nodded, not looking at him as he took the shot lifted off the porn video in hand again. "Where'd you get the picture?"

"One of your friends in that fraternity printed it out for me after showing us the video."

"*Us?* Caitlin saw it too?"

Cort Wesley nodded. "But it's all right, 'cause she's a Texas Ranger. I figure the next question she'd ask you is when exactly you first spotted this girl, Kai, you recognized from the video."

"At Viva."

"That be the place across from Spats, both managed by your friend Theo."

The boy's eyes widened, then narrowed again when holding them that way made his head hurt. "Theo? Is there anyone at Brown you *didn't* talk to about this?"

"I was with a Texas Ranger, remember?"

"Where's Caitlin again?"

"She had to go back home for some Ranger business. I already told you that."

"When?"

"A while ago."

"I don't remember. I got a concussion, don't I?"

"That's what the doctor says."

Dylan shook his head deliberately. "Avoided one all season in football and look what happens. Sucks." He paused and steadied himself with another series of deep breaths. "I want to call Caitlin."

Cort Wesley handed him his phone. "Give it your best shot, son."

Dylan held the handset, smirking. "I thought you were gonna get a new one."

"What's wrong with what I've got?"

"Dad, it's a piece of shit. You don't even have any apps on it, except that flashlight one you never use."

Cort Wesley was left staring at his oldest son as if the boy had just landed from another planet. "How do you know I don't use it? I can't wait until you have kids of your own, son."

"Why?"

"So you can share in my misery."

Dylan had the phone pressed up against his ear now. "Very funny, Dad."

"You see me laughing? I want to hear more about this Kai."

"Like what?"

"You met up with her the night you got jumped."

"That's right."

"She texted you after your meetings and she met you at Spats." Dylan nodded.

"Your pals in the fraternity had the feeling she was in trouble or something, that you were trying your best to help her."

"She was in trouble for sure," Dylan affirmed and extended the phone back toward Cort Wesley. "Straight to voice mail."

And that's when all the lights in the hospital went out.

35

SAN ANTONIO, TEXAS

Caitlin shoved Sharon Yarlas all the way behind her and whipped out her SIG Sauer. One of the clowns being photographed brought a young boy in close against him for cover, fumbling his own pistol from its holster in the process.

Thoughts and visions whiplashed through Caitlin's mind, holding on the image of the clown makeup melting off the impersonators' skin, revealing splotches of flesh color amid the white. She shot the trailing clowns first before either managed to get off a shot. Her bullets punched them backward, into and over seats where several train riders bore the brunt of the impact.

The rest of the car, though, thought this was hilarious, part of the show for which they'd purchased an overpriced ticket. Well, not so overpriced anymore it seemed, what with a gal Texas Ranger shooting it out with four clown gunmen in a pretend gunfight.

Applause rippled through the car as the clown holding the boy in one hand and a pistol in the other got off a shot that splattered an EXIT sign and sent shards of the red letters spraying in all directions. Several ended up in Caitlin's hair, clinging there, and drawing more applause from an audience captivated by the show that now featured trick shooting.

One of the clowns she thought she'd put down for good was stirring in the aisle and the fourth had thrown himself over a seat. He opened fire from there, kill shots for sure, if Caitlin hadn't stooped low, dragging Sharon Yarlas down with her. She couldn't shoot him through the cushion since the seat behind which he was crouched was occupied by a red-haired girl busy recording the whole thing on her cell phone, impervious to the bullets flying around her. To a man, woman, and child, no one in the car had yet realized this was very much the real thing.

Until Caitlin dropped down all the way to her stomach, SIG steadied in two hands, and shot the clown square in the face, sending gory pieces of blood and bone flying through the air. The corpse was thrown backward onto the riders he'd squeezed himself among, coating them in brain and skull matter.

The applause stopped.

The screams began.

Caitlin rolled sideways, fortunate to avoid the misaimed bullets fired by the clown still clutching the boy before him as a shield. No way she could risk a shot now, certainly not from her back where she'd ended up, so Caitlin did the next best thing.

She shot out the car's overhead skylight, one of the many new features added since she'd ridden the train as a girl. The safety glass disintegrated in a single instant, raining shards downward all over the clown where they settled into his red wig, the pieces shiny against the matte finish of his hair. Still dragging the boy with him, he shook them free, firing off shots until his revolver clicked empty, while retreating to the door separating this car from the next.

He surged through it as Caitlin pushed herself back to her feet, greeted by errant fire from the wounded clown leaking blood out his baggy white costume. She was dimly aware of desperate cries and screams, the riders gone invisible to her after ducking down beneath their seats for protection.

Caitlin fired two shots purposely low into the floor before the wounded clown, stilling his fire long enough to take better aim and put her last three bullets into him, one blowing part of his scalp into a wall patch between two windows. Then she started down the aisle, becoming aware of the screams and cries coming from the car through which the final clown was now moving with his young hostage in tow.

A hand suddenly reached out and grasped her arm.

"That's my son, Ranger, my son!" a man blared, eyes wide in panic. "Please, please!"

Caitlin shook herself free and moved on.

36

The room's only illumination came from the streetlamps breaking the darkness beyond and the glow of headlights cruising along nearby Route 95 that splashed moving shadows across the walls of Dylan's room.

"Where's your goddamn gun?" Dylan asked, sitting further upright in bed.

"Back home, son. Airlines got a thing about civilians carrying them on flights."

Dylan looked down at Cort Wesley's phone, which he was still holding after his call to Caitlin that had gone straight to voice mail. His finger rolled across the screen, activating the flashlight app that shone on a white-coated figure, a doctor, standing in the doorway.

An Asian doctor.

He started into the room, was halfway through the door when he whipped out something black and shiny from beneath his lab coat. Cort Wesley recognized it as a mini-submachine gun, with a sound suppressor affixed to its barrel, as he threw himself into motion, crashing into the door and slamming it hard into the Chinese gunman, pinning whatever kind of gun it was against the wall. Cort Wesley jerked the door backward, cracked an elbow into the smaller man's skull, and then went for his weapon. He had reached and managed to grab hold of the cold steel much too easily, he realized, because the Chinese gunman had let him.

Cort Wesley let the weapon go flying from his grasp and felt a blow slam into his ribs with the force of an iron bar. He recognized the move as some kind of martial arts strike, thrown with an open hand so what hit him was the palm and heel with enough force to rattle his ribs. Cort Wesley felt the air burst out of him, but clung to his calm even as his breath fled him.

The Chinese man was a whirling blur of muscle and bone, no features Cort Wesley could lock on to long enough to focus a strike. And before instinct could take over, the smaller man unleashed a wild flurry of blows that Cort Wesley blocked, deflected, dodged, ducked under, yet still felt enough land to leave him dazed and disoriented.

Cort Wesley felt the back of his head slam into something that shattered on impact and realized momentum had carried the two of them into the bathroom. Mirror glass rained all around him, the biggest shard of it catching the dim reflection of a can of disinfectant spray sitting atop the toilet bowl. Cort Wesley groped for it, missing on the first two flails and nearly knocking it to the floor with a third, until he locked it into his grasp with the fourth.

The Chinese man was twisting in close, for what Cort Wesley vaguely recognized as a move that would snap his neck like a twig, when he found the activator and snapped the can before the smaller man's eyes as he hit it. He sprayed and kept spraying, his assailant wailing up a storm as his deadly hands sprang upward to his burning eyes.

Cort Wesley gave no quarter from there, pummeling the smaller man's ribs and face, and then driving him backward, back into the room where only Dylan's bed stopped his pitch and held him upright. He seemed to be slumping to the floor, Cort Wesley just realizing the bed was empty, when a knife flashed in the Chinese man's hand.

Spittle flew from the man's mouth, his eyes wide with fury, as he slashed the knife sideways, its blade struggling to glint in the near darkness of the room. Cort Wesley narrowly avoided the first blow and managed to deflect the second, but a third followed a feint that left a gash down his side. Light exploded before his eyes, the pain following fast, and Cort Wesley felt his wounded side was freezing up solid. Hobbled, he was still able to knock the next blow aside while managing only a halfhearted counter with his other arm.

Then he saw the knife rearing back, nothing he could do to stop its surge from the angle at which it was coming. Still he tried to twist, tried to get his arm up when . . .

CRACK!

. . . the muffled sound coming from inside him, it seemed, until the Chinese man froze in place before him. His eyes locked open and glassy before he keeled over forward to reveal Dylan perched on the floor holding the silenced mini-machine pistol in hand. Holding it steady in case the would-be killer moved again.

Cort Wesley moved gingerly across the floor as hot pain continued to seer his side where the knife had grazed him. Dylan clung to the weapon, holding it straight and still as if he still had a target in his sights. A thin wisp of smoke bled from the barrel and drifted past him before dissipating in the stale room air.

He took the mini-machine pistol from his son's grasp, the boy only then snapping alert as if roused from a dream. He met Cort Wesley's gaze, but couldn't hold it.

"We gotta move, son."

He helped Dylan to his feet as a vast shadow appeared in the doorway, blocking what little light the corridor had to shed.

37

SAN ANTONIO, TEXAS

The clown was halfway down the aisle of the rearmost train car, revolver in one hand and hostage boy in the other, when Caitlin surged through the door and caught him in her sights.

"Let the boy go and drop the weapon!" she called out, SIG steadied before her.

The clown was almost to the back door marked EMERGENCY EXIT, no place else to go from there.

"*Now!* You hear me? Let him go *now!*"

Caitlin wanted to shoot then, but the boy was just too close and she was still too far away to be sure of hitting the right target.

"Last chance!" she shouted anyway, thinking of something else.

Her hand was already stretching upward, reaching for the emergency brake pull her grandfather had told her about yanking one day to forestall a robbery on a train even older than this one. She pulled downward and heard the screech of the train's huge brakes engaging just before the initial jolt of displaced gravity threw all the passengers forward.

Including the clown.

But he latched on to a handhold just in time, the boy separated from his grasp as the clown burst through the door at the train's rear and vanished an instant ahead of Caitlin's bullet shattering the glass window. She figured he'd jumped off the train for sure, but reaching the remnants of the window provided no view of him fleeing beyond, meaning he'd chosen another route of escape from the slowing train: The roof.

With that, Caitlin surged through the door and grabbed hold of the highest ladder rung she could grasp, following the clown's path up onto the train's roof.

The train's speed was down to probably twenty miles per hour and still slowing when she crested the ladder's top and pulled herself onto the roof of the rearmost car, spotting the clown already atop the center car now. The slowing clip allowed him to twist sideways and fire her way, missing with two shots and then a third.

Caitlin knew how hard hitting a moving target while moving yourself was. So she lurched to her feet and chanced sprinting straight for him before he could jump off. The clown emptied the revolver's cylinder, none of his shots even coming close. Caitlin opened up with her SIG in response, each report sending a pang through her eardrums, bullet after bullet skewing off target as the clown used a speed loader, slammed the cylinder back closed, and started firing anew.

She felt the heat of one and then another of the clown's bullets hiss right past her and slowed enough to steady her aim before letting loose with her next salvo. Waiting until she reached the break between the third car and the second, the train down to fifteen miles per hour, maybe ten when she hit her trigger again as the clown's gun locked empty and he sank a hand into the baggy pocket of his Western clown suit.

Before he could find a fresh speed loader, impact literally picked him up and threw him over the edge of the center car down to the break between it and the lead car Caitlin and Sharon Yarlas had boarded. She backed up to give herself enough of a start to easily leap from the top of the trailing car to the center one, bending at the knees as her boots touched down.

The train's slowing pace made it easy to cover the car's distance quickly and she reached the break with the lead car to find the clown's body pinned between them, lying faceup with his eyes locked open. Caitlin saw that he'd sweated most of his makeup off and crouched to get a better look because what she'd glimpsed standing didn't seem possible. But it was, as revealed by the clear view afforded her now.

The clown was Chinese.

38

PROVIDENCE, RHODE ISLAND

Coach Estes stood in the doorway to Dylan's room, flanked by a dozen of Dylan's teammates on the Brown University football team, maybe more.

"Thought we'd stop by to visit," Estes said, just starting to grasp the busted-up conditions of the room.

"We're gonna need some help getting out of here, Coach," Cort Wesley told him.

"Just tell us how," Estes offered, his gaze finally locking on the Chinese man dressed as a doctor Dylan had shot dead.

The hospital floor was a study of chaos, just catching up to the sound of gunshots and reports of a violent struggle in a patient's room. A parade of doctors, nurses, and attendants rushing in all directions through darkness broken only by emergency lights shining down from their wall mounts. They seemed not even to regard the sight of Cort Wesley wheeling his son's bed down the hallway, enclosed now by a dozen Brown football players, led by the school's head coach, whose big frames rendered it invisible.

Cort Wesley was hardly surprised when he saw three more Chinese coming straight at him from the head of the hall, backup for the man left dead in Dylan's room.

"Now!"

With that, Coach Estes and the Brown football players darted sideways and Cort Wesley sent the hospital bed speeding straight for the three Chinese men who froze briefly at the ruffled mattress and bedcovers rolling their way.

Dylan had exited the room on wobbly feet between three massive offensive lineman more accustomed to blowing holes for him through opponents' defensive lines. The three Chinese had managed to free their guns. But the empty bed speeding toward them proved enough of a distraction to give Cort Wesley the instant he needed to steady the mini-submachine gun he'd drawn from under a sheet.

He opened fire just as the Chinese gunmen found their triggers and took all three out with a succession of single shots sprayed side to side, fighting against barrel jerk and sway that blew heat up into his face with each report. The gun was a piece of shit really, but from this distance it was good enough to do the job. The hospital bed had rammed the wall, one wheel oddly still spinning, when what looked like the whole Providence Police Department burst through a stairwell door just beyond the dead bodies at the head of the hall, guns leveled and ready to fire.

PART FOUR

"You may withdraw every regular soldier . . . from the border of Texas . . . if you will give her but a single regiment of Texas Rangers."

—Sam Houston

39

"Drop it! On the floor now!"

Cort Wesley had already shed the mini-submachine gun and was halfway there before the cop's order was even finished. He was placed under arrest and transported to the Providence Police Department, after the knife wound he'd suffered was dressed. Turned out to be little more than a scratch.

"I guess I shouldn't be surprised," Detective Finneran said, shaking his head, his expression stretched into a grimace from what might have been a bad case of heartburn. "This kind of shit followed you here just like it followed our favorite Texas Ranger."

"Not exactly. Those shooters were coming to finish the job on my son. I'm not there at the time, you'd be investigating his death instead of theirs."

"But you were there and we've got four dead bodies to prove it." Finneran paused, something changing in his expression. "Your son recognize any of them?"

"He didn't get a very good look," Cort Wesley said, not bothering to inform the detective that Dylan had actually shot one of the gunmen himself. "But you can bet the two incidents are connected."

"Can I? Is that because you know something you're not telling me?"

"That girl's the key, Detective," Cort Wesley told him. "The one my son left the bar with."

"We were proceeding on the assumption that she may have set him up, that the attack was a robbery gone wrong."

"Seems pretty obvious you can rule that out now."

"Not to me, Mr. Torres."

"It's Masters and I don't think I'm reading you here."

"Well, I read *you* as the kind of man who attracts trouble. You say the men you killed came after your son when it could just as easily have been you."

"Am I under arrest?"

"I've got four bodies to account for."

"That doesn't answer my question."

"It's the best I can do."

"Then can I have my cell phone back to make a phone call?"

"To the Ranger? I've already brought her up to speed on what happened."

"How gracious of you."

"Not really. I just wanted to make sure she was back in Texas. Looks like she got into a pretty big scrape of her own—with Chinese gunmen too."

"I need my phone," Cort Wesley said, rising.

40

SAN ANTONIO, TEXAS

"You wanna tell me what all this is about?" Cort Wesley asked Caitlin, after each had caught the other up on the events that had just transpired. "What we did to piss off the entire nation of China."

"We got a Ranger already up at Luke's boarding school in Houston just as a precaution. You say they got you and Dylan separated?"

"According to Detective Finneran, it's routine in matters in-volving a shooting, multiple in this case."

"Dylan recognize any of the shooters from that beating he took?"

She heard something change in Cort Wesley's breathing on the other end of the line. "He killed one of them, Caitlin."

"Oh, shit . . ."

"Shot him dead and likely saved my life."

"You talk to him?"

"They got me back at the station and he's still at the hospital. Got Finneran to station a cop at the door, though. In feudal times, Chinese assassins always worked in groups of four. You wanna tell me what kind of shit we stepped in this time?"

"It all goes back to that girl Dylan told people he was helping out, Cort Wesley. We find her, we'll have our answers."

"Easier said than done."

"My guess is we've got several people not telling us everything they know. But I have great faith in your powers of persuasion."

"Providence police won't be happy at my continued involve-ment, Ranger."

"That concern you?"

"Not even for a second," Cort Wesley told her.

Caitlin spotted a crime scene technician rushing up to Captain Tepper, holding something in his hand.

"Call you right back, Cort Wesley."

41

SAN ANTONIO, TEXAS

Tepper had taken charge of the crime scene set up around the train that had been stalled on the track bed for hours now. Lights had to be set up to make sure no evidence from the gunfight was missed. The tall, freestanding lights were the kind construction crews used in night work, overly bright with a foglike sheen sprayed from their powerful bulbs. The team would probably be on scene much of the night, mostly inside the train collecting evidence in the form of fingerprints and shell casings, working to confirm Caitlin's version of events with fancy laser measuring devices that could pinpoint from where exactly each bullet had been fired.

Caitlin had worked with Sharon Yarlas to evacuate the stopped train in as calm a manner as possible. The museum grounds were a good three miles back and buses were ordered up to retrieve the riders who were promised a full refund and free ticket to return anytime they wanted.

Caitlin reached Captain Tepper amid the spill of the floodlights, just as the crime scene tech was handing him an evidence pouch.

"All the victims had a few of these in their pockets," explained the man whose ID badge, dangling from his neck, identified him as Ramirez. "Mean anything to you?"

"Pink flower petals," Caitlin said, regarding the contents of the pouch.

"I believe he was asking me, Ranger," Tepper groused. "They look like pink flower petals," he told Ramirez, handing him back the pouch.

"Any idea why all four of the gunmen would be carrying them on their persons?"

"Isn't that what you're supposed to tell us, son? Why don't you get those over to Doc Whatley at the Medical Examiner's Office and let him have a go at this?"

"Will do, Captain. Oh, and one more thing. Each of the suspects had the same number of petals in their pockets. Exactly four."

42

Caitlin saw Guillermo Paz's truck parked under the umbrella of elm tree branches. The moonlight splayed their shadows over the shiny paint and windows, making it look like the massive pickup was in the grasp of some multitentacled monster.

She watched the driver's-side window roll down at her approach. "How'd you know, Colonel?"

"I had a vision, Ranger, a bad one. Full of darkness and fire and things that looked like clowns."

"Clowns," Caitlin repeated, as if to reassure herself she'd heard him correctly.

"Does that mean anything to you?"

Caitlin regarded Guillermo Paz's huge shape filling the entire driver's seat almost to the car's roof. She felt the warm dampness rising out of her skin again, touching the sweat-darkened portions of her shirt. Through all the hours spent at the crime scene around the train, she'd been unable to feel anything but hot. The lingering effects of the gunfight, along with worry over exactly where this was headed now that Dylan was clearly still in danger, had conspired to keep her body temperature in the red.

"I went to a circus once as a boy," Paz continued suddenly, "not to watch, but to pickpocket the wallets of men at the concession stands. I think I was fourteen at the time, right after I killed the man who murdered my priest. I wasn't very good at it. People took too much notice of me. I guess I stood out even then. The clowns had whips they used on the animals, elephants mostly, to make them do what they were supposed to. The whole time with smiles painted onto their faces. I learned a lot that day, Ranger."

"What do you know about the Triad, Colonel?"

"They are what passes for the Chinese mafia."

"Four Chinese tried to kill me today. They were disguised as clowns."

Paz showed no surprise, no reaction at all. "The outlaw too?"

Caitlin nodded. "Up in Providence where that ambush had already put his son in the hospital. Only they weren't dressed as clowns there."

She could see Paz squeezing his leather-wrapped steering wheel. "I got in my truck and it brought me here. I don't remember the route. I think maybe my mother was doing the driving."

"I'm going inside, see if I can grab some sleep."

Paz nodded. His long, tangled hair looked shiny in the moonlight and his clothes smelled of a load of wash done with too much laundry detergent. A car passed by on the street, both of them tensing as its headlights pierced Paz's eyes, which looked like black spheres wedged into his skull.

"I told you about my vision, Ranger."

"You said you saw darkness coming."

"I was wrong," Paz told her. "Because it's already here."

Caitlin started to turn away, then thought of something and swung back. "Ever cover the Chinese in your studies of philosophy, Colonel?"

"For sure, though without very much success at all."

"Does the number four have any special meaning?" she asked him, thinking of the flower pedals recovered from the pockets of each of the Chinese gunmen, of which there had been four as well.

Another car drove past them on the street, its headlights reflecting off Paz's liquidy black eyes and brightening the space between him and Caitlin.

"The number four symbolizes death," he told her.

43

"When can I get out of here, Dad?"

"How's your head feel?"

"I told the doctor it felt a lot better."

"You lied to him, in other words."

"I think this place is making it worse. Just back me up on this, okay?"

First thing that morning, Finneran had shown up with coffee in hand at the holding cell where Cort Wesley had spent the night.

"Peace offering?" Cort Wesley asked, easing himself upright.

"More like a going-away present. You're a free man, cowboy. How is it guys like you and this Texas Ranger end up with friends in the highest of places?"

"I have no idea what you're talking about."

"I'm talking about Washington. Word got passed down from on high this morning that we needed to cut you loose. So get yourself on an airplane, cowboy. I never want to see your sorry ass in this state again."

But Finneran didn't step aside when Cort Wesley approached the cell door to take his leave.

"I pulled your file," he said instead. "At least I tried to. Got plenty from the state of Texas but nothing out of the national databases, and that includes the FBI's."

"You're in my way, Detective."

"I know a rigged deck when I see one, cowboy. My lieutenant told me to back off. Apparently somebody caught wind of the fact that I was looking into your background and didn't like it. But the way you operate, even your friends in Washington won't be able to pull your ass out of the fires you keep setting."

"I'll take that under advisement."

Cort Wesley had taken a cab to the hospital, not about to ask Finneran to snare him a ride. Dylan was sitting up when he got there, his bed raised as upright as it would go. He was using a handheld control that also connected him to the nurse's station to scan through the channels. Just like home. The blinds were open and the sun's angle was starting to push fresh light through the window, illuminating a trail of wet footsteps from the bed to the bathroom.

"Doctors want to hold you for further testing and observation. I told them we were leaving today."

Dylan nodded. "My clothes are in the closet. I want to get dressed. I hate these hospital things they make you wear."

Dylan deactivated the mute button, then put it back on before even a word had been spoken on the screen. The sun framed his face with a halo, making his skin look the way it did when he came in after a run. His long black hair was wet at the ends, evidence of a recent washing that left him smelling vaguely of antiseptic hospital soap. It hung in slow-drying tangles past his shoulders. Cort Wesley watched the boy twirl some stray strands that had collected near his cheek around his finger, release them, and then twirl them all over again.

"We were talking about that girl Kai before the shooting started yesterday."

Dylan switched the television's sound back on and turned it up as far as it would go.

Cort Wesley sat down at the foot of his son's bed. "Your mom never told me much about you mostly because I didn't ask. But what I remember most of what she did tell me was that you were fond of picking up strays. Started with squirrels and progressed all the way to dogs and cats. Like you could never stand to see any-thing left on its own."

Dylan rolled his eyes. "So?"

"That proclivity seems to have grown up with you. I think what attracted you to this girl was that she was a stray. You recognized her from that video and thought maybe you could save her just like you saved all those animals back before when you were a little kid. But this time you got a little more than you bargained for and I'd like to hear what that was exactly."

"She said she had family back in China and was turning tricks to raise the money she needed to bring them over."

"And you believed that?"

Dylan shrugged. "Not for a minute, but I didn't think it was any of my business. It was just kind of cool, recognizing her from that video in a bar. She didn't even bother denying it, kind of played along like she was glad I knew who she was—well, what she did anyway."

"That's because she probably saw you as a mark, income for the evening."

"It wasn't like that."

"Then what was it like?" When Dylan remained silent, Cort Wesley decided to fill in some of the blanks for him. "You made the first contact but the night you got jumped, she texted you. Your friends from that fraternity said it seemed important. I'd like to know what changed, why she reached out to you if it wasn't about money."

"It wasn't about money."

"Then what?"

Dylan blew out his breath and then sucked in some air to replace it. "She called me after that first night, wanted to meet up. Said she wanted to talk."

"About what?"

"About you, Dad, but Caitlin mostly."

"Me? *Caitlin?*" Cort Wesley managed, trying to make sense of that. "What'd you tell her about us?"

"Nothing, nothing at all."

"That means Kai must've checked you out, found the two of us in your background."

"She saw your pictures in my room, and on my phone too. Caitlin really interested her, the fact that she's a Texas Ranger and all. Then the night she texted me she mentioned some of the things the two of you had done, the bad guys you'd taken on."

"What else did Kai tell you that night, son?"

"That she wanted me to take her home with me to San Antonio. Said she had a job only the Texas Rangers could handle. Something about a serial killer."

44

SAN ANTONIO, TEXAS

"I'm a little busy here in case you didn't notice, Ranger," was how Doc Whatley greeted Caitlin the next morning when she showed up unannounced at the Medical Examiner's Office inside the Bexar County Forensic Science Center, which occupied three floors near the Merlin Minter entrance to the University of Texas Health Science Center at San Antonio.

"Looks like you didn't get any more sleep last night than I did."

Whatley frowned at her. "I was just about to go home and try to steal a few hours when you showed up."

"Then let's make this fast, Doc. What can you tell me about the case I didn't know yesterday?"

"Which case would that be?" he asked with a sigh, the strain and pressure cracking his voice more than the fatigue. "We got a whole buffet line to choose from, Ranger. I was already trying to find some link between those serial killings," Whatley continued, "other than the fact that all the victims were Chinese, when the bodies of four homeless men showed up. All found within the jurisdiction of this office and all four without a mark on them. No visible cause of death to make things any easier on me either."

"Did you say four?"

Whatley nodded. "Is that important?"

"Just tell me how this is our problem?"

"It isn't our problem, it's *my* problem. I haven't been able to ascertain a cause of death yet, other than just to tell you whatever it was killed all four of them in a virtually identical manner. So if you want to know why I haven't got the answers you came here for, blame the San Antonio Police Department and sheriff's department for carting the bodies over." Whatley shifted about uneasily in his desk chair, searching for a comfort that eluded him. "What was it you wanted anyway?"

Caitlin sat down before him, so Whatley wouldn't have to look up at her. "You were gonna look into those flower petals found in the clown gunmen's pockets last night."

"They're camellias," Whatley told her. "But what's even more interesting is that I found oil from the flowers in the stomachs of all four of those Chinese gunmen from the train shooting."

"You mean they *ate* them?"

"Drank, probably. In some kind of elixir, tincture, or even tea. The Chinese have these things called tea ceremonies, you know."

"I've heard of the Japanese doing that, not the Chinese."

"Well, the Chinese do it too. They have ceremonies for pretty much all purposes, so I imagine partaking in one prior to going out to kill a Texas Ranger may be among them. And there's something else that might interest you. See, the camellia is a fairly familiar flower in the south, particularly in southern Louisiana where the climate is perfect for it. But the flower is native to China." Whatley paused here, as he always seemed to do just before making his point. "And that's where this particular strain originated."

"You mean it was imported?"

Whatley nodded, his face brightening with color in the sun starting to burn stronger through his office window. "And, of course, such imports, even of seeds, need to be registered and inventoried in order to make it through Customs. As far as I can tell, Ranger, only one such entry in all of Texas has been made in the past two years."

"Care to tell me where I can find these flowers, Doc?"

45

PROVIDENCE, RHODE ISLAND

"You see what I'm getting at here?" Cort Wesley said to Theo, the stout, burly manager of Spats and the other establishment across the street where Dylan had first met Kai.

"I'm glad to hear your son's doing better," Theo said, continuing to remove the chairs from atop the tables to ready the sports bar for lunch. The wall-mounted widescreen televisions were tuned to an assortment of sports channels, on mute right now.

"It seems you're ignoring me, Theo."

"You're not a cop, Mr. Masters. You're not even a customer."

"My son is. And I'm the one who pays the credit card bills he's been racking up here, on booze mostly thanks to that fake ID he's got now."

Theo lowered another chair to the floor and then regarded him. "I've told you everything I know."

"No, you haven't. But that's about to change. We're going to talk some about Kai, you and me."

"Kai?"

"The Chinese girl's name. You didn't know it?"

"I never asked."

"Well, you might not have known who she was, but you pretty much admitted you knew *what*. Yet you still let her patronize both establishments."

Theo lowered another chair to the floor. "I don't know what you're getting at, Mr. Masters."

"You let her do business inside places you run because I don't think you had much of a choice. You got something going with somebody and I want to know who that is."

Theo stopped his labors and backed off a bit, studying Cort Wesley as if seeing him for the first time. A ceiling fan twirled slowly over them.

"You should get on a plane back to Texas," Theo advised.

"Sorry, no can do on account of unfinished business that starts with you. And if you don't help me with my business, I'm gonna end yours by doing my own personal ID check starting tonight. I imagine your patrons would just love that. So what's it going to be, Theo?"

A thin shaft of light formed a dome around Theo's bald plate down to his forehead, seeming to carve his face in two. "I'm protected, Mr. Masters, by the same people who handle high-end call-girl traffic like Kai. People you don't want to mess with."

Cort Wesley took a step closer to him, blocking out the light. "I'll be the judge of that. Why don't you tell me where I can find them?"

46

New Braunfels, Texas

"Thank you for seeing me, Mr. Zhen," Caitlin said to the founder of the Yuyuan Corporation, surprised that he was able to meet with her so quickly. "I appreciate the courtesy very much."

"No thanks are necessary, Ranger. Our policy is to cooperate in any law enforcement investigation fully and promptly. Our policy is to hold nothing back whatsoever."

"Would that be the company's policy or your country's, sir?"

He smiled behind the bamboo desk in his sprawling office that might have matched the square footage of Caitlin's entire house.

The office was laid out in elegant but minimalist fashion. Yuyuan's American corporate headquarters occupied all of an eight-story building on Old San Antonio Road just off Route 35, which connected New Braunfels to San Antonio thirty miles to the southeast. It was located on the grounds of what had been envisioned as a sprawling office park, abandoned when the economy cratered, leaving Yuyuan as the lone standing structure amid land cleared but never further developed.

The building seemed a perfect blend for the tree-rich landscape, its modern design dominated by curved lines as opposed to the angular ones of typically generic office buildings. Yuyuan's American headquarters seemed to grow out of the ground instead of being built upon it. The building's ground floor was shaded to match the tan ground color, darkening with each successive level. Much of that was an illusion bred by the structure's sloping design and reflective windows when struck by the harsh Texas sun tamed by its neutral colors.

Long and rounded to follow the building's exterior curves, Li Zhen's office had been built to take advantage of the best of both the afternoon and morning sunlight—though if the currently raised rattan shutters were an indication, that light could be shut out in mere moments. Strange, then, how Zhen had placed his desk in the one corner of the office that didn't get any sunlight at all. Even now he regarded Caitlin from a nest of shadows while three separate shafts of light joined up in the very spot she was seated.

"Both, Ranger," Zhen said, his smile holding. "I am at your service. Just tell me how I may serve you."

"Well, sir, this may sound a bit odd since it concerns flowers."

"Flowers, Ranger?"

"Imported from China. I believe they're called camellias, and I couldn't help but notice that beautiful garden you've got on the grounds here from that glass elevator."

"Thank you," Zhen said, no smile this time and his gratitude didn't sound very genuine.

Caitlin leaned forward. Her chair, one of four matching ones lined up in front of Li Zhen's desk, was elegant but stiff and boasted no cushion. Already forcing her to shift about in search of comfort, however brief.

She let her eyes fall on a series of very old black-and-white photographs set beautifully on the wall behind Zhen's desk, all enlarged and displayed in elegant bamboo frames that were a perfect compliment for the remainder of the office's decor. As the office's sole wall hangings, Caitlin thought the pictures still looked out of place until she realized they featured various scenes from the mid- to late 1800s of work on the railroads that ultimately stitched the country together. The pictures were grainy, some of the clarity sacrificed in favor of size, but all featured a sampling of the Chinese workers greatly responsible for supplying much needed labor. One looked to be a posed group shot, the rest taken in the midst of heavy, backbreaking work, sometimes with Caucasian foreman and railroad men in suits caught in the frame with their expensive trousers tucked into boots.

"Looks like we've got something in common, sir," Caitlin said.

Zhen cocked his gaze behind him to follow hers. "The railroad?"

Caitlin nodded. "My great-grandfather was a Texas Ranger too, and William Ray Strong had occasion to cross paths with some pretty mean types who worked those camps."

"That name rings a bell," he recalled. "Perhaps my ancestor crossed paths with yours."

"You had relatives here at the time?"

"I did, Ranger," he said, his eyes lingering on the old photographs. "My great-grandfather as well."

"I wasn't aware of that," she told him. "It wasn't in any of the press materials I reviewed on you and your company before coming out here."

"Because such documents are propaganda, concerned only with the present." Zhen stiffened ever so slightly. "And the truth is that part of my background is not a happy story."

"I suspect the same could be said for many who laid those rails, Chinese and Caucasian both."

He twisted back around, turning away from the photographs coldly as if they'd never hung there at all. "My great-grandfather came to America with an invention he sought to sell to the owners of the railroad. It took him months to get a meeting, only to have them steal it right out of his grasp. He was left with no recourse, no hope, no one to file charges with, no one even to listen to his story."

"My great-grandfather would've listened."

Caitlin could see Li Zhen getting anxious, clearly pained by the story at which he'd only hinted. "And been helpless to act against the railroad, just like everyone else at the time." He cleared his throat, closed his eyes briefly as if to wash his mind clear of the thoughts. "But I don't suspect the fates of our ancestors is what brought you here today."

"It isn't, sir," Caitlin said, eyes straying yet again to the wall of perfectly arranged pictures.

One especially, featuring a shot of rails being laid and ties pounded, caught her eye. It was a tall, angular shot that showed the line seeming to extend all the way to infinity. And something about the way the Caucasian work bosses were standing reminded Caitlin of pre–Civil War shots of Southern plantations.

"What brought me here," she continued, finally letting her gaze rest back on Li Zhen, "is that an oil from the strain of the camellia flower that's native to China was found in an examination of the remains of four men, all Chinese, killed in a gunfight yesterday. Maybe you heard about it on the news."

"I don't watch the American news, Ranger."

"Well, sir, I can't say I blame you. But if you did you'd know the shoot-out happened at the Texas Train Museum located in San Antonio. And you'd also know that I was the one who killed them."

Zhen just looked at her, nodding almost imperceptibly. It looked as if he wasn't going to say anything at all until he spoke without any gesture or signal.

"I am relieved to see you survived such an attack, but don't see what it has to do with your visit here to Yuyuan today."

Caitlin glanced out the window, in the garden's direction as best as she could recall it. "A supply of camellia seeds from China was delivered to a Yuyuan address two years ago, sir. I was wondering if the flowers grown from them make up part of your company's gardens."

"I'd have to ask our designer."

"You don't know yourself, Mr. Zhen?"

"Not within the degree of certainty you seek, Ranger."

Caitlin shifted in the stiff chair again. "Know what strikes me most about your beautiful office, sir?"

His gaze gestured her on.

"Its sense of order. Everything in its place, everything exactly where it's supposed to be."

"A guiding Chinese principle in design," Zhen affirmed, nodding, "undertaken in the hope it may extend to life itself. Imagine if we could arrange our lives as neatly and surely as we arrange our rooms."

"Well," Caitlin said, coming to the very edge of her chair, "that's exactly my point, sir. I need to tell you I find it strange that a man who values order to that degree wouldn't know all the flowers contained in his garden."

"I didn't say camellias weren't present among hundreds of other species of flower. It's the source of the seeds I can't be certain of."

"So if it turns out flowers from your company gardens produced the oil that ended up in the stomachs of the four men I was forced to shoot yesterday, I'm sure your concern would match my own."

"It would indeed, Ranger. It could just as easily be that a company employee ordered the seeds for their own garden, of course, but we must be sure of our facts and not jump to any hasty conclusions."

"Understood, sir."

Zhen seemed to be searching for a response when, again, his words emerged abruptly. "It is a good thing we understand each other, yes?"

"It is."

He rose, polite hand extended stiffly toward the door. "Then I will check with my designer about the contents of the company gardens. Please leave a number where you can be reached with my assistant."

"Thank you, sir, I'll do that," Caitlin said, rising too. She held her hat in her hand and Li Zhen seemed to be studying it for some reason. "I do have one more question, though, for you."

Li nodded a single time.

"Do you know the significance of the number four in Chinese numerology?"

"I believe it represents death."

"Because I couldn't help but notice there are four chairs set before your desk, sir. Should I read anything significant into that?"

Caitlin had just reached her car when she felt her cell phone vibrating in her pocket.

"I was just gonna call in, Captain," she told D. W. Tepper, who was well aware of where he must have reached her. "Something about Li Zhen doesn't sit right with me."

"Why am I not surprised?"

"Maybe because you've come to trust my judgment in such matters."

"More likely because I felt the winds of Hurricane Caitlin blowing as soon as you told me where you were headed after you saw Doc Whatley. But save the dirty details for later, Ranger. I need you back here fast, so fast I'm gonna start smoking and not gonna stop until you arrive."

"I'm climbing behind the wheel now, Captain. What's going on?"

"Old friend of yours from Washington is on his way in for a visit and I don't want you leaving me alone with him any longer than necessary."

"Oh, shit . . . Not *him*, Captain."

"Yup, it's him all right, sure to be dragging the usual shit behind him on a chain. And I want him out of here before the stink sets in like it always does when he comes around."

"What's it about this time?"

"You're not gonna believe this, Ranger."

"Try me, D.W."

PART FIVE

"I reported to the sheriff that the enemy had crossed the river . . . gone to the La Parra and gathered these beeves, that I had found them at the marsh, they had fought, and that I would now place him in charge of their bodies."

—Captain Leander H. McNelly

47

"Do you have a reservation, sir?"

"No," Cort Wesley said, brushing past the manager of Providence's University Club into the main dining room, "but I don't think I'll be staying long. I just need to ask one of your guests a question."

The club was located in a private arch nestled on a plateau between the city's downtown area and the campus of Brown University, a favorite lunchtime haunt of power brokers, politicos, and those who fancied themselves to be either. Cort Wesley had come in search of one in particular: a man named Nicolas Dimitrios, better known as Nikki D, who Theo had informed him owned the two college-area venues he managed along with a whole lot of other nightspots in town.

Theo's description made it easy for Cort Wesley to spot Nikki D as soon as he entered the main dining room. The man looked to be about his age, with the waves combed and oiled out of his brushed-back hair, a ring for every finger, and olive-toned skin. Dimitrios was in the company of two other men he didn't know but recognized the type all the same. Their Italian suits shined in the room's lighting, their shoulders seeming stuffed under the pads and ties thrown back behind them in order to avoid wearing their meal upon them. Living, breathing stereotypes.

Cort Wesley approached straightaway and took the fourth chair at the table, sliding it into the absence of a place setting before a glass of water with melted ice.

"Hey, Nic, sorry I'm late," he greeted, taking a hefty sip of water and feeling the condensation collected on the glass moisten his fingers. "Glad you boys started without me."

"I think you've got the wrong table, friend," Dimitrios told him.

Cort Wesley returned his gaze, while studying his two guests. The one on the left had a fleshy nose and a ridge of scar tissue over his forehead. An ex-boxer probably now with reading glasses held on the tip of his nose, as if he'd forgotten to remove them after studying the menu. The one on the right did everything stiffly, from the way he used his utensils to the way he blinked and reached for his ice-laden drink that looked like scotch. His face was a blank canvas, utterly devoid of emotion because clearly he was a man who had no use for it.

"No," Cort Wesley said to Dimitrios, setting the water glass back down, "this is the right table because you're the man I need to see."

Dimitrios looked trapped between both thoughts and intentions. He was eating a salad with lots of colors and stopped his next forkful halfway to his mouth and returned it to the plate.

"I'm going to ask you politely to leave."

"You can ask any way you want, hoss, but I'm not going anywhere until we talk." He looked toward the other two men at the table who were studying him from behind their flat expressions and noisy breathing. "See, fellas, my son got mixed up with one of Nikki D's girls. Since he's buying you lunch at this swanky club, I'm assuming you know all about the side racket he's got going and you might even be the guys behind this protection he's got. But he doesn't have it from me." Cort Wesley turned his gaze back on Dimitrios. "See, my son ended up in the hospital, half beaten to death."

"I have no idea what you're talking about."

"That's why I'm going to make this as simple as I can for you, Nic. The girl my son got involved with was Chinese, mid-twenties probably, who told him her name was Kai. You're going to tell me where I can find her, then I'm going to get up and walk out. It'll be like I was never here."

Cort Wesley could see Dimitrios's eyes, too tiny for his head and too light for his coloring, flashing, his mind putting things together. The two goombahs, Left and Right, looked at each other, starting to plot their own response.

"So what do you say, Nic?" Cort Wesley asked the Greek.

"I say to get the fuck away from my table."

"That wasn't the answer I was hoping for."

"Only one you're going to get, all the same."

"All the same," Cort Wesley said, catching the goombahs across the table starting to move, "I don't think so."

48

San Antonio, Texas

The man Caitlin knew only as "Jones," although it had been "Smith" once, sat behind Captain Tepper's desk with a pair of shiny cowboy boots crossed on the blotter.

"With all the time I spend in Texas," he greeted, without rising or extending a hand at Caitlin's entry, "I figured I'd finally get myself a pair."

"Why don't you try growing a pair instead, Jones?" she said, stopping just short of the desk.

"You don't even know what brought me in for a visit this time."

"I know it can't be good. And I'd like you to take your boots off my captain's desk."

"And what if I don't?"

"This conversation will be off to an even worse start than usual."

Jones smiled, sat up in Tepper's desk chair, and eased his feet back to the floor. "Where was I?"

"Just leaving."

"You mean, you really haven't missed me?"

"I always feel like I need a shower after our visits, Jones. Why don't you just fill me in on the shit you dragged in with you this time? I could practically smell it when I walked in the building."

"It's you doing the dragging today, Ranger. I'm just along for the ride, watching you self-destruct in true Caitlin Strong fashion. In so far over your head you can't even see the surface any longer."

"You are a walking cliché, Jones."

"You told me that once before."

"Apparently you didn't take the cue."

The blind over the office's single window was yanked all the way up, exposing Jones to a bright swatch of light in a world where he'd come to much prefer shadows. His face was flat and freshly shaven, with a dollop of shaving cream clinging stubbornly behind his right ear. Even in the light, Caitlin couldn't quite make out his eye color, as if Jones had been trained to never look at anyone long enough for anything to register. He was wearing a sport jacket over a button-down shirt and pressed trousers that looked like a costume on him. His hair, normally tightly cropped and military-style, "high and tight" was the nomenclature as she recalled, had grown out just enough to make his anvil-shaped head look smaller.

She'd met Jones for the first time overseas when he was still "Smith." Figured him for CIA back then, but he was with some shadowy subdivision of Homeland Security these days and had pretty much carte blanche to protect the homeland any way he saw fit. That included utilizing the services of Guillermo Paz and the band of killers the colonel had assembled for any purpose Jones deemed worthy. Caitlin's path had crossed his on several occasions since he became Jones and none had ended particularly well. He reminded her of a cat who shows up scratching at your door, show-

ering you with love until it's time to move on to the next house offering a bowl of milk.

"You broke the rules again, Ranger, a big one this time," Jones
told her.

"Yeah? Which rule is that?"

"I played football in college, you know."

"I didn't."

"In practice and scrimmages the quarterback always wears a
different color jersey, gold usually, to remind his teammates never
to hit, not even to touch him. No exceptions. He's protected at all
costs."

"So?"

"So you the hit the quarterback, Ranger."

She leaned over the desk. "Come again?"

Instead of answering, Jones rose stiffly from Captain Tepper's
old chair, moved to the window and lowered the faux wooden blinds
that were probably older than Caitlin was. When that failed to shut
out enough of the light to make him comfortable, he worked the
slats closed. The result, by the time he settled back in the chair, was
to cloak him in the shadows that made him far more comfortable.

"Li Zhen is protected," Jones told Caitlin, even his voice sounding more confident and relaxed. "He and his company are working
with the United States government. You've heard of us, I assume."

She tried to see him as clearly in the shadows as she had in the
light, her imagination filling in the blank spaces that averted her
vision. "I must have missed the man's golden jersey. My visit was
routine. Just following up on a few leads."

"Right," Jones said musingly, "flower petals."

"Connected to four gunmen who shot up a historical train ride."

"Until you gunned them down in typical Caitlin Strong fashion, the frontier gun*man* reborn in a woman. Only this isn't the
frontier anymore." He shook his head. "Man, who's really the walking cliché here?"

"Those gunmen had camellia petals in their pockets and oil from
the same flower in their systems. We traced that flower to Yuyuan."

"Conclusively?"

"If you call the only importer of the seeds from China on record conclusive, I suppose so."

"Of course, it's inconceivable to think anybody might have imported camellias without the proper paperwork."

"Where you going with this, Jones?"

"I thought I told you that already."

"I must have been paying attention to something important at the time."

"You will case and desist on Li Zhen and Yuyuan." Jones popped up out of Captain Tepper's desk chair dramatically. "There, that wasn't so hard, was it?"

"We're not finished."

"Yes, we are. I'm keeping it short and sweet this time. That pressure you feel on your shoulders is the weight of all of Washington bearing down."

"You're in bed with Zhen."

"So to speak," Jones acknowledged.

"Too bad I didn't know the two of you were acquainted or I would've used you as a reference."

"Wouldn't have mattered, Ranger; he doesn't know me as Jones."

"You back to being 'Smith' in his eyes then?"

"Brooks, Ranger. He knows me as Brooks."

49

PROVIDENCE, RHODE ISLAND

The two goombahs, Dimitrios's luncheon guests, needed to reach across the table to get to him, and Cort Wesley was ready when they did. The one on his left was closer and banged the table hard enough to spill his water and dump his lunch onto the tablecloth.

He must've been left-handed because his stretch came all the way across his body.

Cort Wesley latched on to the man's fingers, squeezing and twisting at the same time. The move was meant to freeze him more than anything, enough so that Cort Wesley was able to use his left hand to grab hold of the man's wrongly angled shoulder and yank. He came across the table as if utterly weightless, directly into the path of the wine bottle the man on the right lashed out like a club. It impacted on his skull with a *thwack*, didn't break, but sent a shower of merlot spraying into the air through its open top. Much of it landed on Dimitrios, stunning him, his white dress shirt blotched with red.

The goombah with the wine bottle realized he was in no-man's-land too late to do anything about it, a wannabe tough guy used to bullying, dominating others by intimidation to the point where he figured this part was cake. It was anything but, though, something Cort Wesley knew all too well, just like he knew guys like this. He didn't wait, seizing the advantage by punching the second man square in the face, feeling his nose mash under the blow. The man didn't so much go down as melt into the floor.

Cort Wesley swung toward Dimitrios, who was cowering in his chair, frozen between motions. Around him the rest of the dining room had grown eerily quiet, those nearest the table having jumped up to put as much distance between them and the melee as possible.

Cort Wesley leaned over, close enough to the Greek to not have to raise his voice much. "I figure we've got two minutes before the cops show up, say ninety seconds to be on the safe side. That's ninety seconds before you're in the worst pain you've ever felt in your life. You follow me so far?"

Dimitrios nodded, eyes sweeping about the dining room as if in search of someone closing in to help. But Cort Wesley's ears had already told him what Nikki D's eyes were about to.

No one was coming.

"Where can I find the Chinese girl, Nic, the one my son called Kai?"

Dimitrios looked as if he was thinking about stalling, then quickly changed his mind. "All that happened, I had nothing to do with it!"

"I know. That's why you're still talking through your teeth. Seventy-five seconds, Nic."

"The syndicate."

"The what?"

Dimitrios seemed like he didn't know how to say what he needed to, his thoughts chopped up as a result. "Like a subscription service. We get girls. From all over the country. Rotated in and out."

"Who runs the show?"

"I don't know."

"Under a minute now, Nikki."

"*I don't!*"

"Tell me something you do."

"New York. The city."

Sirens wailed in the distance.

"I'm listening, Nikki," Cort Wesley told the man who looked so scared it seemed his eyeballs were pulling back into his skull. "What am I gonna find there?"

"Dealers."

"Drug?"

Dimitrios shook his head. "Something else," he said, Cort Wesley's mouth dropping when Nikki D told him what.

50

SAN ANTONIO, TEXAS

"Wait a minute," Caitlin said, her eyes having adjusted to the lower level of light in Tepper's office, "you're working with Li Zhen *directly?*"

"We're working with Yuyuan, yes."

"We as in Homeland Security."

"That a statement or a question?"

"It doesn't require an answer."

Jones sat back down and leaned forward, into the light spilled downward by the room's single overhead fixture. The fixture was dusty, the result being to turn his face into a patchwork quilt.

"You own a cell phone, Ranger?"

"You've used my number."

"So I have. It was a figure of speech. The third generation wireless network became the fourth generation wireless network, and already people were clamoring for the fifth. If you weren't too busy shooting people, you'd be aware that the fifth generation wireless network went active this week."

"The subject came up during my last stretch at Quantico. The government had just awarded the contract to build the five G to Yuyuan. The instructor, someone with experience comparable to yours I imagine, called that the dumbest thing he'd ever seen in his life."

She could feel Jones stiffen, something in the cadence of his breathing changing, however imperceptibly. "Because someone with experience like mine wasn't there to tell him we had no choice."

"What's that mean?"

"There isn't an American company with the wherewithal to handle the job. Sad but true. Cisco failed to get past even the pre-liminary round, leaving us with Alcatel, Siemens, or Yuyuan. All three of those are foreign, last time I checked."

"I believe the point the instructor was making was that doing business with the French or Germans has its advantages over the Chinese."

"Curtly spoken, Ranger, but it also has its disadvantages. On merit, technological capacity, and the ability to build a network ca-pable of delivering the goods made Yuyuan far and away the best choice. And they delivered under budget and ahead of schedule. By almost six months, meaning the network beat the new phones and software to the market."

"Which means you're effectively giving the Chinese access to every bit of data and information that travels over the Internet."

"They've already got it," Jones told her. "Who do you think built the four G network? Not Yuyuan, but another Chinese company named Shenzen was responsible for maybe three quarters of the work after everybody else involved dropped the ball. Why do you think it took so long to get the network up and running country-wide? We're talking a cluster fuck of biblical proportions. Trust me. I know because I was front and center, and determined not to repeat that fiasco with the five G."

"Ah, the fox guarding the henhouse . . ."

Jones canted his head to the side like a confused dog. "Am I missing something here?"

"I was just about to ask you the same question, Jones. You'd never make a call like this, approving a Chinese corporation to build a five G network, unless there was something in it for you. So why don't you just come clean and tell me what you, what Homeland, is getting out of this?"

Jones rose, back into the light now. "Back off, Ranger."

"You or Li Zhen?"

"One and the same as far as you are concerned."

"Even if he's behind those gunmen both here and up in Rhode Island yesterday?"

"You let us take care of things." Now it was Jones doing the staring. "Just like I took care of your boyfriend."

"You want to be more specific?"

"How'd you think he got released from police custody, Ranger? He's a free man thanks to some well-placed calls from yours truly. Don't bother to thank me."

"So, what, I'm supposed to see this as a trade-off?"

Jones started for the door and then stopped. "I don't give a shit. I'm telling you this is under control. We took care of your boy-friend and now we're going to take care of Li Zhen. Enough said on the subject."

That left Caitlin shaking her head. "Not in my mind. The Chinese are where they are today because everyone who thinks they're playing them ends up getting played themselves. Guess that's you now, Jones."

"Cut me some slack, Ranger. My department is up to the task."

"Maybe, maybe not."

"You mind telling me what it was Li Zhen did that crawled this deep up your ass?"

"Are you capable of being objective? Because all this started after Cort Wesley's oldest got involved with a Chinese girl mixed up in the porn industry and turning tricks. The boy gets his head bashed in and two days later, Chinese hit teams come gunning for Cort Wesley and me carrying flower petals from Yuyuan's garden."

"You don't know that."

"I will once I get a search warrant to have a real close look-see. In the meantime why don't you tell me why Yuyuan and your friend Li Zhen would go to guns over a prostitute in Providence, Rhode Island?"

He ignored her again. "This isn't some rogue creature that crawled out from under a rock near your boot. This is an operation with major significance to Homeland Security. I can only insulate you so long and so deep."

"When have you ever?"

He shook his head again. "You have no idea."

"So enlighten me, Jones."

"Go back to that serial killer you're chasing, Ranger. It's a lot safer."

"How'd you know about that?"

But Jones moved into the hallway instead of responding, his expression more sad than angry. "Same way I heard about that stunt you pulled at the cemetery."

"I didn't see it as a stunt at all."

"Oh no? When was the last time a law enforcement official bulldozed a couple dozen people into a drainage trench?"

"That Beacon of Light Church has been terrorizing innocent

people all across the whole country and no one's done a damn thing about it that stuck. Guess I'm a prisoner of my own convictions."

"That's not the problem. The problem is you're beginning to buy into your own bullshit. You think that because of who you are, shit like plowing into people with a John Deere is going to wash right off you without leaving a stink. But even Wild Bill Hickok met his match, Ranger."

"As I recall he was shot in the back."

"Right," Jones nodded, his expression turning to what, for him, was somber. "That was my point."

51

FIESTA, TEXAS

They were shooting a girl-on-girl scene, Li Zhen's favorite years ago, when making films like this was his profession.

Especially when the performers really were girls, as opposed to women. Not kiddie porn here in America, of course, but skirting as close as possible to that without drawing the wrath of the FBI and a myriad of other agencies.

The studio was located in Fiesta, a few miles outside of San Antonio, in a nest of office buildings not far from the Six Flags Amusement Park. The office park had been turned empty and dark by the recession, but was absolute state of the art. Enough to make Hollywood itself proud. The shell company Li had formed to finance the studio's creation spared no expense when it came to equipment, especially cameras and lighting. And right now that lighting revealed two sultry young women not even out of their teens pleasuring each other in ways even Zhen's grandest imaginings could not conjure. Instead he imagined himself with them, between them, inside them. He noticed they'd shed their schoolgirl uniforms off to the side: plaid skirts and white blouses, just like the group that had stood at the rear of the ribbon-cutting ceremony the other day.

As per his request.

Zhen felt the familiar stirring, eyes beginning to close to surrender to the darkness of his thoughts when he heard heavy footsteps approaching through the quiet.

"So it's true," came the voice of General Mengyao Chang, and Zhen turned to find him standing in semi-darkness, outside the reach of the camera lights.

The director yelled "Cut!," Chang having spoken just loud enough to ruin the shot. Zhen held a hand up before the director could protest further.

"You have returned to your former ways," the general continued. "Tell me, did Chinese government money pay for all this?"

"We both have our jobs to do, General," Li Zhen managed, trying to appear unperturbed. "What we do outside of fulfilling our duties is our own business. Or would you prefer that I remind you of some of your own proclivities?"

Chang forced a smile. "That will not be necessary, so long as we understand each other."

"We do, General," Zhen agreed, steering Chang further back into the darkness so the shoot could continue, "but learning of my inability to leave my former life entirely behind could not be what brought you halfway across the world without advance notice of your coming."

"Power is a curse as well as a blessing," General Chang told him, his voice quieter now. "A mentor once told me those with power are like pillars holding up the rest of humanity. As such, distance must exist between them."

"Wise counsel," Zhen nodded. "Perhaps you should take note of it yourself, considering I am responsible for much of the power you now possess. You were only a colonel that night I came before the Triad."

"Should I remain thankful you chose Governor Chen to demonstrate your capabilities?"

"Not at all. I chose Chen because I knew he'd be the hardest to convince. I knew you, on the other hand, were a pragmatist then as you are now. Which tells me your visit is anything but random. Or pleasant."

"That depends."

"On what?"

"If our nation's interests remain paramount in your heart."

Chang clasped his hands tightly behind his back and Zhen realized the color of his suit was the same greenish color as the uniform that fit him better. It could not be a good thing that the general had showed up in Texas unannounced, catching Li Zhen unprepared. Of all the affronts in Chinese manners, surprise was considered one of the worst since it precluded much valued preparation. Li Zhen knew that was a sign, a message in itself, especially with Chang coming here since he could've just as easily have waited for Zhen to return to Yuyuan, the company's entire workings supervised by the general's department in the Chinese government.

Chang continued to maintain an active presence inside the Triad as well, overseeing the organization's tremendously profitable move into Russia's lawless far east, covering such areas as illegal logging and fishing in addition to control of the region's many casinos. Yuyuan was now the sole supplier of slot machines and all electronic gaming for Vladivostok and beyond, thanks to that relationship. An unholy alliance perhaps, but an alliance to be treasured all the same.

"Concerns have been expressed," Chang continued. "Serious concerns raised about your judgment and behavior."

"Our contact in Homeland Security, Brooks, summoned you, didn't he?" Zhen asked, noticing four members of Chang's private security force dressed in plainclothes just inside the lone entrance to the studio.

"How I learned of your indiscretions is not of concern. What is of concern is how you may have placed at risk an operation crucial to the future of our nation."

Zhen remained silent, waiting for the general to continue.

"You know of the pleasure I take from riding roller coasters, *Xiānshēng* Zhen?"

"I do."

"Once, not far from here, I rode one that goes backward as quickly as it moves forward. An interesting symbology, don't you think? Since moving in reverse can only mean an acknowledgment of error and one's inability to correct it. An acceptance of that which is wrong."

"That is not what all you see before you is about. And the product reaped from places like this has helped make you a very rich man far more than your gambling interests have."

"I don't like your tone," Chang said, recoiling slightly. "Perhaps you forget your true heritage, to whom you are vastly indebted for overcoming it. You came to us no more than a cheap pornographer, peasant scum with a movie camera, and our backing allowed you to become everything you are today. Yuyuan isn't yours, it's *ours*. Your presence here serves us, something else you seem to have lost sight of."

"Serves you? By that I'm sure you mean the fifth generation wireless network we are building that will provide China with a treasure trove of America's greatest technological secrets and research. They think their defenses render them immune," Zhen added, managing a slight smile, "not realizing we constructed those defenses as well. Through our subsidiaries, of course."

"All the same, like that roller coaster I just spoke of," Chang countered, studying him closely in the spill of the refracted light off the big kliegs, "sometimes experience in life is enhanced by traveling backward. It has been decided that you should return to China and retake your seat as head of Yuyuan's offices there."

Zhen reminded himself not to raise his voice and risk ruining another shot. "I would respectfully remind you that my place is here."

"We cannot allow the arrangement made between our government and the Americans to be compromised, *Xiānshēng* Zhen."

"You mean the arrangement *I* made, don't you?"

"There is only one 'I' in China and it is not you. Far, far from it. As when riding a roller coaster, each rise is followed by an even swifter fall. But on a roller coaster, as in life, the next rise is just ahead. Am I making myself clear to you?"

"What is clear to me, General, is that you are here because my American contact must have expressed his concerns to you. And you would take his word over mine."

"You have become a liability, *Xiānshēng* Zhen," Chang said, his voice laced with a grim finality. "You will be allowed to save face, but you will not be allowed to save it here. You will return home and do so without delay. On the same return flight that I am taking a few hours from now. I already have your ticket. You can meet me at the airport."

"You know the proverb that says the rise may be slow, the fall fast, but no one stays at the top between them for eternity?" Zhen asked him.

"No, but it is a wise lesson to keep close in mind."

"My thoughts exactly," Li Zhen told General Chang.

52

SAN ANTONIO, TEXAS

Caitlin had pulled the Venetian blind back up and was standing by the window when Tepper came to reclaim his office.

"The man walked right past me on his way out the door. Felt like a snowman come to life," he said, plopping into his chair. "I swear, Ranger, this man's body temperature could keep your beer cold."

"We ever relocate headquarters, let's make sure not to send him the forwarding, Captain."

"Do I need to ask how it went?"

"Off. I don't know any other way to put it. There were times in our talk where he wasn't even the same asshole both of us know.

Like he was reading somebody else's lines. And he brought up the serial killer we're chasing."

"Guess nothing escapes the attention of Homeland, does it?"

"Question being, why would he care? I don't see any threats to national security in the murders of five prostitutes, unless he also knew Li Zhen's family history in the United States has connections to the old Trans-Pecos rail line. I don't know why he'd even bring it up otherwise, do you?"

"I'm trying real hard not to bother, Ranger, and you should do the same. That's all I've got to tell you."

"How about telling me what happened after my great-granddad and Judge Bean finished with that engineer at the railroad worksite?"

Tepper shifted about uneasily in his chair, as if Jones had left some oily residue behind on the fabric. "I was hoping you'd let that one go."

"I did, until I saw pictures of those old railroad days plastered over the walls of Li Zhen's office."

Tepper lit up a Marlboro, as if to dare Caitlin to stop him. "Uh-oh, the Category Ten winds of Hurricane Caitlin are beginning to blow."

"What happened next in Langtry, D.W.?"

Tepper took a deep drag on his cigarette. "Well, here's what I recall from the story passed down through the years. . . ."

53

LANGTRY, TEXAS; 1883

"Now, lookee what we got here. . . ."

William Ray Strong swung toward the bulbous shape of what looked like an upside down bowling pin, massive across the top with spindles for legs approaching the mess tent where Kincannon told them to wait. Proudly displaying a badge on his lapel that

William Ray didn't recognize. He wore a three-piece suit with the top and bottom buttons missing from the vest. The Ranger pictured them bursting off him and taking out an eyeball or maybe breaking somebody's nose.

"It's a genuine Texas Ranger and a fake judge," the man who looked formed of jelly continued, reaching them.

Roy Bean snickered at that. "Was he talking about you or me?"

"Both of us, I suspect," said William Ray.

"I'm John W. Bates, chief of the Southern Pacific Railroad Police," the bowling pin announced, hooking his thumbs in his lapels. "And right now you are standing on land owned by Southern Pacific. That places you in my jurisdiction."

William Ray took a step forward to meet him. "This was still Texas last time I checked."

"And you may be chief of the railroad police," Roy Bean added, "but I'm the duly elected law for the county in which we're all standing."

"Duly elected?" William Ray posed quietly.

"Well, close enough," Judge Bean replied in a hushed tone.

In response to the Ranger's request to see the man who'd sewn on the tent flaps, Kincannon had summoned Bates to the mess tent jammed with wooden slab tables laid out amid the dozen posts pile-driven into the earth to hold the grime-strewn tent up.

"We're here about the murders of those four Chinese women," William Ray told Bates.

Bates rolled his thumbs around, then planted them back on his lapels. "I was meaning to look into that myself, but I've been too busy dealing with hostile locals to bother with dead whores."

"Yeah," said Judge Roy Bean, "those locals seem to have a problem with the Southern Pacific stealing their land out from under them to make room for the railroad."

"We don't steal it. We pay market price per acre. It's called eminent domain."

"And what do you call the four women killed here in the past couple weeks?" William Ray asked Bates.

"Not my problem."

"How's that?"

"Chinese strike is slowing us down. I got a thousand other workers in this camp already gonna lose bonus money on account of that. It's all I can do to hold them back from taking matters into their own hands."

"As opposed to the hands of those Pinkerton men we heard were coming," noted Judge Bean.

"Sheriff can never have too many deputies, under the circumstances."

"Is it true the Chinese weren't paid for building that dam?" William Ray asked.

"Far as I know, they were hired to build a rail line and they'll be paid for doing that as soon as they're back on the job."

"And once they are, will the man who proclaims himself to be the law for the railroad stop ignoring the murders of these Chinese women that happened under his watch?"

Bates thrust a stubby finger at him. "You watch your tongue, Ranger."

"Got any suspects, Chief?"

"Not that I'm about to share with you."

"Speak with any potential witnesses?"

"No, sir, I haven't," Bates said, sounding proud of that fact.

"What about the families of the victims?"

He shook his head. "Not my concern."

"You know what *bahk guai* means, Chief?" William Ray asked him.

"Nope."

"It means 'white devil'—who your Chinese workers believed killed these women. You'd know that if you'd bothered to ask. Since you haven't had the time or opportunity to do so, I don't suppose you'll mind the judge and me picking up the slack," William Ray said. "At least until these Pinkertons arrive."

Bates smirked. "You're a Texas Ranger. You got the right. I just wouldn't expect to get anywhere if I were you."

"You mind if I get back to my work?" Kincannon asked, although it was unclear to whom his question was posed.

"We asked to meet you as a courtesy," William Ray said to Bates, standing there like an extra pillar to hold up the tent. Then he swung toward Kincannon. "The judge and I will see that man who done the sewing now."

Kincannon looked to Bates for a reaction. "Chief?"

"Let 'em waste all the time they want, Mr. Kincannon."

"You're welcome to join the judge and I for the interview, Mr. Bates."

"I got better things to do with my time, like pick at the warts your damn climate grew on my feet."

William Ray ignored him. "Mr. Kincannon, if you'd be so good as to point us in the right direction."

"He's right over there yonder," Kincannon said with a thrust of his finger.

"Where?" Roy Bean asked.

"Sitting at that table sewing them flags we hang from each train with the Southern Pacific trademark. You can't miss him," Kincannon continued. "He's the blind man."

"Yup, I been working the railroad somewhere or other since they crossed the Mississippi," Abner Ecklund told William Ray and the judge, not even missing a beat on his sewing. "Doing this and that, mostly that."

He looked to be around sixty, though it was hard to tell thanks to the mottled scar tissue that ran across his forehead, brow, and all the way down to his cheeks. It encased much of his eyes as well, reducing them to sightless slits leaking pus and mucus that dried in a jagged line down from the corners. The light streaming in through the open tent didn't quite reach the section where Ecklund was seated, which, of course, didn't seem to bother him. But it was enough to reveal a deep brownish cast to his skin and hair mottled

in kinky waves. William Ray figured him for a mulatto, much re-
viled in these parts, recalling how Rangers had come upon the
corpses of more than one dragged to death after being lashed to a
horse. He looked at the scars layered over Ecklund's face like a second skin and pictured it dragging across a dry creek bed of stone
and petrified wood. The thought made him cringe.

"You got a true talent, sir," the judge told Ecklund, breaking up
William Ray's thoughts.

"Thank you kindly. What about the two of you, what is it you
boys do brought you here?" Ecklund asked, still without missing a
beat on the Southern Pacific flag he was sewing. "I know you're new
'cause I don't recognize your voices. And I know all the people here
by their voices."

"I'm the local presiding judge for the county," Bean said, "and
this here's a Texas Ranger."

"We're here about the murders of some Chinese women in and
around the camp," William Ray picked up. "Only clue we've got is
some stitching the killer did to all the bodies. I recognized it from
those tent flaps you sewed."

It was hard to read a man without eyes, but William Ray could
have sworn Ecklund's expression turned sad. "How many victims
this time?"

"*This* time?"

"Not the first instance this has happened in a railroad work
camp," Ecklund told them, finally interrupting his sewing. "Not
the first instance at all."

"Guess you don't see me as a suspect," Ecklund continued.

Judge Bean and William Ray Strong just looked at each other.

"That was supposed to be a joke," the blind man told them.
"'See.' Get it?"

"How many other times?" William Ray asked him.

"Twice in camps I was working, twice more I heard about through word passed around." Ecklund turned his sightless gaze on the Ranger. "Always Chinese women with their heads sewn on backward, right?"

William Ray nodded, then said, "Yes," when he remembered the man couldn't see.

"And you recognized my stitching from those tent flaps?"

"I can't say for sure, sir, but it's a safe assumption from my experience. You had some medical training, I'm guessing."

"Sure did," Ecklund beamed proudly. "Back in 1870-something or other when I was working the Transcontinental. Cheyenne attacked a work crew scouting the land by pushing receptacles into the ground to see what comes up so we could plan the next leg of the route. We had one doctor who wasn't worth much and one nurse, a Christian missionary, who was. She's the one taught me how to stitch flesh, taught me how to use feeling to replace sight and, damn, if she weren't right. Got so I could see the wound I was stitching in my head. That woman convinced me it was no different from stitching wool really, so long as I could learn to work a smaller needle."

"How many others this missionary nurse teach to do that?" Bean interjected.

"None I'm aware of, Judge. See the typhoid got her before the Cheyenne or the winter ever had a chance to. I was with her when she went. She thought I was her dead husband and I went right along with it. I believe she was a pretty woman, though I couldn't say for sure."

"How many men have you taught?" William Ray asked suddenly.

"Couple here and there."

"Any in this camp right now?"

"Just one," Ecklund told him. "But I wouldn't pay much heed to him."

"Why?"

"I can't say, Ranger. Don't have the stomach to be dragged over land again. . . ."

Ecklund's voice drifted off, his ears perking up as he heard something ahead of the judge and William Ray. He turned with Judge Bean to find a host of hardscrabble men with shoulders bursting out of their shirts coming up on them. Looked to be eight at least, each as big as the next and all holding what looked to be cut-down pieces of lumber for rail ties discarded because of wood rot. William Ray lurched up from the chair, instinctively placing himself in front of Roy Bean.

"We're here to tell you boys that you don't belong here," the biggest of the men said, addressing William Ray first before moving his gaze to Judge Roy Bean. "We don't recognize your law or your authority and we don't give a goddamn about those Chinese who don't think enough of this country to handle their load."

William Ray made sure the speaker could see his hand holding rigid just over the Colt holstered on his hip. "Then it's a good thing the state of Texas does, friend."

He noticed Chief Bates standing just by the main entrance to the mess tent, grinning with clearly no intentions of intervening. William Ray figured these men for his deputies.

"I ain't your friend," the big man said. "And your hand moves any closer to that pistol, I'll bust your fingers into porridge mix."

"Only if you're faster than me, son."

"You won't be faster than all of us standing here. And I ain't your son neither. Two of you need to ride out of here and leave railroad business to the railroad. We don't need word of dead Chink whores gumming up our works, already three weeks behind schedule."

William Ray grabbed Judge Bean by the suit coat, dragging him backward toward the quickest exit between two heavy posts holding the mess tent up. "Well, I'd never want to be a bother, so we'll just be on our way."

And with that he laid his boot into the nearest post hard enough to crack it and send the bigger part pitching inward. That section of the tent collapsed onto the big man and his gang, their beefy frames outlined in canvas as they struggled futilely to free themselves.

* * *

Chief Bates slept on a cot squeezed behind a sliding curtain in the back of his office. That evening, he lumbered up the four steps leading to a narrow, flap-tented structure built up on a wooden base. His nightly rounds had finished in his usual stop at the saloon, where the Irish proprietor never charged him for a drink. He'd plop himself down on the feather mattress that smelled of his own sweat and let the sun wake him in the morning.

But a Colt Peacemaker shoved against his face and then into his mouth changed his plan.

"This is all legal and proper, right, Judge?" William Ray asked Judge Bean who was standing off to the side just out of reach of the flickering lantern light.

"Be hard for Chief Bates to testify otherwise with his head missing. And the action does conform to that writ of habeas corpus I got here in my pocket for sure."

"That's right," said William Ray. "So, Chief, what we got here is a list of all the other railroad camps where Chinese women have been murdered. Mr. Ecklund told us he taught a man to sew who was in all of them to the best of his recollection. Since he wouldn't tell us who that be, we thought we'd ask you. Hell, you should be thanking us, sir; we're letting you do some God's honest police work. Nod if you're okay with giving us an answer as opposed to me splattering your brains."

Bates nodded.

"What exactly is a writ of habeas corpus, Judge?" William Ray said, as he and Roy Bean walked back to their horses.

"I haven't got a goddamn clue, Ranger. But it sounded good, didn't it?"

54

Tepper stopped when the phone rang. He answered and listened briefly before replacing the receiver.

"That was Doc Whatley. He'd like to see you right away. Notice I didn't ask him what it was about."

"I need you to have Young Roger check out something for me, Captain," Caitlin said, handing a slip of paper across his desk.

"What's this?" Tepper asked, squinting to better regard it.

"The URL link to a porn video."

"For Young Roger?" he followed, befuddled by Caitlin's request.

"I need him to find out everything he can about who produced it and where. I can't even find the site on my computer. Keep getting a message that it doesn't exist."

Tepper shook his head and laid the piece of paper down at arm's distance, then reached for the pack of cigarettes he'd laid down on the desk blotter to find them gone. "You a magician now too?"

"Am I missing something here?"

"No, Ranger, I am: my cigarettes."

Caitlin crouched down to retrieve a pack that must've been lying on the floor. "Here you go."

"Thanks," Tepper said, taking the pack from her and tapping it on his desk blotter. "Hey," he called, when she was halfway through the door, "it's empty."

55

"Not sure about this one, bubba."

Cort Wesley looked toward the ghost of Leroy Epps, once again standing by the window of Dylan's hospital room. "Neither am I, champ," he said, and looked down at his sleeping son again, not wanting to wake him. "No root bear today?"

Epps grinned, his teeth full, white and showing no signs of the rot held over from his mortal life. *"Things seem to sell out even where I be these days. By the way, that was one slimy hombre you just talked to. There ain't no hell, bubba, but he's living proof there should be."*

"Dealers," Nicolas Dimitrios had told Cort Wesley back at the University Club.

"Drug?"

"Something else: people."

"Human trafficking," Cort Wesley realized, as the sirens screamed closer, his cue to make his exit fast. "They supply you with women."

"And more," Dimitrios said, looking down. "They supply *every-one*," he added, looking up again.

"Everyone?"

"Coast to coast. Like a fucking franchise. You wanna do business, you do it with them or not at all. You run a big enough operation, they find out you're not cutting them in and your establishment gets torched."

"Where can I find them? Give me a name, an address."

When Dimitrios didn't respond, Cort Wesley jerked the man toward him by the lapels. "You really want to make me ask again, hoss?"

"My wallet," the Greek mumbled.

Cort Wesley jerked it from his pocket and pushed it against Dimitrios's chest. He fished a black keycard from one of the compartments and handed it to Cort Wesley in a trembling hand.

"The Flatiron Building on Fifth Avenue," Dimitrios managed. "Twenty-third floor. You'll need that card."

Cort Wesley had managed to get back to the rental car just in time and drove off right past the quartet of Providence police cars screeching to a halt before the University Club seconds apart. His heart was hammering so hard against his chest he had to pull over as soon as he was back up around the Brown University campus, careful to park in a lot just across the street from the Rockefeller Library, between a white truck and van both marked FACILITIES MANAGEMENT. Cort Wesley opened the windows and took a series of deep breaths, trying to calm himself when he noticed Leroy Epps seated in the passenger seat.

"Want me to drive, bubba?"

"Why don't you go to the cafeteria and get me a bottle?" Leroy Epps continued in Dylan's hospital room, wetting his lips as if he were thirsty. *"I'll watch the boy here for you. Want me to wake him up? I can do it in a dream."*

"Let him sleep."

"Why is it we like watching our kids sleep so much, bubba?"

"You don't ask me a whole lot of questions, champ. Usually it's me doing the asking."

"That's on account of the fact that I got most of the answers I need already and most of the ones you do too."

Cort Wesley watched his sleeping son flick some hair away from his closed eyes, his hand staying on the pillow when he was done. "I think it's because they're safe, maybe the only time the bad stuff can't hurt them. We hover over them in the false belief we've got a measure of control over their lives, that we can keep the demons away."

"Well, that's about as smart a way as anybody could put it. You hit all the right chords with what you said. Makes me think you don't need me coming around as much as you think you do. You got the same answers I do. All having me around does is let you pose the questions."

"I never did like you much anyway, champ," Cort Wesley winked.

Leroy Epps's eyes followed Cort Wesley's to Dylan. Plenty of times when he appeared the whites of those eyes were stained with blood and broken veins thanks to the diabetes that had ultimately killed him. But today they were blisteringly white, almost as if old Leroy had used some heavenly concoction to bleach them.

"Know what I regret most? Dying in the god-felootin' prison. Makes you stop appreciating what the world outside looks like, all it's got to offer. You see my point?"

"No."

"Goes like this. We don't value all the good we got until we're looking at it through barbed wire. 'Course I got a grand view of things from where I be now, though I don't always like what I see."

"Like right now, champ?"

"I heard what that sumbitch wearing red wine over his clothes had to say on that account. Sounds like you're up against some pretty bad hombres this time. That's why I need to question where you take things from here."

Cort Wesley followed Leroy Epps's gaze back to Dylan. "Doctors say he's fit to travel."

"Question being is he fit to travel where you're fixing to take him?"

"He's safer with me."

"You want to believe that, bubba, be my guest."

Dylan stirred, his eyes peeling open to find Cort Wesley looking down at him and a fresh change of clothes at the foot of the bed.

"How you feeling, son?"

"Better."

"For real this time?"

The boy yawned then stretched. "For real."

"Then get dressed," Cort Wesley said, noticing his old friend was nowhere to be seen, having slipped back into the ether. "We're going on a little trip."

"Where?" the boy asked sleepily.

"New York City. Take ourselves a bite out of the Big Apple."

56

San Antonio, Texas

Guillermo Paz stood in the sun at the farmers' market on the grassy outskirts of Olmos Basin Park just short of the thick woods that rimmed the property. It was a simple scene in his mind, laid out over what might have been the infield of a former Little League baseball field since the canopied tables of fresh fruits and vegetables were placed on gravel stretches inlaid amid thick, uncut grass. This particular market offered truly field-to-table produce picked anywhere between only a few minutes and a few hours before going on display. As such, pickup trucks and vans dotted the scenery, giving the otherwise pristine setting a cluttered look that kept it from being a throwback to the simpler times Paz sometimes believed he was searching for.

He spotted a man wearing a black jacket over his white priest's collar, walking with a canvas bag in hand ready to be filled. The man was taller than Paz had expected and walked slightly hunched over as if hobbled by back pain, one of his legs dragging a bit on alternate steps. He had thick white hair plastered to his scalp, the waves combed out with oil that had dried to the texture of concrete. The warm sun didn't seem to bother him at all and Paz saw him clinging to it as opposed to the available shade.

He caught up with the priest casually, joining in step with him, the man becoming aware of his presence when Paz's shadow swallowed up the light.

"Hello, padre," Paz greeted. "We haven't actually met before, not officially anyway."

The priest froze, looking as much through Paz as at him, as if he didn't believe him to be real.

"A woman at the church told me I could find you here. I told her it was an emergency. I hope you don't mind me stopping by."

The priest continued to stare at the man who, up until that moment, he'd only glimpsed through his church's confessional screen. A mystery and an enigma now revealed in flesh and blood with nothing between them.

"You mind if I walk with you, padre?" Paz continued.

The priest nodded, his lips quivering slightly. "We share God's earth, and its bounties, together, my son," his familiar voice intoned, cracking a bit. He looked at Paz as if not sure he was really there, seeming to need confirmation in the stares others cast the huge man's way.

"Glad to hear you say that, truly grateful. But I don't deserve such consideration. Not at all."

"Perhaps this is a conversation better had in our normal setting," the priest said, stiffening a bit.

"Oh, I didn't come to confess anything, padre, at least not yet. I came to apologize."

"Apologize?"

"For turning in other directions, for not appreciating the guidance you've given me. First, there were those college classes I audited; that didn't go well. More recently, I've been teaching English to immigrants mostly to think out loud to myself until some great cosmic realization strikes me in front of a classroom of people who can't understand a word I'm saying. But if I spoke to them in Spanish, I'd have to have something to say that was important to them instead of to me. Does that make sense?"

"Actually, it does," the priest said, nodding as he shifted his still empty canvas handle bag from one hand to the other.

Around them, the farmers' market was comfortably cluttered, the air rich with the smell of flowering plants, fresh greenery, and vegetables thriving on the vine, tree, or bush mere minutes before.

"You know what I was thinking of when I saw you walking, padre?" Paz asked him, not giving the priest a chance to continue.

"What, my son?"

"That priest back home in the slum who I witnessed being murdered for just walking down a street like you were. He was carrying a bag just like that, full of bread. You remember me telling you about that?"

"I remember you telling me how you killed the man who murdered him. How you never forgot and waited until you were old and strong enough."

"But that's the point, isn't it, padre? How do we know we're strong enough to suit the task before us?"

"My son?"

"I work for the Americans now, for the good guys, you might say. I'm not asked to burn or strafe villages or generally destroy the lives of anyone who opposes the government. They send me out after people who are a lot like I used to be, determined to do harm often for its own sake with no regard for the toll on humanity it takes."

"That sounds like a noble transition."

"It should be, but it's not. It feels the same, leaves me just as empty and rudderless. I think I realized why when I watched you walking. I was a boy again, back in the slum, standing outside the church while the priest walked toward me. I saw the gang coming before he did, saw them grab for the bread stuffed into his bag. I ran to help but I was too small and too slow, and by the time I got there they'd stabbed him to death because he resisted. The bread ended up in the street, covered in dirt and grime. I wanted to chase after the gang, but I stayed with the priest instead. I was with him when he died. I ever tell you that part?"

The priest before him today shook his head, trying to stand up straighter as they continued to walk, the crowd seeming to part in Paz's path.

"I want my actions to have meaning," Paz told him. "I want to feel like I did when I killed the gang leader with his own knife. I have it with me now. Would you like to see?"

The priest shot a hand forward the way a cop stopping traffic might. "That isn't necessary, my son. And you only come to me when, how do you say it, the storm clouds are gathering."

"Can't even see them this time—that's how thick the darkness is that's coming."

"Your Texas Ranger again?"

"That's why I needed to see you, padre. The darkness threatening her is different and I feel I'm a part of it somehow."

"How can that be?"

"I'm not sure yet. Not long after I witnessed the priest's murder, I found myself running with other boys as lost as I was. I didn't realize for a time they were part of the same gang that had killed a man who wanted no more than to do good by a poor village's children. But I didn't quit. I stayed in the gang and that's how I eventually found my priest's killer."

The priest stopped before a display of baskets of bloodred tomatoes piled high and angled outward. "I come here every Saturday," he told Paz. "And every Saturday I find myself marveling at how those stacks of tomatoes don't collapse and roll underfoot everywhere. You know why?"

"Because buyers choose only from the very top of the piles."

"And what would happen if they reached down and took one from lower?"

"Trouble."

"Exactly," the priest said, letting himself smile. "This darkness that's coming springs from someplace just as deep. That's why you can't see or define it. It's hidden, ready to topple everything perched above it. I'm actually gratified to see you with no confessional screen obscuring my vision."

"Why's that, padre?"

"Because I can see for myself that you do what you do without hatred or malice in your heart. You are a soldier serving God's army, even if He does not always announce himself as the general. This darkness that's coming?"

"Yes, padre?"

"It may be all-powerful, but it is spawned by evil men who seek nothing but destruction."

At that, Paz reached down and plucked one of the tomatoes from low in the stack. He lifted it toward him, unleashing a blood-red avalanche that reminded Paz of molten lava running downhill. The tomatoes bounced and rolled and splattered underfoot, people left comically dancing and darting to dodge from their path.

"Just like that," the priest said.

"Just like that, padre," Paz echoed, feeling a smile spreading across his face.

"You must stop them, my son," the priest continued. "Go with God."

Part Six

"*Arrested John Wesley Hardin, Pensacola, Florida, this P.M. He had four men with him. Had some lively shooting. One of their number killed, all the rest captured.*"

—J. B. Armstrong, July 1877

57

SAN ANTONIO, TEXAS

"Something about these dead girls just isn't right," Frank Dean Whatley told Caitlin Strong inside his lab at the Bexar County Medical Examiner's Office, where he'd brought her as soon as she arrived.

That lab never changed, at least not in Caitlin's memory. It was sparkling clean everywhere, not a speck of dust or grime anywhere to be found, the cheap tile floors so shiny she could see the outline of her shadow. It smelled of the powerful antiseptic cleaner Whatley insisted his staff use after every examination and procedure in a concerted desire to pay homage and respect to those who crossed his slabs. It was almost as if he was trying to make some kind of moral amends, especially to the victims of crime who had already been treated with the ultimate indifference and cruelty.

The body of the victim found the other night at the Menger Hotel on the River Walk was lying on the steel, mirror-like slab right now. She'd been covered just past the breast line by a white sheet, neatly folded over at the edge to reveal fine, perfectly aligned stitching where Whatley had reattached her head so she was facing in the right direction.

"No luck identifying any of the victims?" Caitlin asked him.

"None at all. Normally you find some clue in their personal items—a parking ticket, a doctor's prescription, a sales receipt—but not in this case. At first, I figured that was the work of the killer. Now I'm not so sure, like maybe these young women didn't want to be ID'ed."

"Or somebody else didn't want them to, Doc. What about that expensive perfume the latest victim had in her purse?"

Whatley frowned. "Available in that size in maybe a thousand stores across the state, not to mention mail order. Too many websites and inventories to bother checking."

"But you've got pictures of all five victims, right?" Caitlin asked, thinking of something.

"Sure."

"Send them over to Young Roger," she said, referring to the young tech whiz who was already checking on the porn website she couldn't find on the Internet. "Tell him I'll explain what I want him to look for later."

"Well, I can tell you one thing now, Ranger—at least, I think I can: all five of these young Chinese women were foreign nationals."

"How can you be sure of something like that?"

"It's not hard if you know what to look for. Skin pigmentation, different concentrations of triglycerides and phosphates in the blood, even bone structure. It's all there to find for someone willing to spend the time to look." Whatley looked down at the latest victim, seeming to study her utterly blank face that looked peaceful in stark contrast to the terrible death she had endured. "So the victims were foreign nationals, but there's no record of their photos ever being logged into the ICE, Immigration and Customs Enforcement, system off passports. You want to explain to me how that can be?"

"Only one way I can: they were smuggled in, by a human trafficking ring in all probability."

"Well, judging by the contents of their stomachs, their hairstyles, and the vaccines in their systems, they've been here awhile, a few years at the very least."

Caitlin looked at Whatley, trying to discern the message in his droopy eyes. "What is it, Doc?"

"My initial reasoning was that the victims were strangled while lying facedown on the bed with their killer on top of them. Follow me?"

"Seems plain enough."

"That's what I thought. I was hampered by the fact I never actually examined or autopsied the other victims, but I had the most recent one, from the Menger Hotel, to work with and that was enough for me to determine that she was strangled while upright, likely standing."

Whatley felt the need to draw in some breath, as if short of it, before continuing. Caitlin waited, still unsure where he was going with this.

"This was suggested by the amount of fluid collected, and its placement, in the lungs," the Bexar County medical examiner resumed. "And the angle of the ligature marks I found indicate that their killer was standing *behind* them when he did the deed. I've always found that to be more important than just about everybody else in the field believes."

"So we've got a profile emerging," Caitlin concluded, trying to determine how this new piece fit into the puzzle she was assembling in her mind.

"Speaking of which, you remember that thread I found at the Menger?"

"Sure, you thought it was the material used to sew the victim's head back on."

"Turns out I was wrong. It was a hair—well, an artificial hair. The kind you'd find in a wig or a toupee."

"So our killer's bald. You could have told me that over the phone."

"There's something else," Whatley told her. "And that's what I needed to tell you in person because it's something the likes of which I've never seen before. This victim and the four others, they'd all had hysterectomies performed. Two of the other medical examiners didn't even make note of that in their reports until I pointed it out from my examination of this victim. But that's understandable, I suppose."

"Why?"

"The scarring was very minor, hardly noticeable."

"You lost me, Doc."

"Somebody went to a lot of trouble and spent a lot of money to make sure it was done right. But that's not all." Whatley looked at her with eyes so big and moist they were almost tear-filled. He started to suck in a deep breath and then abandoned the effort. "The operations were performed a whole bunch of years ago, Ranger, while they were still little girls."

58

Connecticut, Route 95

"I don't get any of this," Dylan told Cort Wesley, after waking up grouchy, groggy, and feeling cramped in the passenger seat of their rental car as it headed south, through Connecticut, along rain-swept Route 95.

"Your head hurt again?"

"My head's fine."

"Doesn't look that way to me."

Dylan squeezed his eyes closed. "Then stop giving me a headache."

"Okay, we'll talk later."

"No, say whatever you want now. Tell me I was an idiot for letting this girl sucker me the way she did. But how was I supposed to know she was mixed up in something like that?" the boy asked. "You have any aspirin?"

"You've taken enough."

"So you're a doctor now too?"

Cort Wesley focused on the road ahead. "You couldn't have

known what she was mixed up in, no way," Cort Wesley said to Dylan, his hands tightening on the steering wheel, which felt hot under his grasp.

It was a dreary day, cold rain filling the air and turning the roads slick. While Dylan was asleep, Cort Wesley left the radio off so as not to disturb him, the only sound that of the windshield wipers swiping the rain splatter off the glass.

"What did Kai tell you about herself exactly?" he resumed.

"Not much. She figured I knew everything I needed to about her already. But remember how you told me to watch people's eyes?"

Cort Wesley nodded.

"Hers were always shifting about, like she thought somebody was watching her."

"What about the night you got beat up?"

Dylan frowned. "Don't say it that way."

"How would you like me to say it?"

"That I got jumped. By two guys at least."

"Get back to that night."

"I got her text after my meetings. She wanted to meet up."

"At Spats. Your idea or hers?"

"Mine. She met me there and told me there was something she needed to tell me. Just not in the bar."

"You think she was running some kind of game on you?"

"Game?"

"A con. You know, playing you."

"Why?" Dylan posed defensively.

"You never pegged her for what she was?" Cort Wesley asked instead of answering his question.

"And what was she?"

"Porn actresses do it for money, son. Seems a simple enough conclusion."

Dylan rolled his eyes. "She never asked *me* for money, Dad."

"Whose idea was it to walk in that direction?"

"Dad . . ."

"I mean it, son."

"I insisted on walking her back to where she said she lived. We must've gotten jumped on the way."

Cort Wesley could feel himself getting angry again. "You mean, *you* got jumped," he said to Dylan. "Kai must have run off."

"What was she supposed to do, Dad, stay and get the shit kicked out of her too?"

"She never called the cops, Dylan. The nine-one-one was placed by a neighbor, dialed just before a passing student made the call too. What's that tell you?"

"I don't know. What does it tell me?"

"I hate when you repeat what I say, son."

"Tough."

"I ever tell you a man only repeats a question when he doesn't want to face the answer?"

"Could you be any more evasive?"

"Nice word—evasive."

"Comes with having a kid in the Ivy League, Dad. I think I remember these guys grabbing for her and me intervening, just like you would if somebody did that to Caitlin."

"She knew who Caitlin was."

"I tell you that already?"

Cort Wesley nodded. "In the hospital, when you mentioned Kai's interest in you had something to do with a serial killer. Don't you remember?"

"The hospital's kind of a blur. She brought that up when she got to Spats that night. Said she needed to talk to Caitlin. Said there were women being murdered in Texas and she knew who was doing it."

"You ask her how?"

"Never got the chance. She knew about Caitlin, she knew about you. Not easy stuff to find out by just entering my name in Google. I asked her about that."

"What she say?"

"Not much. Can I have an aspirin or not?"

"I already told you no."

"I guess I forgot that too."

Cort Wesley turned to shoot Dylan a look, making him climb up the bumper of a minivan and necessitating a last-minute stomp on the rental car's brakes. He felt the antilocks engaging with a body-rattling quake, slowing just short of a collision.

"Jesus, Dad, why don't you let me drive?"

"Because the docs said you may still have some lingering effects from the concussion. That it might impair your judgment."

"Really?" Dylan asked, making a sound stuck somewhere between a snicker and a chuckle. "So what's your excuse? Now, how 'bout that aspirin?"

And Cort Wesley fished in his pocket for the bottle.

59

SAN ANTONIO, TEXAS

Caitlin sat in her SUV for a time after leaving Doc Whatley's office. She hadn't let on in front of him how much such a violation of these young women, when they were barely in their teens, bothered her.

Someone wanted them to have sex and lots of it.

That same someone didn't want to ever worry about them getting pregnant.

And now five of them were dead, murdered in the same way as another string of Chinese females in 1883; those bodies likely buried not far from where the railroads blazed a trail across the country into present day.

Caitlin finally gunned her engine and, as much to distract herself as anything else, flipped on her scanner and ended up tuning in just as something was happening at San Antonio airport. She was already tearing down the road for the nearest ramp to the freeway when her cell phone started chirping.

"You on your way to the airport?" Captain Tepper asked through the Bluetooth.

"How'd you know?"

"Because you've got a sixth sense for this shit, to the point where I'm starting to think you're actually the cause of it all just to give you an excuse to drive me bonkers."

"Stay away from the Marlboros, D.W."

"Only if you promise not to shoot anyone today."

"Depends what I find at San Antonio International. Why don't you give me a hint?"

60

NEW YORK CITY

"You want me to come *inside* with you?" Dylan asked, not believing what his father had just said.

"I got a plan," Cort Wesley told him, "and you're a part of what I've got in mind, assuming you're up to it."

"I'm up to it. So what is this place exactly?"

"Not sure, son. A safe bet would have it that Kai's part of an operation that's headquartered right here."

They stood on the pedestrian plaza lined with tables on the Broadway side of the wedge-shaped historical icon known as the Flatiron Building at 175 Fifth Avenue. Cort Wesley's eyes continued to gaze up toward where he needed to go: the twenty-third floor, Nicolas Dimitrios had said, just before handing Cort Wesley the black keycard he held in his pocket now.

So just how was it he counted only twenty-two floors from the outside?

"There's something else we need to talk about," Cort Wesley continued, feeling the words corkscrew in his throat.

"You don't have to say it, Dad."

"You don't know what I was going to say."

"Something about me shooting that guy you were fighting with. I don't even remember doing it. I went for that gun and next thing I know it was jerking in my hand. Guess it was the concussion."

"You took him down with the first shot, son. Not an easy thing to do."

"That what you wanted to tell me?"

"You . . . okay with what you did?"

"I told you, I don't remember doing it."

"You killed a man, Dylan."

"I've seen people die before, Dad," the boy said pointedly. "Why do we have to talk about this?"

He could tell Dylan wasn't being evasive; the boy just didn't see the point of belaboring the issue. Cort Wesley figured his apparent detachment from the deed stemmed from a combination of witnessing his own mother's shooting and all the violence to which he'd been exposed since. Then again, maybe it was a genetic thing, handed down from generation to generation. Cort Wesley's dad once told him he'd killed his first man in a prison yard where he'd been stuck as a sixteen-year-old boy, doing time with hardcore criminals after being tried as an adult for armed robbery. It was either that or give himself up to the man in ways he wasn't about to. And, after splitting the guy's skull open with a chunk of concrete that had broken off from the base of the steel fencing, nobody bothered Boone Masters again. Cort Wesley, on the other hand, had killed his first man in self-defense; well, defense of a girl who was attacked while they walked down the street, turning the attacker's own knife against him.

He'd been sixteen at the time too. Paid the matter no more heed than Dylan was now. The boy showed no ill effects, seeming to brush killing a man off with ease. Had he seen and experienced so much of the like to have become immune to its effects and accepting of its necessity as a result?

Goddamn, he thought, *most parents only have to worry about teaching their kids about the birds and bees. . . .*

Cort Wesley returned his attention to the Flatiron Building and the task at hand. A far more subtle approach than going in with guns blazing was called for in dealing with whoever was distributing high-end call girls through the country from the twenty-third floor that didn't, apparently, exist.

"You ready, son?"

"You haven't told me the plan yet, what I'm supposed to do."

Cort Wesley grinned. "I think you're gonna like this. . . ."

Inside the lobby, Cort Wesley nodded at the security guard behind a small counter and flashed the black keycard in front of a scanner. A light glowed green and he pushed his way through a turnstile with Dylan by his side.

There were six elevators and Cort Wesley chose the one farthest down on the right because the cab door was already open. He laid a hand against the door to keep it that way for Dylan to enter and then joined his son inside.

Cort Wesley studied the panel to find, not surprisingly, no floor marked twenty-three. He still had his black keycard in hand and looked for another scanner to wave it before, but none was immediately evident.

"Let me try," Dylan said.

He snatched the card from his father's grasp and angled it in front of a lens higher up on the panel that Cort Wesley had taken for a security camera. As Dylan held the black access card near it, though, the lens glowed blue and the elevator doors closed. A moment later, the car was in motion, streaking for a floor that shouldn't have existed with the two of them as the only passengers.

"Those jeans are too tight," Cort Wesley said suddenly, not exactly sure why.

"That's the way they're supposed to fit."

"Well, son, it looks like you already outgrew them from where I'm standing." Cort Wesley stole another glance, in spite of Dylan's caustic stare. "I can almost tell the last number you dialed on that throwaway cell phone we grabbed down the street."

"Oh, man," the boy muttered, as the elevator continue to zoom upward, making no other stops.

"I saw your credit card statement. How is it they cost so much when there's so little to them?"

"They don't cost that much, Dad."

"That's because you're not paying."

Dylan gave his father a long look, as if sizing him up. "You look naked."

"What's that supposed to mean?"

"You're not carrying a gun."

The elevator reached the twenty-second floor and kept climbing.

"And you've got no idea what we're going to find up there. What if it's a trap?"

A bell chimed as the elevator stopped on the twenty-third.

Cort Wesley eased Dylan behind him and pressed up against the front of the cab, out of sight from anyone who might be waiting when the door slid open.

"We'll know soon enough, son."

61

SAN ANTONIO, TEXAS

"Gate Seven, Ranger!" a TSA supervisor called out when Caitlin reached the security checkpoint at San Antonio airport's international terminal.

Two TSA workers escorted her through, bypassing the scanners and X-ray conveyor. The checkpoint had pretty much ground to a halt since the sudden death of a Chinese diplomat farther down the concourse just prior to his boarding a flight back home. Captain Tepper actually wasn't sure he was a diplomat, just that he was Chinese and dead reportedly of natural causes.

Which begged the question why a Texas Ranger was required at the scene.

Caitlin saw the reason as she approached Gate Seven in the imposing form of Consuelo Alonzo, deputy chief of the San Antonio Police Department. Alonzo had risen quickly through the ranks of the department, becoming the youngest woman ever to make captain three years prior to her recent promotion to deputy chief. And she was rumored to be in line for the job of public safety commissioner that came with a plush Austin office, a job that would place her, among other things, as chief overseer of the Texas Rangers. Alonzo had overcome an appearance often referred to as "masculine" by even supporters, and much worse than that by her detractors. Caitlin put little stock in the rumors pertaining to Alonzo's personal life and her own sexual preferences, knowing she'd born the brunt of similarly caustic attacks herself.

This was Texas, after all, where a woman needed to work twice as hard, and be twice as good, in a profession ruggedly and stubbornly perceived to be for men only. Caitlin and Alonzo had had their differences over the years, but had maintained a mutual respect defined by their professionalism and the sense that their own squabbles only further emboldened those who sought their demise.

"Congratulations, Deputy Chief," Caitlin greeted as she drew closer, having not seen Alonzo since her formal appointment.

"Save the pleasantries, Ranger," Alonzo snapped in a tone typical of their past dealings. "You're only here so I don't have to explain to anybody why I never called in the Rangers. So make sure you face the media when we let them in."

"I can see you're really enjoying your new position."

Alonzo ran a hand through her spiky hair. She was heavyset and had once set the woman's record for the bench press in her weight class. She'd also done some boxing and was reputed to be the best target shooter with a pistol in the entire department. They might never be friends, or even allies really, but Caitlin knew far more made them alike than different professionally.

"Why don't you tell me exactly why I'm here?" Caitlin said,

drawing close enough to Alonzo to smell peppermint-scented gum mixing with hair gel that smelled like flowers. She recalled it hadn't smelled that way prior to her promotion.

"Because we're gonna need all the political cover we can get on this one," Alonzo explained. "The deceased was a high-ranking Chinese official and, apparently, his government had no idea he was even here."

"This official have a name?" Caitlin asked her.

"General Mengyao Chang."

General Mengyao Chang had been talking on his cell phone when, according to witnesses, he was shaken by a crushing pain consistent with a heart attack and then collapsed. Efforts to revive him by members of his security detail, as well as by a Chinese doctor who happened to be at the gate, failed. He was pronounced dead by the San Antonio paramedics who'd followed the airport's own emergency personnel to the scene. As far as Caitlin could tell, everything had been handled just as it should have been. The body had not been removed from the scene because General Chang's security contingent refused to release it.

Right now the corpse lay covered on a gurney still enclosed by paramedics determined to protect it from the heated back and forth currently ongoing between members of the general's entourage and Deputy Chief Alonzo herself, who was trying to deal with having three men addressing her in Chinese at the same time. Caitlin had moved off to the side, closer to the covered corpse with Alonzo no longer paying attention to her.

"I understand the victim was on his cell phone when he died," she said to the nearest paramedic.

"It was still in his hand when we arrived on the scene," the paramedic confirmed. "Never saw one quite like it before. I think one of the detectives already bagged it."

"You think you might be able to get it for me?" Caitlin asked him. "I'd like to have a look for myself."

* * *

The paramedic was right. The phone looked to be a Chinese-made, upgraded model without a brand name on it; thin, sleek, shiny black everywhere with rounded edges. She'd just given it back to the paramedic who'd handed it to her when a pair of men who might've been twins appeared on either side of Caitlin.

"We need you to come with us," the one on the right said, the two of them snapping matching wallets open that identified them as officials from the State Department.

"Right away," added the one on the left.

"I'm here on direct orders," Caitlin told them, rotating her gaze between one who was thin and the other whose bulbous upper body had swallowed all semblance of his neck. "Why don't you take this up with my captain?"

The one on the right, the thin one, started to reach out to take her arm. "We already have, Ranger. If you'll just come with us, we'll explain everything."

62

NEW YORK CITY

The elevator doors opened into a spacious but simple reception area with no one laying in wait for Cort Wesley. He breathed easier and noted a pair of plants atop a thin pile carpet set before a glass wall and matching doors. No furniture whatsoever unless you counted the big wide shapes of two men standing on either side of those double doors, out of sight from anyone inside.

"Hey," Cort Wesley said innocently, pretending to be out of breath as he approached them, "I'm sorry I'm late."

He pulled Dylan along with him, the men watching both of them in confusion.

"My appointment was for, oh, fifteen minutes ago," Cort Wesley told him. "This is my son. He wants to be a model. He's the one looking for representation, not me."

The two men looked at each other.

"I think you've come to the wrong place," one of them said.

"No," Cort Wesley started, coming right up to them in an utterly unthreatening manner. "See, they gave me this to make sure I could access your floor."

He flashed the black access card, then purposely dropped it. When the man on the right stooped to retrieve the card, Cort Wesley slammed a knee square into his face, then lashed a vicious sidewinder of a strike with the side of his hand into the second man's groin. The second man doubled over, letting out a gasp that sounded like the air escaping a balloon. He didn't have much hair, but Cort Wesley grabbed what he could and slammed him into the glass wall.

He felt, or imagined he felt, the glass buckle, giving like a sponge. When the man's eyes still clung to consciousness, Cort Wesley smashed his skull against the glass twice more. He saw his eyes go glassy and let him slump the rest of the way down.

By that time, the first man was stirring, starting to lumber back upright with his face covered in blood from his shattered nose. His effort ended when Cort Wesley slammed his interlaced hands into the back of the man's skull where it met the neck and spine. He could feel the big shape stiffen, back arching as he crumpled to the carpet below.

Cort Wesley crouched and retrieved the black access card from where he'd dropped it. Then he led Dylan to the double doors and waved the card in front of a lens identical to the one the boy had spotted in the elevator. A click sounded, and the doors snapped electronically open.

Once through the glass doors, Cort Wesley swung left toward a reception desk where a woman rose in befuddlement at his approach.

"Can I help you?"

"You sure can. I'm here about representation." Cort Wesley stood aside so the woman could get a better look at Dylan. "For my son, not me."

"How did you get in here?"

Cort Wesley flashed his black card.

"I mean past the guards," the woman said, peering beyond them as if expecting the two currently unconscious men to appear.

"I told them I had an appointment," Cort Wesley said nonchalantly. "About getting representation for my son." He squeezed Dylan's shoulder. "He wants to be a model, but he looks more like an actor or rock star to me. What do you think?"

The woman was hitting a button on her phone over and over again. "I think you must be in the wrong place."

"You came very well recommended, though."

"I don't believe I got your name, sir."

"But I want to make it clear as crystal," Cort Wesley said, ignoring her, "that I want no funny stuff." Then he hardened his voice, let the woman glimpse him as he really was. "Anybody looks at my son the wrong way, it'll be the last sight they ever see."

That's when four men stormed down a dark hallway from whatever lay beyond the woman's desk. The two in front looked like Wall Street traders and a bulky one in the middle could have been a clone of the two who'd been parked outside the glass doors. But it was the fourth who grabbed Cort Wesley's attention. Dressed and coiffed right out of a fashion magazine, with a genuine tan, combed-back hair perfectly oiled, and eyes with the smallest pupils of anyone Cort Wesley had ever seen, as if the whites were in the process of swallowing them. His ears were pressed so tight to his head that they looked glued in place.

"You need to leave, sir," the big man in the middle said, beefy hand stretching forward as he advanced ahead of the others.

"Huh?"

The hand found Cort Wesley's arm. "You and the faggot need to leave. You don't belong here."

Cort Wesley twisted his hand off. "Don't touch me. I'm just here because I heard you—"

The big man grabbed his arm firmer this time and steered Cort Wesley back toward the entrance in the reception area, cutting off his words. "Now."

Cort Wesley let himself be pulled straight to the door, watching the man's eyes widen in befuddlement when he realized the two guards who were supposed to be posted there were nowhere to be seen.

"Don't come back," he said, pushing Cort Wesley through the doors and Dylan right after him.

The door closed and sealed behind him. Cort Wesley watched the big man talking on his wrist-mounted microphone and got one last look at the man with the slicked-back hair and glued-on ears, their stares holding briefly before he drifted out of sight.

"What's next?" Dylan asked him inside the elevator.

"You'll see."

"Why don't you just tell me?"

"I need to have a little talk with their boss," Cort Wesley said, the elevator hitting its cruising speed.

"The oily-looking guy who looked like Euro trash?"

"I don't know what Euro trash looks like, but that's the one."

"Do I look gay?" Dylan asked suddenly.

"Huh?"

"That guy called me a faggot."

Cort Wesley looked at his son wryly and winked. "I told you those jeans were too tight."

The elevator opened on the lobby level.

Cort Wesley led Dylan out, moving straight for the revolving door exit when he unobtrusively yanked down on a fire alarm, a deafening screech sounding immediately.

63

The men from the State Department brought Caitlin to a sterile, windowless room normally reserved for interrogations of foreign nationals flagged by ICE agents. They sat at a steel table outfitted with slots for both hand and leg restraints, the two men seated across from her on the left and right as if they rehearsed their positioning. For some reason the disparity in their sizes made her think of the old comic team of Laurel and Hardy, Hardy being the bigger one.

"You are to have no further contact with Li Zhen," today's Oliver Hardy told her.

"He has something to do with that dead Chinese general?"

"Mr. Zhen filed a formal complaint with the State Department accusing you of acting toward him in a threatening manner and intimating his involvement in a series of killings."

"You referring to the four Chinese gunmen I killed on a train yesterday or the ones shot dead up in a Rhode Island hospital?"

Neither Laurel nor Hardy seemed at all moved by her question.

"Mr. Zhen enjoys certain protections afforded by the Foreign Nationals Protective Act," said the man who reminded her of Stan Laurel, the smaller member of the famed team.

"Even though he isn't protected by diplomatic immunity," added Hardy, "he is served by many of the same rights he is alleging you violated."

"You are under orders to cease and desist all further contact with Mr. Zhen under any and all circumstances."

"Should you have any further questions you wish to pose, forward them to our office and we will pass them on with a request the answers be furnished in writing."

Caitlin looked from Laurel to Hardy and back again, then just shook her head. "Do you guys have to practice this act, or does it just come natural?"

"That's a direct order from the secretary of state." Hardy.

"Violating it would be grounds for the department filing federal charges against you and ordering your immediate arrest." Laurel.

"And which department would that be?" Caitlin asked them both. "State or Homeland?"

The two men stood up in unison.

"You have your orders, Ranger," Laurel told her.

"Is Jones behind this? Oh yeah, you boys may know him as Brooks in these parts."

"TSA officials are waiting outside to escort you from the terminal," Hardy said, instead of answering. "Refusing to comply with their instructions is also a federal offense."

Caitlin joined them on her feet. "You boys afraid to handle the chore yourselves? Afraid what might happen when we're out of the terminal and officially back in Texas?"

Laurel and Hardy flashed almost identical smirks.

"What's General Chang got to do with Li Zhen and Yuyuan?"

The two men started for the door.

"You boys curious at all about what brought Chang to Texas and who he was talking to on the phone when he died?"

One of them opened the door. "You have your orders, Ranger," from Laurel.

"Step foot in Yuyuan again without authorization and you'll face five years in federal prison," from Hardy.

"You can't walk all over Washington the way you do with Austin, Ranger."

"A fine mess, then, isn't it?" Caitlin caught their utterly blank stares and just shook her head. "Never mind."

The two men started through the door in step.

"Your captain's been informed of this meeting," Laurel informed her.

"So has the governor and director of public safety," Hardy added.

"Hey, you forgot to mention the president."

The two men stopped, one slightly ahead of the other.

"Yes," from Laurel, "we did."

"But he's been informed as well," Hardy told her.

64

NEW BRAUNFELS, TEXAS

Li Zhen often lost track of time when he was down in the sublevel from which he would trigger what Qiang had called *Qǐshì*, Chinese for the apocalypse.

He'd thought the deal he had made years before with the Triad to assume this new social standing would have vanquished the obsession of a youth and manhood spent among lessers. Had his great-grandfather not been cheated by the Americans, had he received the due his invention deserved instead of having it stolen, no arrangement with the Triad would have been necessary. His great-grandfather would have returned to China a rich, powerful, and respected man with a stature that his forebears would reap for centuries to come. Instead, he was first humiliated and then killed, further sentencing the family he left behind to live as peasant scum with no hope of rising to the higher social standing he sought in coming to this country in the first place.

And now that country would be held accountable. Now that country would pay for the sins that had rendered Li Zhen's dreams hopeless even before he was born.

Qǐshì . . .

Now this spiteful country would reap what those railroad men had sewn. This was their making, not his. In laying the tracks that joined the vast frontiers of America together, they were actually laying the seeds of their own eventual destruction.

Li Zhen heard his name being called, wondering if it might not be his great-grandfather speaking to him through the years, until it sounded again in his ear through his Bluetooth device.

"Yes," he said, clearing his throat.

"The Texas Ranger is back," Qiang told him.

65

New Braunfels, Texas

"Thank you for seeing me, Mr. Zhen," Caitlin told the head of the Yuyuan company, from the same chair she'd occupied in her initial visit.

"I'm already going to place a phone call to officials at the State Department, Ranger. I imagine they will send federal marshals to take you into custody."

"You may want to rethink that call, sir, since my visit here today concerns your own personal safety."

Caitlin watched Zhen lean forward, the motion as stiff as his posture. "*My* safety?"

"I believe you might be in danger. It concerns General Mengyao Chang."

"I have been informed of his tragic passing, Ranger, but don't see how that could possibly endanger me."

"Actually, I believe General Chang may have been murdered, sir."

"I was informed all indications pointed to a heart attack."

"Not all indications. That's why I'm here," Caitlin told him. "Your safety's more important to me than some edict from the State Department."

"I appreciate that, Ranger, but don't see what—"

"General Chang was on the phone to an identified party back in China when he was stricken," Caitlin interrupted. "But a number of other calls on his phone's log were to you. Was it business between him and Yuyuan that brought him to Texas?"

"I met with General Chang earlier in the day. I'm sure you understand I am not at liberty to discuss the topics of our discussion. He was supposed to stop off at Six Flags Fiesta to ride the park's roller coasters, a kind of obsession for the general—at least, that's what he told me. We met in Fiesta actually so he could make the stop before going home. You may want to report that to those overseeing the investigation, Ranger. General Chang was an older man who probably shouldn't have been riding roller coasters at all. There could be a connection."

"And what exactly was your connection to him?"

"You realize I am under no obligation to answer your questions."

"I am, sir, and, like I said, I took the risk in coming here because of my concerns for your safety on the chance my suspicions are well founded."

"I appreciate the courtesy, Ranger. In China, it's no secret that the interests of business, the military, and the government are all intrinsically intertwined. General Chang was the military representative to whom I reported on a regular basis."

"That's interesting, sir, since the travel documents I had a look at indicate the last time General Chang was in Texas goes all the way back to the time Yuyuan opened its offices here."

Caitlin's gaze moved behind Li Zhen to the wall of old black-and-white photographs from the frontier railroad days.

"One of your pictures is missing," she noted.

Li did not turn to follow her gaze to the wall. He looked like a man trying not to appear surprised.

"It was a shot that caught the work in progress on one of the many railroad lines Chinese immigrants helped build," Caitlin continued. "I thought I recognized it as somewhere in West Texas."

"A lot to conclude from a single photo."

"It was the scrub brush, Mr. Zhen. Only Texas has it, or, at least, it's the only state that has it where the railroads were building at the time."

"My great-grandfather, Tsuyoshi Zhen, spent many years in your state, working those rails. Did I mention that?"

"You mentioned the owners of the railroad cheated him out of some invention."

"Not just some invention," Li told her, with an edge of bitterness and animus creeping into his voice. "It was his life's work and they stole it from him."

"My great-grandfather spent some time in one of those work camps investigating the murders of Chinese women at the hands of the Old West's first recorded serial killer. You know anything about that?"

Li Zhen's expression didn't change, remaining utterly flat and noncommittal. "I believe I do," he said, rising from his chair. "Allow me to share it with you. . . ."

66

LANGTRY, TEXAS; 1883

William Ray Strong stayed in one of the six bedrooms over Roy Bean's combination saloon and courthouse that were normally occupied only for an hour or so at a time. He was awoken not long after dawn by a knock on the door and opened it to find the judge standing there.

"I brought you some coffee," he said, handing William Ray a hot, steaming mug, the contents of which looked thick as tar.

"Didn't think we were intending to get this early a start."

"Tell that to the railroad men downstairs waiting for you, Ranger."

*　*　*

William Ray dressed quickly and headed down the stairway that doglegged to the right with the rest of his coffee in hand. He spotted four men all in suits, two standing and two sitting. The two who were sitting sat patiently next to each other, each in their forties or fifties. One wore tiny wire-rimmed spectacles. The other, who was somehow familiar to William Ray, didn't.

The two men standing, meanwhile, stood slightly back from them. Their suit coats dangled over the bulges of their holsters and William Ray had them made as private security, Pinkerton men in all probability since the company supplied both the Trans-Union and Southern Pacific railroads with most of their hired gunmen. There was no shortage of need for their services, especially on the plains, but these were the type better suited for dealing with settlers and farmers unwilling to cede their land based on the eminent domain principle upon which the railroad relied.

The two seated men rose briefly in unison at William Ray's approach, his gaze following them even as he watched to see if the Pinkerton men brushed their coats back to expose their pistols.

"Nice to meet you, Ranger," the older of the two said, extending a hand across the table.

William Ray laid his cooling mug of coffee down on the table and took it. "Normally, when I shake a man's hand I'm already familiar with his name."

"John W. Morehouse, Ranger, and this is Christopher Allen Bookbinder. We operate the Southern Pacific Railroad."

"By operate I don't suppose you mean drive the trains."

"Hardly," Morehouse said, his teeth so white when he smiled it seemed as if he'd wet them down with paint. "My father was one of the founders of the Southern Pacific and Mr. Bookbinder here serves as our project manager, quite a job given how much rail we're laying at any given time over any number of sites."

William Ray let his gaze wander over them to the two men standing in the shadows cast by the morning sunlight streaming in through the side windows. "You didn't introduce them."

"Because their names aren't important."

"But their presence must be, or they wouldn't be here. I thought you looked familiar, Mr. Morehouse. I've seen your picture in the papers. I've never seen their pictures in the papers," the Ranger continued, tilting his gaze again toward the Pinkertons, "but they look familiar enough too. You come all the way out here from New York?"

"We were already here on other business when we received word of the visit you paid to our worksite yesterday. Stirred the pot a bit, didn't you?"

"Just doing my job, sir."

"And that's why we're here now, doing ours. Spare you time and trouble in the process."

"Time and trouble kind of goes with my job too," William Ray told him. "Isn't that right, Judge?" he continued when Roy Bean took the chair next to him, laying a massive mug of beer before him, plopping it down so hard that a bunch of the foam at the top sprayed into the air.

"Take it from me," the judge said, toasting Bookbinder and Morehouse, "this man is a genuine pain in the ass. His bad side is a place you don't want to be, any more than you want to mess with any Texas Ranger."

"You caused quite a commotion," Morehouse said to William Ray. "I thought it prudent we have a talk to set the scales right." He shifted in his chair enough to be able to look back at the two Pinkerton men. "And these men accompanied us to demonstrate to you that we are well capable of policing our own and handling the kind of situation that has arisen in the camp you visited."

"Where were they a couple weeks back?"

"Pardon me?"

"The first victim was killed almost two weeks ago, but I'm guessing this is their first trip to the camp." William Ray leaned forward. "See, their shoes are clean and their suits don't have a single speck of mud or dust on them. And their pants are wrinkled in the places that tell me they just finished a long train ride."

"Makes sense," said Roy Bean, draining a hefty portion of his beer in a single swig and mopping the suds from his mouth with his sleeve.

"But here's the problem," William Ray resumed. "Your Pinkerton men must've been on their way west before the judge and I showed up at that worksite. I seem to recall your chief engineer, Kincannon, telling us they'd been sent for to deal with that strike by those Chinese workers."

"That's none of your business, Ranger. None of this is your business."

"That's funny, because last time I checked this was still Texas, and that makes it my business."

Morehouse frowned, looking toward Bookbinder who handed him an envelope. "Then maybe you should have a look at this, Ranger. Save all of us some trouble."

He handed the envelope to William Ray who saw it had been neatly slit open at the top, recognizing it as a Western Union wire. Though the envelope was open, the wire looked otherwise undisturbed as he slid it out and unfolded it a third at a time.

"In case you have a problem with any of the words, Ranger," Moorehead said flatly with no apparent derision, "it's from the governor of Texas, John Ireland himself, ordering you to cease and desist all investigative efforts as they pertain to the Southern Pacific Railroad here in your great state."

William Ray handed the telegram to the judge initially without comment. Then he regarded the man wearing the pressed woolen suit across the table.

"Pays to have friends in high places, doesn't it, Mr. Morehouse? Tell me, did you make any contributions to our recently elected governor's campaign?"

"I did indeed, Ranger. Then again, the Southern Pacific made an equally substantial contribution to his opponent."

"A fine strategy, sir."

"Thank you."

"And so is keeping a lid on the fact that you've got a murderer loose who's killed Chinese women at several of your work camps and will go on killing unless justice is done."

"We are perfectly capable of looking after our own, Ranger."

William Ray leaned across the table, shoving his coffee mug out of the way to make room for his elbows. "If that were the case, there wouldn't be four dead young ladies in Langtry, sir."

Morehouse leaned back in his chair and folded his arms across his chest. "Has a complaint been filed, Ranger?"

"The murdered women weren't exactly feeling up to the task of filling out a report."

"Then if no complaint was filed, what's your cause for investigating?"

"That's on me," said Judge Roy Bean, seeming to lick at the suds down the sides of his now empty stein of beer. "I caught wind of what was transpiring from a customer of mine who delivers beef to the site. He overhead a few men talking."

"Well," said Morehouse, slapping his open palms on the table hard enough to make the rest of William Ray's coffee jump in its mug, "there you have it. Since no official complaint has been filed, Ranger, you had no real call to intrude on the camp, land duly owned by the Southern Pacific, I might add, in the first place." He pointed toward the telegram upon which William Ray had planted his elbows. "I believe the governor came to his decision in full awareness of that fact. Enough said." Morehouse rose and replaced his bowler hat. "I appreciate you both doing your best to uphold justice in this fine state."

"I believe I recognize you from someplace other than the newspapers," William Ray said, looking up at him now. "Can you think of a time we may have met before?"

"I don't think I would have forgotten you, if that were the case, Ranger."

"I was thinking the same thing, Mr. Morehouse. That's what bugs me."

"Maybe I have a familiar face."

"I suspect you must."

"Well, then, we'd best be getting back to work."

Morehouse turned and walked toward the door in lock step with Bookbinder under the protective shadow of the Pinkerton men who didn't take their eyes off William Ray for a single second.

"Mr. Morehouse?" he called just as Morehouse was starting through the door, waiting for him to stop and turn. "Just make sure no harm comes to any of these Chinese on account of this strike."

"I've got a railroad to run, Ranger, and right now they're stopping me from doing that."

"Then pay them what you owe for the construction of that dam. Last time I checked, slavery was illegal in this country."

"Well, sir," Morehouse said, with a snarky grin, "that depends on your perspective, doesn't it?"

"We still headed over to that camp?" Judge Bean called from the bar where he was refilling his mug, after Morehouse and the Pinkertons were gone.

"We sure are, Judge," William Ray said, checking his Colt. "Those boys must not know much about the Texas Rangers. And something else."

"What's that?"

"I believe I remember where I recognized Mr. Morehouse from."

William Ray Strong and Judge Roy Bean reached the site just as work was starting up again laying track. The entire camp seemed to be working—everyone but the Chinese, that is, who, to a man, remained on strike, which was sure to keep the Southern Pacific from meeting its daily quota.

They rode in single file, one behind the other, the eyes of the workers gaping at the sight once again of the Texas Ranger riding high in the saddle with one hand on the reins and another perched near enough his Colt to have it drawn in a blink. William Ray spotted a number of Pinkerton men scattered strategically about, lean-ing against posts, cigarettes dangling from their lips, with a few holding shotguns just tight enough. They all wore suits, some cov-ered by long barn coats just beginning to soak up the grime of the street, but none had their Pinkerton badges pinned to their lapels.

William Ray made a point of ignoring them through the course of his leisurely approach to the camp, heading straight to the tent forming police headquarters where the bowling pin form of Chief Bates was perched on the stoop shaking his head.

"I was hoping you'd change your mind, Ranger."

"Came back as promised, Chief," William Ray said, as he dis-mounted, "to get that name from you."

William Ray didn't need to follow Bates's eyes to know the Pinkertons were coming, the lot of them converging here from what-ever posts they'd been standing. "You wanna talk in your office, Chief Bates, or right out here on the street?"

"I don't want to talk to you at all. I said everything I had to say yesterday and your brains got too much range shit stuck in them to regard my words with the impact you should have."

"You sure take a long time to say a quick thing, sir," William Ray told him. "As it turns out, guess I should've blown your brains out last night."

The Pinkertons had enclosed him and Judge Bean in a neat semi-circle, the Ranger still paying them no heed whatsoever.

"You know, Judge," he called out loudly instead, "I don't think Chief Bates here got word of the parade."

"Don't appear that way," said Bean from his saddle, unflustered by the guns steadied his way.

"It's in the judge's honor," William Ray told Bates. "An annual tradition we're gonna call Roy Bean Appreciation Day. Since this is his county, we thought we'd run the parade straight through here so you folks can enjoy it too."

And with that a flood of pounding hooves sounded just ahead of the wave of riders armed with pistols, Winchesters, and shotguns storming through the camp to take up positions behind the Pinkertons.

"This here's the planning committee," William Ray continued. "The judge has a lot of friends, don't you, Judge?"

"I do," Bean said, spitting a huge wad of tobacco to the gravel below.

"Some of these came all the way from El Paso. Why, the judge even closed his establishment for the duration of the parade so these men don't even have any drink inside them yet. But their respect for Judge Roy Bean more than allows for their sobriety, not long for this world since all drinking is free in his saloon once the ceremony is done. So, Chief, what say you and me have a talk while the rest of these boys get acquainted with each other?"

Bates's expression wrinkled in displeasure. "All this for Chinese whores?"

"Last time I checked, whores are still people, Chief."

"Why bother, Ranger?"

"Because I don't see anybody else about to. Now, about that name you were going to get for me . . ."

William Ray found the young man to whom Chief Bates directed him in the mess tent, seated at the same table where he'd noticed him the day before while interviewing Ecklund.

"You'd be David Morehouse," the Ranger said, hovering over him. "I met your father just a few hours back. You sure look a lot like him. I was wondering if I could have a word with you."

The young man gazed up at him, but his eyes still seemed somewhere else. They seemed unable to focus on William Ray, staring at him the way a young puppy does until it learns how to use its eyes. He had a boy's eyes that wouldn't stop twitching and hair dangling past his shoulders that looked much too long for his narrow face, so gaunt that his skin seemed stretched over his skull.

"They stung me," the young man said. "Stung me all over. I was out in the brush when they attacked."

In point of fact he didn't look as much like his father as William Ray had remembered, not much at all other than the eyes. But that was more than enough to form the resemblance that had occurred to him as soon as he saw John Morehouse seated in Judge Bean's saloon. Identical shade of crystal blue and held in the same narrow bent, looking somehow sardonic.

Looking into David Morehouse's eyes, though, the Ranger saw something that wasn't right; very wrong, in fact. The young man couldn't hold his gaze on anything for very long, and when he tried the lids turned all jittery and he ended up squeezing his eyes closed.

"Hornets," he continued, speaking in a boy's plaintive tone. "They're everywhere. That's why I come in here. I'm hiding from them."

"You been in other camps 'sides this one, son?" William Ray asked, addressing David Morehouse that way even though the young man was only a few years his junior.

"Hornets," he repeated, "always hornets. Swat 'em, swat 'em, swat 'em . . . That's what I do."

William Ray knelt so he was eye to eye with the young man, his face a mask of comfort. "You wanna show me where they are?"

"Why?" Posed fearfully.

"So they can't hurt you again."

"They stung me bad."

"I know."

"Over and over again."

"Gotta stop that from happening ever again, don't we?"

William Ray laid a comforting hand over the back of David Morehouse's trembling one. But the young man yanked it away instantly and tucked the hand behind his back, as if to hide it.

"Hornets hurt me bad."

"Show me where they did it."

"Hurt me bad, bad . . ." With that, David Morehouse began to tap his forehead against the hard wood of the table in perfect rhythm with his repetition of the word. "Bad, bad, bad, bad, bad, ba—"

William Ray grasped hold of him in midmotion and held the young man steady. He could feel something like electricity dancing on the surface of David Morehouse's superheated skin. It felt like holding on to a basket of snakes. Every nerve of the young man's body seemed to be on fire, sending signals to a brain that was misfiring worse than a Colt pistol soaked in mud.

"I want my daddy," he called out suddenly. "Where's my daddy?"

"Right here, son," a voice announced before William Ray could say anything further.

He rose from his crouch and turned to find John Morehouse standing there, board rigid and flanked by the Pinkertons the Ranger remembered from Roy Bean's bar. He pushed his coat back to ready his Colt for a draw. But Morehouse seemed uninterested in him, moving straight for his son without giving William Ray another look.

"The hornets, Daddy, the hornets!" his son wailed when he reached him. "You promised to make them go away, Daddy, you promised!"

"They came back, but we'll do better this time, I promise."

William Ray backed off, leaving Morehouse to console his son until the man's gaze chased him down.

"You find what you wanted, Ranger?" the man asked him, hugging his son now.

"Your boy needs help, sir."

"And that's what he's getting."

"I mean real help."

John Morehouse regarded him hatefully. "You're trespassing, Ranger. This is Southern Pacific Railroad land, and I want you off it." He eased his son up from the table and half-led, half-dragged him toward where the Pinkertons were still standing. "Take your judge and gunmen with you and leave, before I contact the governor."

William Ray tapped his hat against his leg, watching David Morehouse's limp frame pressed against his father. "What's he mean by hornets, sir?"

"That's not your concern; none of this is."

"Except for those murders, sir. This stopped being Southern Pacific land the moment women started dying. You might have been able to cover that up in those other worksites in other states, but that won't wash here. Know why?"

John Morehouse stopped and looked at him in silence.

"Because other states didn't have Texas Rangers," William Ray told him, eyeing his sobbing son. "And whoever it is did the deed needs to be held accountable for it before more women die."

67

NEW BRAUNFELS, TEXAS

"I guess such behavior runs in your family," Li Zhen told her, when he'd finished. "First your great-grandfather violates a direct order from the governor of Texas and now you violate an order from your country's State Department."

"Justice may be blind, sir," Caitlin said, "but she's not stupid."

Zhen looked at her through the bright sunshine in Yuyuan's gardens that were invisible from the street or parking lot. He'd led her down here to hear the story on one of the rattan benches inlaid amid the brick walkways that spiraled through the gardens like the yellow brick road in Oz.

"Beautiful place to share a very ugly story," Caitlin told him, gazing about.

Zhen took a deep breath and let it out slowly. "I come down here at least twice every day to remind myself that there's beauty in the world no matter how much the ugliness threatens to dominate. The artificial smells, the recirculated air. Take a look around you, Ranger. Some of these flowers have existed in nature unchanged for millions of years. They've managed to outlive every other species on the planet. Sometimes I come down here and ask myself what makes them better than us. How they've been able to survive for so long."

With that, Zhen reached around to the outside of the bench and lifted a pair of microtip pruning snips from a hook. The razor-sharp steel glistening in the sunlight, Zhen squeezed the handle to make the pointed tip open and close directly before Caitlin.

"I like to do some pruning every day," he explained. "Otherwise dead growth could threaten and overcome the living."

Zhen moved on toward a nearby set of flowering plants, Caitlin taking his explanation as an unspoken invitation to join him. He maneuvered himself before the plants, positioned so that the pruning snips were in easy range of her.

"Seems like you can't see the dead plants without looking well below the surface," Caitlin noted.

"All things have a right to survive, Ranger. It's a fine line we walk."

"And snip," she added, watching Zhen start to clip away at a series flowers that looked smaller, drier, and slightly discolored when compared to those that were flourishing.

He seemed to be having trouble managing the effort. Then the snips slipped from his grasp and Zhen looked up at her after stooping to retrieve them.

"Life can only thrive when the weak are trimmed back," he said.

"Is that a fact? And who gets to decide on such relative merits?"

"I don't believe they are relative at all." Zhen stood back up and looked directly into Caitlin's eyes, the tip of the pruning snips just short of her denim shirt. "Weakness and decay are not hard to spot." He continued to hold her gaze for a long moment before he started snipping away again at the stale undergrowth that fell in clumps to the ground. "And then what we discard gives back of itself so the strength can endure."

Caitlin angled the brim of her hat to keep the sun from her eyes. "Like those first waves of Chinese that ended up discarded themselves."

"We were enslaved, Ranger. The Civil War ended, and then we showed up."

"Slavery didn't end with the Civil War, Mr. Zhen. The railroads took plenty advantage of blacks as well. I think you wanted to tell that story down here because the whole story is so dirty, like it can't shake off a sheen of grime from itself. But I noticed something as you were telling it. You mind if I have a go at those, sir?" Caitlin asked, eyes aiming for the pruning snips.

Startled by her request, Zhen handed the snips reluctantly over.

"The way your eyes narrowed when you got to the part about John Morehouse, head of the Southern Pacific at the time," Caitlin said, as she picked up the work just where Zhen had left off, doing her best to imitate his motions exactly. "I was looking into the whole period last night when I couldn't sleep, seeing what names came up. There was one that stuck in mind, a Chinese inventor who came over in the 1860s to see if he could sell the railroads on his latest invention. Something that would allow them to transmit Western Union telegrams over long stretches of land strung along poles that would run parallel to the tracks."

Zhen didn't interrupt or comment, so Caitlin continued as she snipped away at the dried petals and stems from which the color had bled out.

"See, the railroads and Western Union saw what they wanted to do with Morse's invention, but they couldn't figure out how to maintain the integrity of the signal over long distances at a time. All the experiments kept failing no matter what they tried."

"Wire," Li Zhen said suddenly.

"Sir?"

"It was wire, Ranger. The railroads and telegraph people couldn't figure out how to push the signals reliably along because the wire they were using was too thick."

Caitlin brushed the planting free of the dead flower parts her pruning had freed. "That Chinese inventor had developed a thinner wire that was actually stronger and more resistant to the elements than all the brands that had failed. That's what he was trying to sell to the railroads. I believe that would have been your great-grandfather, Tsuyoshi Zhen."

Zhen nodded, just once.

"And the man he tried to sell his invention to, that would have been John Morehouse of the Southern Pacific, wouldn't it, sir?"

Caitlin could see Zhen's polished veneer starting to crack. She imagined she heard the sound of plaster breaking away from its cast.

"My great-grandfather brought his life's work to John Morehouse in good faith, and the railroad stole it for their own use, giving him no credit or money. There was nothing he could do. He was left penniless," Zhen continued distantly, looking straight up into the sun without so much as squinting. "Not even the money he needed to get back home. He had placed all his faith in his invention and the integrity of the Americans, and for all his efforts and intentions he ended up working hard labor side by side with men for whom a dollar a day in wages was a dream come true. Ironic, isn't it, Ranger?" Zhen asked her, after a pause that felt longer than it really was.

Caitlin looked up from the fresh area through which she was working the snips. "What, sir?"

"That so much today is spoken about theft of your intellectual property by my country. How we are waiting at every turn with an ear to every door and cup to every wall, listening in order to appropriate all your greatest technological and intellectual property secrets for our own use. When in fact it was your country who launched a big part of its progress toward the twentieth century by stealing from *us*."

"A favor your country has repaid numerous times."

Snip.

"You try my good graces, Ranger. Perhaps I should've contacted the State Department when I first learned you had returned."

"What stopped you?"

Snip.

"Our shared history, I suppose. But there is one more thing as well."

Zhen rose and led Caitlin along the winding path, past elegant rock gardens and majestic waterfalls that pushed water downward to be recirculated in a constant loop. He stopped before a magnificent collection of multicolored flowers that included a selection of the pink ones she recognized all too well. He extended his hand outward and Caitlin returned the pruning snips to him.

"You asked me about our garden's camellias in our last meeting, Ranger," he said, working like a surgeon around a lush flower. "I'm going to provide you a sampling to see if these flowers match the petals found in the pockets of those gunmen."

"Thank you, sir."

"Don't bother thanking me, Ranger. I do this because I know it will yield nothing but further embarrassment for you. Consider it a parting gift to add to your disgrace."

With that, Zhen eased the collection of petals, leaves, and stem parts to Caitlin who held open a plastic evidence pouch in which to hold them. "This makes me think of something I spotted when I was pruning those flowers."

"What's that?"

"A perfect bud just starting to flower. Right there among all that decay, there it was."

"I don't believe I see your point," Zhen told her.

Caitlin sealed the evidence pouch, staring at him again. "That there's plenty of strength below the surface we can't always see."

"Something you'd be wise to remember, Ranger."

"Something both of us would, sir," she told him.

68

"Nice place to meet, Colonel," Jones said to Guillermo Paz inside the Alamo, the main building better known as the chapel that had been elegantly reconstructed based upon drawings, descriptions, and stories drawn from firsthand accounts. "I imagine you feel right at home here."

Guillermo Paz continued to stroll about the angular setting, full of alcoves and corners jutting out here and there. One of them, he knew, was where the only survivors of the battle were found in hiding, women and children Santa Ana freed to forever hold the tale in their minds. Among these was Candelaria Villanueva, who claimed to the day of her death at the age of a hundred and twelve that she had served Jim Bowie until he was shot dead on the very cot on which she'd nursed him. Paz pondered what it was like to live that long but quickly dismissed the thought since he didn't really believe anyone ever died; at least their spirits didn't.

"I find myself wondering which side I'd rather have fought for," he heard himself saying.

"The winners," Jones said. "Haven't I taught you anything?"

"The Texans were massacred, yes, but their deaths sewed the seeds for Santa Anna's eventual demise and disgrace. So maybe the distinction is not as simple as it seems."

"Nothing's simple with you, Colonel. That's why you need to get back to work. And I've got a nasty job for you and those cut-throats you've put together. Keep them raping and pillaging the locals for a time."

"All my men go to church, Jones," Paz said flatly. "If they aren't capable of making a change in their lives, they aren't right for my employ or my company." With that, he started to gaze about the chapel again. "The only actual structure still standing from those times is the Long Barracks out back. Everything else is a re-creation, a carbon copy, a facsimile."

"Another point I must be missing here, Colonel."

"Look in the mirror and you'll see what I'm getting at."

"You need to get moving, Colonel," Jones said impatiently. "Looks like this assignment came up just in time."

"I'm not taking it."

"You don't even know what it is."

"Something more pressing has arisen."

Jones stopped and looked up to meet Paz's black eyes, his own only reaching up to the big man's chin. "You need to hear me out on this."

"I'm busy."

"It involves Caitlin Strong, Colonel, and we don't have a lot of time."

Part Seven

The operations of the companies will be directed, more than has heretofore been the case, to the suppression of lawlessness and crime. . . . [Officers and privates] are required and expected to use unremitting diligence in hunting up and arresting all violators of the law and fugitives from justice wherever they may be or from whatever quarter they may come.

—General Order 15

69

Caitlin had stopped at Doc Whatley's office to drop off the evidence pouch containing the camellia flower parts from Yuyuan's gardens, when he closed and locked his office door behind them.

"What's wrong, Doc?"

"Remember I told you about those dead homeless men found without a mark on them?"

"I do."

"Their bodies are gone."

"Come again?"

"You heard me. I had them stored in freezers under John Doe IDs. This morning they were gone. So unless we got ourselves a zombie problem on our hands, I'm thinking of putting in my retirement papers."

"You don't figure county officials were behind this?"

"Not without me signing off on the forms. And there's something else. Remember I told you about them being found with no clear indication of the cause of death?"

"Sure."

"I may have a clearer indication now, thanks to the death of that Chinese diplomat in the airport terminal."

"He was a general in the Chinese army, I believe, Doc."

"Well, according to the Chinese government, he's a diplomat—at least his body is supposed to be treated as such. And we're not having this conversation, Ranger. If anybody asks, *anybody*, it never happened."

"It's not like you to be so mysterious, Doc."

"We were allowed to store the body while the diplomatic issues were worked out. Weren't allowed to touch it, at least with a scalpel, though—that was the condition."

"You follow it?"

"Not exactly. I guess a little of you has rubbed off on me, Ranger. Anyway, what I found makes no sense at all. That's what you need to hear about."

70

NEW YORK CITY

"You stay back, you hear me?" Cort Wesley said to Dylan while the crowd from inside the Flatiron Building spilled out onto the pedestrian plaza on the Broadway side of the building in response to the fire alarm he'd pulled.

"Dad," the boy started to protest but Cort Wesley cut him off.

"Just do it, son." Cort Wesley continued to study the emerging crowd, locking his gaze on the sharply dressed man he'd recognized from the nonexistent twenty-third floor, and readying the pistol he'd taken off one of the big guys upstairs. "I seen all I want to see of you in a hospital bed."

Cort Wesley slithered through the crowd, making himself thin and light. It wasn't anything he'd ever been taught and he couldn't say exactly how he did it.

That crowd proved even more of a gift when he realized the man with the orange-toned flawless skin had been separated from the two thugs with whom he'd emerged from inside the unseen section of the offices upstairs. Cort Wesley spotted them gazing deliberately about, then refocused his gaze on his target, his mind charting a course his body followed as if on autopilot.

Before he knew it, he was close enough to the man to smell his fancy aftershave mixed uneasily with too much dry-cleaning solvent used to launder his suit. Pistol pressed hard into the man's ribs.

"Straight ahead, hoss, and don't stop for anything unless I say so."

71

SAN ANTONIO, TEXAS

Doc Whatley locked the door to his analysis lab too, after ushering Caitlin inside.

"Ever seen a cell phone like this before?" he asked her, his breathing coming fast and his gaze never far from the locked door.

Caitlin gazed at the cell phone through the plastic evidence pouch. "It's General Chang's. I recognize it from the airport but I've never seen one like it before."

"That's because it's from China. Not even available here. But it's not the one belonging to the victim at the airport, no, and that's what I can't make any sense of at all."

He moved toward a locked drawer and fumbled for the right key on his ring that still contained a good dozen of them. It took him several tries to get the drawer open and remove a trio of evidence pouches that contained cell phones identical to the one he'd just shown Caitlin. Whatley laid all four out in a neat row on the counter and backed off wordlessly, as if what Caitlin was about to see spoke for itself.

"Where'd these come from exactly?"

"Those four homeless men whose bodies flat out disappeared into thin air."

"All died of unexplained causes, you said."

"Just like the victim at the airport, near as I can tell."

"General Chang grabbed for his chest just before he keeled over in the terminal. Based on that and other signs, paramedics were pretty sure it was a heart attack."

"Same for the four homeless men."

"Whose bodies are now missing."

"And what the hell were they doing with those cell phones, Ranger?"

The more Caitlin ran it through her mind, the less sense it seemed to make.

How could the deaths of four homeless men possibly be connected to the death of a high-ranking Chinese general? More to the point, what were those homeless men doing with cell phones at all, much less of a Chinese variety not commercially available in the United States?

Caitlin had just started down the stairs to exit the building when she saw Young Roger stepping around the stairwell straight for her.

"We need to talk, Ranger," he said, file folder tucked tight under his arm.

72

NEW YORK CITY

"You have any idea of the world of hurt you're going to be in?" the man asked, coming awake bound to a desk chair in a Chelsea Hotel room a few blocks away from the Flatiron Building.

"That's good, Mr. Mareno," Cort Wesley said, tossing the man's wallet aside.

Cort Wesley had already drawn the blinds and left only a single lamp on, angled so it caught Mareno's face, making the bronze tone look as if it could be peeled off like a Band-Aid. He'd checked into the room in the newly renovated, formerly fleabag hotel before heading over to the Flatiron Building, the semblance of his plan having already taken shape. They called such places "boutique" these days, but to Cort Wesley that was just another world for "old," right down to the radiator fed by old-fashioned steam pipes and the network of fire escapes attached to the building's exterior with rust already peeling through their fresh black paint.

"You make that up yourself or did someone write it for you?" Cort Wesley continued.

"That boy you brought upstairs to my office, are you fucking him or something?"

"You're nothing more than a pimp, hoss, and no fancy office on a floor that doesn't exist can change that." Cort Wesley looked down at the man tied to the chair, his hands laced behind him. "Know how you can really tell when a man is scared shitless? When he tries to talk tough like you are."

"You think I'm scared?" Mareno smirked.

"You're not?"

Mareno smirked again. His skin looked powdery dry, more like a mask stretched over his skin. "I'm too busy picturing what's going to happen to you down the road. And not too far down it either."

"Really? Then maybe you should look down, not too far toward your crotch."

Mareno did and noticed the substantial bulge there that looked like a folded-up sweater had been stuffed down his pants. "What the fuck?"

"Believe I detect a note of fear in your voice, hoss." Cort Wesley sat down on the edge of the bed and faced the man. "I know you've heard about all those fancy tortures we got—water boarding, electrocution, and the like. But when you're in the field you learn to be a bit more creative."

Cort Wesley watched Mareno swallow hard.

"Know what's down there?"

The man just looked at him.

"Dry ice mixed with salt to slow down the chilling process. I'm guessing your privates are starting to feel a bit cold at the moment, aren't they?"

The man's eyes were blinking rapidly.

"Here's what happens from this point, hoss. You don't talk to me, tell me what I want to know, we just sit here and watch your privates freeze up solid. Know how long you can last before your prick and balls are done for good, no different than a snowman's nose?"

Mareno didn't respond.

"Me neither," Cort Wesley told him. "But based on what I've seen of frostbite, I'm guessing maybe twenty minutes. So you and I, we're gonna do some talking, or I'm gonna stick a sock in your mouth, walk out the door, and lock it behind me. By the time they find you, your prick'll be a Popsicle that'll break off as soon as they stand you up." He stood up towering over Mareno, giving his last statement more time to sink in. "So, you wanna start or you want me to?"

73

SAN ANTONIO, TEXAS

"You ever hear of the Deep Web, Ranger?" Young Roger asked, inside Doc Whatley's office after they'd appropriated it for their meeting.

Whatley had been in the midst of putting a PowerPoint presentation together and had forgotten to turn off the pull-down screen on which it was projected. The result was to light both Caitlin's and Young Roger's faces in the spill off the gleaming white background.

"I believe it came up during one of my trips to Quantico, but not much stuck," Caitlin told him. "Another version of the Internet, something like that, as I recall."

"Kind of," Young Roger said, tilting his head from side to side. "And that explains why you couldn't find that porn site when you plugged in the URL. You need a special browser called a Tor browser to access the Deep Web."

He was only twenty-nine but looked even younger. Though a Ranger himself, the title was mostly honorary, provided in recognition of the technological expertise he brought to the table that had helped the Rangers solve a number of Internet-based crimes ranging from identity theft to credit card fraud to the busting of a major pedophile and kiddie porn ring. He worked out of all six Ranger Company offices on a rotating basis. Young Roger wore his hair too long and was never happier than when playing guitar for his band the Rats, whose independent record label had just released their first CD. Their alternative brand of music wasn't the kind she preferred, but Dylan told her it was pretty good.

"In a nutshell," Young Roger continued, "the Deep Web was actually invented by our own government to create a clear and unobstructed path by which they could communicate secretly with their own people in the field without worrying about electronic eavesdropping. But it didn't take long before it became a haven for drug traffickers, financial looters, a whole lot of new-age criminals wielding an Internet currency called Bitcoin and—"

"Don't tell me, pornographers."

"Kiddie porn included. The Deep Web provides a secure, untraceable means by which the freaks can conduct their business without fear of recrimination or reprisal. Ranger, we're talking about a second wholly independent Internet beneath, or alongside, the real Internet with its content never showing up on Google and its URL addresses bounced around so much as to be utterly untraceable."

"So that link to the porn video I sent you . . ."

". . . took me into the Deep Web. Actually, it took me nowhere at first, which made me figure the site had simply been taken down. Then I played around a little more and realized it was a matter of the location being disguised by the data being run through an intricate system of relays. Each time it switches, another layer of encryption gets stripped away until, by the time the site finally lands, only someone intricately familiar with negotiating the Deep Web can find it."

"So you found the video, have I got that right?"

"Along with plenty more that could provide the link to others and, eventually, the originating point of the posting. Then we'll know exactly who was behind the software. I can tell you one thing for sure already: this wasn't the only porn video that followed the same general route, not by a long shot. Whoever posted it on the Deep Web has done it before and that's sure to help me nail them."

"Any connection to those murdered Chinese girls, Roger?"

"I've only managed to track the relay route so far, but that's next on my list to follow up. I did look into this Li Zhen like you asked, though. His file's sealed on all relevant databases for national security reasons. Dead end."

"I figured," Caitlin told him, hardly surprised given Zhen's connection to Homeland Security. "Thanks for trying, anyway."

"Hold on, Ranger. Since when do I let dead ends stop me?" Young Roger asked her. "Any traditional files on Zhen may be sealed but, like you figured, Interpol's were a whole different matter. Turns out they had plenty on your friend Li Zhen, thanks to his links to Chinese pornography. Apparently, he was a pioneer of expanding his horizons into the field of Internet porn years back."

"So why didn't Interpol arrest him?"

"They could never make anything stick, especially the more serious Web-based material. But I did learn Zhen's wife died twenty-eight years ago. Interpol's file includes mention of two daughters too, one born in 1989 and the other in 1976; on July Fourth, if you can believe, the day of the Bicentennial. The older one committed suicide at the age of seventeen in 1993. But here's the strange thing. The younger one seems to have disappeared, fell off the face of the damn planet, right around the time Yuyuan got started. I believe her name was—"

"Kai," Caitlin completed before he had a chance to.

*   *   *

Caitlin was so distracted by fitting the pieces of what Young Roger had told her into the puzzle she was assembling, that she almost got hit by a car walking across the parking lot on the University of Texas Health Science Center campus. She skirted another car screeching into reverse and climbed into her SUV, which she'd parked in a shady spot in the corner.

She'd just gotten the key into the ignition when movement flashed in the rearview mirror, and a hand grasped her shoulder from the backseat.

74

NEW YORK CITY

"You want to order up some room service?" Cort Wesley asked the man tied to the chair. "Maybe check out the offerings on Pay-Per-View? Gotta figure out some way to pass the time if you're gonna keep giving me the silent treatment."

Mareno looked down at his groin again. He held his eyes closed for a long moment, then opened them slowly with all trace of bravado, of resistance, missing now.

"You tell me what I want to know and our business is done, hoss. I pull that dry ice out of your undies and I'm gone from your life."

"And I'm supposed to believe that?"

Cort Wesley couldn't help but smile. "Oh, I get it. You think I'm gonna punch your ticket because I'm scared you'll track me down otherwise." He shook his head. "I'm not that easy to scare and if anyone comes after me as a result of this, it's you who'll pay the price."

"What kind of accent is that? You sound like a cowboy."

"Texas. And right now this cowboy is pissed off that your traveling whorehouse almost got my son killed."

"Son?" the man asked, eyes flashing as if the pieces were finally falling together for him.

Cort Wesley dragged an armchair over from the corner and sat down angled close to his hostage. "So you wanna keep up the chit-chat while your balls freeze, or you wanna get down to business?"

"You have no idea who you're messing with here, what we'll do to you."

"Right now, it's just you." Cort Wesley hesitated to let his point sink. "You starting to feel a bit of chill down there where the sun don't shine yet?"

The man looked down, his gaze telling Cort Wesley he was.

"Your balls are running out of time, hoss. So let's make this quick. Where'd the Chinese girl come from?"

"I don't know who you're talking about."

"Goes by the name of Kai. Pretty enough to turn my son's head spinning. You remember my boy, don't you? He's the one someone involved with you beat to within an inch of his life. You wanna tell me what the girl had to do with that, where she fits into all this?"

Mareno swallowed hard, looked down below his waist again.

"Tick, tick, tick," Cort Wesley said. "I figure you got maybe ten minutes before the pain kicks in, fifteen before you're gonna be a soprano. You don't impress me as a man cut out for this kind of shit. Just talk to me so you can go back to pushing your pencils, running your numbers, and fucking up a lot of innocent kids' lives."

"Kai was sent to Providence," the man said abruptly, his voice turning shrill. "But ten days ago she dropped off the map."

"Ten days," Cort Wesley repeated, recalling mention by Caitlin, of something else that had happened around that time, but he couldn't remember exactly what.

"We lost contact with her," the man tied to the chair was saying. "She must have figured out how to disable her tracker."

"Tracker?"

"GPS chip we install to keep tabs on the merchandise."

"Where?"

"Underneath the skin on her forearm. We've been looking for her ever since."

"She ended up back in Providence," Cort Wesley told him. "But you know that already, since your men kicked the shit out of my kid."

"Uh-uh, cowboy, not us. Whoever found Kai, whoever hurt your kid, must've dug up their leads some other way. We didn't even know there was a problem until we got a call that she hadn't shown up on set."

"What set?"

"Another porn video."

"Being shot where exactly?"

"What's the difference?"

Cort Wesley pulled his chair closer to Mareno again. "I walk out of here, hoss, you won't need one of your girls to give you a blow job anymore—you'll be able to do it all by yourself 'long as your freezer's working. Now answer my question: where was this video supposed to be shot?"

Mareno spoke through a smirk that had spread across his expression. "Your own backyard, cowboy: Texas."

75

NEW YORK CITY

Dylan waited in the lobby, on lookout like his father had told him. He'd bought a magazine at the newsstand, but wasn't really paying any attention to it, his mind upstairs with his father and the man whose tan colored his face orange.

He had found a chair with a view of most of the lobby and the street beyond the hotel entrance and watched the people come and go. Around him workmen toiled, continuing the updates on the lobby that included the fresh carpeting and new furniture in the section in which he was seated. He was digging the heels of his boots into the brushlike surface of the knap when a beautiful Chinese woman came through the door.

It looked like Kai, a lot like Kai, enough to set Dylan's heart fluttering the same way it had the first time he'd laid eyes on her. Just a trick of his imagination conspiring with his vision and the lobby's dull, atmospheric lighting, he decided.

The more the boy looked, though, the more the woman really did look like Kai. And then she was heading his way, Dylan's breath starting to bottleneck in his throat with the certainty that this was no trick of his imagination or vision at all.

"We need to go!" she said, voice hushed, as soon as she reached him. "Hurry!"

"Huh?" was all Dylan could manage, leaving him feeling lame and stupid.

"They're coming. I saw them on the street. There's no time."

"Coming for . . ."

"You and your father. Hurry, please."

Dylan felt himself rise. "I've got to warn him," he said, the only words he could muster, prepaid cell phone in hand in the next instant, but Cort Wesley's phone went straight to voice mail.

"Now, please."

Dylan's eyes fixed on the alcove housing the elevators. "Just stay here. I'll be right back."

Kai grabbed him by the arm before he could move, holding him in place. Her grip was deceptively strong and she'd grasped his arm at the elbow, pressing in a way that he began to feel it go numb. Then her eyes bulged, Dylan catching four men in sports jackets worn over dress shirts without ties making their way through the lobby.

"Kiss me!" Kai said, in more of an order than a request.

"Huh?"

"Do it!"

And when he couldn't, she did it for him, leaning in and kissing him hard on the lips. Kai eased him into a slight spin that obscured both their faces from view, backing off only when the four men disappeared into the elevator alcove.

"I know people who will help us," Kai said, her voice steady but hushed. "We must leave."

Dylan couldn't take his gaze off the elevator bank. "I need to help my dad."

"You need to come with me," Kai told him.

And then Dylan saw the gun in her hand.

76

SAN ANTONIO, TEXAS

Caitlin had her SIG out, already turning when she saw none other than Jones struggling to lean forward. The hand that had found her shoulder was trembling now, the rest of him a quivery mess with blood soaking through his shirt and jacket from clearly more than a single wound.

"Jesus Christ!"

"Only surprise," he managed through dry lips, his voice cracking, "being it wasn't you who did it."

"Who did?"

He slumped back in the SUV's backseat, everything about him looking smaller, all the intimidation and bravado that defined him leaking out with the blood. "I fucked up, Ranger, I fucked up bad."

Caitlin gunned the engine. "I'm getting you to a hospital. . . ."

"No," he wheezed louder, trying to reach out for her again, but failing. "No hospitals, unless you want to get me killed for sure."

"While that's tempting, Jones, I know a doctor who owes the Rangers a favor for helping to keep him out of jail. Guy's name is de la Cruz. Rangers busted him a few years back," Caitlin continued, already reversing fast and then jamming the SUV into gear, "for performing unsanctioned plastic surgery procedures. I saw pictures of some of the people who came in for facelifts and came out looking like they were wearing Halloween masks."

Jones tried to smile and failed. "Is that the best you can do?"

"Don't worry, it's not like you need to have your nose fixed," she said, going for her phone.

Caitlin ended the call and dropped her phone in the cup holder. "He's waiting for us," she said, tearing down the road now for de la Cruz's house in East San Antonio. "What the hell happened, Jones?"

"What happened was you were *right*. Dead-on, one hundred percent bull's-eye, your aim true as goddamn ever."

"Make sense, Jones."

"You're right about me too, Ranger. I like to believe my shit don't stink, but that doesn't mean I need to carry somebody else's load."

Caitlin screeched into a turn, nearly colliding with one car and then another, and just managing to right the SUV and speed on. The former doctor, Juan de la Cruz, was fifteen minutes away in a part of the city still patrolled by gangbangers. Any more than fifteen and Jones looked like he might bleed out.

"You're babbling, Jones. Keep quiet until we get there."

"This isn't babble, Ranger, it's the truth. Maybe the first time you ever heard me tell it. I had things wrong."

"You're talking about Li Zhen, this whole deal for his company to build the fifth generation wireless network," Caitlin said, stopping short of telling Jones what Young Roger had just told her about Zhen's background.

"You don't think we did it out of goodwill to better international relations, did you?"

"Not even for a minute. But who's *we*, Jones?" Caitlin asked, checking his condition in the rearview mirror.

"Usual suspects. Kind of people who make me look noble and honorable. I guess it's the price of doing business in the world we live in."

Caitlin flew through a yellow light and then risked a red, cars spinning out all around her. "About what?"

"Oh, everything maybe, but especially Yuyuan. This whole thing is bullshit. The deal isn't about business, it's about Li Zhen. I should have seen it, but missed all the signs."

"Signs of what?" Caitlin asked him.

No response.

She took her eyes off the road to twist round and jostle him gently in the backseat. His closing eyes snapped open again, full of life for the moment.

"Signs of *what?*"

"Li Zhen played us," he said, picking up his last thought, as if Caitlin had said nothing at all. "Dangled something we couldn't hope to resist before us and we jumped on it like a dog in heat."

"You're not gonna die until I kill you, Jones, and I swear I'll do that unless you say something I can understand."

"Elections, Ranger. Is that plain enough for you?"

"What about them?"

"Only that thanks to Yuyuan's fifth generation network, we'd be able to fix any one of them we wanted."

77

NEW YORK CITY

"Now I'm gonna ask you this one more time," Cort Wesley continued, "and if you don't answer me, I'm gonna get up and walk out of here, and leave you to figure out how to piss for the rest of your life."

"Kai came from China," Mareno told him, sweat starting to bead up on his powdery, bronze features, "the syndicate there."

"Run by who?"

"The Triad," the man said, glancing downward again. "Chinese organized crime."

"I know who they are."

"Can you loosen my belt?"

"Not until you tell me more about Kai."

"There's nothing more to tell."

Cort Wesley slid his chair closer until he was almost in the man's face. "I'm not going to ask you again, hoss," he continued, his voice gone smooth and flat.

Mareno said nothing, his lips quivering again behind whatever he was thinking. Paying him no further heed, Cort Wesley rose stiffly and walked toward the door in a measured step, never looking back.

"The Triad turns them into sex slaves as young girls," he heard the man say, as his hand hit the doorknob. "I'm talking nine or ten years old. They don't want them any older, feel it takes that long to train them properly."

"Like dogs, you mean. Human fucking trafficking," Cort Wesley said, feeling the contents of his stomach curdle at what he was hearing. "Keep talking."

"What else can I tell you?"

"Everything you know about Kai. More than you've said already."

"The Triad doesn't kidnap or steal—they don't have to in China when boys are all anybody wants to raise. They barter. You want something from them, they take something from you. A deal is a deal."

"And you're just an honest broker, that it, hoss?"

"I'm a consolidator. We've got twenty more offices like mine across the country, well over a hundred across the world. The Triad's only one of our suppliers. These girls come from everywhere, even right here in the U.S. of A. It's big business. Huge."

"I'm going to bring it down," Cort Wesley said, hands clenched into fists at his sides, his spine coiled in tension and neck held so rigid that his head was beginning to throb.

The man's gaze turned pleading, desperation starting to set in. "I'm starting to feel it now. Come on, help me out. For fuck's sake, get this shit out of me!"

"Kai ran away for a reason. She came back to Providence for a reason. Nothing happens without a plan. I want to know what all this is about. I want to know what she's up to and why my son almost got killed for it."

"Look, I told you all that I know. You want any more, there's someone else you need to track down—the person who told us we could find Kai in Providence."

"Tell me more, hoss."

"All I've got is a phone number, a man who took a personal interest in finding her. I don't know his name. The number he gave me doesn't even exist anymore."

"You remember it?"

"Just the area code: eight-three-oh. Ring any bells?"

Cort Wesley felt the iron bands through his neck and shoulders tighten even more. "It's Texas. New Braunfels."

Cort Wesley could tell from the desperate, pleading gaze stretched across Mareno's taut skin that the man had told him everything helpful he knew. He wanted to get back to Dylan, back to Texas and the hell out of New York where just walking down the street left you covered in a film of grime clinging to air choked by car exhaust.

"Hey," Mareno called when he turned the knob and pulled the door open. "Hey! You forgetting something here?"

"It's just a couple bags of frozen peas, hoss," Cort Wesley told him, moving into the hallway. "Minute or so in the microwave and they'll be good to go."

He'd started to close the door when the gunfire began.

78

Caitlin waited in the screen porch fronting Juan de la Cruz's home in East San Antonio while the former doctor worked on Jones in a back bedroom. She sat in a ratty chair, the fabric upholstery holding a musty smell from the moisture reaching it through the screen. It felt vaguely damp to her, but she'd chosen it for the vantage point it provided of the street and surrounding neighborhood. Twice she'd taken out her cell phone to call Captain Tepper to request backup, but had returned the phone to her pocket on both occasions.

What, after all, was she supposed to tell him? Beyond that the possibility existed that Homeland was "watching" her phone, anticipating that Jones might have reached out to her after the attempt on his life failed.

The third time Caitlin took out her phone, she dialed Cort Wesley's number but it went straight to voice mail. He was on his way to the Flatiron Building when they'd talked earlier, but since then nothing, adding to Caitlin's discomfort and the anxiety that felt like fingernails scratching at her skin since Jones had finished describing the connection between Yuyuan and Homeland from the backseat of her SUV.

"Elections, Ranger. Is that plain enough for you?"

"What about them?"

"Only that thanks to Yuyuan's fifth generation network, we'd be able to fix any one of them we wanted."

Jones had sucked in a breath and let it out in a long wet wheeze that sounded like the air was coming through a dozen different holes. "Comes down to homeland security, Ranger."

"Doesn't it always?"

"This was different. Look around you. Americans are capable of doing more damage to this country than any foreign power could ever do."

"We've been through this before, lots of time."

"Just the preliminary rounds, Ranger. Forget about homegrown terrorists and right-wing fringe groups plotting insurrection and civil war. They're inconveniences; uncomfortable and unsettling, but inconveniences all the same and nothing more."

"As opposed to what?"

Jones was trying to recapture his breath again. "Politics, Ranger."

"Losing blood makes you even more cryptic than usual, Jones."

"Politics in general, and elections in specific, are the biggest threat out there. Anybody can run for office and pretty much anybody does these days, no matter how fucked-up in the head they might be."

"Comes with the country, Jones."

"Really? You can line up all the terrorists hiding in our midst and all the crazy preachers building an army on the lunatic fringe and they wouldn't even compare to the damage the wrong elected officials can cause."

"Wrong," Caitlin repeated.

"You just nailed the watch word. You can't solve everything with a gun," he said finally. "Sometimes you need a different weapon. It's not so much making sure the right people get elected as making sure the *wrong* people don't. We're not trying to stack the deck here, Ranger, just make sure the country gets dealt a fair hand."

"And that's supposed to make me feel better?" she'd asked him.

And now Jones was fighting for his life because he'd bucked the system he helped create. In ironic counterpoint, Caitlin, the very person who trusted him the least, had become the only person he could trust at all.

So she remained vigilant and ready, her eyes sweeping the street for anything out of place: person lingering too long by a window, a car driving by more than once, a delivery truck crawling along as if in search of an address. Then a screen door with a bad spring slammed behind her and Caitlin spun in her chair to find the former physician Juan de la Cruz standing at her side. His bloodshot eyes regarded her and he reeked of both the alcohol he'd been drinking and the clinical variety soaking through his skin.

"You can see him now."

79

NEW YORK CITY

Cort Wesley spun back into the hotel room, fortunate the door had not closed all the way.

"I warned you, you dumb hick!" Mareno blared.

The pistol he'd taken off one of the man's guards palmed now, Cort Wesley kicked over the chair to which Mareno was still bound.

"Hey!" Mareno cried out, after his head smacked the carpet.

The door burst inward in the next instant ahead of a hail of submachine-gun fire. The bullets seemed to hit everything at once: walls, windows, drapes, furniture. Two figures surged into the room, ready to continue the spray when Cort Wesley lurched out from behind the door. Neither man had a chance, requiring only a pair of bullets each. One's finger clamped reflexively on the trigger as he fell, stitching a jagged design of bullets across the ceiling and far wall in a neat arc. He fell atop Mareno, Cort Wesley leaping over both of them when the next three men charged into the room abreast of one another.

Cort Wesley reached the window of the old hotel that opened onto a fire escape, its glass fractured by the initial barrage of bullets, and crashed through it as a fresh trio of fire streams traced his path. Cort Wesley hit the ledge hard, already rolling toward the ladder extending downward. He dropped down it to the next platform, pistol steadied in both hands when the torso of one man emerged from the window above followed by a second.

Cort Wesley got off four shots in rapid succession, but the jerking of his initial target's body conspired to spare the second man his bullets. The result was a fresh spray of automatic fire unleashed his way before he could get off any further rounds. The echoing twang of the steel jacketed rounds sparking off the iron rails turned his ears to mush, and Cort Wesley fought against the urge to return fire blindly. He had only the single magazine of fifteen for the nine-millimeter Glock, plus the one in the chamber. He hadn't been keeping a mental tally of shots fired, figuring he'd used four inside the room and another four out here so far, leaving him eight bullets.

Eight bullets for the two remaining gunmen. Plenty normally, but he had little maneuverability in such narrow confines, complicated further by his adversaries' holding the high ground. When the next spray of automatic fire burned closer to him, he had no choice but to fire three shots upward. That held the remaining gunmen at bay long enough for him to slide down the handholds of the ladder to the next level down. Just starting another drop when one of them loomed overhead, submachine-gun barrel angled downward straight for him.

Cort Wesley released one hand and fired upward with the other. He took the man in the throat with the first bullet and under the chin with the second, but not before the barrage clanged close enough to his hand grasping the rail to strip it free and send him plummeting. He hit the next platform hard, his momentum carrying him over the edge still three stories up. Dangling with one hand holding on and a second clinging fast to his weapon. And then the fire was spitting at him from two directions at once, both above and below, clinking off steel and heating up the air around him.

Cort Wesley saw what he had to do, where his only chance at survival lay, even as the impossibility of the maneuver struck him. Not that it mattered, since he was already committed to the action in both mind and body. He managed to unlatch the hook on the ladder, letting its rungs unfold and stretch straight for the sidewalk. His firing angle above cleared and he found his trigger halfway into the plunge. Dimly aware of the fourth gunman pitching up and over a platform rail, falling straight past him and beating him to the concrete.

His ladder stopped ten feet from the sidewalk. Cort Wesley's Glock was already steadied by then, firing his final bullet downward in the same moment he felt the clunk of the ladder's sudden end jolt him to a stop. It was an improbable shot, if not an impossible one, the angle going against physics, especially with fire pinging and clanging all around him, the heat of the bullets so intense it was impossible to say whether he'd been hit or not.

Click.

The Glock's slide locked the very moment the gunfire ended below, fading echoes of it all that remained. A glance showed him the final gunman sprawled on the sidewalk with blood running out from beneath him.

Cort Wesley dropped down to the sidewalk himself to the sounds of brakes squealing and car horns blaring ahead of the mind-numbing grinds of metal squashing against metal. He thought he heard sirens too, picking up his pace as he looped around the block back to the hotel lobby to find Dylan.

He felt a warm sense of relief, when he reached the lobby to find chaos, but no bodies spilled on the fresh carpeting. Then Cort Wesley's insides knotted up again when a fresh reality dawned on him:

Dylan was gone.

80

"You saved my life, Ranger."

"Glad to hear that, Jones," Caitlin told him. "Now make it worth my while. Let's start with who did this to you."

Jones was lying on an exam table in de la Cruz's back bedroom, propped up on a bunch of pillows matted with blood. An open window pushed the soft breeze against the drawn blinds that robbed the room of light save for an overly bright fixture burning overhead. He flashed the annoying smirk Caitlin had come to know so well, a gesture that seemed ill suited to his current condition.

"What's the difference?"

"You intend to let them get away with it?"

"My intentions are meaningless. The shooters are already off the map. I took them down myself. Guess nobody told them I didn't always ride a desk."

"Where did this happen exactly, Jones? No report was called in."

The smirk flashed again. "I'm sure it was. Then it got buried."

"By whose shovel?"

Jones shook his head. "Forget it, Ranger."

"You of all people should know that's not in my nature."

"Then make it your nature. Trust me, you'll never get the people behind the shooters. They're untouchable."

"Then let's move on to what they're trying to do, how you ended up on their enemies list."

"Simply stated, we've lost control of the government. Elected officials can no longer be trusted to do the right and obvious thing, because they don't belong there in the first place."

"It's called democracy, Jones."

"Not when you've got a zillion gerrymandered districts and radical fringe elements on both sides that seem determined to bring the government down. They're growing in power, not declining." He tried to sit up farther, grimaced, then lay back down slowly. "Blame hatred if you want, blame the Internet, blame natural political cycles—I don't care. What I care about is the fact that if we can't trust these bozos to do things right in office, then we need to find a way to keep them from ever getting there."

"What's this have to do with elections, with Li Zhen and Yuyuan?"

"Only everything, Ranger, thanks to that fifth generation network. Guess they didn't cover the future in your last professional development visit to Quantico," Jones added, managing a smirk.

"I see you're feeling better."

"You always bring out the best in me."

"Get back to what they didn't cover at Quantico."

"Simply the fact that within a very few years time election results will be transmitted wirelessly over the Internet, in plenty of cases by the voting machines themselves once they turn digital, which Homeland has already allocated the funds for."

"Uh-oh . . ."

"I think you see the point, Ranger."

"Homeland made sure the contract was awarded to Yuyuan," Caitlin concluded, "because Li Zhen's going to help you rig elections."

"Rig is a strong word."

"What would you call it?"

"Electronic influence to make sure elected office is held as much as possible by those who have an IQ higher than eighty and actually care about doing the country's business."

"Very patriotic of you."

"I wasn't alone," Jones told her. "This operation had support all the way to the top."

"How high is that exactly?"

"You know," Jones told her, "I really don't know myself."

Caitlin moved closer to him, cataloging his wounds based on the gauze wrappings that were leaking blood in places. Looked like he'd been shot three times, although sometimes the way bullets jumped about inside a person made it difficult to be sure. She was still struggling to get used to the harsh scents of rubbing alcohol and clinical disinfectant that permeated de la Cruz's illegal operating room.

"What made you sour on the plan?" she asked Jones.

"You, Ranger, after you made your usual mess of things. Only this time you exposed Li Zhen as someone we definitely needed to get out of business with in my mind. I can live with his secrets, even his lies, but he's hiding something bigger. The whole time we thought we were playing him, I think he was playing us."

"Of course he was playing you. Giving Yuyuan control of the five G network means opening the door to pretty much any secret or new technology the Chinese want to steal."

Jones looked unmoved. He shifted slightly, still enough to make him wince in pain and steady himself with a few long breaths.

"We'd already figured that into the equation, considered it a zero-sum game."

"A sacrifice you were willing to make, in other words."

"That's right."

"No, Jones, it's very far from right, the polar opposite. You people are willing to go so far to accomplish what you want that you just can't turn back anymore. The road's collapsed behind you because you blew it up."

But Jones had something else on his mind. "I ordered Zhen to back off and he still tried to have you and Masters killed. Then I asked General Chang to intervene on our behalf by sending Zhen back home and he ended up dead."

"You think Li Zhen killed him?" Caitlin asked, not giving away any of her or Doc Whatley's own conclusions.

"It doesn't seem possible but, yes, I do."

"Oh, it's possible all right."

Jones sat up straighter on the table, ignoring the pain that was even more obvious in the increased spill of light that reached him as he winced and then grimaced. "I know that look, Ranger."

"Then turn away."

"Hey, show a little gratitude here. I tried to do right by you; Masters and his sons too."

"What about his sons?" Caitlin asked, feeling the familiar bite of cold hold on her spine. "Are you saying they're *both* in danger?"

"You think I'm bad, you should see the guys I report to."

"You mean the ones who tried to kill you."

"The very same, Ranger, but I took care of it before the shooting started."

"Took care of *what?*"

"I made sure the outlaw's other son is protected."

"Luke?" Caitlin asked, as a flutter moved through her and left her feeling light-headed. "You tell me what the hell's happening or I'll do some damage de la Cruz won't be able to fix."

"Nothing's happened to him yet, and nothing will," Jones assured her. "I sent Paz."

81

HOUSTON, TEXAS

Luke responded to the knock on his dorm room door at the Village School to find two men standing there he didn't recognize and the Texas Ranger assigned to guard him nowhere to be seen.

"You need to come with us, son."

"Are you guys Rangers?" the boy asked.

"They sent us."

"Then where's Bill?" Luke backpedaled into his room. "His last name's Toddman. You must know him."

The two men followed Luke inside and closed the door behind them.

"Pack whatever you need," the same speaker told him. "Make it fast."

In the mirror atop the dorm room's bureau, Luke could see the other man's face twitch. He'd shut off the room's lights to save energy, working only by the light of his computer and that cast by the saltwater fish tank reflecting the sun streaming in through his window overlooking the courtyard. He'd chosen the Village School himself after Dylan had been accepted to Brown University. Luke wasn't half the athlete his older brother was, but he was twice the student, and he knew he'd need all of that to follow Dylan to an Ivy League university, maybe Brown too. The Village School filled a sprawling campus wrapped around a new high school building, the second phase of which had just opened for business when he arrived on campus. His dad had bought him a fish tank twice the size he'd asked for, taking up a hefty portion of his desk, but providing his dragon fish plenty of room to swim in and out of the various lairs he'd laid inside meticulously, like an interior designer for aquarium environments.

"Did my dad send you?" Luke asked, as he grabbed his backpack and dumped out its contents of textbooks, pads, empty snack wrappers, and energy drink bottles.

"Just pack your stuff."

"Was it Caitlin?"

Neither man said a word. The one who'd said nothing at all so far moved to the window.

"Maybe we should wait for Bill," Luke said, trying to sound dumb and innocent, something about this feeling all wrong to him.

"Don't make us tell you again," from the man by the window, speaking for the first time.

"Matter of fact," said the other, "let's just leave. Forget about packing. We'll pick up whatever you need. Safety first, right?"

Luke greeted his question with a slight nod, fear scratching at his spine and chilling him at the core. Then he felt the men come up on either side of him, each taking an arm.

"For your own good," one of them said.

Then he was being led toward the door, the other man jerking it open.

Guillermo Paz stood there, high as the top of the doorframe, grinning.

"*Mala idea*," he said. "Bad idea."

Then he was in motion, faster than anyone Luke had ever seen, faster than any*thing* he'd ever seen.

Paz was standing there. And then he wasn't.

The two men were holding Luke. And then they weren't.

Luke heard something clatter to the floor. Looked down to see a pistol stripped from one of the men's grasp and realized Paz was holding them both at the fish tank. His huge hands closed on the back of their heads and shoved their faces under the water, holding them there effortlessly as they writhed and kicked. Not even breathing hard while he drowned them.

"So," Paz asked Luke, the men starting to still, "you like your new school?"

PART EIGHT

They traveled swiftly and lightly, unencumbered to anything that could not be carried on horseback. They subsisted on wild game (or horse meat in lean times) and slept in the open under a blanket with the saddle for a pillow. Like all ranging companies, they bore no flag and sported no uniform. The Ranger's "usual habiliments," noted one, "were buckskin moccasins and overalls, a roundabout and red shirt, a cap manufactured by his own hands from the skin of the coon or wildcat, two or three revolvers and a bowie knife in his belt, and a short rifle on his arm."

—Robert M. Utley, *Lone Star Justice:*
The First Century of the Texas Rangers

82

"How'd you know where to find me? You been on my tail or something?"

Kai shook her head. "Not exactly."

"What then?"

"They planted a GPS tracker in me," she said, holding up her arm to reveal a thick wrapping of gauze. "I got it out and stuck it on something I knew you'd always have with you, being from Texas and all." She looked down at the boots he was wearing. "And it looks like I was right. Anyway, I used the signal to follow you."

Dylan scraped the souls of his boots on the park grass, as if trying to scratch the tracker off. "I'm gonna take a guess here," he said to Kai, seated close enough next to her on the bench in Columbus Park to smell the sweet scent of jasmine rising off her flawless skin. "You wanted something from me all along. That's how all this started."

"Yes and no," Kai conceded emotionlessly.

"Can't be both, girl."

"Stop talking Texas."

"What's that mean?"

"Calling me 'girl.' Dropping your subjects."

"You're not my teacher. I don't even know what you are," the boy said, not bothering to hide his frustration. "And why can't I call my dad? Give me back the phone he got for me."

"Not yet, because they could be tracking your father's phone."

"There you go again. Who's 'they' . . . girl."

"Are you trying to upset me?"

"I'm just trying to get some answers."

She flashed a brief smile. "You did pretty well getting something else out of me back in Providence."

"Yeah, but was it real?"

Her stare scolded him. "What do you think?"

"I don't know. That's why I asked."

Upon reaching Chinatown via the subway, they'd made straight for Columbus Park just beyond the Lower East Side, a history-rich section of Manhattan that was a part of the infamous Five Points a century and a half before. Columbus Park was actually built in that violent era, although now it was home to tai chi classes and residents lounging with their pet songbirds nearby.

"I need to know my dad is okay."

"He is."

"You can't know that."

"Yes, I can," Kai said, taking a shallow breath. "Because he's Cort Wesley Masters."

"That's what I meant before about whether it was real or not between us—because it was my dad and Caitlin Strong you really needed."

"I didn't notice that picture until after."

"After what?"

"Do I really need to tell you?"

Kai left things hanging there, allowing Dylan to invent whatever she was feeling in his own mind. His head began to throb and a sudden pang left him feeling dizzy and nauseous.

"What's wrong?"

"Nothing. Just what happens when somebody jumps you and rattles your brain."

"I'm sorry."

"You ran away."

"And they chased me instead of killing you."

"So I'm supposed to thank you now?"

Kai lapsed into silence, Dylan studying her closer. He wanted to be angry, but she was just too beautiful. The way her hair tumbled to her shoulders, the roundness of her mouth. Her eyes that seemed wide, barely Asian while highlighting her almond-toned skin and complexion so smooth it looked lifted from a painting. The dark, resin-coated jeans that rode her hips and hugged her like a second layer of skin. She looked like an actress, or a model, the way she held herself, the way she moved.

Then again, Dylan thought, recalling her actual profession, *she had to be both pretty much. . . .*

"You plan on answering my question?" he asked, the words much harsher than his tone.

"Which one?"

"I don't remember. There's a lot of things I don't remember since that night, like why I let you get inside my head."

Kai flirted with a smile that didn't quite break. "As I remember, it was because you were trying to get inside me."

"Why'd you text me the night of the beating?"

"Because I thought your father and that Texas Ranger could help me, help me get him."

"Get who, Kai, get *who*?"

She checked the sky, as if reading the time by it. "Time to go," she said, rising from the bench.

Dylan remained seated, afraid if he stood up the world would start spinning and he'd pass out. He felt chilled, a damp cold sweat breaking out on his face. "Where?"

"Texas."

83

Kai remembered the night they came for her. She'd been playing with her dolls, laying them out neatly on her bed. Her favorite ones were the oldest of all, handed down through the family for generations after being hand-sewn by a long-dead relative with a penchant for breathing life into his work. There were seventeen in that particular collection, each beautifully fashioned and realized.

And yet Kai recalled them being uniformly sad in expression, their stitched faces that of straw-stuffed beings who'd known much strife and pain in their lives. Their finely sewn expressions carrying the weight of the world, along with a quiet wisdom. When she imagined her dolls talking to her as an even younger girl, it was always these that spoke in the clearest voices.

After she was taken away, she missed those dolls the most. She would beg her "keepers" to retrieve them for her, after she'd been snatched from her life with only the clothes on her back. In later years Kai would learn this had been done so her life might be started over again, effectively from scratch. There could be no anchors to the past whatsoever, nothing to stoke memories better left behind as well.

Kai didn't have the dolls, no, but she kept close hold of those memories. And when the sadness set in with the reality of her plight, it was the memories to which she turned. Closing her eyes and imagining the dolls talking to her, striving to ease her pain and console her. But they had few truly happy words to offer, as if somehow the sum total of their own experiences had been sad as well. Kindred spirits, then, which may have explained why those old dolls were the ones she kept closest in heart and mind.

There were few memories left from that actual night, nothing really except for her father looking out the window, casting her a final gaze as the car in which she'd been placed pulled away. Not a wave, not a smile, not a tear. Just an empty stare out the window no different from the way he looked when he was waiting for a delivery to arrive. He was there, then he was gone and so was she.

What did I do wrong?

For so many months, if not years, that question had haunted her thinking. She had no memory of her mother, and her father never spoke of the woman who'd birthed her to the point where Kai wondered if she was somehow to blame. Was that what she was being punished for now? Her father had never been the same after the death of her beloved older sister, always her father's favorite who'd followed her mother to the grave not too many years before they took Kai away. The oldest dolls she loved the most had belonged to her sister originally, and Kai vividly recalled the night her sister had left them in her room atop her bed.

Why? Kai had asked her.

Because I don't need them anymore. They're yours now.

And soon after that she was gone, following Kai's mother into the afterlife and turning those old dolls into her best friends.

The men brought her to a big house far away from the city, more like a palace really. It was surrounded by a gate, the grounds covered in lavish gardens. Other girls around her age shared the house with her. On numerous occasions, some went away and others took their place without notice or fanfare. Kai learned their names as best she could, but the girls were uniformly kept to themselves, together only for schooling that was much different from what she'd come to know in the school she'd attended near her home. Languages and geography and history were the focus, especially languages. Kai learned English first, then Japanese, followed by Spanish. Originally, she'd assumed the big house was just a boarding school; only once months passed with no visitors, including her father, ever appearing did she realize it was more like a prison, a jail, a reformatory.

What did I do wrong?

No one ever told her, no matter how many times she asked. They taught her gymnastics and other sports, but mostly gymnastics. Kai excelled, much better than the other girls, the least gifted of whom she realized were usually the ones there one day and inexplicably gone the next. She learned tai chi as well, loved it for the art's ability to help whisk her away in her mind to someplace else. At first that someplace else was home. Later, when it became clear *this* was her home, she went other places in her mind that almost made her life tolerable.

Almost.

The big house had four floors but Kai's life was confined to the first in her initial months. She heard sounds coming from the floors above, strange sounds, through the nights when she stirred restlessly in search of sleep. Her room, in contrast to the room at what had once been her home, was stark. Bare walls, only a single window that was covered with a grille that shut out much of the light even on the sunniest of days; a bed, a desk, a chair, a lamp. That was it. No television, no radio, no tape or CD player like the one on which she used to play music at home. The only music in the big house came from someone playing a piano somewhere, a piano Kai could never remember actually seeing.

She accepted her routine, grew used to it because she had no other choice. Then one night when sleep wouldn't come, she was stirred from her bed by soft sounds coming from outside. Kai moved to her window and watched a girl a few years older than she dashing across the majestic lawn on a path bisecting the lavish gardens. Kai watched her reach the steel fence and try to scale it, failing twice, almost succeeding a third time when dark-clothed men were suddenly upon her, yanking her down. Kai heard the older girl's muffled cries and screams through the thick glass, pressed herself against the wall so as not to be seen watching. And when she peered out again a few moments later the girl and the dark-clothed men were gone.

Kai never saw the older girl again, but the men, or others just like them, were always about keeping their presence as scarce as possible. That led her to conclude all the girls brought here were indeed bad, that this was a place girls who misbehaved were brought. She was a stellar student, her father always telling her how proud he was of her accomplishments, so her sentence here couldn't be because of school.

Then what was it? Where had she misbehaved so badly to have her father send her away like this?

A mistake, it had to be a mistake! But her protestations to that effect inevitably fell on deaf ears and Kai gave up making them. In her dreams on the nights that she was able to find sleep, the mother she had no memory of came to her. But her shadowy, spectral shape offered no reassurances of Kai's plight, gave no explanations for it at all, and made her feel no better at all.

For good reason, as it turned out.

84

ALAMO HEIGHTS, TEXAS

The finished basement room was covered in pictures, four walls of them. The girl Li Zhen couldn't take his eyes from at the film studio the day of General Chang's unfortunate passing moaned softly as he entered her on the circular bed. That bed was the only piece of furniture on the otherwise stark floor, and it spun slowly to allow Zhen a view of all the pictures papering the walls. The basement's thin light rising from recessed bulbs fixed in all four corners illuminated a single individual portrayed at all stages of her life, from infancy to her teenage years when death had stolen her from him.

Two years back he'd purchased this eight-thousand-square-foot red-stone mansion that sat on four and a half lush acres in Alamo Heights. The previous owner had been a waste management tycoon, a Mexican immigrant Zhen recalled, whose arrest and subsequent incarceration had led to the price being drastically reduced. The property, originally owned by a drug dealer before the waste management baron, featured a pool, tennis court, tree house, and two-stall covered barn. The soundproof basement, complete with steel-reinforced walls now plastered with portraits of Zhen's only true love, had not been among the features advertised.

He had arranged those pictures clockwise chronologically, so the slow turn of the bed allowed him to relive his true love's all-too-short life. The girls he had Qiang bring to him here were no more than surrogates for the girl captured in those portraits. They all made for poor facsimiles, some posing a greater challenge to his imagination than others.

Today that challenge proved especially great, the typical reverie and release Zhen experienced in these moments lost to thoughts of Caitlin Strong. She seemed not to stare at so much as through him, and Zhen was left with the terribly uncomfortable sensation that she could see all the way to his soul and the truths it revealed.

Including the truth about his one true love in whose pictures his mind normally feasted in times like this.

Zhen believed in fate above all else, but right now the message such fate carried was distinctly unpleasant. No amount of the sights revealed by the slowly turning bed could relieve the discomfort he felt over Caitlin Strong's dogged pursuit of him. Then, suddenly, her face replaced that of his true love's across the walls. Zhen looked down and the Texas Ranger was beneath him, eyes boring into his soul and seeing what no one had ever seen before.

I'll kill you.

Zhen wasn't sure whether he spoke the words or only thought them. But then his fists were in motion, pounding and pounding. Feeling the crack of bones breaking and squish of flesh splitting, as blood flew into the air.

85

Cort Wesley ducked into one of a million Starbucks in Manhattan when he saw it was Caitlin calling. "Just give me a sec, while I get somewhere quiet," he said. "I just walked into a Starbucks that has two floors, if you can believe that."

"We've got them here in Texas too, Cort Wesley."

"We do?"

"Paz just picked up Luke at school. He's fine."

"Well," said Cort Wesley, "one of two ain't bad."

He'd been walking the streets ever since, sensing Dylan was okay as dusk approached but having no way to be sure. Unless . . .

"About time you realized I was here," Leroy Epps said, suddenly by Cort Wesley's side, walking in perfect rhythm with him.

"You got the answer I'm looking for, champ?"

"Depends if you asks the right question, bubba."

The last of the bright sky didn't have a cloud in it. The sun's weakening rays hit Leroy Epps and seemed to pass straight through him. But Cort Wesley noted his old friend still squinted as he faced him, his eyes narrowed into slits that left only a glimpse of the whites visible. He wet his lips, as if the sun was drying them out.

"No riddles today, please," he heard himself saying.

"Wasn't a riddle, just a fact. And you know I can't answer that kind of question, even if you did ask it. Them's the rules."

"Since when did rules matter to you?"

"Since I got here, bubba. You want the kind of liberties I got extended to me, you don't want to risk upsetting the balance of things. It's so damn

*delicate you just wouldn't believe. 'Sides, you don't need me to answer a
question you already got figured yourself."*

And with that Leroy wet his parched lips again. Cort Wesley
thought they looked cracked, bleeding in a few spots as if Leroy
had been chewing on them. He also realized people he passed were
staring his way, a big man who looked out of place here to begin
with in a heated conversation with himself. He touched a finger to
his ear, pretending to have a Bluetooth piece there.

"You wanna explain that to me clearer, champ?"

*"You know what you feel in your heart, bubba. Don't need it said by
me or any other. That's the problem with folk when they're still walking
the earth 'stead of kind of passing through it like I be. You learn to trust
only what you can see and touch. But trust me when I tell you that don't
even begin to scratch the world's itch."*

"How about the future, champ? Any words of wisdom there?"

"Same as it always be," the ghost of Leroy Epps told him. *"Cloudy
with a chance of clearing up later."*

"That's not a big help."

*"Future's easier to see than folks realize, bubba. Like climbing a stair-
case, it's not just about looking ahead but remembering the steps you took
to get you as far as you got. Make sense?"*

"Not really."

"It will. Fact is it has already."

"How's that?"

*"How is it you figure you survived at this game 'long as you have?
How many gunfights you walked away from, not even counting today's? You think that's an accident, luck? Bullshit's what I say, 'cause
there's no such thing as either. You made it this far on account of you
letting what's behind you tell you what's ahead. Sorry I can't be more
helpful."*

"Me too," Cort Wesley said, his skin suddenly tingling and the
breath starting to constrict in his chest.

Leroy swiped his tongue across his lips again, eyes widening
toward something across the street. *"Say, how about you grab me a
bottle of root beer at that stand over there? You used to pay to have the*

guards smuggle it into the Walls for me after I took sick. I'm not sure if I ever thanked you for that."

"You still get thirsty, champ?"

"No, sir. I just like the taste and the smell. You can't wait to need something to want it. Comes down to terms and nobody's better at dictating those than you. Dispensing a little whup-ass just like you did in that hotel earlier today. What's your heart tell you about your boy?" Leroy asked thumping his own chest with the same fist that had knocked out twenty-six fighters after he turned pro.

"That he's out there. And he's not alone," Cort Wesley added, with no clear grasp as to why.

The ghost grinned.

"Why you smiling, champ?"

"Folks don't see everything that's in front of 'em 'cause it'd mess with their minds too much if they did. The more you see, the more you know."

"Well, am I right? Is someone with him? Is it that Chinese—"

Cort Wesley felt a drop as he stepped off the curb, realizing too late he was walking straight into traffic. He felt a hand grab him and draw him back onto the sidewalk, but when he looked back to thank whoever had done it, there was no one there.

"Thanks, champ," he said out loud, not caring if anybody heard.

86

San Antonio, Texas

Caitlin hung up the phone, her third call to Cort Wesley in an hour completed and making her even more anxious than the first two.

"No sign of Dylan," she told Jones.

They'd relocated to the Juan de la Cruz's front room immediately behind the screen porch, the former doctor having vacated the premises on Caitlin's instructions.

"But," Caitlin continued, "according to the NYPD detective I talked to, a young Chinese woman was spotted approaching him in the lobby just before the shooting started upstairs." She studied Jones's expression, waiting for him to respond. "This doesn't surprise you."

"You didn't do your homework."

"On what?"

"Not what, Ranger, *who*."

"Li Zhen?"

"Yes. And no."

"Is this what I saved your life for?"

Jones laughed and kept laughing even when pain stretched across his features and it seemed he might split the neat stitches de la Cruz had left over his bullet wounds.

"I must've missed the joke," Caitlin told him.

"No, this time you *are* the joke, Ranger, because you've got everything turned around. Who do you think they were coming for next? You'd be dead now if I hadn't offed the team that came for me."

"How many, Jones?"

"Three. At the airport. I was flying back to Washington to pull the plug."

"On your own people," Caitlin surmised.

"They're not my people. I don't have people. That's why we get along so well, Ranger. Deep down inside we're the same."

"Only on my worst days," she told him. "What'd you do with the bodies?"

"They were waiting for me in a parking garage—that's where it all went down. They got off their shots and I got off mine." He stopped, suddenly out of breath. Several long moments passed before he got it back. "They're in the trunk of the car I parked in that lot outside the Medical Examiner's Office, maybe three down from where I found your SUV."

"How'd you know I was there?"

Jones tried to flash his smirk, but his expression wouldn't cooperate. "Your captain told me after I threatened to pay him a visit. I don't think he likes me very much."

"Can't imagine why. Get back to Li Zhen." Caitlin rose, hands planted on her hips with heat flushing through her cheeks. "I'm gonna go out on a limb here and say that Zhen handed his one surviving daughter over to the Triad's sex trade in return for them setting him up at Yuyuan. She ends up turning thousand-dollar tricks in the United States for a human trafficking network Cort Wesley found headquartered in New York City. They sent her to Providence where she met Dylan who ends up getting his head bashed in by thugs looking for Kai after she apparently strayed. Have I got this right?"

"Pretty damn close."

"Then let me ask you this, Jones: did you know Li Zhen used to traffic in porn when you went into business with him?"

"I didn't go into business with him, Ranger; I went into business with Yuyuan for what their fifth generation wireless network could do for Homeland."

"Know something?" Caitlin asked him. "You've spewed so much sanctimonious shit in your time that it just rolls off your tongue now. I wish you could hear yourself, Jones, I truly do."

He tried to stand up, grimaced badly, and plopped back down to the wood-framed couch covered in upholstered cushions showing various discolored patches of stain in the sunlight.

"What's this all about exactly?" Caitlin resumed.

Jones pushed himself to his feet, wincing badly this time. "I need some air. Help me out onto the porch, Ranger, and we'll take a little trip back into history, all the way to 1883."

87

El Paso, Texas; 1883

"I can't let you into Mr. Morehouse's room, Ranger," the hotel clerk said. "He doesn't just run the Southern Pacific, he owns this hotel."

Judge Roy Bean tapped the folded-up, chewing tobacco–stained paper he'd laid on the reception desk counter. "You know what a search warrant is, son?"

"I do not, sir."

"It's a document that permits a judge to order a search of a man's residence and possessions under the provisions of the Fourth Amendment. I filled this one out myself upon the request of the Ranger here."

"Judge, I still can't—"

"You'll be jailed unless you do—my jail in Langtry, son, which is a place you definitely don't want to be."

The clerk tapped his teeth against his upper lip. "I should really cable Mr. Morehouse for instructions."

"No, son, you shouldn't."

The clerk shrugged and reached behind him for the right key.

The morning after meeting David Morehouse, son of the head of the Southern Pacific Railroad, William Ray Strong and Judge Roy Bean rode into El Paso and to the hotel that served as the company's headquarters. As a result, it boasted no vacancies, just about all its rooms rented out to railroad officials to make use of as they saw fit. One of these was a suite rented out to John Morehouse himself, his son David living in the suite's adjoining bedroom.

The clerk escorted them to Morehouse's top-floor rooms and unlocked the door.

"Should I go inside with you?" he asked William Ray Strong and Roy Bean.

"No, son, you should most certainly not," the judge said in what sounded like an order. "The Ranger and me will be just fine on our own."

The clerk nodded grudgingly as the two men entered.

"What was that paper you said was a search warrant?" William Ray asked the judge.

"A marker from a man who lost bad at cards last night," Roy Bean told him. "Sumbitch was such a piss poor card player, I didn't even have to cheat."

*   *   *

It didn't take them long to locate David Morehouse's bedroom and not much longer to find exactly what they'd come looking for.

"Boy didn't even bother to hide the evidence," Judge Bean said as William Ray removed the items he'd spotted in the bottom drawer of the clothes bureau and laid them out neatly atop it.

Both men found themselves looking at a collection of fine sewing needles of various sizes, some with thin or wiry material still threaded through them. William Ray couldn't tell if it was the same material used to sew the female murder victims' heads back on, but it was close.

"Don't look much the kind of needles you'd use for stitching, though," the Ranger noted. "Look more like the kind used for sewing."

"Sure," Bean snickered, "sewing a head back on. Not like he's gotta worry much about a fine line or causing further pain to the victim."

"All the same," William Ray told him, taking a fresh inventory of the assortment of needles they'd found in the bottom drawer, "this looks more like a seamstress's collection for easy work along with the finer, more delicate kind."

"Finer, more delicate kind would work pretty dang well on a neck, don't you think?"

"I suppose."

"So what's got your britches in a huff?"

"Something don't feel right, Judge, that's all."

"Hell, Ranger, we got four bodies with their heads stitched on backward in this camp and who knows how many more in those others. This dumb-ass kid's the devil in disguise, I tell ya. You want to argue the point, go right ahead."

William Ray nodded and started tucking the evidence into a saddlebag. "What do you say we ride back out to the camp and go from there?"

* * *

The crew was in the process of moving the railroad farther down the line, trying to make up as much lost time as the unseasonable wet weather had cost them. The workers were crowded onto the empty train cars of the steam engine–driven locomotive that moved with them for the two-mile jaunt, the buildings and businesses constructed on their behalf shrinking in the distance.

But Chief Bates's office, with RAILROAD POLICE HEADQUARTERS stenciled over the doorframe, was just where it had been. William Ray and Judge Bean found him inside with his boots kicked up on his desk, alternating between a cigar and cup of tar-black coffee while a pair of deputies flanked him on either side.

"I come here as a courtesy, Chief," William Ray said with the judge just behind him, "to inform you that I am placing David Morehouse under arrest for the murders of the four Chinese women in this camp."

"Is that a fact?"

"Don't make me repeat myself."

Bates chewed on his cigar, seemed to be giving consideration to William Ray's words. "Sorry, Ranger, I can't help you."

"Why's that?"

Bates removed the cigar from his mouth long enough to sip some of his coffee that left a dark ring on his upper lip. "On account of the fact that the boy ain't on the premises any longer. His father found a proper place for him to reside. Boy ain't right in the head, you know."

"I did get that impression, but it doesn't change the need for justice to be done."

William Ray was still staring Bates in the face when the echo of gunfire, constant and unbroken, crackled beyond the shack.

William Ray Strong had never ridden a horse faster than he did the quarter-mile out to the camp where the Chinese workers remained on strike. The volley of echoing gunshots had slowed to single volleys by the time he leaped down with Colt in hand amid the litter of bodies and gun smoke drifting with the breeze.

He shot two Pinkerton men just as they were sighting in on a Chinese man trying to flee with a child in his arms and wife by his side. The Pinkertons fell to the ground over their Winchester rifles with great coats billowed to both sides. Two more rushed him and he shot them too, spotting the figure of the man he knew as Su dashing straight into the open space between a series of clotheslines to scoop a crying toddler up from the ground. Fresh gunfire rang out and William Ray watched Su's spine arch as he was hit. The force of another round doubled him over, but he staggered onward still clutching the toddler until he reached a shrieking woman who took the boy from his grasp and ran off into the brush where other Chinese had scattered to escape the massacre.

William Ray watched Su keel over dead and used his final bullet to gun down one of his killers. The Ranger stood right there in the open while he reloaded, as bullets whizzed past him on both sides. He snapped the cylinder back into place, drew the Colt's hammer back and sighted in on another gunman who'd shot Su in the back. The man opened up with his Winchester from thirty feet away, missing three times before William Ray fired twice, his second bullet taking the man square in the heart.

He used three more shots to clear a path to the cover provided by a pile of cut wood for burning, and reloaded again as wood shards and splinters flew through the air behind a torrent of return fire. William Ray cursed himself for not bringing his own rifle into the battle. His horse had bravely stood its ground, but was too far away to chance the effort now, leaving him with these fresh five shots and the ten additional bullets in his belt. He popped out from the right of the pile to return fire, then twisted to the left where he caught another Pinkerton by surprise.

If nothing else, the fire he was drawing ought to give any remaining Chinese time to flee, but he couldn't get sight of all those downed bodies, women and children and some of those Christian missionaries among them, out of his mind. Then a storm of horses thundered into the camp, led by John Morehouse himself.

"Stand down!" he cried out. "Stand down now!" Then, after the Pinkerton men's gunfire was reduced to no more than echoes, "Come out, Ranger Strong. It's over."

William Ray emerged from behind the woodpile with Colt steadied straight on Morehouse, who was seated atop a draft horse that towered over the scene. A tall, rail-thin, mustachioed man wearing the badge of a federal marshal sat on a horse next to him with a half dozen gunmen spread out just behind them, all with badges pinned to their lapels.

"You're under arrest for ordering these killings, sir!" the Ranger shouted up at Morehouse.

At which point, Judge Roy Bean rode up, stopping his horse so short, he nearly fell off, then lost his balance and fell into a patch of mud once he dismounted.

"And I look forward to presiding over your trial!" he snapped at Morehouse, dropping both hands to his mud-soaked knees to catch his breath.

"This land doesn't belong to Texas anymore," Morehouse told them both quite calmly. "It belongs to the Southern Pacific under the jurisdiction of the United States government under President Chester A. Arthur. Isn't that right, Marshal Stoudenmire?" he asked the tall man on the horse next to him.

"It sure is," the tall, rail-thin man said.

Morehouse surveyed the scene of fallen bodies, dissipating gun smoke, and Pinkerton men emerging into the open, shaking his head in feigned disgust. "And do you feel yourself capable of dispensing proper justice in this matter, Marshal?"

"I sure do," Stoudenmire told him.

"Then you can start with those Pinkertons I didn't kill," William Ray yelled up to him, "all of them guilty of murder."

Stoudenmire surveyed the scene. "That's a matter of opinion right now, pending a proper investigation."

"By which point the killers could have scattered to the ends of the earth."

"A man's innocent until proven guilty, Ranger."

"Meaning the Southern Pacific only enforces laws that suit its best interests."

"That doesn't matter one way or another," Morehouse said, looking back at William Ray and the judge. "Now, you boys may not know that the county seat was recently moved from Ysleta to El Paso, giving Marshal Stoudenmire here full discretion in upholding the law of the land here in Langtry as well."

"How recently was that?" Judge Bean asked him.

"Last week, give or take a few days," Morehouse said, barely containing his smile.

"Well," said William Ray, "I didn't know about the change in the county seat, but I know all about Marshal Stoudenmire," he continued, striding toward the man who looked like a skeleton with clothes draped over his painted-on skin. "I believe you shot a by-stander during a gunfight at the intersection of Overland Avenue and El Paso Street in April of 1881."

"It happens," Stoudenmire said, unmoved.

"Not to the Texas Rangers, it don't. So you still a lousy shot or you been practicing?"

"You're trespassing on railroad land, Ranger," Morehouse picked up. "It's now up to Marshal Stoudenmire to investigate and resolve this terribly tragic incident to the full extent of prevailing law under joint railroad and federal authority."

"Where's your son, Mr. Morehouse?" William Ray asked instead of arguing the point further, positioned so to spare himself further sight of the massacre's victims.

"My son's whereabouts are of no concern to you."

"We found the sewing needles in the bottom drawer of his bureau, sir. Your boy was taught to sew in another camp by that blind man who makes your flags here, the same camp where the first set of murders took place."

Morehouse stiffened atop his horse. "Damn shame, all these

Chinese women getting killed and nobody seeming to care. I've been looking into these alleged murders personally, Ranger. It may interest you to know that my son wasn't even present in the Cheyenne, Wyoming, camp or the one in the Oklahoma plains. He's not your killer, so I sent him away before you could frighten him any further."

"And I'm just supposed to take you at your word on that?"

"I'm sure you'll check the story out and find out I'm telling you the truth. So go ahead, waste your time."

Morehouse climbed down from his horse gingerly, his movements looking rehearsed and well practiced, and he was quickly joined on his feet by Marshal Stoudenmire and his deputies. "You don't understand how the world works these days, Ranger. The time for cowboys and gunfighters is gone. The frontier's dead because the railroad killed it."

"And you think I'm just gonna forget my investigation because of that?" William Ray heard fresh sobs and cries of shock and sadness, turning to find survivors of the massacre rushing to their downed loved ones, hoping against hope to find them still alive. "You think I'm going to let the butcher who killed these women go free?"

"It's over, Ranger," Morehouse told him. "And who cares about a bunch of Chinese whores anyway?"

William Ray reared back and punched Morehouse square in the mouth. The man went down as if his legs had been yanked out from under him, Stoudenmire and his deputies getting their pistols steadied on William Ray while he continued to glare at John Morehouse.

"Thank you, Ranger," Morehouse said, grinning through the blood seeping from his mouth. "You just made my point." He kept his eyes fastened on William Ray Strong as he continued. "Marshal Stoudenmire, please place this man under arrest."

88

"How'd you know all that?" Caitlin asked, once Jones had finished.

"We're Homeland Security, Ranger," he managed, fidgeting in the old wicker chair that seemed to creak or crackle every time he moved. "We know everything."

Night had fallen in the course of his telling the story, a shroud of darkness descending on the neighborhood to the accompaniment of high-revving cars cruising the streets with blaring music emanating from their open windows.

Somehow the coming of that darkness left Caitlin feeling anxious and uneasy. "So the true murderer was never caught."

"For all I know it was Morehouse's son. But I can tell you the murders stopped after that. And what's the difference after so many years?"

"Because it's happening again, just like it did back then in every detail. And only somebody familiar with those details could be doing it."

"You mean anyone with access to the same files I do. That's a lot of names."

A car backfiring on the street beyond left Caitlin's hand just short of drawing her SIG Sauer and opened Jones's eyes wide again.

"Did you know Morehouse stole Chinese technology to make the telegraphs work coast to coast?" Caitlin challenged.

"I know that's what Li Zhen claims."

"I think Li Zhen killed General Chang," she said suddenly.

"Come again?"

"Our medical examiner has linked Chang's death to the deaths of four homeless men. Identical circumstances for the most part that'll go down as natural causes—a heart attack, something like that. What they call it when they don't have another term. The homeless men were all carrying cell phones. That seem strange to you?"

"It's been known to happen."

"How about the fact they were Chinese models not currently available here in the States? How about the fact that Chang was carrying an identical phone on his person? How about the fact that you called in Chang to shut Li Zhen down and then he dies in a most convenient manner at a most convenient time?"

"Where you going with this?"

"I'm not sure yet," Caitlin told him. "You wanted to rig elections, get the right people into office or, at least, make sure the wrong people lost. That was enough to turn a blind eye to what Yuyuan and China were going to do with control over our fifth generation wireless network."

"I already told you all that."

"But you missed something. This was about something entirely different for Zhen all along."

"I told you I had a feeling about that, but nothing else. Explains why I tried to shut the bastard down."

"Zhen thinks America ruined his life way back when John Morehouse stole his great-grandfather's invention and then perpetrated that massacre that took the man's life and likely left the rest of the Zhen family in pretty bad conditions back in China."

"So?"

"So what if Li Zhen's been looking for a way to get even his entire life? What if that's what building the fifth generation wireless network has been about for him from the beginning."

"Any notion as to the specifics?"

"I believe it's connected to however he killed General Chang." Caitlin studied Jones closer. The porch light made him look milk-white in color. "I still say you need a hospital."

"I need my head examined for thinking you'd understand what I was trying to do here. I listened to you, Ranger. I looked into what you said about Li Zhen and I tried to pull the plug. That's why we're both sitting here right now."

As he finished, a dark sedan with rusted underpanels rolled casually down the street.

"So the only people you can call to report this want you dead and probably me too by now," Caitlin told him. "*Your* people, Jones. How high up the food chain we talking about here?"

"They eat strictly gourmet. That clarify things for you?"

"Names would clarify them better."

"Even if I gave them to you, even if I had them, what would you do? Thanks to you, I'm a bad boy, Ranger. I misbehaved. This is on me, and I'll deal with it my own way."

"Sure, with three bullets just yanked out of you."

"And the three men who put them there stuffed in a car trunk. I believe I can still take care of myself."

Caitlin looked away from him in time to glimpse the back end of a black car that just passed the house. Could have been the same rusty one she'd seen moments earlier, but she couldn't be sure.

"You don't like asking for help, do you?" she asked Jones, holding her gaze on the street now.

"You think you can ride into Washington with guns blazing?"

"I think whoever sent the men stuffed in your trunk and dispatched the State Department to warn me off are going to send a whole bunch more. And I don't think they're going to stop at you either. That makes it my fight too. Even if I take down Li Zhen and whatever he's really up to, your friends at Homeland can't risk being held complicit. The men who came after Cort Wesley in New York weren't Chinese, Jones. The war's started already."

Tension settled between them, the moments passing without the rusty sedan reappearing.

"My truck's rear tires are flat," Caitlin said, happening to move her gaze in that direction.

She was feeling for her pistol when her phone rang. She checked the Caller ID before answering it.

"Colonel?"

"We're almost back to San Antonio, Ranger," said Guillermo Paz.

"How close?"

"Twenty minutes."

"Not close enough," Caitlin told him.

89

NEW YORK CITY

Dylan eased the wheelchair along the LaGuardia Airport concourse, steering it toward the gate from where the flight back to Texas would be leaving. Kai sat slumped before him, totally transformed and barely recognizable from the girl who sent what felt like electricity dancing through him, the heavy makeup forming her disguise leaving a powdery residue in the air that smelled like lacquer.

From Columbus Park, they'd headed deeper into the heart of Chinatown, into a world different from anything he'd seen before. It was like entering a foreign country, everyone jabbering away in their native language instead of English. The air smelled of salt and spices from food served out of sidewalk stands or storefronts. The signs on the stores were printed in both English and Chinese, a few just in Chinese.

He let Kai steer him along, found it odd that spotting a fellow Caucasian walking the streets, shopping or just strolling, put him more at ease.

"I'm sorry," she said suddenly.

"About what?"

"About what happened to you. The night you were beaten. It wasn't the first time something bad happened to you. I can see that in your eyes."

"That's true enough," Dylan told her, trying not to catalog all the shit he'd been through these past few years. "But bad things have happened to you too, and I don't need to see them in your eyes."

Kai turned from him back to the sidewalk ahead, stopping at the next building. "We're here."

They entered and walked upstairs to the third floor, where a Chinese man was waiting for them outside an open door, gesturing for them to enter. He spoke no English, leaving all the conversation to Kai.

He took their pictures and an hour later presented them with fresh passports and driver's licenses, along with credentials attesting to Kai's "disability." So too the pictures he'd shot of her had been Photoshopped to age her in accordance with her disguise. Her cheeks were sunken, her hair touched by gray, shoulders turned bony and narrow—the woman Dylan was pushing along the concourse in a wheelchair, in other words. Whoever had attacked his dad at the hotel would know he and Kai were together by now. They'd be watching the primary routes out of the city, including the airports. But they'd never pay attention to a young man pushing a broken woman in a wheelchair, because nobody ever did.

And they hadn't today.

The plane was already at the gate when Dylan and Kai arrived, and they were granted immediate access by just flashing their boarding passes. Left alone in the cabin in the moments prior to general boarding.

"What's waiting for us in Texas, Kai? What's all this about?"

"My father," she told him.

90

Li Zhen was still shaking when Qiang's men arrived to dispose of the body, unable to quell the tremors that rose with the thoughts of what he'd done. Exacerbated further by the fact that he had stood for endless minutes under a stream of frigid water in his shower to punish himself for his indiscretion.

He had lost control. He never lost control.

"It's her," the freshly dressed Zhen said to Qiang as a pair of men carried the body of the dead girl, wrapped in plastic, past them. "The Texas Ranger."

"I . . . don't understand," Qiang told him.

"Did you check the grounds?"

"I have men posted."

Zhen moved to the window. "I think she's coming."

"We are prepared."

Zhen swung away from the glass that had misted up with the condensation formed by his rapid breathing. For some reason his thoughts turned back to coming before the Triad council on the night that changed his life forever sixteen years before. They'd thought the advantage theirs, but he'd shown them different, just as he'd been forced to do so many times over the course of his life. A man of low station, peasant scum, avoiding the defensive posture he so loathed by always attacking. Seizing the advantage, any advantage, to get what he wanted.

But not now, not with Caitlin Strong.

Those moments in the basement when he thought he was killing her were wonderful, rekindling memories of his unlikely, unprecedented rise to power, drawing imaginary lines to envision destinations he wouldn't be denied. And now, on the verge of his penultimate triumph, Zhen found himself a frightened, cowering man reduced to peeking out of windows.

"I want her dead, Qiang," he heard himself say in words that emerged in more of a hiss.

"In time," the giant said.

"I want to do it myself. I must feel the life pass out of her. Stare into her eyes as it fades from them."

"You still believe she is coming?" Qiang asked him.

Zhen started to turn back toward the window, then stopped. "No," he said, massaging his temples as his head started to pound, "I realize she's already here."

91

SAN ANTONIO, TEXAS

"Let me help you back inside," Caitlin said to Jones, twilight having turned to darkness in the sky beyond.

"Fuck that, Ranger," he said, trying to stand on his own. "I don't run from a fight, no matter what."

"You couldn't even walk away from this one."

"You got any more guns stashed in your SUV?"

"A shotgun and an AR-15, only whoever flattened the tires is sure to have taken them."

"Still worth a look."

"The painkillers must be affecting your brain, Jones. You think they're not watching the house right now?"

He looked toward her holstered SIG Sauer. "So we got one pistol . . ."

"And two backup magazines to go with it. Unless de la Cruz has weapons lying around."

Jones focused on the shape of the cell phone pushing out from the pocket of Caitlin's jeans. "Get Paz on the phone. Let me speak to him."

She shrugged. "He's too far away. He'll never get here in time. Captain Tepper's marshaling the forces. Right now, best we can hope for is that the shots-fired call I made holds them off until then."

And that's when the gunfire began.

"Guess we can forget about that," Jones spoke though a grimace as Caitlin dragged him back inside the house.

The gunfire was constant, blistering the air. Plaster and wood rained down on her and Jones from all angles, the glass shards that struck them feeling like icicles. They'd dropped to the floor once back within the house proper, hugging a worn shag carpet.

Caitlin cracked the door back open and, staying on the floor, poised her pistol through it and aimed for the door leading into the screen porch from the outside. She heard shuffling behind her and twisted awkwardly to find Jones lumbering toward the kitchen in a crouch. Fresh blood leaked through his dressings, his face pale and expression frozen in an agony he held back to avoid crying out in the pain that racked him.

"Jones!" she called out.

But he didn't acknowledge her, didn't even turn back.

Caitlin heard a muffled thump and turned back around. A figure sheathed in black lurched toward a window on the house's left side, just crashing through when she planted a bullet dead square in his forehead.

One down, but how many more left to go?

She held her position, the scream of sirens approaching in response to her shots-fired call into SAPD minutes before. Response time to this part of the city tended to be slower, but D. W. Tepper would have the whole of Texas law enforcement here anytime now too, if they could just hold out.

But for how long against firepower that continued to rain bullets into the house, seemingly from all angles at once? The echoes reached Caitlin as muffled rasps, her hearing having taken too much of a beating in the initial onslaught. It was one of the many things nobody tells you about a gunfight before you've actually been in one. Maybe because the people who knew held back the information in the hope you'd never have to experience it yourself.

Caitlin had been in more than her share of gunfights, but never one that found her totally on the defensive, pinned down this way. Forced to rely on the intervention of others for her very survival. She hated that feeling of helplessness, of dependence, more than anything.

She thought she saw another figure dart up the front steps, his head covered in some kind of ski mask caught in her vision. Caitlin fired off four shots in rapid succession, but heard no satisfying grunt or thud of a body falling to the ground.

Then she heard the crash of another door, the back one, bursting open followed by the *pfffffffffffts* of silenced rounds, how many she couldn't say, before an awful high-pitched wailing erupted, fading to a sound like an animal whimpering. Caitlin lunged back to her feet, darting through the fire and emptying the rest of her magazine through the two windows looking out from the house's front room to keep the shooters at bay. She'd just gotten a second magazine jammed home, round jacked into the chamber when she spun into the kitchen ready to start firing anew.

The harsh chemical scent assaulted her an instant before her eyes started to burn. She glimpsed the wounded Jones crouching over the body of one of their attackers, the man's exposed eyes frozen open and colored an awful red. Jones turned toward her, submachine gun with attached sound suppressor in hand.

"Ammonia and bleach, Ranger," he rasped. "There's deadly shit you wouldn't believe under the typical kitchen sink."

What little remaining strength he clung to seemed to bleed

away in that instant and he keeled over to the floor that was slick with the deadly, noxious compound he must have hurled into the gunman's face.

"Jones," she started.

He looked up at her, but that was all.

The blare of sirens screeched through the house, followed by the squeal of brakes and, almost immediately, a hail of heavy, automatic fire.

Caitlin felt sick to her stomach, these cops dying because she had called them and they'd come in response having no idea what they were driving into.

What was I thinking?

She wasn't; the instinct to survive and triumph had won the moment. She'd fallen into what her grandfather had once called a "gunfighter haze" where normal rudimentary thought didn't apply.

Caitlin left Jones where he was with the submachine gun and surged back into the front room, SIG ready to fire on anything that moved. Holding to the hope the cops might still be miraculously alive and that she could somehow keep them that way. The gunfire continued to pierce the night, pinging through her restored hearing and sounding curiously like that old-fashioned popcorn you cooked by shaking it over a stove burner. The night beyond was lit by muzzle flashes tracing toward the house, accompanied by the thuds of impact and crackling of more window glass giving way. Impossible to tell how many guns or how many men firing them. More than she'd ever faced down, that was for sure.

And then some kind of rolling light pierced the darkness, growing in intensity and brightness as an engine's roar drowned out the gunshots and something that looked like a tank thundered into her vision.

92

The lights seemed to be everywhere, turning night to day, leaving Caitlin to wonder if some ephemeral moment was blending heaven and earth. That maybe she'd been shot and this was the great white light that everybody talked about guiding you to the next world when your time was done.

But her time wasn't done.

And these were no heavenly lights; they were attached to a massive truck, not a tank, a whole day-glow bright bank of them that seemed to freeze the gunmen in their steps.

But not Caitlin. She watched the truck just manage to skirt the shot-up SAPD cars and plow into two of the black-clad men without slowing. Impact hurdled them airborne and then the truck slammed into and crushed a third. This as it twisted across Juan de la Cruz's tiny lawn, kicking up a fountain of dirt and grass.

And then the massive shape of Guillermo Paz emerged from the cab, wielding twin assault rifles that looked like toys in his huge hands and seeming to fire everywhere at once. Caitlin burst out through the screen porch door, adding her fire to his, concentrating on the gunmen at the outskirts of his firing angle.

They were on opposite sides of the yard, seemed to have moved around closer to the back, escaping the spray of day-glow brightness that split the night. Caitlin rushed to her right because the gunman on that side seemed to have better hold of his gun, his moves suggesting high-grade military experience. Along the way she glimpsed one of the shooters still in Paz's sights drop down for cover behind a big bulky trash receptacle deposited on the curb. Maybe not registering it was made of plastic until Paz's fire literally blew it apart, pulverizing it back into and over the man, exposing him for the rain of fire that seemed to lift him airborne and toss him free of the light's spill.

By then Caitlin had come to the corner where the house bent to the left on an awkward angle, likely to conform to the property line. She caught the gunman who'd rushed that way just snapping a fresh magazine home and jacking back its slide to fire. Two bullets to the face and one to the throat ended that ambition for good, and she kept her charge in that direction going, hoping to run straight into the other gunman who'd fled Paz's fire.

She could still hear the echoing rattle of his twin fusillades, a brief pause for reloading during which she detected several individual rounds fired off by his remaining targets. The fact that his return fire came immediately and relentlessly made Caitlin wonder if maybe the pause had been a trap meant to get the shooter to do exactly what he'd done, exposing himself to certain death at the colonel's incessant fire.

Caitlin rounded the rear of the house to find the final gunman taking up a shooter's stance with his cut-down assault rifle, likely in Paz's direction. She opened fire without the split second it took to aim and steady, knowing she didn't have it. As a result, a few of her bullets missed and a few more thudded into his high-tech body armor and drew barely a flinch. Just a couple bullets left in this magazine and no time to trade it for her third, when fresh fire from inside the house spun the black-clad gunman one way and then the other.

Jones!

She could barely acknowledge him doing something positive, having put the submachine gun she'd left with him to good use. The gunman he'd shot wobbled one way and then the other, Caitlin just steadying her SIG on him when twin barrages by Paz literally lit up the air before twisting him around and dropping his body in a bloody heap.

Caitlin's mind recorded additional gunfire that was nonexistent, echoes of it banging up against the sides of her mind. It didn't end so much as recede, as if the volume was being turned down slowly. She found herself on the side of the house facing Guillermo Paz with no memory of having walked there, the colonel still surveying the scene with his all-seeing eyes that glowed like a cat's and twin assault rifles held at the ready.

"You told me you were too far away to help, Colonel," she heard herself saying.

"Get behind me, Ranger," he urged, turning so he was backpedaling toward his truck right into the center of the light spill. "I lied, in case they were tuned in to your phone."

"I wouldn't put it past them," she said, when a fresh shape popped up in the rear of Paz's truck, wide-eyed and terrified.

"Luke?" Caitlin managed. Then, to Paz in disbelief, "You brought him with you?"

"There was no time to stop, no place safe to leave him."

Caitlin gazed about her, into the carnage left behind in the bright haze cast by the truck's light array as an army of sirens blaring with flashing lights just reached the outskirts of her vision.

"No place safer than this, Colonel? Really?"

"I'm here and you're here, Ranger," Paz said. "You tell me."

PART NINE

"No peace is too quick, no task too difficult or hazardous. Night and day will the ranger trail his prey, through rain and shine."

—Ranger James B. Gillet (1873)

93

SAN ANTONIO, TEXAS

Jurisdiction had yet to be determined by the time Deputy Chief Conseulo Alonzo arrived on the scene. But D. W. Tepper had beaten her there by nearly two hours and had taken complete charge by first cordoning off the area and then prioritizing the crime scene team's work to include the gunmen's vehicles in order to more swiftly reveal their true identities and who was behind their dispatch.

"Well, Ranger," he groused, after his initial survey of the scene swimming with San Antonio rescue wagons and police squad cars, "I do believe you may have broken your own record with this one." He watched crime scene technicians struggling to keep the positions of all the bodies secure from press and rival law enforcement groups, the corpses alone numbering at least a dozen. "These gunmen look like characters from one of those video games my daughter lets my grandson play. You mind telling me who was unfortunate enough to draw your wrath this time?"

"Ask him," Caitlin said, gesturing toward Jones who was being tended to in the back of one of the rescue wagons, while Guillermo Paz stood nearby as tall as the truck's top.

"Which one? All assholes look alike to me in my old age."

"The smaller one. The bigger one saved my life. Again."

"Charmed life you lead, Ranger."

"It pays to have friends like the colonel."

Tepper boldly tapped a cigarette free of its pack and stuck it in his mouth, as if daring Caitlin to follow her usual custom of plucking it out. Instead of bothering, she turned toward Luke seated in the passenger seat of her SUV, now in need of new rear tires. He cast her a wave, then smiled at Captain Tepper.

"You got a strange notion of babysitting," Tepper noted.

"A couple guys from the same team being loaded in body bags paid the boy a visit at his school."

The captain looked from Luke to Paz, then back to Luke again. "Don't tell me, Frankenstein's monster over there showed up to save the day."

"Drowned them in a fish tank," said Caitlin.

"You're serious, aren't you?"

"Yes, sir."

Tepper scowled, shaking his head as his eyes sought out Paz lurking somewhere in the shadows. "Ranger, you've declared war before, plenty of times, just not against the United States government."

"That's who dispatched the gunmen. Somebody covering their tracks and their asses, not wanting to squander this deal they made with the devil."

"You talking about Homeland Security's intentions to rig a whole bunch of goddamn elections?"

"Prospects of that don't seem to worry you much, D.W."

"I stopped voting when the goddamn politicians stopped even pretending to listen. Doesn't matter who's pushing the buttons or pulling the strings, Ranger."

Tepper regarded her tautly. He looked tired and cranky, having missed a few spots with the Brylcreem he used to slick down his ash-gray hair and trying fitfully to smooth it into place by wetting his fingers in the product's stead.

"They came after Jones," Caitlin told him, "because he realized their plan had run off the tracks and was trying to pull the plug. Won him three bullets."

"I don't know what's a bigger miracle," Tepper said, checking his pockets again for a lighter and shaking his head when the search came up empty. "Jones having survived that or so many encounters with you."

"We're gonna need him to finish this, Captain."

"Right now, I'd settle for somebody making Homeland realize their hit teams aren't welcome in Texas." Tepper started to walk away, then stopped. "Oh, and you need to call Young Roger. He said it was important."

"Your murder victims weren't just high-end call girls," Roger reported, when Caitlin got him on the line. "At least four of the five appeared in porn videos made by the same company that produced the one from the Deep Web."

"I'm guessing you found those other videos."

"You bet. The ones in question all go back between twelve and eighteen months," Roger told her. "But I was able to trace a whole bunch of others the same company had produced going back five years now."

"Five years," Caitlin repeated.

"That important?"

"It's when Yuyuan's American headquarters opened."

"Then here's something that'll interest you: the videos are shot out of a warehouse studio in Fiesta owned by a shell subsidiary."

"Of Yuyuan?"

"Yup. I told you that would interest you. We're raiding the place tomorrow, if you'd like to join in."

"I've got something else I need you to do," Caitlin told him. "Give me an address to have something messengered to you tonight."

"What?"

"Cell phones, Young Roger."

* * *

"I think I'll ride along with you to the hospital, if you don't mind," Caitlin said to Jones, climbing into the rear of the rescue wagon after paramedics had lifted his gurney inside.

"Afraid I might not make it otherwise, Ranger?" Jones asked her, while the paramedics continued to work on him.

"Who's your source on all things Li Zhen?"

"I've got several. What are you looking for?"

"Whatever it is you missed."

94

San Antonio, Texas

Cort Wesley stuffed the phone back in his pocket when he saw Dylan riding the escalator down into the terminal building. He could tell by the boy's expression something was wrong, surely connected to the fact that his flight had landed a half hour before and he was just emerging now. And the girl, Kai, was nowhere to be seen.

He approached the escalator, reaching it just as Dylan hit the bottom.

"She's gone, Dad. Goddamn made herself disappear."

The boy had used the prepaid phone Cort Wesley had bought at a drugstore to call him from Chinatown.

"She's inside talking to the old guy right now," he'd whispered. "I don't have much time. We're headed back to Texas."

"You need to get away from there right now," Cort Wesley told him. "You need to walk out."

"I can't," Dylan said after a pause that felt much longer than it actually was.

"Stop thinking with your dick, son."

"I'm not. Jeez, Dad," Dylan followed, and Cort Wesley could picture him shaking his head and blowing the hair from his face with his breath. "I'm playing this like you. Trying to get to the bottom of things."

"You're not me. How you feeling?"

"Fine."

"What about the headaches?"

"I just told you I was fine. And I can't just up and leave her. Is that what you want me to do? You wouldn't; I know you wouldn't. Hold on, she's headed back into the room. I gotta go. I'll find a way to let you know when we're getting in."

That way turned out to be a text message, a form of communication that Cort Wesley utterly detested. But the text had contained the flight number and arrival time. Cort Wesley was already in the air when it reached him, having taken another airline that would actually land in San Antonio ahead of Dylan's flight.

And now Dylan was here, but the girl was nowhere to be found. They emerged into the cool night, Dylan kicking at the concrete with his boots, looking unsure and confused. Like a kid.

"I don't know how you and Caitlin can keep dealing with shit like this."

"Neither do I."

"We read *Dracula* in one of my English classes. My favorite character was Van Helsing, the guy who brings down the monster. I think I liked him because he reminded me of the two of you."

Cort Wesley looked at the oldest son he hadn't even known for the first thirteen years of his life. Thought of Li Zhen trading his daughter in to the Triad like a car for a better model of life. He figured that Dylan's problem was that he had too big a heart and was able to look past the bad in people to what made them that way. He'd already known too many monsters in his time and Cort Wesley's greatest unstated fear was that the experiences would scar him for life. In that moment, though, he realized they wouldn't and couldn't.

This boy was his son all right, growing up in his image and following the twisted example set by him and Caitlin Strong.

"Jesus Christ, Dad."

"What?"

"Stop looking at me like I've got two heads. I'm getting us a cab."

Cort Wesley waited until they were in the back of the taxi to call Caitlin.

"Is that a siren?" he asked her, pressing the phone tighter to his ear.

"Don't ask. Long story. I'd need maybe an hour to explain. Luke's safe—that's what you need to hear. I've got him with me now."

"You took him out of school?"

"There wasn't much of a choice," Caitlin said, not bothering to elaborate further. "But it all ends tomorrow, Cort Wesley."

"Where are you going to be tonight, Ranger?"

"Where you just left: San Antonio International."

95

SAN ANTONIO, TEXAS

Kai emerged from the supply closet without the wheelchair, walking upright with the same grace and agility she'd kept disguised ever since reaching LaGuardia Airport back in New York.

Ironic that she was costumed to look so much older today, because that's how she'd felt for so long. Worn, beaten, and what little she had left inside her feeling dried up. Little because they'd stripped it away, scrubbed sandpaper against her psyche and spirit to turn her into what they needed her to be.

The abuse she suffered initially had been limited to the psychological, and it was subtle and brutal at the same time. Brutal in how she was denied anything but passing glances and glimpses of the other girls who'd been taken away from their homes just as she had. Without a social support system, Kai was forced to rely on the women who supervised the home for all her emotional needs. They became both parent and friend, teacher and adviser, providing what she needed the most while never answering any of her most pressing questions or addressing the things that kept her awake long into the night. They were her only stimulus, her sole interaction with the world, creating a longing sense of dependence.

Kai trusted the women, believed they loved her, so when they began ever so subtly introducing her to the skills she needed to perfect, she accepted it as natural. Came even to look forward to those sessions since it was then the most attention was paid to her. And when she behaved and responded well to their teachings, she was rewarded with a doll she could play with. Not as nice as the hand-sewn dolls passed down through generations of her family, but something to cling to at night in the cold and dark before she fell asleep desperate in the hope she might meet her mother in her dreams.

Then her schooling moved on to a different kind of doll, a larger one imitating a boy's anatomy. Her teachers informed her that she was going to learn how to make boys happy. She thought initially what followed was very wrong. Though Kai didn't embrace her new lessons, she didn't reject them out of hand either. There must have, after all, been a reason she was being taught these things, and her teachers were relentless in pointing out that this was a great gift she was being taught to dispense. And with each successive mastery of a lesson came more privileges, including her choices of foods, more toys to play with, movies she was allowed to watch. She did what was expected of her and, as had been the case with her studies previously, committed herself to excel.

Weeks and months passed. Her lessons began to include films that depicted sexual acts tastefully and lovingly, watched so often that Kai became unaffected by them. They came to define normalcy to her and, again, she saw no point in resisting. She didn't want to be one of those girls who cried or screamed or tried to run away, and then one day was no longer heard or seen at all. She believed in her heart her father had sent her here for a reason and that someday he would return for her.

That day never came.

But another day did, the beginning of putting her lessons to practice with first young men, mere boys, not much older than her really. To Kai it was no more than a game, another lesson. She had grown up imbued with a desire to excel at everything she did, and why not this? She had been here so long now that it was all she knew, and in the progression saw an end to the process. Her privileges were extended to trips beyond the walls of the house, to malls where she was allowed to buy anything she wanted and taught how to appreciate the best in clothing and jewelry.

Once in a crowded mall she became separated from the chaperone who'd accompanied her. For a brief moment, her heart thumped at the opportunity to run, to escape. But to where and toward what purpose? So she remained just where she was until the woman returned, smiling joyously.

Because she had passed another test.

Because she hadn't run when given the chance.

And she was deemed ready to begin the next phase of her schooling.

They had a party for her back at the home, pretended it was her birthday. Kai had to remind herself how old she was: almost thirteen now. The days marked off in her head, even though she'd long stopped looking beyond one to the next.

Another lesson.

Strive for perfection.

And that's what Kai did and had done ever since.

Be the best.

As her father had taught before she was taken away. And so it was around then that, faced with the reality he was not coming for her, she decided she'd focus on coming for him. At first she pictured herself asking him why he had done this to her. Later, she imagined making him pay for it. Longing became hatred and she found purpose in the art of lovemaking they taught her by seeing it as a means to the end of tracking him down. Something she could never achieve until fate placed her in the United States and she saw Li Zhen's face plastered all over the media in conjunction with his company's launching of a fifth generation wireless network. And not long after that she came upon a report of a strange murder somewhere in Texas, then another. Murders she recognized from the tortured history of her family that she'd uncovered over the years as well.

History being made to repeat itself and the killings would go on and on, young women much like her senselessly murdered unless she did something. Because Kai felt certain her father was behind the murders. He was a monster. Perhaps her mother and sister had been the lucky ones. But the victims found murdered in a fashion identical to similar victims in America's Old West had not been lucky at all. And there would be many more of them, sacrifices to the times that her father believed destroyed their family's hope, unless she stopped him. Alone now, unless . . .

Unless . . .

Kai found an empty table in the back of a small bar in the terminal and pretended to study a menu resting beneath a sugar caddy. She eased the cell phone from her pocket and pulled up a number she'd lifted off Dylan's phone back in Providence. She started to dial it, stopped, then finished entering the digits. Staring at them for what seemed like a very long time before she pressed Call.

96

SAN ANTONIO INTERNATIONAL AIRPORT, SAN ANTONIO, TEXAS

Caitlin arrived at the Jetlinx private terminal in a detached building just off the tarmac in time to watch the private Lear heading in off the runway. She figured it must have taken off from Houston while she was still at the hospital with Jones. She felt like a kid, face pressed against the window as it taxied straight on course for the glass before veering off into a parking position.

She was through the door and heading for the Lear as its door opened and a set of steps lowered to reveal a pair of plain-clothes Chinese guards standing at the top. She climbed the stairs and eased past them and into the jet to find an old, thin Chinese man rising from behind a table set in the middle of the cabin be-tween four chairs, two on either side facing inward. He nodded and one of the men moved down the stairs to assume a post on the tarmac while the other eased the door closed and took up vigil before it.

"He speaks no English, Ranger Strong," the old man told her, rising. His shock of stark white hair looked chiseled to his scalp, more a statue's than a man's. "So our words will remain secret."

"Thank you for seeing me, Mr. Consul General."

"Please, join me. Sit. Can I get you something?"

"Just the information I requested and you kindly agreed to provide."

The consul general of the People's Republic of China attached to Texas stiffened. "Kindness has nothing to do with it. It has become a matter of practicality now that Li Zhen has betrayed both our nations. Understand, Ranger, that only information rel-evant to Li Zhen's presence in your country was made known to Mr. Brooks and his people. The rest was withheld for obvious reasons."

"And what would those reasons be, sir?"

The consul general leaned forward over the table, smiling reas-suringly. "In China we consider information to be not just a com-modity, but a weapon to be wielded to enforce control and keep underlings beholden and respectful."

"Meaning you have information about Li Zhen you've never shared outside the family."

The consul general's expression wrinkled. "Family?"

"The immediate circle in which you move, sir."

He nodded, grasping her meaning now. "I'm afraid the information you seek is most unpleasant. We would never think of sharing it with anyone if the stakes did not call for it."

"I understand."

The consul general shook his head deliberately, the motion looking almost painful. "No, Ranger Strong, I don't believe you do."

The consul general was right; she didn't. Incoming and outgoing air traffic hammered her ears, and one jet coming in for a landing passed close enough overhead to buckle Caitlin as she walked back to her loaner car. The depths of Li Zhen's depravity defied even her worst expectations, confronting her with the reality of a nemesis whose moral repugnancy rendered him utterly unpredictable. A sociopath for whom morality was a delusion.

And it was left to the Rangers to stop him, no one else was about to help in the little time they had remaining.

Caitlin's phone rang. With no Bluetooth to rely on, she jerked the handset to her ear, expecting Cort Wesley to be on the other end of the line.

"You know who I am," a female voice greeted instead.

"Yes," Caitlin said, feeling a chill surge through her, "I do."

97

SHAVANO PARK, TEXAS

Cort Wesley was sitting on the porch swing when Caitlin pulled into the driveway. She wore only a T-shirt and jeans in spite of the cool bite to the fall air.

"Luke and Dylan are both inside," he told her, the swing rocking slightly. "Guess this is what it takes to bring us all back together."

Caitlin looked back at the street, then continued climbing the porch steps. "I don't see Paz's truck."

"He's here."

"You saw him?"

"Didn't have to." Cort Wesley dug a heel into a slat and stopped the light sway of the swing. "Man, Ranger, you look white as a ghost."

"That's because I just spoke to one, Cort Wesley."

"Hello, Kai," Caitlin said into her phone, the words feeling like marbles banging up against the sides of her mouth.

"I'm sorry Dylan was hurt."

"He could have died. It would've been your fault."

"I didn't have a choice."

The phone felt cold in Caitlin's hand and against her skin. "Criminals say that all the time."

"You think that's what I am?"

"It's what you're acting like, and I'm not talking about how you make your living."

"You know I had no choice in that."

"I'm starting to get a real notion and I'm sorry, I truly am."

"People say that all the time, too."

"Difference being," Caitlin said, still seated behind the wheel of the loaner with the engine off and the windows starting to fog up, "I mean it." She stopped and took a deep breath, unsure of exactly what she going to say next until the words began to spill out. "I watched my mother gunned down when I was a little girl. I've got no memory of that, but it's with me every day of my life, and maybe all these gunfights I keep getting in are about getting back at her killers. But I can't get all the monsters, Kai, nobody can."

"You feel my pain, is that what you mean?"

"Not at all. But I know what pain feels like and what it can do to a person. And it's done the same thing to me it's done to you."

"What's that, Ranger?"

"It turned me into something I can't control. Me not running from a fight, gun or otherwise, was never about being brave. It was about that night my mother was killed and doing to others what I couldn't do to her killers while hiding in a closet."

"A shrink tell you that?"

Caitlin tried to swallow, but her mouth was too dry to manage the effort. She started to reach for a water bottle tucked into one of the loaner's beverage holders, then stopped.

"I've never shared that with a single other person, but I know you can relate to what I'm saying. Thought it might be helpful for you to know you're not alone."

"Your father didn't trade you in like you were an old car."

"No, but Jim Strong pretty much ignored what I witnessed, like he was hoping I wouldn't remember. I only wish he was right."

"I remember too. All too clearly. It never stops hurting."

"And it never will, no matter what you do here or anywhere else. The pain never goes away and sometimes the more you try to get rid of it, the worse it gets."

"Dylan's lucky, Ranger," Kai said after a pause.

"To be alive anyway."

"I meant because he's got you."

"You've got me too, Kai, and that's a promise. I know you're in San Antonio. Let's meet up, just the two of us."

"I called to warn you, Ranger," Kai said flatly, instead of continuing to engage her. "I'm going to end this tomorrow."

"Don't talk like that."

"Stay away from Yuyuan," she continued. "Dylan and his father too. I've been waiting a very long time for this day."

"Your father's a monster, Kai."

"That's the point."

"No, the point is you don't have to be one too. You're the victim in all this. Dylan saw in you the same thing I'm hearing, so let me help. Just me. No cops or other Rangers, I promise. . . . Kai?" Caitlin waited again. "Kai?"

Caitlin looked down at her phone and saw the call had already ended.

* * *

"She called you?"

"Memorized the number off Dylan's phone. Said she was going to handle things tomorrow. Told me, all of us, to stay away from Yuyuan."

"Handle things," Cort Wesley repeated stiffly

"That was my thought too."

"You think she can pull it off?"

"I wouldn't put anything past her. I'm betting she's spent a good portion of her life getting ready for this day."

"You feel bad for her."

Caitlin let some of her breath out and took a seat next to him on the porch swing. "Don't you?"

Cort Wesley started to shake his head, then stopped as something dawned on him. "I believe I finally get why you and Dylan are so close. Because the two of you are the goddamn same. You both think you can save the world, one person at a time."

"You don't think we should bother trying?"

"I think it's a waste of time. Not because people can't be saved, but because they don't want to. I spent four years in prison, Ranger, so I've seen that firsthand. Know something? You can actually *smell* hopelessness. I thought it was just my imagination until I visited someone in the pen and there it was again, same as my time in the Walls."

"So, what, you want me to learn the scent?"

Cort Wesley kicked the swing into a slight rocking motion again. "It beats hearing what you want to and seeing what you want to. Because not everybody deserves to be saved. You wanna believe they can, because it justifies the way you go about your business."

"You're way off base here, Cort Wesley."

"Am I? How many have you ever told about witnessing your mother's death? But that didn't stop you from telling Kai. Anything to help you win her over, put another trophy on your wall of those you've saved instead of bagged."

Caitlin looked at him for what felt like a long time. "You finished?"

"I don't even remember what I just said," he said, leaning backward with a sigh.

The swing coasted to a stop. "Then let's focus on tomorrow."

"What do you think Kai's got planned for Li Zhen?"

Caitlin leaned forward, the color flushing back into her face. "I don't care, Cort Wesley, because we're gonna get him before she can."

98

NEW BRAUNFELS, TEXAS

Li Zhen clutched the phone tighter to his ear, numbed by what the man on the other end had just told him. "What do you mean *raided*?"

"Texas Rangers stormed the studio," the man said, still trying to catch his breath. "I barely got away. They had a warrant. They took everything. I tried to call our lawyer, but he isn't picking up. I didn't know what else . . ."

Zhen found himself feeling cold again, just like yesterday when no amount of frigid water could wash away the weakness and frailty revealed by his killing a girl who became Caitlin Strong to him. His hands ached even more than they normally did, his split knuckles swollen to twice their normal size.

"Texas Rangers," he repeated under his breath, when the man's voice drifted off.

"That would be me," he heard a voice call from the doorway.

Li Zhen pocketed his phone, identical in all respects to General Chang's.

"That's an interesting phone, sir," Caitlin continued. "Available only in China would be my guess, produced specifically to run on the new fifth generation network Yuyuan built."

"Should I be looking for my pruning snips, Ranger?" Zhen managed, fighting against the urge to launch himself against this woman just as he had the whore who'd morphed into her the day before. Kill Caitlin Strong just as he had killed her likeness.

"You won't need them to hear about what we uncovered."

"I assume this concerns me."

Caitlin nodded slowly. "It's the reason why I'm here to arrest you."

She had served the arrest warrant to the guards downstairs who, under threat of arrest themselves, had escorted her up here to a private laboratory that took up the entire corner section of the building's top floor and was reserved for Yuyuan's fledgling pharmaceuticals division. The floor was lined with various reptile, insect, and even a few plant exhibits on display within cages or terrariums placed on stands. Caitlin had the sense she was in some sort of living museum, except for the room's warm, humid conditions that were conducive to the various species collected.

Zhen moved to a case inhabited by horned toads, eased back a slot in the top and poured in a dish of dead insects. "Perhaps you'd like a snack, Ranger."

"Already ate, sir, but thanks just the same," Caitlin told him.

Zhen closed the slot. "You have no authority to arrest anyone here," he said indignantly. "My company lawyers have been adamant about that."

"Oh, I didn't tell you. It's an *international* warrant for arrest. I'm serving it on behalf of the Chinese government."

Zhen's expression turned utterly flat, his face the texture of granite as he moved toward a larger terrarium case where a series of snakes coiled about a miniature jungle scene. A small case resting next to it held three small mice.

"The warrant was secured just this morning by something called a people's procuratorate," Caitlin continued, as she watched him, "on behalf of one of your country's consul generals."

Zhen removed one of the mice from the case by the tail. Still pretending to ignore her, he dropped it into the terrarium and then repeated the process with the second and third mouse, while the trio of snakes inside twisted and turned through the glass.

"Black mambas, Ranger, the most poisonous snakes on the planet. But their poison, which invokes instant paralysis, has also had miraculous effects on study animals suffering spinal cord damage, actually spurring the regrowth of damaged nerve tissue."

"Sounds promising, Mr. Zhen. But it doesn't change what brought me here."

"I understand there is a black SUV parked outside the entrance with three men inside," Zhen said suddenly, clasping his hands behind his back.

"They're Rangers, sir. Backup, in case I need it."

Zhen nodded, unmoved by her words as he moved away from the terrarium where two of the snakes had already taken the mice in their mouths. "What do you see before you, Ranger?" he asked.

"Bugs, sir, lots of them. And some lizards thrown in for good measure."

Zhen smiled, the way a teacher might to a student whose mind was dwarfed by the scope of his knowledge. "That is because you see only the obvious: the creatures behind the glass, but not the power they have and hope they will someday bestow on mankind."

"I'm really not interested, sir."

"You should be, Ranger, you should be," Zhen said, stopping before a fish tank long enough to sprinkle in some flakelike food across the top, and then moving on to a cage laden with sand and brush and filled with yellow scorpions. "Behold the Deathstalker, the most toxic and deadly of any in the scorpion family. But we are only now beginning to realize that its venom also offers treatment for a wide variety of cancers."

Caitlin took a few steps forward to close the gap between them. "I noticed you didn't bother feeding them, sir."

"The Deathstalker is a cannibal, Ranger. But they feast only on others in their species who die of other causes. The ultimate in both self-preservation and natural selection, wouldn't you say?"

Without waiting for her to respond, Zhen moved on to another glass case, where groups of frogs sat abreast of one another, their jowls puckering as they uttered their familiar call. "And these are African tree frogs. They secrete saliva that once absorbed through the skin causes hallucinations, delirium, seizures, and sometimes even death. But that same saliva may hold a treatment to retard the devastating effects of ALS disease. Do you see the point I'm trying to make here?"

"I'd really like to get on with this, Mr. Zhen, if you don't mind."

He stiffened. "Things should never be taken at face value, *Cat-lan* Strong," he said, seeming to take pleasure in purposely mispronouncing her name. "You see what's before you and nothing else."

"You want to know what I see, sir? I see a monster who traded his ten-year-old daughter to the Triad to secure his own fortune."

"Is that what I'm being arrested for?"

Caitlin froze her stare upon him. "Know what I learned last night?" she said, recalling her meeting with the Chinese consul general who'd flown down from Houston. "That your wife died two weeks *before* your daughter was born. Did you have her killed, Mr. Zhen? Did you have her killed because she was going to expose you for what you were?"

Li Zhen continued to stare at her, but his expression had lost its confidence and he was blinking rapidly now, fighting to steady his breathing that had turned short and rapid. "Is that what this people's procuratorate warrant is accusing me of?"

"No, it accuses you of rape and incest. Your oldest daughter committed suicide because of what you did, so if you ask me murder should be added to the charge too. How many times did you rape her, how many times did it take before she got pregnant?"

Caitlin stopped long enough to continue holding Zhen's stare until he turned away.

"She was Kai's real mother."

99

A Polycom conference phone sat in the middle of the table, wires strung across the top of the table connecting it to the wall jacket and power outlet. A single light glowed green, as D. W. Tepper strode into the room.

"Sun's barely up and I'm already pissed," he said between a scowl. "Just got word there's a protest planned outside Yuyuan for today. Highway Patrol says they're gonna shut the freeway down no later than noon." Tepper aimed his next words toward the conference phone. "You hear us okay, Doc?" he asked Bexar County's longtime medical examiner.

"Loud and clear," Whatley replied.

"How 'bout you, Mr. Jones?" Tepper followed to the man from Homeland Security, currently at an undisclosed medical facility under guard of Colonel Paz's men, who, besides the Texas Rangers, were the only ones he could trust right now.

"You miss me, Captain?"

"Not at all, but it is nice not to be butting heads with you for a change. Amazing what getting shot up tends to do for the soul. Young Roger, the floor is yours."

Young Roger brushed the long hair from his face and leaned forward. "I spent much of the night examining the cell phones Ranger Strong messengered to me and didn't find what I expected to."

"What's that mean?" Caitlin asked him.

"Well, I started with what you told me about the victims, particularly the most recent one—that Chinese general. What you were suggesting is death by ventricular fibrillation. Does that jibe with your findings, Doc?" Young Roger asked, aiming his words toward the speakerphone.

"Well, I wasn't able to do much more than a cursory exam of General Chang, but it definitely jibes with what caused the deaths of those homeless men," Whatley reported.

"Okay," Young Roger resumed, "what we're talking about is essentially using electrocution to cause a heart attack. Now, a low-voltage AC current traveling through the chest for a fraction of a second can induce ventricular fibrillation. Fibrillations can be and usually are deadly because all the heart muscle cells move independently. You end up with contractions so strong that the heart muscle seizes up and stops moving altogether."

"You mind backing up a bit, son," interjected Captain Tepper. "I believe my heart muscle's been seizing up ever since Hurricane Caitlin here returned to the Texas Rangers."

Young Roger leaned farther over the table. His long hair fell in front of his face and he brushed it to the side again with a swipe of his hand. "Think of it this way, Captain. The heart muscle is actually driven by low levels of electrical current—that's what an EKG, or an electrocardiogram, is actually measuring when they hook you up to a machine in the doctor's office."

Tepper hocked up some mucus and swallowed it back down. "Haven't had one of those in years, son," he told Young Roger. "Not since the paper spit out a flat line and the nurse told me I must be dead."

"When the electrical signals become too weak or inconsistent with age," Young Roger continued, "you can stimulate the heartbeat with a pacemaker." He stopped and rotated his eyes around the table. "What happened to the Chinese general and these homeless men is like a reverse pacemaker—that's what those cell phones essentially were. The point I made earlier was that it doesn't take much electric current at all to cause significant physiological damage, including a heart attack. To give you an idea what I'm talking about, it takes a thousand times more current to trip a circuit breaker than it does to bring on respiratory arrest. Right, Doc?"

"Young man," came Whatley's surprisingly clear voice over the speaker, "you are dead on in your assessment. A bad pun, I suppose, in this case."

Captain Tepper puckered his lips and regarded the cell phone tucked into plastic and centered between them with clear disdain. "You mind telling me how a device that small, and battery operated no less, could put out that kind of voltage, son?"

"Voltage," Young Roger told him, "has nothing to do with it. It's all about electric *current*. OSHA estimates it takes as little as exposure to one hundred Ma, or milliamperes, to cause ventricular fibrillation and probable death. So I turned my attention to how a device that small could generate even that level of current. Doc, you notice the phones in question were no longer in working order?"

"I did," Whatley confirmed. "Tried to turn them on and nothing happened. I assumed the batteries were just drained."

"Close, but not quite. See, all the phones were equipped with chips that had burned out. There were no visible signs of that, but when I tested the chips, it was clear that they were no longer functional. Now, what you need to know about chips like this is that they only use a small portion of their cores at any given time; otherwise, they'd fry." Young Roger picked up one of the phones through the plastic and held it up for all to see. "What I think Yuyuan figured out was how to utilize the entire core of the chip at once to concentrate an electrical charge of sufficient current to kill whoever was holding it at the time."

"So the phone rings," Caitlin started, "the victim answers it, and the person on the other end triggers this chip."

"More than likely, there wouldn't be a person on the other end, but a machine. A router capable of sending the signal to the chip the split second the receiving phone is answered. All the killer would need to do is program the number."

"But the victim would have to be holding it," said Cort Wesley. "Have I got that right?"

"Not necessarily," Young Roger answered. "It's a matter of conductivity. Skin makes for an ideal conductor, but kept in a pocket, with only a thin layer of material separating the phone from the skin, could work just as well. So could a phone held in a typical belt clip or holster."

"So why did Li Zhen need to build the entire five G network to pull this off?"

"A few reasons, starting with something called system spectral efficiency, which basically refers to the data volume per area unit. That, coupled with higher bit rates in larger portions of all coverage areas, will combine to allow users in previously outlying areas to download more data much faster. For our purposes, that means a clearer and sharper signal, less degradation from its point of origin along a broader bandwidth."

"In a language we can all understand, if you don't mind, son," said Captain Tepper, shaking his head.

"It's the difference between firing a bullet through the air instead of through water," Young Roger elaborated, taking the sample phone in hand again through the plastic. "If I dial your phone right now from this very room it could take up to ten or fifteen seconds for the call to actually go through. In Li Zhen's case, each one of those seconds would weaken the signal his satellites are sending to the point where it might not, probably wouldn't, be strong enough to generate an electrical charge sufficient to cause ventricular fibrillation. But with the five G network those delays would be effectively eliminated."

"But you're forgetting one thing here: the phones with these killer chips haven't been released yet," Captain Tepper noted.

Young Roger pondered that for a moment. "How long has it been since Yayuan was awarded the five G network contract?"

"Five years, give or take," came Jones's voice over the speaker.

"So they could have been installing the chips in question," Caitlin started before Young Roger had a chance to, "in the billion or so other phones China's been manufacturing annually for the last five years."

"Only the ones meant for American import," Young Roger elaborated.

"So you're saying he could, conceivably, push the button even before his fifth generation network is fully operational," concluded Cort Wesley.

"At maybe twenty to twenty-five percent efficiency, but yes, sure he could."

"Meaning he'd kill only twenty million Americans instead of a hundred," Caitlin noted, her voice sounding dry, as if her mouth was suddenly coated with dust.

Young Roger's nod dissolved into a shrug. "But a fully operational and integrated fifth generation network would allow the transmitted signal to travel in a more direct path, with far greater integrity and far less likelihood of interference or disruption. And the resulting increase in bandwidth allows for tens of thousands of calls to be placed in the same moment without crashing the system or diluting the signal."

"In others words," Caitlin elaborated, "Zhen will be able to kill a hell of a lot more people in a much shorter time frame."

"Right as rain, Ranger," Young Roger said. "And at that point it's possible the victims wouldn't even need to answer their phones. So long as it's powered up, and in close enough proximity to the body, the number ringing alone could be enough to activate the chip. Seventy percent of all the mobile phones in the world are manufactured in China, over a billion handsets last year alone. And components, especially the chips, account for maybe ten to fifteen percent more."

"So let me get this straight," Tepper said, pushing his hands through his hair and leaving more of it wedged out in all directions like garden weeds, "all the killer needs is a phone number for his intended victim and the family's planning a funeral."

"Simply stated, yes."

"You hear that, Jones," Caitlin couldn't resist chiming in, "what Homeland's deal with the devil has wrought. Li Zhen was playing you all along, delivering exactly what you wanted so you wouldn't bother to ask the questions you should have been."

"You think I could have anticipated all this?" Jones's voice, more strident and indignant, sounded hollow all of a sudden over the speaker.

"I don't think it ever occurred to you to bother," Caitlin told him. "That's the problem with people like you who give no quarter when it comes to what they claim is defending the country: you see what's before you and nothing else. Li Zhen pulled the wool over your eyes and you didn't even bother to notice."

"I took three bullets when I tried to shut the whole thing down, Ranger, in case you've forgotten."

"I once shot a pit bull that had sunk its teeth into a boy's arm," recalled Captain Tepper, swiping his tongue over his palm to wet his hair down anew. "Put six bullets into him and they still had to surgically remove the dog's jaws from the boy's arm at the hospital. Sounds like Li Zhen's got the same attitude, and I'd like to hear now how we go about dealing with that."

"Same way you dealt with the pit bull," Caitlin told him. "Pretty much."

Jones chuckled through the speaker. "So you plan on just walking into Li Zhen's office with this warrant you managed to procure from the Chinese consul general attached to Houston and slapping the handcuffs on him?"

"As a matter of fact, Jones, I do."

A cell phone rang, no one at the table sure whose it was.

"Don't answer that," D. W. Tepper said from the doorway.

100

New Braunfels, Texas

"Your oldest daughter's name was Jiao," Caitlin continued. "I believe that means delicate, tender. Beautiful too. Have I got that right, sir?"

Zhen made himself hold her stare, wondering if she'd seen his basement in Alamo Heights. All the pictures of his one true love, Jiao, plastered over the walls.

"I hear rapists in your prisons get even worse treatment than they get in ours," Caitlin told him. Sweat, wrought by the room's fetid conditions, was beginning to bead up on Li Zhen's forehead.

"You can't prove any of this," he said finally, his expression remaining flat and calm. But the way his fists kept clenching and unclenching told Caitlin he was fighting to retain control.

"What's wrong with your hands, sir?" she asked, noticing his swollen, split knuckles. "Looks like you've been in a scrape."

Zhen clasped his hands behind his back again. "It's nothing. Just a scuffle. It's not your problem."

"No, sir, it's not, and neither are you. You're China's problem once I turn you over to consulate officials and they get you back there. I do have a question, though: did General Chang ever learn the whole truth about Kai, who her mother really was? I wonder if it would've rendered her less appealing to the Triad's pervert division."

Zhen shook his head, trying to muster his typically sententious smile but failing utterly. "An old Chinese proverb councils that it is better to light a candle than to curse the darkness. You curse the darkness, Ranger. These allegations and insinuations will never have any light shed on them. I will be exonerated and you will be disgraced."

"I prefer the proverb that goes something to the effect that if you've never done anything evil, you don't have to worry about the devil knocking at your door. But in your case he might as well be breaking it down."

"You're just like your great-grandfather, Ranger."

"I wish the same could be said for you, sir. Tsuyoshi Zhen, your great-grandfather, was gunned downed saving a child's life in the midst of that massacre at the hands of the Pinkertons. And this whole thing, this plot of yours, is about revenge for that, along with John Morehouse stealing his invention. I'm not saying you don't have call to hate this country because of that, but killing innocent people makes you a lot more like your great-granddad's killers and less like him."

Li Zhen stood there rigidly, as if chiseled out of the floor. "Your great-grandfather couldn't stop them back in 1883 no more than you can stop me today."

"That's a matter of opinion, sir. Maybe you haven't heard how the story ended."

101

El Paso, Texas; 1883

William Ray Strong was in an El Paso jail cell, not bothering to sleep as dawn approached, when Judge Roy Bean burst through the door accompanied by six men William Ray recognized as regulars in his saloon.

"Who's in charge here?" the judge demanded in a drunken slur.

An older, overweight deputy who'd been snoozing with his boots crossed atop a desk lurched awake in his chair, dropping the shotgun laid across his lap to the floor.

"That'd be me," the man said, stumbling to his feet and laying his palms flat on the desktop for support.

Bean shot William Ray a look and flashed a wink. The Ranger could smell the whiskey rising through the pores of him and his men, mixing with the sour stench of perspiration after a long night of drink followed by the ride here from the Langtry saloon.

"I got something for you," Bean resumed to the deputy, drawing some papers out of his jacket pocket. He staggered drunkenly toward the old deputy, his path straightening just before he reached the man and passing the mottled mass of pages to him. "This here's a writ signed by the county commissioner ordering you to place your prisoner in my custody. On account of the fact that crimes he committed in my jurisdiction done supersede yours."

"What crimes are those?"

"Public drunkenness, disturbing the peace, and assaulting a federal deputy."

"Who would that be?" the older man asked, looking up from the pages out of which he could make no sense.

"You," the judge said and punched him hard enough in the face to push the man back into the wall where he smacked his skull and slumped downward, eyes growing glassy. Then Bean looked toward William Ray with a shrug. "I was running out of patience."

"Remind me never to cross you, Judge," William Ray said, as Bean jerked a key ring from the deputy's belt and flipped through the assortment for the right one to open the cell.

"When this is over, Ranger, you and me are gonna sit down and drink us some whiskey."

"First things first," William Ray told him.

By the time John Morehouse learned of William Ray Strong's escape and return to the camp, he was nowhere to be found. Then an out-of-breath boy rushed up to him with a report of something going on at the site of the earthen dam constructed to stem the flow of floodwaters built up through the unseasonably wet spring. Morehouse gathered what was left of his Pinkertons and rode out to the dam, accompanied by Marshal Stoudenmire and his deputies.

They found Texas Ranger William Ray Strong there standing alone atop the man-made berm holding back the torrents of water that would otherwise flood the entire length of the northern spur the Southern Pacific was building.

"You're trespassing, Ranger," Morehouse charged, staring up into the sun. "Another charge to add to those filed already. I'd say you can consider your career finished."

"I tried to do this the right way, sir."

"How's that?"

"By arresting you for the killings of all those Chinese you'd cheated out of their wages, those Christian missionaries too. You know the term *bahk guai*?"

"Can't say I do, Ranger."

"It means 'white devil' and that's exactly what you are for believing the laws of the nation and state of Texas don't apply to you or your railroad."

"Are you finished, Ranger?"

"Not quite, sir."

With that William Ray eased a hand down to his belt, the Pinkertons tightening their grasps on their weapons, until the Ranger came away with a cigar instead of a pistol. He lit the fresh stogie with a match he shook out in the air and tossed aside before beginning to puff away. Then he crouched down and retrieved what looked at first glance to be a string of wire from the top of the earthen dam, but at second glance looked like something else entirely.

"Have you lost your mind, Ranger?" Morehouse yelled up to him, heart beginning to hammer against his chest. "Is that a—"

"Yes, sir, it's a fuse, connected up to a whole bunch of dynamite I borrowed from your supply depot. I hope you don't mind. I filed a requisition with the Rangers via telegraph to make sure you get compensated appropriately, so you don't need to worry none on that account."

Morehouse froze, Stoudenmire froze, the Pinkertons froze.

"Shoot him!" Morehouse ordered. "Shoot him now!"

"Bad idea, sir," William Ray warned before a single finger could find its trigger, cigar tip holding just short of touching the fuse.

Morehouse jerked a hand up to signal his men to hold up and followed the length of the unspooled fusing as far as he could. "You can't do this. You have no idea of the damage you'll do, how far you'll set us back."

The Ranger stood over them, silhouetted by the sun, puffing away on his cigar again and impervious to the guns still held upon him. "I believe I've got a very good idea," William Ray said down to him. "My father was one of the first Rangers ever sworn in after their duties became official. One of the lessons I learned from him before he went off to fight in the Civil War and never came back was if you can't get someplace one way, you find another." With that, William Ray touched the tip of his cigar to the edge of the fuse that immediately caught, sizzled, and began to burn. "This is my other way. Only choice you got left, Mr. Morehouse, is whether you want to ride away or swim."

William Ray Strong and Judge Roy Bean had galloped just out of range of the blast, watching it from a plateau just short of the hills overlooking the scene. The dynamite ignited in not one, but several rippling explosions that blended into each other. Brief bursts of explosive flame were drowned out by thick smoke that cleared in the morning air to reveal the tons of earth piled before the overflow's onslaught falling aside. Peeling away to let first streams and then torrents of water flood outward from the blown dam, following the line of rails and ties as far as the eye could see.

William Ray watched it rushing across the landscape as long as he could, figuring it would wipe out pretty much everything the Southern Pacific had built for the entire length of this northern spur, washing away miles and months of work.

"That ought to teach them," William Ray noted, still working on the same cigar.

"What exactly?" Bean asked him.

"That you don't mess with Texas, 'specially the Rangers." He tossed his cigar aside, looking as if he had a sour taste left in his mouth. "It ain't much, but it's better than nothing."

102

"So this whole thing, this plot of yours, is about revenge for that massacre that claimed the life of your great-grandfather," Caitlin finished, after looking at Li Zhen for a long moment. "That and John Morehouse stealing Tsuyoshi Zhen's invention."

Li Zhen moved closer to her, positioned in a way that made him seem part of a terrarium containing African tree frogs set immediately to his rear. "You feel too much, *Cat-lan* Strong," he said, letting his face freeze again just short of a smile. "We have a saying that life is a tragedy for those who feel but a comedy for those who think."

"And you're the one laughing, is that it?"

"You tell a good story, *Cat-lan* Strong. I will give you that much. But that's all it is—a story."

"Hold on, I haven't finished yet. Haven't even gotten to the part about you murdering five Chinese call girls exactly the same way as somebody in that camp did. They were also porn actresses who worked out of a studio the Rangers raided this morning, if you haven't heard. A studio leased out to a shell company that leads straight back to Yuyuan."

Zhen's porcelain expression seemed to crack, right down the middle in Caitlin's mind, from the way the light struck his suddenly narrowed eyes above which furrows had dug into his brow.

"You killed those girls along the rail line the Southern Pacific built through Texas. The daughter you pawned off to human traffickers dropped out of sight right around the time the murders started. She knew it was you, got involved with Dylan Torres because she thought his dad and me were the ones who could put a stop to it. The arrest warrant I'm serving for your government doesn't mention any of that, but I suspect rape and incest should put you away for plenty long enough on their own."

Zhen seemed unmoved by her conclusions. "I think you're bluffing. I don't believe the warrant is valid because my government would never risk embarrassment by cooperating with you on such a foolish venture."

"I understand you stuck a soldering iron in their privates after you strangled them, Mr. Zhen," Caitlin countered, trying to taunt a rise out of him. "Was it because your own tool doesn't heat up much anymore and probably hadn't since you raped your oldest daughter? John Morehouse cut your great-grandfather's balls off by stealing his invention, just like the Triad sliced off yours by making you trade your daughter for Yuyuan. How's that deal feeling right about now?"

Caitlin waited for Li Zhen to respond, was surprised when he didn't.

"So William Ray Strong never got his killer," she resumed, "but I got mine. And wherever my great-grandfather is now I'm sure he must be real pleased you didn't get away with killing women and sewing their heads on backward like somebody back in those railroad camps did."

Zhen's expression had gone utterly flat again. "I imagine that would be a challenging task."

"Not for a man with your degree of practice, sir."

Zhen smiled tightly. "What about a man with rheumatoid arthritis?" he said, holding his hands up to reveal gnarled, swollen fingers and knuckles that looked like lumps of mottled flesh even without the bruising suffered yesterday. "Do you really think a man with hands like this could manage the kind of murders you're describing?"

Caitlin felt the breath seize up in her chest, recalling how much trouble Li Zhen had had working the pruning snips out in his company's garden. As much as the condition of his hands, she could tell he was telling the truth from his eyes, the gleeful gleam that flashed at refuting the most strident allegation she'd come to level against him.

But if Zhen wasn't the one leaving bodies along the old rail line, then who was?

She had gotten it wrong today, just as William Ray Strong had in 1883 when he suspected David Morehouse of that spate of killings.

"You've lost, *Cat-lan* Strong," he said, and moved toward the far wall beyond all the display cases lining the floor. "Come witness the price of your defeat."

Once there, Li Zhen waved a palm in front of what must have been some kind of scanner, because the wall receded to reveal a wide, crystal-clear, wall-length window overlooking the front of the complex.

Caitlin joined him before it, readying a pair of plastic handcuffs.

"Look down," Zhen told her.

Caitlin spotted her SUV parked in front of the entrance, a trio of shapes barely discernible inside. Beyond, Old San Antonio Road had now been closed off entirely by the swelling protest that had forced her to loop all the way around in approaching Yuyuan. And then she glimpsed a trio of black-clad figures rush toward the three figures inside her SUV, opening fire with their submachine guns.

Zhen came up alongside her. "I think I will accelerate my plans."

Part Ten

REWARD!

FIVE THOUSAND DOLLARS FOR DEAD BANK ROBBERS
NOT ONE CENT FOR LIVE ONES

—From a placard in a Texas bank window, 1928

103

The trio of black-garbed shapes had cut through the light, sweeping past a FedEx truck parked by the entrance. Eerily miniaturized from this distance looking down, the whole scene was rendered even more surreal by the fact that the thick glass muffled all sound of their gunfire.

Orange flashes burst from the muzzles, followed by a constant stream of color burning through the sun-drenched air. The men moved as they kept shooting, no quarter or square inch of space spared. Their bullets tore into the SUV, Caitlin following the three figures inside jumping and jerking about as the bullets pulverized them.

"Now, you are alone," Li Zhen taunted. "How does it feel, Ranger?"

She drew her own pistol and leveled it straight at him. "We're leaving, sir, with you under arrest."

Zhen didn't move, his gaze still focused downward through the window, not even bothering to regard her as if unaffected by her intention.

"I'm not going anywhere," he told her.

"You just murdered three Texas Rangers. You just declared war on the state of Texas."

Zhen finally turned her way again, his expression flat and smug. "I will never see the inside of a jail or a court, and you know it. It will be reported that you and the other three Rangers died in a traffic accident, something like that. Your vehicle exploded, leaving no remains at all."

Caitlin held her SIG Sauer steady on him. "How's that exactly, sir?"

"Turn around, Ranger."

Caitlin did, found herself facing two average-sized men flanking a giant bald figure in the middle. All three had guns trained her way, their thick swatches of Triad tattoos visible in exposed patches of their skin.

"The big guy's name is Qiang, I believe, Mr. Zhen," Caitlin said, holding her gun just as steady. "There's an international warrant out for him for the bombing of a government building in Taiwan. I guess I'll just have to arrest him too."

"Arrogance inevitably destroys those who let it consume them."

"You should know, I suppose. Not that it matters, because you're always going to be the man who took his own daughter to bed and fathered a second one. No amount of money or power can ever change that. And you know what's worse? Given the chance, you'd do it all over again, without any hesitation at all. Have I got that right, sir? Look at me and tell me I'm wrong."

"You think you're any different, hiding your weakness behind your gun? Shooting anyone who opposes you so you need not face the truth."

"You're talking about self-loathing, Mr. Zhen, and the truth is I've known my share of it. And by acknowledging that, you learn to stop hating yourself. You should really try it sometime."

The two smaller Triad gunmen were approaching now, while Qiang hung back. Caitlin eased her hands into the air, SIG dangling from a single figure looped through its trigger guard. She felt one man take it from her grasp while the other jerked her arms down behind her back, quickly fastening her own set of plastic wrist cuffs in place.

"There is no dam to bring down on me, *Cat-lan* Strong," Zhen said, taking the SIG in a swollen hand that seemed to have trouble holding it. His porcelain expression bent into a snarl that morphed into a tight, toothless grin.

The two Triad soldiers dragged Caitlin between a set of display cases toward the elevator.

"Take another look out that window, Mr. Zhen," she said, twisting toward him.

Zhen turned his gaze back out through the glass just as the Triad gunmen outside down below jerked open the pockmarked, bullet-riddled doors of Caitlin's SUV to inspect their handiwork. They froze, backing off with guns lowered, gazing at one another in befuddlement at the sight revealed before them.

Zhen squinted, seeing what they had seen but still not believing it. He twisted round, the elevator door sliding open even though none of his men had pushed the button. He was still searching for words when Guillermo Paz burst from the elevator cab, submachine guns held in either hand spitting bullets.

104

NEW BRAUNFELS, TEXAS

Paz had entered the parking garage through a storm drain built under it that connected a catch basin to a nearby river for run-off to avoid flooding. He'd found the elevator just about where the architectural plans for the complex revealed it to be, following it to the floor where tracking software installed on his smartphone indicated his Texas Ranger was located. The phone and software had been provided by Homeland Security, and Paz never bothered himself about how it worked exactly.

He only cared that it did.

His initial bursts took out the men on either side of Caitlin

Strong, Paz swinging toward the massive shape recorded at the edge of his consciousness in the same moment pistol fire opened up his way. He launched himself airborne to avoid it, hitting the floor still in motion, sliding across the tile toward the cover of the larger display cases holding various kinds of insects and reptiles.

Paz heard glass shattering, display cases ruptured by his fire, the big man's, or both. The rupture of the case had freed thousands of fire ants to scurry across the floor, the pack seeming to move as one, converging on him. Paz swept wave after wave of them aside as he positioned himself to return the big man's fire.

But that fire, he realized, was trained not on him, but on the case behind which he rested. More glass shattered, freeing a trio of snakes Paz recognized as black mambas, infused with venom that could kill a man within seconds, two of them with just-swallowed mice bulging from their skin, and a third with a mouse still inside its open mouth. They slithered across the floor, riding atop the fire ants with tongues sweeping the air.

Other shapes seemed to dance before him, skirting his line of vision. The man Paz recognized from pictures as Li Zhen glided past him and took Caitlin Strong by her cuffed wrists, dragging her with him into the elevator with the Ranger's own pistol pressed against her skull.

Before Paz could react, the door started to close and the giant he now recognized as an extremely well-regarded assassin and killer named Qiang opened fire, blowing apart the glass of an aquarium filled with fat-faced fish that paralyzed larger prey so they could enter and eat them from the inside out. The jets of water from the tank propelled the fish across the floor, turning it slick and murky with the fire ants swept away while the fish flopped, clinging desperately to life. A similar variety native to South America were known to kill a few fishermen every year for doing no more than trying to extract the hook from their mouths. More seasoned men of the sea had learned never to dump the product of their nets without wearing gloves thick enough to resist such toxic bites.

Paz remained pinned to the floor, below the next line of the big man's fire. But he stayed in motion, sliding through the water, his clothes soaking up fire ants while he was careful to avoid touching the fat-faced smiley fish whose grins promised death. He rammed into another display case, toppling it over backward and freeing what looked like some kind of toads with horns rising over their faces to hop across the floor, drawn to the thickest pools of water.

Paz steadied one of his submachine guns on Qiang's position, opening fire to find the big shape nowhere to be seen an instant before two terrariums standing side by side were spilled over in unison. Paz pushed himself backward across the floor, his palms torn bloody by shards of shattered glass, leaving a splotchy trail in his path as the enraged black mambas slithered across the floor toward him.

105

New Braunfels, Texas

The three gunmen were backing up toward the FedEx truck when Cort Wesley burst out the rear doors, flak jacket buried beneath his blue uniform top and assault rifle clacking away. He saw enough of them to know they were Chinese, Triad soldiers in all probability, but not enough to tell anything else.

But he could feel their shock, the very thing that had helped render them vulnerable to his surprise attack. Shock at what they had viewed inside Caitlin's SUV after shooting the hell out of it:

Mannequins, seated inside in place of men. Decoys.

Cort Wesley had wielded an M16 more times than he could count, had killed with the deadly rifle pretty much every time he'd fired it. Today that fire had a hollow ring to it, drowned out in large measure by the protest that had shut down the road directly in front of Yuyuan. He kept the trigger working until the magazine emptied, slapping a fresh one home just in case before starting forward.

The three Triad soldiers lay in blood pools so thick, the coppery stench almost made him gag. It was a smell Cort Wesley had never gotten used to. That was the thing about gunfights; everything in life seemed to change, evolve, except them. They were always the same, as far back as Cort Wesley's experience allowed him to recall. The sense of the assault rifle jerking slightly in his grasp, its weight much heavier than anyone who'd never wielded one could possibly imagine. The feel of super-heated air from the expended bullets pushed back at him by the forward gravity created by the expended shells.

Cort Wesley wanted to smell the flowering dogwood trees and the fresh scents cast by the elms and oaks layered into the ground around the complex. He wanted to suck that into his nostrils to replace the blood stench taking root there now. But it wouldn't go away, lingering and loitering in his nose as well as consciousness as if to remind him he'd just snuffed out three lives. He wished it hadn't been necessary. He wished somewhere down deep it bothered him more.

In the road fronting Yuyuan, meanwhile, as many as five thousand protesters had gathered for a rally against Zhen's company. Cort Wesley realized the police detail assigned to secure the area was understaffed and woefully unprepared to deal with such numbers and ferocity. Barely a thousand were expected to show up and the additional four thousand left the participants pressed shoulder to shoulder, all facing a stage that was currently empty.

Cort Wesley reached the SUV's shot-out windows to find the stench of burned plastic replacing that of spilled blood. The three mannequins dressed as Texas Rangers right down to the Stetsons and badges had taken so many bullets, parts of them had practically melted. Charred holes marked bullet entries in dangling plastic limbs. Two of the mannequins' heads were missing and the torso of a third had taken so much fire that it was mostly just a jagged hole where its chest and much of its stomach should have been.

Li Zhen had taken the bait just as hoped for and expected. Caitlin was right; the man's weakness lay in his arrogance, his sense of invincibility and entitlement. Cort Wesley figured there must be some Chinese proverb counseling against just that. But he wasn't much for quotes and proverbs, much more comfortable with a rifle than a moral and, with that, he swung back around and charged toward the building's entrance.

106

NEW BRAUNFELS, TEXAS

Zhen slammed Caitlin's head against the elevator cab wall once and then again, as it bottomed out like a Disney ride, zooming downward. His breathing had picked up, turning rapid and shallow, noisy through his mouth. His eyes continued to glow hatefully, wide with indecision and uncertainty over encountering the utterly unexpected.

"I want you to *see!*" he hissed into her ear. "To bear witness!"

The plastic ties binding her wrists together from behind left her unable to deflect or counter his blows.

"Where we going?" she asked, finding her voice. "Hell?"

"No," Li said, as the elevator door slid open. "The future."

Paz and Qiang continued to exchange fire, the motion of both constant, each managing to stay just ahead of the other's bullets. A final volley from Paz shattered yet another display case and freed desert scorpions to scurry across the floor. Their stingers were raised ominously as they advanced like an army, the clacking sound they made as they moved en masse sounding oddly like the crackling of fires burning in the hillside slum Paz remembered from cold nights in his youth.

Qiang's final stitch of fire, meanwhile, obliterated the glass of a case holding what Paz recognized as African drum ivy, the deadliest plant known to man. It was more of a vine really, with thick, full leaves that looked like pincers and extracted a noxious white vapor known to cause almost instant death. The drum ivy's deadly defenses were activated by proximity; Paz heard what sounded like a hiss and just managed to evade the escaping vapors that fluttered through the air in a thin cloud, dissipating.

Then he glimpsed Qiang storming across the floor, seeming to soar through the air, the two of them meeting in the room's center atop crackling glass with creatures scampering or buzzing all around them.

The lobby doors forming the entrance to Yuyuan had been locked down, so Cort Wesley shot out the glass with a fusillade that cost him his second magazine. Then he crashed through the solid panes fractured along spiderweb-like lines into the sprawling reception area. Soft music formed an insane background to the sounds of gunfire when he opened up on more Triad soldiers who seemed to be coming from everywhere at once.

And that's when time froze, nothing but the staccato bursts of sound and glimpses of movement registering with him at all.

Time changed. Places changed.

But not battle, one exactly like the last and the next. Context, location, and purpose always distinct, while sense and mind-set remained the same.

And Cort Wesley took to this one, just as he'd taken to all the others. Nothing was forgotten, each piece of every other battle he'd ever fought leaving an indelible mark. There was the sense of the assault rifle vibrating slightly as it clacked off rounds, warm against his hands, steady in his grasp. The sight of the muzzle flash, strange metallic smell of air baked by the heat of the expended shells, and his own kinetic energy. The world reduced to its most basic and simple. There was the gun, his targets, the glass and wall between them, and nothing else. Welcome and comfortable in its familiarity with all thinking suspended and instinct left to command him.

"Dad!" Cort Wesley heard Dylan say in his tiny earpiece. "Dad!"

His son's call from outside on the outskirts of the massive crowd gathered to protest Yuyuan sounded more like an echo in Cort Wesley's ravaged ears. The boy was here because he was best able to identify the big wild card in all this:

Kai.

"She's here, Dad, she's here!"

Cort Wesley heard his son's words with an illusionary beat between each of them, making it feel as if his brain and body were detached from each other. "Keep her out of the building!" he ordered, picking up only splotches of his own words. "You hear me, son?"

Dylan slid down a slight rise just over a man-made arroyo used to collect rainwater washed off the nearby four-lane. The tree cover obscured whatever was happening at Yuyuan from him, but he was pretty sure he'd detected the clack of gunfire, light and tinny from this distance with so much additional noise around him. He lost Kai amid the slog briefly, than spotted her again as she moved in lithe, supple fashion through the tightly packed crowd, seeming to glide.

He started toward her through the clutter of humanity, not sure exactly what would happen when he got there; what exactly he'd say or do. Dylan knew she'd used him to get her out of New York, but didn't much care right now. His head was pounding again. His mouth had gone bone dry. He was sweating like crazy even though he didn't feel warm and all he wanted to do was get the girl aside and talk her down.

The crowd thickened the closer Dylan drew to Kai, approaching from her rear flank so she wouldn't spot him before he reached her. She was so beautiful even amid these conditions, the focused intensity he'd glimpsed in her expression, resolve coupled with self-assurance, only adding to the infatuation that had almost gotten him killed.

Dylan was still eight feet away when a fissure opened in the crowd, a clear path between him and Kai when he saw the lighter flash in her hand.

* * *

Caitlin felt Zhen drag her from the elevator by her cuffed hands. Banks of dull overhead lights snapped on, illuminating a sprawling floor of computer terminals, servers, and mainframes. She recognized what looked to be routers and relays nestled on a floor dominated by a long series of wall-sized monitors broadcasting the constant scrawl of ten-digit combinations that could only be phone numbers across the nation being stored by Yuyuan satellites orbiting hundreds of miles overhead. The room was utterly devoid of humidity, feeling chilly and airless to her.

"This is where the end of your country begins," Zhen clamored, dragging her across the floor by her hair. He plopped her down in the first chair they came to and jerked her head backward with a final tug of her black locks, his dry odorless breath pouring into her. "This is where my family gets even! My destiny, my fate."

"Murdering tens of millions of innocent people?"

"It would have been *hundreds* of millions if your interference hadn't forced me to activate my plan ahead of schedule," Zhen corrected and pressed the SIG against her temple, the muzzle of the barrel feeling like ice. "The signal will go out over the four G network, not nearly as effective but a satisfying result just the same."

"Why not just kill yourself, Mr. Zhen? It's what you really want, probably since the first time you slept with Jiao. You want to blame America for you being reared in poverty, go ahead. But this country had nothing to do with you raping your daughter. She was only thirteen when Kai was born. Tell me, did you ever rape her too?"

But Zhen's mind was somewhere else, not seeming to have registered her words at all. "Just a few strikes on the keyboard and it begins," he said. "My satellites waiting to receive the data in order to transmit a signal that will automatically dial those cell phone numbers ringing right here in your country at a hundred thousand per second. You are about to bear witness to the end of life in the United States as you know it."

"Only until you're dead, Mr. Zhen," Caitlin said, trying to remain composed, not ready to concede anything, keenly aware Zhen was having trouble keeping the pistol steady in his arthritic hands, which grew shakier with each passing second.

He moved his face closer to hers. "You'd like that, wouldn't you, for the simplicity it suggests? The way it was in the time of our grandfathers. But those times are long past. The satellites operate remotely. Once the operation is triggered, your country's fate becomes inevitable. My death will mean no more than your life, *Cat-lan* Strong. You will witness me bringing that to be, witness me—"

But before Zhen could utter another word Caitlin slammed her forehead into the bridge of his nose, Zhen sent reeling backward with her pistol flying from his grasp.

107

NEW BRAUNFELS, TEXAS

Cort Wesley had momentarily forgotten about Dylan's warning that he'd spotted Kai, lost in the environment of spilled bodies, pooling blood, and a wailing alarm that only just reached the edge of his consciousness. That mind-set was the only way to survive this kind of battle time and time again.

But for now anyway he was the only man standing. The lobby belonged to him, his ground to defend. Shapes of Chinese gunmen, provided by the Triad no doubt, continued to emerge from different points in different moments. But they were ill prepared for this kind of fight, especially against a professional as seasoned in battle as Cort Wesley was. They were killers, yes, but killers used to being met with far less resistance, if any at all. The shots several managed to get off flew wildly off kilter, which in Cort Wesley's lexicon meant missing him by more than a foot.

He could feel their fire dancing through the air, sizzling past him. Could almost imagine being able to follow the errant path of their bullets the same way he could the vapor trail of a jet passing overhead. Then a single bullet found his body armor, knocking a measure of his wind out and twisting him to the side. But he caught the shooter in his next burst as the man tried to launch himself airborne behind an indoor rock garden. Cort Wesley ejected the spent magazine and rammed a fresh one home in less time than it took to find his next breath.

Then he heard something—no, not heard so much as *felt*, the floor starting to quake beneath him as if the earth was ready to open up and swallow the world whole. His gaze twisted toward the lobby's glass front wall to see the endless wave of humanity streaming toward the building.

Dylan had seen Kai touch the lighter to the packages of firecrackers, had done the very same thing himself on enough occasions to know what was coming next. Her eyes met his and held there in the last moment before . . .

Pop! Pop! Pop! Pop! Pop! Pop! Pop! Pop!

The Fourth of July had come early, the staccato crackle of the fireworks racking his head to the point he had to close his eyes briefly to chase away the pain. But it must have indeed sounded like gunfire to the masses gathered, because the crowd suddenly whipsawed in all directions at once, seeking routes of flight denied by the congestion. Left to charge in the only direction available: straight across the road toward the Yuyuan complex, the hate that had brought the members of the crowd here further fueled by relentless, unstoppable panic.

Dylan felt himself jostled one way, and then another, his head feeling like somebody was banging golf balls around inside his skull with each impact. His stomach lurched and he felt dizzy, woozy, on the verge of passing out. He almost lost his footing, managing to glimpse Kai slicing a path through the crowd, angling herself toward Yuyuan. He fought the nausea down and took a single deep breath to settle himself enough to pick up the chase.

"Dad!" he yelled into the wrist-mounted microphone his father had given him. *"Dad!"*

But there was no response.

Paz clung to his balance and drove Qiang backward into a still whole display case. The back of his bald head crashed through the glass and what looked like giant hornets buzzed at him from a hive that had ruptured on impact.

Paz held Qiang there as long as he could, until the hornets attacked the back of his hands. The stings felt like sharp pinpricks, the pain radiating inward and then seeming to spread across the interior surface of his skin. Paz realized his hands were seizing up on him from whatever poison the stingers contained, Qiang's face a mass of blistering boils from the stings that had closed one of his eyes and swelled one side of his mouth to the size of an apple.

Qiang seemed to have trouble breathing as he mounted a desperate shove backward that Paz was powerless to counter with his cold, tingly hands, his fingers rendered stiff appendages he couldn't flex into fists or even rotate. Qiang's one working eye bulged with a rage fired by the pain pulsing through his blood to every part of his body, as he continued thrusting Paz backward.

Paz twisted, trying to add his own force to the equally big man's momentum. His hands, though, weren't up to the task, the result being to strip him of his balance. He felt himself canting for the tile, his legs losing their grasp on it as well. But he managed to loop his stiff hands behind Qiang's head, taking him down too.

Impact rattled the floor, sending a bevy of desert scorpions scurrying from their path amid the shattered glass. Qiang landed on top, hands closing on Paz's throat when an African tree frog opened its mouth wide and secreted a foul-smelling ooze straight into Qiang's face. It stitched a neat line across his brow, looking as if it had been painted into place, Qiang's one working eye twisting up as if to look for what struck him. He jerked a hand upward to try to wipe it off in the same moment Paz recovered enough feeling in one of his hands to grab hold of the Chinese man's shirt and yank him to the side.

Paz twisted, turned, rolled, straight into the path of two black mambas converging on him.

Caitlin didn't bother going for the pistol: with her hands bound behind her there was no point. She followed up her head butt of Zhen by shoving her shoulder into him, driving both of them backward for the wall. Her intention was to create enough force to break his ribs on impact, disabling him. But Zhen surprised her, twisting deftly just enough to pitch both of them over a counter.

Caitlin fell hard to the floor with him atop her, nothing to cushion her fall. She took the brunt of the impact on her shoulder, feeling something crunch inside the joint itself. Zhen hammered her twice with open-handed blows to the neck and head that left her stunned, even as blood from his shattered nose showered her in rhythm with him jerking from side to side.

Caitlin felt his knobby, gnarled, swollen fingers struggling to close on her throat. She kicked at a raised platform near which they'd landed, kicked and kept kicking until a big computer console resting there dislodged and came crashing down upon Zhen.

108

NEW BRAUNFELS, TEXAS

The crowd was everywhere, Dylan powerless to do anything but move within its flow. It was like being swept forward in some vast tsunami of churning feet and desperation. He felt light, as if he were floating, and wondered if he was on the verge of passing out.

Each foot of progress he made toward the front of the mass and Kai was negated by a shift sideways or backward, mandated by the flow of unrestrained panic that had taken on its own life. The crowd didn't so much move as one as form into separate ripples linked by some invisible connective tissue that kept it somehow whole.

Dylan, having lost track of Kai, realized he'd been swept up in a flow that had taken him across the street toward a wall of glass off which the sun reflected in blinding fashion.

The entrance to the Yuyuan building.

The rumble in Cort Wesley's mind had become audible, deafening by the time the crowd reached the glass. Momentum pressed the first wave so tight against the facade that those comprising it were trapped there, suffocating as they struggled fitfully to wedge themselves free.

The effort proved futile, no one was going anywhere with so much weight and impetus shoving in against them. In his mind, Cort Wesley could feel, almost see, the heavy safety glass buckling. A glance far to his left revealed the gardens Caitlin had told him about beyond the glass, Cort Wesley starting that way in the last moment before the entry doors at last gave and caved inward behind the force of an endless mass surging through.

Paz just managed to avoid one snake by twisting left, then another by jerking forward, both of their jaws left snapping at the air. A third with the mouse just clear of its mouth came at him from the side and Paz snatched it out of the air by the neck as it pounced, feeling it writhe in his grasp, tail whipping from side to side as it tried to free itself.

But Qiang had regained his footing and loomed over him as well, having hoisted a glass terrarium with a glass bottom now swimming with what looked like tiny spiders. Paz hurled the snake up toward Qiang just as he was prepared to unleash it, enough to throw off his timing and send the case crashing downward just to Paz's right. It exploded upon impact, tiny spiders and more shards of glass sprayed in all directions.

Paz avoided both by lurching back to his feet just as a desperate and nearly blind Qiang managed to find his throat with one flailing hand and then another, driving Paz backward hard and fast.

The monitor slammed into the back of Li Zhen's head, its now cracked screen seeming to drive his stunned form downward. This allowed Caitlin to twist aside and brace herself against a divider between two workstations and regain her feet. She saw her SIG across the floor a dozen feet away and scrambled toward it, while Zhen fought to regain his footing with blood now dribbling down his forehead.

Caitlin was still conscious of the cool wash of the air-conditioning over the room full of machines, in stark contrast to the fetid air of Zhen's terrariums upstairs, promising death to millions and millions if she failed to stop the computerized instructions and data from being sent to satellites orbiting overhead.

With Zhen still dazed, Caitlin dropped and slid across the floor toward her SIG Sauer, back-crawling the last stretch of the way to ready her cuffed hands to grasp it. She felt her fingers brush against the steel and kept groping, managing to get it up and as close to steadied on Zhen, who was wobbling back to his feet, as she could manage.

She fired twice, aiming in the opposite direction of the one in which she was facing and missing wildly. Fired three more times, finally getting her shooter's bearings when Zhen pounced and she felt the pistol wrenched from her grasp, twisting to find him looming over her.

"You stop nothing! You achieve nothing! You *are* nothing, *Catlan Strong*!"

Her name spoken as an afterthought, her pistol held in his trembling, deformed hands. Li Zhen was just about to fire when a new voice echoed through the emptiness over the quiet whir of the machines.

"Hello, Father."

*   *   *

Cort Wesley was halfway to the entrance to the gardens when he glimpsed his son trapped amid the mass just back from the glass wall. Dylan hopelessly snared, caught in a vice between the crowd's expanding force forward and the building's glass facade. The boy's eyes met his, the panic filling them enough to drive Cort Wesley to tilt his assault rifle upward and blaze a stitch of bullets across the glass atop the crowd and back again. The glass spiderwebbed, its integrity compromised, the crowd crashing through it in a heap when it ruptured entirely along invisible fault lines.

Cort Wesley found himself amid the mass of humanity. He clung to his footing as he swept through the struggling pile until he spotted Dylan's long hair sweeping from side to side, while the boy fought to free his legs pinned by bodies that had collapsed atop them.

Cort Wesley reached down and jerked his son free, hoisting him airborne and then half-carried, half-dragged him toward the entrance to the gardens.

Paz felt Qiang's thumbs closing, pressing, contracting the cartilage over his throat. The man's one functioning eye bulged with rage, his features swollen to monstrous proportions, his face barely recognizable as human anymore.

Paz started to reach outward, realizing in that moment the seconds left to him weren't enough to pry the powerful grasp from its place. Then he noticed exactly what Qiang had slammed into, the contents in the shattered terrarium immediately above him.

Paz reached up and closed both hands over thick swatches of African drum ivy, tore it from its bounds and lashed it forward. Pressed it into Qiang's swollen face.

Hssssssssssss . . .

Paz wasn't sure if the sound made by the deadly vapors being unleashed actually came from the plant or were a product of his imagination. It didn't matter.

Only the effects did.

Qiang released his grasp almost instantly, flailing wildly for the noxious vines still pressed against his face. He recoiled, hands dropping to reveal his skin bubbling and puckering as if coming to a boil. The big man's one eye started jerking from side to side, his entire body struck by a spasm before it seized up all at once and he keeled over at Paz's feet like a felled tree.

Cort Wesley and Dylan charged along the narrow path cutting through Yuyuan's gardens. The sky had clouded up, a storm in the offing that seemed to wash the color out of the scene.

Cort Wesley ran with the assault rifle shouldered and his Glock nine-millimeter pistol in hand, preferable in close quarters, ready in case more Triad soldiers were laying in wait. He had no idea where the path or the gardens led, certain only he couldn't go back toward the chaos of the lobby.

A gunman lurched out to his left. Cort Wesley took him down, then swung immediately to his right, shooting another. They seemed to be coming from all angles, Cort Wesley firing as if this were some sort of crazed video game. He felt Dylan pressed up against him, his son needing him for balance to avoid falling, and Cort Wesley loosened his grip on the Glock so he could loop an arm protectively around the boy.

"I've got you, son, I've got you!"

Dragging Dylan onward, Cort Wesley jerked the assault rifle downward and started clacking off shots from it in place of the Glock. Swinging one way, then the other, then back again, an imaginary bell chiming in Cort Wesley's head as his score continued to climb.

He tightened his grasp on Dylan and drew the boy to the right, off the path where he'd glimpsed a fence obscured by heavy vines.

It looked easy enough to scale by using the vines for climbing leverage. And that's exactly what father and son did, cresting over the top and dropping down on the far side of the complex just as an explosion shook the Yuyuan building at its core, coughing smoke and rubble into the air.

109

Zhen didn't fire, trapped between intentions and actions, the pistol stopping somewhere between Caitlin and Kai.

"Do you recognize me, Father? How many years has it been?"

Li Zhen didn't answer her. His eyes widened. His face broke out into a strange leering grin, his mind in a place Caitlin didn't want to consider, while he continued to regard his daughter as if she were just another actress on an audition reel.

"You have exceeded my expectations," he said coldly, calmly.

He seemed to delight in the sight of her, the pistol in his hand forgotten. Caitlin imagined him looking at Kai now but seeing her as the little girl he'd handed over to the Triad in exchange for the standing he enjoyed today. She stood before him with a radiance and beauty that defied the hatred that drove her.

"Why don't you shoot me, Father?" she said, an overstuffed backpack slung from her shoulder. "Kill me as you killed Jiao. You remember her, don't you? I wish I did more clearly. But it's been so long and I had nothing to remind me of her, not a picture or keepsake, when you let them take me away."

Caitlin lumbered back to her feet, noticed the elevator door was still open. Even in the dim lighting dominated by the glow of the big wall screens with numbers scrolling across them, she could see how beautiful Kai was, how Dylan could have fallen for her so quickly. Her complexion looked more like something lifted off a magazine photo. But her expression today was frozen somewhere between acceptance and sadness, so flat and smooth that Caitlin wondered if a smile had ever broken it. It wasn't just her training, the ability to coerce and seduce. It was an innocence and vulnerability forever suppressed and yet somehow still lurking just below the surface.

"Because that would be a terrible waste, to strip the world of such a beautiful flower."

"Tell that to my sister. When I finally learned the truth, everything made sense. But that doesn't change the fact I never learned how to feel, or how to enjoy it. I guess you were training me for the life you finally sold me into without even realizing." Kai stood there, shaking her head. "But you don't believe you've done a thing wrong, do you?"

"I knew I'd see you again. I knew fate would bring you back to me, knew that someday—"

"You'd come back for me," Kai said, cutting him off with her own thought. "That's how I survived the first months, by convincing myself you'd come back. I dreamed about that day just as, later, I dreamed about this one. I've followed you, Father, studied your every move. Made it my life's work to learn everything there was to learn about you. That's how I found out the truth about my sister . . . and myself. I even uncovered the plans for this building, this secret level so befitting a man whose life is nothing but secrets. I'm glad I got here in time to stop you from destroying any more lives."

Caitlin watched Kai approach her, a small knife appearing in her hand. She felt the young woman ease her cuffed wrists upward and heard a brief grating sound as Kai sliced through the plastic.

"Leave," she said, meeting Caitlin's gaze.

Caitlin glanced at the gun trembling within Zhen's arthritis-riddled hands. "I can't do that, ma'am."

"Leave," Kai repeated coarsely. "This doesn't concern you."

Caitlin backed off to keep both father and daughter in her line of vision, shaking her hands to restore the blood flow as best she could. "Listen to me. Do this and you're no different from him. You can be better, you *are* better."

Kai's gaze darted briefly to her. "I can get the only one who matters, the one who left me for dead a long time ago. It's time for him to pay for what he's done, all the pain he's caused."

Kai eased the backpack from her shoulder and dropped it to the floor. Something clacked together inside. Caitlin imagined plastic explosives wedged into tight packs, or maybe something cruder, like dynamite. Just as her great-grandfather had used a hundred and thirty years before to blow the earthen dam and destroy the latest rail line built by the Southern Pacific.

"Please, leave," Kai said to Caitlin. "So you can tell Dylan I'm sorry."

"You reached out to him because you wanted my help. Well, here I am. We can still do this the right way."

"The true crimes my father's guilty of carry no sentence," she continued, addressing Caitlin while staring at Li Zhen. "They inserted things into me to train my body, larger each time until I was deemed ready. I was twelve years old at the time. And when I was thirteen, the rapes began. On a daily basis . . . sometimes more. I made them think they'd broken me down. But they didn't, and I had you to thank for that, Father. Because in order to find you, I had to survive."

"You want me to say I'm sorry," Li Zhen managed finally. The murky lighting struck his face in a way that seemed to divide it into shadowy sections, ready to fracture. "You want me to drop to my knees and plead for forgiveness. But I'm not sorry. I lost the ability to be sorry a long time ago."

"You lost the ability to be *human*," Kai blurted out to him, her voice cracking and growing less sure. She swung back toward Caitlin, resolve starting to weaken however slightly. "Go. Now."

"No."

Caitlin saw that Kai was holding a handheld detonator, maybe three inches in length and narrowing at the bottom with a red plunger riding its top. "Please, so he doesn't claim another life."

Caitlin sidestepped, placing herself between Kai and Li Zhen. "Exactly my intention."

Li Zhen struggled to steady the pistol on her, the barrel quivering. "I'll kill both of you."

"Know what I think?" Caitlin said to him. "That you're weak

and a coward at heart. You slept with one daughter because you didn't have the strength to resist the sickness inside you and gave up the other to the monsters of the Triad. My guess is you were glad to give her up because you thought it would hide all the bad you've done. But it didn't make you any less a monster or a coward."

Zhen seemed to forget all about his daughter, focusing his aim and eyes entirely on Caitlin, as if to make some kind of twisted point. Caitlin watched the shaky, swollen finger that was poised over the trigger start to move.

But then he moved his free hand to one of the keyboards instead, gun still trained on her as he prepared to initiate a command sequence and steadied a single finger into place. "I think I'd rather see you witness me activate the plan. All those phone numbers you see scrolling on the screens before you dialed in minutes, your country dying a slow and agonizing death. My family's revenge at last."

He had fallen into her trap, attention divided, a man lacking familiarity with a firearm. Caitlin twisted slightly to the left, angling for her charge. If a lucky shot found her, then so be it. But Zhen's plan would be stopped.

And then Kai, moving with a dancer's speed and grace sped past her, brushing up against Caitlin just enough to knock her off-kilter. Throwing herself on her father and taking him to the floor.

Kai looked up, her father dazed but struggling to free himself beneath her. Caitlin saw the flatness, the emptiness in her gaze. Followed it downward.

To the detonator in her grasp, Kai's eyes flashing an unspoken message as her thumb moved into place.

Caitlin burst into motion, charging for the elevator. She twisted around once inside and caught one last look at Kai, their eyes meeting as the doors closed automatically. The elevator began its rapid ascent, several seconds passing before a blast shook the cab sideways, then up and down. Caitlin remembered noting the elevator walls cracking before she was hurled forward into the darkness that swallowed her.

110

EL PASO, TEXAS

"Sinners repent or more will die! Sinners repent or more will die! Sinners repent or more will die!"

A few days later, her arm in a sling and her ears still ringing from the percussion of the blast at Yuyuan, Caitlin approached Reverend William Bryant Tripp across the parched ground of Concordia Cemetery just outside El Paso. The Mexican border lay barely a hundred yards to the south and she'd forgotten that this historical landmark lay on desert grounds. That was in stark contrast to the lush foliage of contemporary facilities like Mission Burial Park in San Antonio, where she'd last confronted the leader of the Beacon of Light Church.

Tripp twirled a finger though his handlebar mustache as he watched her approach, separating himself from his chanting throng to meet her well before it.

"Have you come to apologize in person, Ranger?"

"No, Mr. Tripp, I've come to place you under arrest."

He smiled smugly. "We measured this time. We're a thousand feet away and then some," he said, gesturing toward the quiet graveside ceremony for another young soldier killed tragically, this time in a helicopter crash stateside.

There were just a handful of people in attendance, and Caitlin couldn't help but wonder if the fact that the sideshow circus of the Beacon of Light Church showing up might have discouraged other friends and family members. A special exception had been granted to allow the young man to be buried on these historic, sun-scorched grounds with other family members who'd also served their country in centuries past. Unusual to say the least, but so were the crumbling concrete markers and broken wooden crosses that littered the dry dusty earth.

Tripp shook his head. "Haven't you learned your lesson by now?"

"Oh, I'm not arresting you for trespassing or disturbing the peace—nothing like that. I'm arresting you for murder."

A flyer with the logo of the Beacon of Light Church drifted between them on the breeze.

"And who exactly did I kill?" Tripp asked casually, twirling a finger through the other side of his mustache now.

Caitlin held the brim of her Stetson against the stiffening breeze and swept her gaze about the sprawling flat grounds that stretched all the way to a mesa set to the west. "Lots of Chinese are buried here, you know, almost all of which worked the railroads."

"I wasn't aware of that, Ranger."

"I'm surprised you'd even set foot here in view of that, Mr. Tripp, given your general distaste for that culture."

"It's *Reverend* Tripp, and I'm not sure what you're referring to."

"Yes, you are. You raised the issue yourself back at Mission Burial Park in San Antonio. How your church members, your very ancestors, served as missionaries in those railroad work camps trying to convert the Chinese to Christianity. You called them 'heathen hordes.'"

"Which makes the cause of my forebears no less noble, Ranger."

"But that cause stopped in 1883 after that massacre in Langtry killed a whole bunch of them along with plenty more striking Chinese railroad workers. Ugly, little-known part of Texas history, Mr. Tripp, that took the lives of women and children too."

"What's that have to do with you coming all this way to accuse me of murder?" He glanced beyond her dramatically. "Or should I be looking for another bulldozer somewhere on the grounds?"

"*Sinners repent or more will die! Sinners repent or more will die! Sinners repent or more will die!*"

"Not this time, sir," Caitlin said, raising her voice over the chanting that had grown suddenly louder as a young man's casket was lowered into the dusty ground a thousand feet away. "I raise that issue because your hatred for the Chinese is a matter of record.

I think you blame them for getting your ancestors killed in that massacre. I think it's something that's haunted you for a long time until you decided to take your own revenge."

"What are you accusing me of exactly, Ranger?"

"The murder of five Chinese call girls in five different cities along the original rail line built by the Southern Pacific. I checked, Mr. Tripp. Turns out you were there to disrupt a military funeral in each and every one of them when the murders took place."

Tripp stared at her for what seemed like a very long time.

"That's ridiculous," he said finally.

"We've got security camera footage from all five hotels where the murders took place showing a man who meets your general description," Caitlin told him. "Except for the fact he was clean-shaven."

With that she reached out, grabbed Tripp's mustache by one of the handlebars and yanked, tearing it off and leaving a sticky layer of residue behind.

"Just like you, as it turns out," Caitlin finished.

Tripp swiped a finger across his bare upper lip, trying hard to show no reaction at all. "That's hardly enough evidence to arrest me."

"Maybe so, Mr. Tripp." She flapped open a plastic evidence pouch and dropped the fake mustache inside. "But we found a piece of artificial hair in the Menger Hotel that I believe is going to be a perfect match for this. Another was recovered at the Lubbock murder scene I'm betting will match up too."

"*Sinners repent or more will die! Sinners repent or more will die! Sinners repent or more will die!*"

Tripp's features had frozen up solid. He stared at Caitlin hatefully, trying to muster up some bravado he couldn't find.

Finally he took a step backward, closer to his chanting faithful, his spine stiffening. "You just bought yourself one of the biggest lawsuits in Texas history."

"I don't think so," Caitlin said, shaking her head. "See, my great-grandfather had the wrong man pegged as the killer of Chinese women murdered in that camp where the massacre took place, just like I did for a time. I think the real killer back then was really one of the missionaries out to punish those Chinese prostitutes for their sins. If William Ray Strong ever considered that notion, he probably would've figured out that same missionary was present in all the camps where murders took place. Playing God, just like you decided to do a hundred and thirty years later. Guess ruining the funerals of young American heroes wasn't enough for you."

"Sinners repent or more will die! Sinners repent or more will die! Sinners repent or more will die!"

Caitlin slid her gaze over to the members of the Beacon of Light Church. "I wonder how your supporters over there would react if they knew about those movies you must've watched to find your victims. I'd have a story ready for them too, if I were you."

Tripp ran his tongue over his upper lip, expression wrinkling at the taste of the remaining glue. A thousand feet beyond, family members were now tossing handfuls of parched earth atop the coffin of their loved one. A few were looking toward the chanters and their picket signs held high toward the sky, squinting into the sun with fists clenched by their sides. A man and a woman Caitlin took to be the young man's parents stood holding between them the ceremonial American flag with which they'd been presented.

"The state of Texas will be hearing from my lawyers, Ranger."

Caitlin used her good hand to whip the handcuffs from her belt. "You can call them from the car, sir."

EPILOGUE

Their influence was worked not by recklessness or foolhardiness, but by the steadiness of their purpose and performance—and by the sureness among both the law-abiding and the law-breaking, that thought of self would never deter the Ranger from fulfilling the commitment of his vows as an agent of the law, order and justice.

—President Lyndon B. Johnson, 1965

The reception to honor first responders was held in the Crystal Room of the White House, sponsored by the secretary of homeland security who was busy holding court in a corner while Caitlin hovered nearby. She'd abandoned the sling but she still wasn't hearing too well out of her right ear.

"Ranger," the secretary called, spotting Caitlin and starting over.

Caitlin heard only half the word, the rest lost to her damaged hearing. She liked the fact that the secretary was a woman too and they'd gotten along quite well in the past, having met while she'd been at Quantico for her annual two-week stint on homeland security issues.

"Do you have a moment?" the secretary asked, steering her toward a set of French doors that led out onto a patio, its outdoor furniture removed for the season and fall leaves beginning to gather in clusters. "There's something I want you to know. The Chinese government has agreed to disable the two satellites launched by Yuyuan to transmit the signal to all those cell phones. In a few days, they'll be nothing more than junked steel floating in the sky."

"You mind asking them to wait a bit longer on that?"

"Why?"

"I have my reasons, ma'am, but it might be better if you didn't hear them. Truth is we've got other fish to fry anyway, and I came here today to make sure you got that grill going as well."

The secretary gazed back through the French doors, as if wishing she'd never stepped outside. "I don't believe I understand."

"I believe you do. I'm not saying you were involved in, or had any knowledge of, the alliance between Yuyuan and your office. Let's call it a rogue operation that may leave some echoes."

"Echoes, Ranger?"

"Sounds that ring out for a time after what spurred them's long done."

"I know what an echo is."

"Then I'm sure you know we can't afford any here. That means whoever else is involved needs to be gone. That means no blowback or somebody going back to guns to cover their tracks."

With that, Caitlin handed the secretary an envelope.

"You'll find a dozen names inside, ma'am, all listed as John Does after being killed in a gunfight in East San Antonio. Right now it's down as gang related."

"Right now," the secretary of homeland security repeated thoughtfully, taking the envelope stiffly in hand

"We've positively ID'ed the victims. Dig a little deeper and I'm sure we'll find a treasure trove of black-ops experience that's better not made public. I believe it's in your best interests that remains the case."

The secretary stiffened. "You've made your point, Ranger. And for the record none of this was necessary. This whole matter ceased to exist the moment I was informed that there were those in my department operating as lone wolves. That's not acceptable and won't be tolerated."

"I appreciate that."

"Then can we go back inside?" the secretary said, folding her arms across her chest. "It's a bit chilly out here."

"One more thing, ma'am. Our medical examiner can't confirm that either Li Zhen or his daughter were killed in that blast at Yuyuan.

If Li Zhen did manage to survive, I want you to know we're gonna find him no matter where he's at or what it takes. Anybody in your office knows anything that can help, I'm sure they'll be in touch."

"I'll pass along a directive to that effect." The secretary of homeland security started back again for the French doors and this time Caitlin let her. "The Rangers always get their man, don't they?"

"Close enough, Madam Secretary," Caitlin said, looking her right in the eye.

"I know there's a reason why we came out here today," Cort Wesley said, as he and Caitlin walked toward the graves of her grandfather and father in Mission Burial Park, the cemetery located on the San Antonio River where they were buried side by side shaded by flowering cottonwood trees in clear view of the historic Mission Espada.

"Can I ask you a question, Cort Wesley? When you talk to that old friend of yours from prison—"

"Leroy Epps." Cort Wesley nodded.

"—Leroy Epps. You believe he's really there?"

"*Gaw head, bubba. Tell the lady,*" he heard Leroy's voice chime in from alongside him.

"Yes, I do."

"Then maybe that's why I felt the need to pay a visit here. Maybe my dad or granddad will do the same."

"*Tell her it don't work that way. But this sure is a nice place to spend a man's passing years.*"

"I'll tell her, champ."

"What was that, Cort Wesley?"

"Just saying that I wouldn't count on it."

Three weeks had passed now since the explosion at the Yuyuan building and ten days since Caitlin had visited the White House. She pretty much had all the range of motion back in her shoulder and had regained almost all of her hearing. Her sleep was still racked by nightmares and she spent more than her share of nighttime hours dozing on the front porch swing until the autumn chill chased her inside. Dylan had returned to school at Brown but Luke, for the rest of this year anyway, was back at public high school here in San Antonio, deemed to be in the best interests of all.

"I've glimpsed them here from time to time, I know I have. But they've never had anything to say."

"Maybe 'cause there's nothing you really need to hear, Ranger. Maybe 'cause you got things pretty well figured out on your own."

"You believe that?"

"Compared to me, you bet I do."

Just off to his right, Cort Wesley thought he caught Leroy Epps wink. Then he moved his gaze toward the road where Guillermo Paz's massive pickup truck was parked in a shady spot not far behind his.

"How long is he gonna follow you around?"

"Until we get Li Zhen."

"Unless he's dead."

"Paz is certain the man's still alive. Says he saw him in a dream. To me, that's as surefire as DNA."

"What about Kai?"

Caitlin shrugged, a bit sadly. "Not yet."

Her phone rang and Caitlin raised the handset to her right ear, through which she still heard better. She listened briefly to the voice on the other end, then lowered the phone slowly.

"Turns out the colonel was right, Cort Wesley. Li Zhen survived that blast for sure. We found him."

"You know where he is?"

"Not exactly," Caitlin said, "but close enough."

Mareno emerged from the elevator and approached his office on the top floor of the Flatiron Building. He had tripled security since his near-fatal encounter with the cowboy and its aftermath. The shit had hit the fan in Texas all right, but fortunately he'd been downwind from the stink. He'd even come to believe his network would be able to emerge from the whole mess scot-free. The luncheon he'd just come from had gone surprisingly well, reassuring him he could remain unscathed.

One of the new security guards, a man Mareno didn't recognize and looked Latino, held the door open for him, catching a second guard's reflection in the glass. Latino too.

Where were they getting these guy from?

His assistant was not at the front desk and he continued toward his office, passing two more armed guards on the way. Mareno had just registered the anomaly that they looked Latino as well when he stepped into his office, bolting the heavy security door behind him.

"Hey, nice place you got here."

Mareno swung and saw the figure of a massive man with shoulder-length hair gnarled in shiny ringlets squeezed into his desk chair. The man removed a flash drive from a USB port on the side of his computer and rose, his huge shoulders blocking out a measure of the sun that had been shining in Mareno's eyes.

"The existentialists had it all wrong about life being meaningless," Guillermo Paz told him. "Point is a man's gotta find his own meaning, and times like this is where I get mine." He stepped out from behind the desk, letting the sun burn into Mareno's eyes anew. "You mind if we make this quick?" Paz asked, glancing at the flash drive he was holding. "There's a lot of young women who need my help, all over the country by the look of things. This is gonna be fun."

Paz turned to stare briefly out the window offering an expansive view of the Manhattan skyline.

"Hey, amigo, you think the reports will say you only fell twenty-two stories since this floor doesn't exist?"

Dylan found himself sleeping a lot upon returning to school. Lingering effects of the concussion he tried to ignore kept catching up with him every time he overexerted himself. Brown let him cut back on his course work, taking an incomplete in one class and dropping another, which left him plenty of time for the naps he had no choice but to take—sometimes two or three a day.

During one, out of nowhere Dylan dreamed about Kai. She was standing over him just like when he was in the hospital. He heard her voice just as he had then but, again, couldn't make himself answer her. He awoke feeling strangely refreshed with the pleasantly warm sun shining into his eyes. Sat up and stretched his arms, knocking something from his chest in the process. Looking down, he smiled and dabbed a sleeve against his eyes that had suddenly turned moist.

Then Dylan leaned over, retrieved the pink rose from his bare dorm room floor, and held it close.

For Li Zhen, it was not so much about defeat as delay. He believed wholeheartedly in the old Chinese proverb that a journey of a thousand miles begins with one small step. What he'd built at Yuyuan had ultimately turned into that one small step, with the rest of a great journey still ahead of him certain to yield great rewards.

Delay, not defeat, he thought again. Why else would he have survived such an explosion if fate was not firmly on his side? His wounds, most of them anyway, would heal in time, but not the wounds he'd someday inflict on the United States.

A different day, a different plan. His destiny as inevitable now as it was before.

Delay, not defeat.

Li's phone rang, a call he'd been desperately awaiting coming at last.

"*Nǐ hǎo*," he answered. "Hello."

On the other end of the line, Caitlin Strong nodded to Young Roger who sat behind a console he'd constructed from data that survived the blast at Yuyuan. He flipped a single switch to activate the signal from the Chinese satellite still orbiting overhead.

"Good-bye, Mr. Zhen," Caitlin said.

AUTHOR'S NOTE

I did a page like this in *Strong Rain Falling* and kind of liked laying out for you the book's origins and where fiction breaks from fact. Since you've just flipped the last page (not counting this one), it's no spoiler to tell you from where the concept for *Strong Darkness* sprang.

Sometime in 2013, early I think, *60 Minutes* ran a story on a Chinese company called Shinzen that has its American headquarters in Plano, Texas (coincidentally). Turned out that Shinzen actually built the fourth generation, 4G, wireless network many of us use today every time we pull out our cell phones. Yup, a Chinese company. I kid you not. Some stuff is too incredible to make up. So Shinzen became Yuyuan, the 4G network became the 5G and, *voila!*, *Strong Darkness* was born.

As you probably figured out, I had a blast teaming Caitlin's fictional great-grandfather William Ray Strong with the very real Judge Roy Bean and pitting them against the forces of the Southern Pacific Railroad. So much has been written about the famous hanging judge (who really did only hang a single man), I hope I've done justice to him here. The remnants of his saloon can still be found in Langtry, Texas, called the Jersey Lilly now. And the first case Bean ever heard as a judge was that of Joe Bell who was brought before him by, you guessed it, the Texas Rangers, in July of 1882.

As for the Trans-Pecos rail line, it was indeed completed in 1883, originating in El Paso and finishing in San Antonio. Since that geography didn't mesh with the story I wanted to tell, I invented that "spur" the Southern Pacific was building to link up with a line to the north.

The Deep Web, meanwhile, is very much real. I'm sure we'll all be hearing lots more about it down the road. In the meantime, check out the November 11, 2013, issue of *Time* magazine to learn enough to scare you as much it scared me.

Oh, and those who have as deep an abiding interest in the Texas Rangers as I do may know that Company F, formerly based in San Antonio, is now based in Waco. But I've left Captain Tepper and Caitlin based in San Antonio because, well, I love the city and it makes for a great setting. Call it dramatic license.

Hey, remember how you used to stay for the credits of the old James Bond films just to see JAMES BOND WILL BE BACK IN . . . Well, you can look forward to Caitlin's next adventure, *Strong Light of Day*, right around this time next year. Can't tease you with what it's about, because I've got no idea myself yet. But I will once it's time to get started. That's a promise from writer to reader, as sacred a bond as there ever was.

So be well until next we meet.

Providence, Rhode Island; December 2, 2013